To Colleen,
with all best wishes,
Joanne Dobson

The Kashmiri Shawl
A Novel

Joanne Dobson

Cobb Hill Books

ISBN: 1495442136
ISBN 13: 9781495442131

For
Jordan McKinley Kohomban
And
Abigail Elisabeth Kohomban

ONE

New York
August 1860

A sudden cloudburst off the Hudson River slapped a curtain of rain against Anna's filthy windowpanes. Water rushed downhill from Broadway into the shallow gutters and puddled between the cobblestones; within minutes, she knew, Liberty Street would be a stinking aqueduct, teeming with refuse. In the lines of the flowery verses she published in the ladies' magazines, Anna would have termed the puddles a pellucid jonquil gold, but in truth they appeared to her something more in the nature of horse-piss yellow. Once she would have turned her eyes, ladylike, refusing to see, much less acknowledge, this evidence of crude animal function, but those days were long past.

She'd just plucked the penknife from a cracked china cup on her writing table in order to sharpen the point of a new quill, when footsteps suddenly pounded up the narrow flight of drugget-covered stairs that led to her room. The penknife slid from the quill, puncturing the tip of her forefinger. A sharp tapping sounded at the door, and Anna sucked in her breath. She caught up a soiled flannel pen-wiper, dabbing it at her finger, mingling blood with ink and ink with blood.

Another knock. More urgent. Who could it be? No one ever called on Anna, forgotten in her high front room in this unfashionable Manhattan boardinghouse. She'd chosen this place for its obscurity, deliberately settling apart from those upright Christian men and women with whom she'd once so eagerly sought acquaintance. She'd also resumed her maiden name: Anna Roundtree, who had so prayerfully departed to India more than ten years earlier as helpmeet to the sainted missionary, Reverend Josiah Roundree, had become once again, Anna Wheeler.

All she'd wanted since her ignominious return alone from Calcutta was to vanish into this great city, to leave no more than the merest ripple on the surface of its life, to seek at the very least a modest support with the productions of her pen.

Again the knock came, louder. As she stood and turned to move apprehensively toward the door, her eye flicked past the window, then flicked back: in the street below she saw a hansom cab, its steaming dapple-gray halted at the curb. The tall silk hat of a gentleman emerged from the cab, followed by said gentleman's shoulders in a light waterproof overcoat. Then the urgent banging on her door resumed, and she forgot about this well-dressed caller two floors below.

Pressing a worn cambric handkerchief against her finger to staunch the thin trickle of blood, she unbolted the door to her room. The lingering smell of her landlady's stewed mutton entered, along with a thin, red-haired Irish woman of the type often seen on the sidewalks selling apples. The visitor yanked off the rain-drenched plaid shawl that was plastered to her head and shoulders.

"You don't know me, and I don't know you, Missus," the young woman whispered. She was lightly freckled, with skin so translucent Anna could see a vein throb in her temple. "But we've met before. Then, one day last month, I seen ye on Broadway and followed ye home."

Anna shivered, momentarily chilled. "Followed me?" Anna thought of herself as invisible. If anyone had asked about her appearance, she would have described herself as nondescript, which was not, in fact, quite true—given her large, stunning gray-green eyes. Nonetheless she dressed in faded cotton, befitting both her impecunious state and her intense desire not to be observed. Invisible. Yes, she wanted above all else to be invisible.

"I wanted to know where you lived," the woman said. "I've had ye on me mind."

"Me? But I've never met you." Anna studied her visitor with the close attention afforded by her missionary medical training. Like so many of New York's Irish, the woman seemed almost a starveling.

"Oh, yes, you have. I'm Bridey O'Neill." Her perusal equaled Anna's in intensity. "'Tis a midwife I am, and I was at the Five Points Mission when your time come."

Anna started, then cast her gaze quickly down the third-floor hallway. The other doors remained shut, but in such close confines who could tell what listeners lurked? She grasped the woman by the arm and dragged her further into the small, drab room, its only splash of color the scarlet, blue, and gold Kashmiri shawl tossed with glowing abandon across the sagging bed. She must be discreet; a woman having only the scant and uncertain earnings of her pen upon which to depend for livelihood was obliged to cling to at least a semblance of virtue. Only the destitute and the very rich could afford the luxury of a besmirched reputation.

As Anna closed her door behind Bridey O'Neill, she half-heard the sound of voices in the entranceway below, the murmurings of her landlady, Mrs. Chapman, and a man's deep questioning tones. But she listened no further; she had no heart for boarding house affairs.

"I've a thing to tell ye about the babe," the red-haired woman continued, dropping her wet shawl in a heap on the floor's cheap rush matting.

"The babe?" Anna gasped and staggered, catching herself against the battered doorframe. A heat born of astonishment flooded her. The long voyage home from India and the extended confinement, she had thought they were lost in the past, remnants, perhaps, of a fever dream. But now—*a thing to tell about the babe*. "Oh, yes," she said. Her voice had gone faint.

It had been a cold day in April two years past with the early leaves half-budded on the trees, when deep in her body the birth pangs had begun.

Those first months home from India had been her darkest ever. She hadn't known how to go about dying, so she'd settled upon death's semblance: a life with no passion whatsoever. She felt numb—as she had since the morning in the autumn of that fatal year when she'd taken ship from bustling, noisome Calcutta, and had then spent four long months at sea. Now, as then, she existed in a condition of elemental emptiness, as if the blank blue of the sky and the blank green of the sea had leached the very color from her soul.

"Miss Parker called me in," Bridey said. "D'ye mind her—Miss Susan Parker?"

"Y … yes," Anna faltered. "The mission worker." Tall, spare and dour, with a giraffe-like neck and intricate, starched, pleated collars, Miss Parker had given Anna sanctuary at the Five-Points Mission on Park Street, just across from the notorious Paradise Square.

Too sick to work at even the simple tasks the Mission required of its inmates, Anna had lain in bed all day, or sat motionless by the single window of the room she shared with a simple-minded girl everyone called Crazy Sal. Nothing could be seen from that window but the back walls of brick houses and a narrow bit of street. But she'd watched the life behind the tenement windows, the women as they went to the pumps and to the peddler's carts. To pass the time, she'd written down in her journal vivid descriptions of the people in the streets. Without that little book her spirit would not have survived.

At first the twinges of childbirth were tentative and dull. She had remained quiet by her window with the closed book on her lap, staring out sightlessly, practicing the deep breathing she'd learned in her earlier labors from Lallia, a Hindu midwife. But soon her spasms swamped her. Heavy and sharp, they threatened to tear her body asunder. Then one anguishing pain had begun deep and low in her belly and built upon itself until someone screamed, and she was in a hot puddle on the floor with Crazy Sal shrieking above her. Anna shuddered at the memory and sat down—*sank* down—on her bed, clutching folds of the bright shawl in each hand.

Bridey O'Neill sat on Anna's one rush-seated chair and continued with her story. "Miss Parker was hopin' to deliver you herself, things bein' as they was, she said, you with no husband and no money. But the child lay sideways and wouldn't budge. You was in pretty bad shape before they called me in to turn it. Once I did, it slid out slick, like a kitten still in the sack."

"And it was dead—" Anna twisted a corner of the shawl. Of course it was dead. All her babies had died within hours, small and pale and early in the Indian heat, all boys, three of them—one with the little black flies at his eyes. Her late husband had said she was insufficiently feminine to be a proper mother, that all the reading and learning had dried up her womanly organs so that she could not bring a child to full term. She'd believed him, then. Josiah was so knowledgeable.

"Nonsense," Bridey snapped. The telling of her story seemed to energize her. "And that was a lie to be sure. It was a big, fine girl, that babe, born squalling like a wildcat."

"A girl?" Something caught in Anna's chest, a fist on her heart. "A girl? And … *crying*?" She could still feel the coarse weave of the birthing sheet between fingers cold with strain. "Bridey, you must be mistaken. Miss Parker said the infant never took a breath."

"And sure that lie has been on my soul ever since the day. I've never seen a child so full of life. But it was just that—" She averted her gaze as if about to address a most shameful issue. "Well, Miss Parker and the housekeeper was all big-eyed, ye know—hissin' to each other in corners, like I didn't have ears to hear." Then she looked directly at Anna. "If I can speak plainly t'ye, Mrs. Wheeler, from the looks on their faces ye'd of thought yourself had give birth to a dog. But she was a pretty little thing, that child. Looked me right in the eye smart-like when I was washing her up. Like she'd know me again if she seed me. Soon's I got her clean and wrapped, Miss Parker grabbed me arm and dragged me into the back room. 'Too bad the child's so poorly,' she blathered. And when I give her the fish-eye, she pulls out her purse and pays me off—double. 'Far's poor Mrs. Wheeler knows, this child was born dead,' she says, and stands in the front door and watches me till I turn down Worth Street. Later that night I was out to the grocery for … for a growler." She cast Anna a sideways glance. "And I seen her slipping around the corner of the Mission with a bundle clutched to her chest." Bridey's eyes were bright with meaning. "Just so." And she crossed her arms loosely as if she were cradling an infant. "And it were screechin' fit to beat the band."

"But—"

"'Twas just, ye see, she couldn't understand it—and, mind ye, I'm not saying how it come about. …" Her gaze left Anna's face uneasily and migrated to the beautiful Kashmiri shawl she clutched. "Ye see, I'm not one who has a right to cast blame on any other woman—if ye understand what I'm about saying. But somehow, for whatever reason …" Her eyes snapped back to Anna's. "… That child was born a darky."

The Reverend Josiah Roundtree had been as blond as an archangel. One afternoon late in the spring of her final year at Mount Holyoke Female Academy, Anna Wheeler walked into the academy's visitors' parlor carrying a vase of glorious pink peonies, and the newly ordained Reverend Roundtree had turned to her from the window, his blue eyes widening with a most gratifying interest. The June sunlight turned his pale hair into a golden aureole. In the height and beauty of his youth, Josiah had appeared saintly and singular of purpose. As Anna, with unsteady hands, placed the vase of lush blooms on the parlor table, a classmate introduced the visitor. Josiah came to Anna with his hands out, then halted abruptly just short of taking hers, as if appalled by his rash impulsiveness. "My dear young lady," he said, after an evident struggle with unsettled emotions. "I feel called, in the most prayerful solicitude, to inquire—are you … are you … saved? Are you washed in the blood of the Lamb?"

Anna knew all about salvation—and all about damnation. Her childhood had coincided with that conflagration of revivalist wildfire known as The Second Great Awakening. In her small town in that area of upstate New York called the Burned-Over District for the frequency and passion of its religious revivals, traveling evangelists had railed that because the Son of God had died for the sins of humankind, we were all born "blood-guilty," depraved, condemned to suffer eternal torment in hell unless saved by having accepted Christ into our hearts. Anna had stubbornly resisted this doctrine. In her heart she was incapable of believing that she had been born a vile sinner worthy of burning forever in a Lake of Hellfire. In this, Anna's heart and her education were at odds. Hadn't she learned from McGuffy's Reader that *In Adam's fall / We sinned all*? Hadn't she lisped that credo with other beginning readers in her hillside schoolroom? Hadn't she sat Sunday after Sunday in the same straight-backed pews listening to the same dire warnings as everyone else in the small Baptist church to which her parents belonged? Yet, she alone, remained silently unbelieving.

One late-March evening, with sleet pounding the plain pebble-glass windows of the church, the eloquent Reverend Charles Finney called upon all who'd ever accepted Christ's salvation from sin to testify to their salvation by coming forward to the altar. Anna, a twelve-year-old apostate, remained stubbornly seated. In later years, when she thought about her childhood at all, it was that agonizing moment she came back to: the entire congregation streaming forward in a singing, shouting—passionate—acknowledgment of having been eternally redeemed from the wages of sin: Elihu Hunter, who starved his horses; Betty Little, who'd consigned her sweet, slow-thinking daughter to the rigors of the county workhouse: Jem Lawrence, who yanked Anna's braids when Miss Hobson wasn't looking. Then there was Anna, who remained unmoved, sitting alone in the hard, straight-backed pew, a small, squirming, seething, sweating ball of resistance. She paid for her resistance at home later with the first of the many "righteous beatings" that were to punctuate her uncompromising youth.

That night, her soul went underground. She could not recognize courage in the solitude of her integrity; rather, she felt that she was cramped in her understanding, that she lacked true spiritual passion. At the age of sixteen, she left home to attend Miss Mary Lyon's Mount Holyoke Female Academy in Massachusetts, her mother's dying words ringing in her ears—"Serve the Lord, Anna. Serve the Lord." But she knew she was incapable.

But at Mount Holyoke, images of the soul's damnation nurtured by more sophisticated evangelists began to plague her with night terrors. Classmate after classmate surrendered herself to Christ, swooning into rapturous submission to Divine Will. Anna understood that she was flawed, but, still, she could never quite bring herself to believe that she was blood-guilty. No matter how hard she prayed for conviction, Anna would never experience the tears, the self-recriminations, the shouts of joy—the true conversion that alone—so they said—would save her soul from the searing fires of everlasting punishment.

Josiah Roundtree—Josiah, alone—roused her soul. Anna was young, tractable, lonely, confused about her instincts. Everything in her short life had conspired to bring her to this moment. In a blinding flash of revelation in that Mount Holyoke parlor, she felt that the Heavenly Father's plan for her life, so long withheld, was at last revealed. In the person of the handsome young minister she had found redemption—or so she thought. In the heat, the light, of the moment she feared she'd swoon right into his arms. From that day forward Josiah's mission became Anna's mission. Her husband's life became her own.

Yes, she was saved, she thought. And she told him so.

A year later, after missionary training, she and Josiah left Christian America together for Heathen India. Josiah would convert the multitudes. And the converted Anna would serve Josiah's every need.

Now, Anna was stunned silent. A child of hers alive and in the world! And … dark-skinned …? Before she could respond to Bridey's revelation, they were interrupted. "*Missus Wheeler*!" Anna's landlady bellowed. Anna opened her door to find Mrs. Chapman huffing up the steps.

"Oh, Missus," the landlady babbled. "It's good I caught you in. Here's a fine gentleman to see you in the parlor—a Mr. Larkin. You must hurry. I've taken his umbrella to drip in the kitchen sink and hung his coat by the stove, he was that soaked. But he don't appear to be a gentleman that has much time to waste, so—"

Then she caught sight of the bedraggled Bridey, and broke off. "Who's this, then?" she shrilled, standing back, staring, hands on ample hips, her bosom rising and falling from the exertion of the climb. The landlady's shrewd light eyes took in Bridey's damp red hair, the muddy brogues, the oft-mended skirts with their mucky hems. "And how'd the likes of you get into my respectable house, Missy?"

The Irish girl drew herself up, rising from the chair. "I come in the kitchen way. Yez was out in the back feeding the goat."

The landlady scowled, and Anna adopted a tone she knew would silence an obsequious woman like Edith Chapman. "The lady is here on my behalf. She is my guest. Please leave us."

"But … the caller!"

Bridey's news was so compelling that Anna couldn't even begin to care about this inconvenient gentleman. "Would you ask the caller please to leave his card? I will see him at a more opportune moment."

Mrs. Chapman was taken aback. The ladylike Mrs. Wheeler, usually so meek, so accommodating. But now, this importunate tone. This … rudeness. She hesitated. "He seems the kind of man who will not be best pleased …" But the expression in Anna's eyes was so cold that the landlady backed away a step.

Anna slammed the door in her face and turned to Bridey, whispering, "She is alive? My baby lives? Who has her? Where can I find her?"

I don't know no more than I just told ye—Miss Parker clutching the kid to her chest and walking out into the night."

"I must find her!" Anna's hands were as cold as those of the iceman who came around to Mrs. Chapman's kitchen twice a week.

"I thought mebee ye'd want to. Now that you know all I do, you can start asking that old crow some questions."

A yearning to see—to hold—her child suffused Anna. "What did she look like, Bridey?"

Bridey's hand gripped the doorknob. "The baby?" Bridey thought for a moment. "She looked like—a surprise. I was expecting a lily-white, like you, and here was this head of black hair and, you know, a little dark girl." She waved a dismissive hand. "If ye want ta talk t' Miss Susan, ye better get on yer way over to the Five Points Mission before it's too late. Afternoons, the old cat is busy pokin' her nose in all over the Five Points with her Bible-readin' and her prayin'. What d' she call it? Winning souls for Christ." Her portrayal of Miss Susan Parker's prissy nasal voice was precise and cruel, with atonal New England vowels flattening out her Irish lilt. "As if we didn't already have the One True Church, and good Father Cleary when we need him. Ye'll catch her at the mission, though, for an hour or so before supper." She swung the door open.

Then a new fear seemed to strike Bridey, and she paled. "Don't let that damn Miss Susan know I told ye. It's hard enough for me living hand to mouth in the Five Points as it is without pissing off the ladies of the mission." She slipped into the hall. The door closed behind her with a little thud.

Anna'd had no word from Miss Susan Parker since she'd left the Mission, a week after her baby's birth—and death, as she'd been led to believe. The mission worker had given her three dollars and a cloth-bound New Testament. She'd ended up being grateful for both: she'd paid the cash to Mrs. Chapman for her first week's room and board; the New Testament she'd slipped under the crooked leg of the wretched writing table in her room in order to steady it.

The thought of venturing into the teeming streets of the notorious Five Points didn't worry Anna as it might have another of her sex and station. She had, after all, spent a year training there for the East India mission field—to heal the lame and the infirm as Josiah had required of her, to treat foul maladies such as cholera and dysentery, to bind putrescent wounds, to deliver bloody, mewling babies of girls scarce out of their own infancies, to dispense pills, potions, and powders at times more harsh in their effects than any illness. Nothing of genteel delicacy was left to Anna. And then, too, Manhattan could offer nothing to equal the miseries of the Indian subcontinent. Who could ever forget the bazaars of Calcutta? The child beggars with their legs lopped off. Skeletal mothers dangling dead babies from their arms as they pled for alms. This latter image galvanized Anna: Babies.

Anna's growing fear was that on the fatal night of her daughter's birth Miss Susan might have taken the baby to the river, the destination of many an undesired child. She'd read it often in the newspaper, some pale drowned infant found stranded on the East River's filthy shore. Would Miss Susan—could she—have conceived of such a cruel and unchristian deed? Until Bridey O'Neill's description of Anna's baby as being dark of skin, Anna had thought it to be Josiah Roundtree's, as blond as a stained-glass Baby Jesus. Given the midwife's testimony, she'd instantly formed a picture of her daughter in the image of the true father: brown eyes, curly black hair, and tea-colored skin. Small wonder Miss Susan Parker had been so appalled.

Anna dabbled her fingers in the water of the chipped porcelain wash basin, then wiped them on a threadbare towel, leaving behind a murky streak of ink and blood. Torn between fear and fury, she snatched a battered straw bonnet from its peg on the wall, slapped it on her head, and set off briskly down the stairs, tying the faded blue strings in a hasty knot. It would be too early to find Miss Parker in, but she'd head for the Mission nonetheless and wait as long as she must for that damned lying, sanctimonious spinster to return. And she wouldn't leave until she learned the fate of her child.

TWO

"Mr. Larkin," Anna's landlady brayed, looming in the hall at the bottom of the stairs and grabbing her appalled boarder by the arm. "Here is Miss Wheeler. You need wait no longer." Propelled by a push from Mrs. Chapman, Anna stumbled into the drab parlor, to find a tall, narrow gentleman in a fine white summer frock coat rising from a green plush wing chair. He gazed at her intently. Over his shoulder she caught a glimpse of herself in the shadowed parlor mirror Mrs. Chapman so prized. Beneath the saggy bonnet, Anna's thick dun-colored hair was restrained in a plain bun, although errant tendrils escaped in the humid air. These wayward curls framed her pale face and large gray eyes in an almost wanton manner. She attempted to tuck a wisp behind her ear.

The visitor granted her a long, slow smile. "At last, Miss Wheeler," he breathed, coming toward her holding out both hands. "I was certain that if I waited, you would eventually consent to see me."

Anna drew back. She had consented to nothing. Who was this presumptuous man?

"I do understand," he said, taking her hand and patting it as if they were old and cordial acquaintances, "the reticent ways of ladies when faced with meeting strange gentlemen." Moving just a smidgen too close to her person, the strange gentleman stopped with a bow. "Allow me to introduce myself. I am William Larkin of Larkin & Bierce, Publishers of Moral Literature for the People." His face was thin, his nose and chin pointed. His crisp gingery hair was cut in sideburns that curved down upon his cheeks, and gold-rimmed spectacles were set low on the narrow nose.

Retrieving her hand, Anna adjusted her bonnet and tipped her head. Anxious to be on her way to the Five Points Mission, she shifted her weight from foot to foot.

Mr. Larkin paid no heed to her restlessness. "Please be seated, dear lady, as I have a matter of some moment to place before you." His voice was high and thin, sounding as if it might habitually indulge in irritation but at the moment was determined upon cordiality. The only matter of moment to Anna was the whereabouts of her daughter—her stolen daughter. Her feet, the wiry sinews of her legs, were primed for dashing from the room, but a sudden burst of common sense kept her fixed in place. She'd heard of Larkin & Bierce, Book Publishers. She'd walked past their fine brick building on Park Row. Now William Larkin himself had called—and had not immediately departed when she refused to see him.

And she was a writer. ... Of course she was a writer; what else was there for an educated, but impoverished and disconnected, woman to do? A woman whose past did not bear too close a scrutiny? A little hand-sewing, perhaps, finishing shirts for the shops on Broadway. But when her vision grew too poor for that? And it would. There were thousands such women. She saw them begging in the streets, thin and hollow-eyed, clutching a remnant of earlier prosperity, a shredded silk reticule, perhaps, or a bunch of ragged flowers on a sagging bonnet. It was a cruel city for an unprotected woman, and Anna clung but precariously to the hems of respectable society. She wrote her verses, sold them to the newspapers and magazines, and lived otherwise what she thought of as a soundless life.

Anna pivoted quickly toward the parlor's arched doorway where the landlady still lurked, eyes wide, reddened hands twisting her afternoon apron into one large knot, mouth agog. "Mrs. Chapman, this is a private matter," she said, pursing her lips. "You may leave us."

The woman huffed, turned on her heel and made to stalk away. The soft *shush* of her housework slippers faded away, but Anna wouldn't have been surprised to find her lingering within hearing distance still.

She sat on the edge of the rose-colored sofa, absently arranging around her the skirts of her one street dress, an old, rusty black silk. "Madame," the publisher said, smiling at her toothily, like a fox. "For the past some months I have seen your poems in the newspapers. Such precision of language—marvelous images, lilting cadences. Such lady-like refinement. I am entranced." Both upper canine teeth protruded hungrily. "And I am further captivated," Mr. Larkin enthused, "by the expression of high intellect subordinated to heart and womanly impulse."

"Thank you," Anna said, casting her eyes down, modestly.

Anna kept two separate notebooks of poems, one with a golden cover for her devotional postings, those soulful verses so easy to write and consumed so readily by the editors and readers of newspapers and magazines, and the other with its garish crimson binding for ... she knew not what. A book of the unwriteable, perhaps, a journal of the everyday. In this latter she noted the raucous cries of the streets—oyster men, newsboys, hot-corn girls. The rank odors of the sewers. The ragpicker's dog-cart heaped high with its reeking load. The waft of fragrant steam escaping from the baker's cart as he raised the lid to dispense yet another pie or hot cake from his rich, sweet store. The cheap prostitute with her empty gaze. A cartman cursing the walkers blocking his way.

And, then, there was a third little book. But, about that compilation of verses, the less said ...

Mr. Larkin leaned forward, his forearms resting lightly upon his thighs. "So ... chaste a vision, essentially feminine, free of all licentiousness."

Anna smiled at him wanly. It went without saying that Mr. Larkin referred to the products of her sunny yellow composition book, not the red one.

Nor the other ...

"So," he said, sitting back again in Mrs. Chapman's worn green chair, "I have come with a proposition I feel will prove advantageous to both of us." He stressed the word *advantageous* in such a delicate manner Anna understood at once it could only mean profitable. Dollars-and-cents profitable.

Suddenly she was interested indeed. A secure income would be of great benefit. For her room in this house she paid from week to week, often uncertain as to what the next would bring. A few days of sickness, a fortnight of dull-mindedness, and she might easily find herself shut out of even this shabby parlor with its narrow painted mantle and dingy net curtains. And, more important to her at this moment, more money for her poems would allow her to support her child well.

If she were to find her child.

She feigned great interest in the sofa pillow next to her, plumping it up and smoothing out the gold strands of its tassels, but now she listened intently as Mr. Larkin continued.

"We, my partner, Edward Bierce and myself, that is, are, as I said, publishers of moral literature for the people, and at this time of questionable productions from our American presses ..." He paused, and removed his spectacles. Then he peered at her, as if uncertain whether or not it was proper to continue with so delicate a subject in the presence of so refined a lady. "Cheap novels," he ventured. "The penny-press with its scurrilous tales." He twisted his thin lips, then continued in a spate of words, as if a flood-gate had been lifted. "The masses of readers have degraded taste and no literary discernment, and there is a great deal of money to be made in sensation fiction written for people of the lower sort. Unscrupulous publishers are rushing to fill the bookstalls on the streets with their trash—blood-and-thunder tales, scandalous stories of ... seduction and impurity. Soul-killing books."

He fixed Anna with a steely eye, and she realized this was not an unfamiliar subject of indignation for him. She nodded to indicate she had awareness of the matter. He mistook her acknowledgment for agreement.

Mr. Larkin cleared his throat as if he were about to deliver an oration to the Manhattan Lyceum. "Now, more than ever, my dear lady, our American populace is in need of the spiritual inspiration accessed by woman's inborn closeness to divine truths. And, Mrs. Wheeler, I would like to publish a book of your verses. Clothed in your elegance of style and my elegant volumes, woman's purest instincts will waft irresistibly across the nation like the holiest of incense, edifying and elevating our citizenry—"

Anna sat up straight, hearing the unspoken words, *and earn us both a great deal of money*. She cut in. "So, Mr. Larkin, you are saying that you think my poems will sell?"

He folded his hands in his lap. "Sell, indeed, and sell well. And you, dear lady, will never again be forced to soil your hands with the ink of the common press."

"Do you truly think that is the case?" She assessed him coolly, although her heart was pounding.

"You, Madam, may soon find yourself to be a very … comfortable woman." The day, though declining, remained warm, and Mr. Larkin took a square of fine white linen from his pocket to mop his face.

There was something of Josiah's sanctimony about this William Larkin, but Anna immediately shrugged off her sense of disquiet. If anyone knows piety and its ways, Anna thought, I do. I must trust myself to manage him. She took a deep breath, held it for a moment, and then let it out. "What is it you want from me, Mr. Larkin?"

Before he bid farewell to Anna, the publisher took from his pocket a fine-grained leather wallet, counted out ten ten-dollar notes, one by one, and stood framed in the parlor door fanning himself with them. "Call at Park Row on Thursday afternoon, and we will make the particulars of our business arrangement official. But, meanwhile …" He handed her the fan of bills. "This, my dear lady, is to demonstrate the sincerity of my intentions." He glanced with distaste around the crowded parlor. His gaze lingered upon the cracked ormolu mantle clock, the set of commemorative George and Martha Washington china cups and saucers on the sideboard, the pump organ that had been squeezed into a corner by the door. He sniffed, and Anna realized the air was still redolent with the greasy odor of stewed mutton. "Perhaps," he suggested, "you would care to find accommodations more … suitable to a gentlewoman."

Anna watched Mr. Larkin cross Broadway, skitter around a lumbering omnibus pulled by four sturdy dray horses, and hail a cab. He even walked like Josiah—Josiah of the later years—in deliberate magisterial steps. Long after the cab's high-stepping black mare and rockaway carriage had eased their way into the stream of traffic and vanished up the thoroughfare, she remained at the window with the fan of bills open in her hand. Only when she heard Mrs. Chapman's footsteps once again in the hallway did she ease the bills into a thin stack and fold it over. By the time the landlady entered the parlor brandishing a turkey-feather duster, Anna had secluded her hand in a fold of her skirt.

Mrs. Chapman's boarding house was shabby and crowded with working people—mechanics, clerks, teachers in the schools—but it was clean and respectable. She offered hearty breakfasts of sausages, pickles, and buckwheat cakes with molasses, and dinners of beefsteaks, mutton chops, and boiled potatoes. More elegant establishments catered to people of independent means and provided in a more genteel manner for them. Lodging houses that served no meals met the needs of what the newspapers called the "lower kinds" of people. And those squalid basement flophouses teeming with the destitute ... Well.

Anna counted herself fortunate to be able to afford her quiet, if unbeautiful, room in which to live and write. She smiled politely at her landlady as she evaded questions about the visitor, then slipped past the older woman and out the front door. Securing Mr. Larkin's bills in her reticule, she determined that she must keep in Mrs. Chapman's good graces for she would not remove from this house anytime soon. There was much else to be done with the money.

THREE

"Miss Parker ain't here no more," said the white-aproned housekeeper at the Five Point Mission's wide front door. She wiped at a spot on the sidelight window with a damp cotton tea-towel.

The Mission was an unornamented four-story brick building on Park Street spread over the space of three large city lots. To the left sat one of the neighborhood's notorious grog-groceries, reeking of liquor even at this early hour. The door opened and a boy of eight or so staggered homeward with a brimming pail of beer. To the right sprawled a lumber yard, loud with the rasp of handsaws. Across the street, shouts and taunts of idle men emanated from the fetid triangle of Paradise Square with its whitewashed palings and stunted trees.

Anna was breathless, hot and damp with exertion, having rushed across the uneven brick sidewalks, avoiding cartmen hawking cabbages and potatoes, ducking beneath wet garments hanging low from heavily loaded clotheslines. At the housekeeper's words her fingertips went cold. "But I must see her." She envisioned Susan Parker's long closed face and obsidian eyes, her prim mouth and twittery righteousness. The tight pleated collars. Miss Susan might, Anna was well aware, deny the baby's existence and refuse to divulge her fate, but Anna would allow no mission worker to stand between her and her child. "I absolutely must speak to her."

"*Must* you, Missy? And what's your business with Miss Parker?" Having achieved a gleaming window, the housekeeper addressed Anna directly. A dumpling of a woman, about forty years of age, she was pasty-faced, with the pitted scars of smallpox.

The dingy white lawn collar and cuffs of Anna's rusty black silk were frayed, and the heels of her shoes worn down. She knew, without even bothering to think about it, that she had been mistaken for some middling servant in a hand-me-down gown—probably a maid for one of the city's better families who had gotten herself with child. Just the type of unfortunate the Ladies of the Mission had set out to help.

As Anna had learned in her own hour of desperate need, the Five Points Mission provided a welcome place of refuge for the destitute of New York City. The founders, well-to-do members of the Ladies Home Missionary Society of the Methodist-Episcopal Church, had a vision: medical care, education, sanitation, hot soup, and edifying discourse, they believed, would transform the lost and tarnished denizens of the Five Points into saved and shining citizens of the great metropolis. And, of course, convert the largely Catholic heathen of Five Points to the Methodist faith and liberate them from certain damnation.

"Well?" the housekeeper insisted.

Anna gave her a frigid stare. "My business is my own," she snapped. "Where will I find Miss Susan?"

"Not here, that's for sure." The woman had busily taken her towel to the brass doorknob.

Before Anna could press her request for Miss Parker's current whereabouts, the doorkeeper was suddenly all smiles, gazing behind her. "Ah, Mrs. Ambrose. Here's a caller for Miss Susan."

Anna turned. A spare woman with sallow skin and white hair in a neat snood walked up the sidewalk. This Mrs. Ambrose was dressed simply in cool gray poplin with embroidered collar and cuffs. Without the hindrance of fashionable hoops or crinoline, her skirts fell smoothly to the tops of neat kid boots. A large market basket on her arm held what looked to be stacks of folded baby linen. Despite her lack of beauty, her sartorial simplicity, and the seeming humbleness of her task, no one in Broadway, or in the Fifth Avenue for that matter, would have taken Mrs. Ambrose for anything other than what she was, a lady of the utmost distinction.

This lady addressed the doorkeeper. "Well, then, Miss Longfield, in the absence of Miss Susan, I will, myself, speak with Mrs. …" She let her words trail off, waved the housekeeper down the darkened hall toward the back of the house, placed her basket on a long hall table and invited Anna in, leading her to a small, plainly furnished parlor. The walls were white, the woodwork painted and grained to resemble black walnut, the uncurtained windows tall and sparkling with cleanliness. Anna's hostess motioned her to a leather-upholstered armchair and settled herself in a straight chair next to a mahogany writing desk, where she fixed a strangely compelling gaze on her visitor. "You are?"

"Anna Wheeler."

A startled surprise greeted her response. "Not Miss Wheeler, the poet?"

Anna was taken aback. Fear of discovery shuddered through her; her face flushed. She had isolated herself so thoroughly from society that she hadn't thought Mrs. Ambrose, a member of the Protestant faithful, would surely have read her poems in the *Christian Herald*.

She panicked, wishing she hadn't so boldly announced her identity. The New York pious were a close community. If she told Mrs. Ambrose who she was and what her business was with Miss Parker, Mr. William Larkin, Publisher of Moral Literature for the People, would be certain to hear of the birth at the Five Points Mission of a child of uncertain origins to Miss Anna Wheeler, inspirational poet. Anna understood immediately that Mr. Larkin would not like anything unseemly, and if he found her life to be irregular, he would not publish her book of poems, and if her poems were not published, she would have no money with which to find and care for her child. There was but one prudent recourse: she must lie.

"No," she responded with but a brief hesitation. "I am not she. I have noted those verses of late in the papers, but I do not know that Anna Wheeler." Her mendacious heart thudded almost audibly in her chest.

"Ah," said Mrs. Ambrose. "Wheeler would not, of course, be an uncommon name. I am Margaret Ambrose." She pulled off fine net gloves. "It is my happy privilege to serve as a Trustee of this Mission. Now, Mrs. Wheeler, …" She gave Anna the benefit of the honorific, *Mrs.*, as most people did, although publishers seemed to like the notion of a virginal poetess and unanimously designated her in print as *Miss* Wheeler. ". . . "You're not the usual sort we get here—may I ask what it is you wish to discuss with Miss Parker?" Mrs. Ambrose leaned forward, smiling as if to take some of the rudeness out of her question. Anna repressed a sharp retort; she knew how precarious her position was, and how little she could afford to alienate a Trustee of the Five Points Mission, at least until she had secured the custody of her lost child.

Mrs. Ambrose matched the gloves palm to palm and laid them in her lap. She raised a reassuring hand. "If you are here on Mission business. ..."

In her own refined manner Mrs. Margaret Ambrose was as much a doorkeeper as was the more impertinent Miss Longfield. Anna sighed. "Two years ago, I was resident here at the Mission—in a time of need. A time, I hasten to say, that is now past. But it is about that period that I wish to speak to Miss Susan."

"I see." Mrs. Ambrose was persistent. "And what was your ... particular need?"

Anna sighed again. "I gave birth to a child—a child who ... who did not survive."

Mrs. Ambrose's light eyes flickered, as if Anna's tale had affirmed some intelligent surmise. She lingered on that surmise for a moment, and then continued. "And ... your husband ...?"

Anna flinched. "I no longer have a husband."

The Trustee's prolonged silence required a response.

"He is dead." She would not rehearse for this woman the tale of tragic martyrdom; she had no desire to be known as the widow of the sainted Reverend Josiah Roundtree, dead at the hands of native mutineers in India during the horrific events of the *Sepoy* Rebellion. Mrs. Ambrose would certainly know of Josiah and know his writings. Indeed, from where she sat, Anna could see a full complement of well-read *Missionary Advocate*s shelved prominently in racks upon a parlor wall. He had written on a regular basis for that journal, compelling reports direct from the mission field.

"I see." Mrs. Ambrose took in the worn dress, the mended cotton gloves. "And you are now without resources?"

"No," Anna replied quickly, her pride stung. "I am not here to petition for assistance. I simply wish to ask a question of Miss Susan."

A small leather-bound New Testament lay on the desk in front of the Trustee. She picked it up and shuffled through it absently. Then, once again, her gaze met Anna's. "You will find her in Tarrytown. The ladies of the Mission have established a home for friendless children at that healthy country town on the Hudson in Westchester County. Miss Susan has taken on the job of supervising the home."

"Ah," Anna said, without thinking of the consequences, "then perhaps that is where—" She broke off immediately. "Then that is where I should seek her. I thank you, Mrs. Ambrose. Now if you would kindly provide me with the address, I shall call on her and ask my question."

An inkstand and pen sat close at hand. Mrs. Ambrose took a sheet of paper from a small stack, writing directions in an elegant script with a gold-nibbed pen. As she handed the paper to Anna, she held on for a moment longer than necessary. Her uncanny eyes probed Anna's. "May I be so bold as to address your spiritual life, Mrs. Wheeler? I sense that you are in some distress. Are you in a state of salvation? Is all well with your soul?"

Anna groaned inwardly. Nothing other than despair had come to replace her earlier reliance on Josiah's faith, and she resented Margaret Ambrose's question. But she must speak, so she answered as honestly as she could. "Mrs. Ambrose, I cannot tell."

Mrs. Ambrose assessed Anna with a fine attention. What she seemed to see was not so much a lost soul wallowing in sin, like the multitudes she habitually encountered in the Five Points, but, rather, a wandering soul whose moral compass had lost its fix on the Lord's true north.

The Trustee's slim pale fingers lingered close to Anna's on the sheet of directions. From years of living with Josiah, Anna intuited what would come next. Her stomach tightened, and she took a deep breath, preparing herself.

Margaret Ambrose took both of Anna's hands in hers and looked sorrowfully into her eyes. "Mrs. Wheeler, let us join our hearts together in prayer, as we petition our Lord to return you to the path of salvation." She bowed her head, as did, after a long few seconds, Anna.

On their outbound journey to India, Josiah and Anna had sailed across the North Atlantic, over the equator, then south around the

Cape of Good Hope, into the Indian Ocean, and past the coral reefs of Ceylon with its off-shore breezes redolent of nutmeg and cinnamon. In their cramped cabin, they held language school, repeating sibilant phrases on clumsy tongues, tracing elegant looped characters with awkward fingers. On deck together they watched the land birds vanish one by one except for a few sheltering in the spars, together they marveled at the flying fish that passed in aerial schools. Phosphorescence danced upon the waves, and they delighted in the antics of a young porpoise alongside the vessel puffing water through its spout. They stood in the bow until the supper bell rang, planning their life of mercy and deliverance among the idol-worshipers of Bengal, anticipating the thousands, God willing, the tens of thousands, Josiah would bring to Christ.

These four months together sailing to India, with Josiah's heart aroused by his vision of salvation for the lost heathen multitudes, had been the Eden of their marriage. She had been beautiful then, she felt. Happy with her husband. Happy in her beauty. Round and rosy and happy and young.

Approaching the subcontinent at Madras, the ship was greeted more than a mile from shore by peddlers on catamarans of bound logs, selling coconuts, dates, and bananas. The half-dozen ladies of the American vessel, merchant's wives, an unmarried medical missionary, and Anna, were gathered at the windows of the state cabin, eager to catch a view of this exotic land. When the first catamaran came into view, all fell silent: the brown-skinned men wore no attire at all except a narrow length of cloth secured at the waist.

"Such extremely ... light clothing," Mrs. Rose, a tea merchant's plump wife, said, her blue eyes wide.

"They appear ... robust and healthy," Miss Howe, the medical lady ventured. "Indeed they do," said Mrs. Eddy, the wife of a Boston spice merchant. "Indeed, they look better than one could have imagined."

Anna said nothing. She had never before seen the adult male form in such a nearly complete state of undress, not even Josiah, who conducted his marital obligations in modest nightshirts. She found these Indian boatmen, with their slender, muscular forms and dark complexions, disconcertingly compelling. A shiver ran through her. "Oh, my," she whispered.

"Wife ..." A strong hand gripped her shoulder. She had not heard Josiah's approach. "Come away from the window." There was a tremor in his voice. "This is no sight for a virtuous woman."

"But, Josiah," she remonstrated, startled, for once, into frankness. "Is there not something marvelously innocent about their scantily clad forms? Indeed, are they not beautiful?"

He glanced out the window, then at her, and then away. Startled, she thought, *Josiah is ... frightened. But are not these the very people he has come to save?* Then hastily she put the thought away as unworthy of wifely devotion.

Now, on the brick sidewalk outside the Five Points Mission, Anna had been prayed for—at some length—by Mrs. Ambrose and invited to attend the weekly Bible Study for the Destitute in Spirit. Her sole intention, however, was to get herself as quickly as possible to the Orphan's Home in Tarrytown where she would find Miss Susan Parker. It was too late to go today—the sun hung low in the heat haze over the river—but tomorrow she would take the steam train from the depot at the corner of Chambers and Hudson. Miss Susan Parker was her sole hope, and Anna must approach the orphanage matron calmly, with full grasp of her own dignity. In Tarrytown, surely, she would learn the whereabouts of her lost daughter.

Pray God in His mercy, she might even find the child there.

FOUR

Having stepped down from the train at the river-town station, Anna straightened her bonnet and shook her rusty-black skirts, releasing a small cloud of ash and a burnt cinder that clunked on the wooden platform. A brass plate on stone pillars across the road from the station announced the long lane that wound uphill to the Hudson Home for Orphans.

Everything about the orphanage grounds was neat and pleasing to the eye, as befitted a well-ordered institution. Privet hedges bordered a flagstone sidewalk. Vegetable gardens spanned a field to the left—long, precise rows of corn and beets and leafy carrots. To the right, ranks of apple trees spread down the hill. In the sweet scent of early-fallen fruit, Anna could smell the coming harvest.

The building itself—three-story, yellow-frame—was clean and spacious, green-painted door and slatted wood shutters closed against the heat of the mid-day sun. Yet it seemed lifeless, with not a single child in sight, especially when compared to the clamor and energy of the orphan asylum Anna had overseen at the Fatehgarh Christian Mission to the Heathen of India. Where were all the children? Their shouts and songs? Then she heard them: from behind the closed door young voices droning in rote recitation of the Old Testament titles: ". . . *Leviticus, Numbers, Deuteronomy ...*"

In the depths of her all-too-human heart, Anna had fostered a phantasmagoric hope: that she would cross the threshold of this orphanage and a rosy-cheeked nursery maid would welcome her, a dark-haired, prattling tot in her arms. "We've been waiting for you," the nursemaid would say, and the child would laugh and hold out dimpled arms—

Instead, a spare figure with a plain face met her at the door, lank brown hair pulled back in a tight bun at the nape of her neck. "Mrs. Wheeler?" Susan Parker queried with a startled rising inflection. Her sinewy hand flew to smooth out her stiff pleated collar before she stepped aside to let Anna in. Then she turned sharply on her heel and marched down the hall to a large room in a rear wing of the building. The shutters were open in the parlor, and sunlight poured in from tall windows. The air was tinged with the scent of beeswax and linseed oil.

Miss Susan motioned Anna abruptly to a chair. She, herself, sat at a cluttered writing desk beside a tall mahogany bookcase, shuffling her papers into a more orderly pile. "It has been, I believe, more than two years since your sojourn at the Mission, Mrs. Wheeler. Have you not yet recovered from your … infirmity?"

"I am well, thank you," Anna said. She set her faded silk reticule down on a small oak table, cleared her throat, and squared her shoulders. "I've come, Miss Susan, to ask you a question about my confinement at the Mission."

Before Anna could finish speaking, Miss Susan was up and out of her chair. "There is nothing I can tell you about your child's unfortunate birth … and death … that you do not already know." She glowered at her visitor. "Now, you must leave."

Miss Susan was so much more hostile than Anna had anticipated; in a crisis of nerves, she found that her tongue, at least momentarily, would not respond to the urging of her brain. As far as Miss Susan's narrow piety could extend, she, Anna Wheeler, was an unchaste woman who had given birth to a misbegotten child of a cursed race. But, tellingly, the matron's strong antagonism suggested more than simple revulsion. It struck Anna that Miss Susan's reaction reeked of fear.

Her purpose fixed, she remained seated and took a deep breath. "I am going nowhere, Miss Susan, until you tell me the truth." She repeated

Bridey's tale of having seen the baby, alive, healthy and squalling, being carried off into the night by Miss Susan herself. "Where is my daughter?"

Miss Susan's fingers were laced together, knuckles as white as her lips. Her voice was tight and cold. "Mrs. Wheeler, you are sadly deluded to believe that your child survived its birth. The housekeeper and I were both present as witnesses to the sorry occurrence. We felt it best to spare you the sight and took the poor little thing off to Potter's field for burial." She picked up a bone-handled pen from the desk and engrossed herself in cleaning its steel nib with a pink flannel pen-wiper. Then she looked directly at Anna. "Further, I cannot believe that you would take the word of a female of low character over ... mine."

Anna would believe Bridey before this soulless automaton any day. She stayed rooted in her chair. "Answer me—where is my child? Do you have her in the nursery here?"

The matron slammed the pen back on the inkstand. "We harbor no colored in this place. Never would we force white children, no matter how degraded by sin and poverty, to associate with the lower races. Deuteronomy 7:3: 'Neither shalt thou make marriages with them; thy daughter thou shalt not give unto his son, nor his daughter shalt thou take unto thy son.'"

Anna knew that this obscure verse was cited endlessly in American pulpits to justify segregation of Negroes and whites, but if she had been sufficiently in control of her mental power she would have retorted that the Old Testament in this case referred solely to the segregation of the Hebrews from the Hittites and Girgashites.

She understood now that there had been no purpose at all in her coming here. Any racial aberrance, such as Miss Susan would consider Anna's child, must in her philosophy be removed from white society. Miss Susan would believe she was doing the Lord's will.

Frustrated and furious, Anna gripped the edge of Miss Parker's desk, her unsteady hands scattering papers across the polished mahogany. Out of the variegated welter of ink on paper, in spite of the tear-wash in her eyes, one familiar bold, backward-slanting script stood out. Her heart stopped. She snatched up the letter.

To Miss Parker, My Dear Sister in Christ,

I address you in the spirit of Christian Love to inform you of God's presence working through us here in India. With the conversion of a full dozen heathen in recent days, the propagation of our Lord's Gospel proceeds apace ...

Anna's heart started up again with a drum-like tattoo. Josiah's handwriting! But no. It couldn't be. The Reverend Josiah Roundtree was dead, his body flung into the Ganges at Cawnpore to rot with a hundred others.

She glanced up at Miss Susan. "How? What?" she choked. Then she looked back at the letter in her hand and the date caught her eye. Her heart slowed. 10 March 1857: two months before the Mutiny. This was merely one of the multitude of Josiah's soliciting letters. Anna had watched him night after night swatting away moths from the light of the oil lamp as he wrote these fulsome missives, one after another, until long past midnight.

Her hand released its death-grip on the page, then instantly tightened again: Was Susan Parker aware that the woman she knew as Anna Wheeler had been married to Josiah Roundtree? Surely not. Miss Susan was not one to keep such knowledge to herself.

"Mrs. Wheeler," the orphanage matron said, "You are beside yourself, in a feverish frenzy. Leave now, or I will call the men from the barns and have you removed."

In the hallway a bell rang. Doors opened. Anticipating—at last—the clamor of childish voices, Anna heard only an unnatural hush, the whisper of felt-shod feet passing in orderly lines over polished floors. Out the window, flashes of color caught her attention: a dozen young boys marched toward a milking shed next to a large barn, their feet encased in wooden sabots. All wore shirts of identical muddy-orange calico. Anna watched the children cross the barnyard in lock step, lined up from smallest to tallest. Abruptly, against every impulse of her heart, she hoped that her daughter was indeed not at this place, had not, in her vulnerable first years of life, been subjected to such soulless regimentation.

"They move as if by machinery," she mused. It was as if the words had engendered themselves; she scarcely realized that she had spoken aloud.

"These are children of the unruly classes," Miss Susan snapped. "Obedience and order are essential to their moral management." She stood tall, looming over Anna, and her voice sharpened. "Mrs. Wheeler, shall I summon the men?"

Anna clenched her teeth, knowing that with her unguarded words about the children she had forfeited even the most forlorn hope of engaging the orphanage matron's assistance. She crumpled her dead husband's letter, threw it down, and rose from her chair. "I know you kidnapped my daughter. Did you drown her in the river like a sack of new kittens?" She swallowed her horror at that thought. "I will certainly, Miss Parker, investigate what legal recourse I have against you."

Anna was aware that the law would be blind to any claims of hers, disreputable and morally besmirched as any investigation would find her to be, but the threat seemed, nonetheless, effective. Miss Susan paled and gasped. But she kept silent.

Anna glared at her, then spun on her heel, strode into the hallway, out through the back door, and down the long steep lane that led away from the Hudson Home for Orphans. A vista lay before her as romantic as any Anna had encountered during her East Indian days, the wide Hudson River and the glorious highlands beyond. Yet all was strictly domesticated, as if the wild and rugged landscape was nothing but an unconscious framework for the true business of civilization: The hills were carved into farms, ripe now with the promise of bountiful harvest and fragrant with the scent of new-mown hay; the river's rocky banks were clustered with homes, churches, and shops, and rimmed with the railroad's iron tracks; the river itself was afloat with commerce, fishing vessels, barges, ferries transporting carriages and carts, cabbages and apples, men and beasts. A steamboat paddled northward against the current, low in the water with its heavy load of travelers and pleasure-seekers.

But all the way down the dusty road that led back to the train station, she saw none of this. Her heart was broken. She feared that in this place and at this time she had come to a dead halt in the search for her lover's child.

Ashok! Oh, Ashok … How I have failed you!

FIVE

It could only have been the hand of God, Anna thought, or of some more wayward Power, that she found the article in the foreign news section of the paper that very evening.

> *Tuesday, August 15, 1860*
>
> *MARTYRED MISSIONARIES.*
>
> *The heinous Indian Rebellion of '57 continues to cast its tragic shadow upon the nations of Christendom. At last, a complete list of the American Christian workers from the Fatehgarh Mission in northern India slaughtered three years past during the bloody massacres at Cawnpore has been made available by the Board of Protestant Foreign Missions. All told, those missionaries to Fatehgarh who surrendered their lives for the testimony of Christian truth were numbered nine. ...*

Had Anna not fled Josiah Roundtree when she did, she, too, would have been listed among the dead. She shivered, though the sub-tropical Manhattan night was far from chill. Smoothing out the *Tribune*, she folded the paper in quarters so that the mission story was uppermost. She knew who these martyrs were; she had lived with them for a decade. She could put faces and voices to the names.

Long assuming that Josiah had died in the carnage of India's gory *Sepoy* Rebellion, Anna was seeing for the first time an actual printed record of his death: an item in a news column, but to all intents and purposes also an obituary. The Reverend Josiah Roundtree slaughtered with his fellow believers by fevered native insurgents. Smudged ink on newsprint his final account. Where was the heavenly Book of Judgment Josiah had so faithfully anticipated? Where was his name written in the Blood of the Lamb?

She sighed, then folded the newspaper. Was this what it had all come to? Josiah's years of preparation, the long, rigorous voyage, the long years in mission service together: all this and, yet, she felt no grief? Had she become so devoid of feeling that she could not mourn the husband to whom she had once submitted her entire being? She tore the *Tribune's* thin sheets into strips and twisted them into paper spills which she set aside for lighting the one whale-oil lamp she allowed herself each night. One last glorious blaze for Josiah's name.

Indeed, no matter how dutifully she tried to suppress it in rigorous self-discipline, she could not deny the unholy sense of liberty in which her innermost spirit exulted.

But such a burst of joy was not to last. All that night, images of her daughter perturbed Anna; a beautiful child, to be sure, but not of a complexion seemly for a respectable white mother. She dreamt about trying to rescue a drowning baby. Running along an interminable wharf, its rotten boards disintegrating beneath her feet, she pursued the watery, choking cries. Then, in an abrupt shift, she thought the baby had been gaffed and hung with the shad and the bluefish and the beautiful flying fish of Calcutta Bay, its plaintive cry lost among the creaks and slappings of the night-moored boats. In a subsequent vision, she, herself, was diving from the docks, slicing down and down through the filth and debris of the urban harbor, reaching desperately for one small, etiolated body—

But, no. No. There must be hope for the baby. Anna, waking briefly in the night, knew she must believe that or go mad. But where could her daughter have been taken? In her dreams, the weary mother took up a different quest, trudging up endless tenement steps, never quite able to reach the roof where she knew the baby hung pinned to a clothesline along with the bloody rags of menstruating women. The cries intensified. She followed them down Broadway where her child toddled unattended, barely escaping the lethal wheels of omnibuses and dray carts. This last dream was perhaps the most terrifying, for Anna had become convinced that she'd awoken from the cottony nightmare and this sharp pounding of her feet on slick, hard cobblestone was real.

Anna woke, this time for good. She was alone in her narrow room, without family, without connections—without even a friend.

And her child's father was lost to her forever.

India
1857

For most of her life Anna Roundtree had lived in the shadows of hellfire. Now, alone in a torrid night among alien people, she was, in reality, fleeing toward it as fast as the East Indian Railway could take her. Since her escape from the Fatehgarh Mission and from her husband's side—for her mad flight had felt like escape, indeed—she'd been traveling for days. Now, abruptly, the narrow, jolting train halted, jarring her from contemplation of her perilous state. Heavy footsteps traversed the train's running board outside her carriage, and porters shouted instructions from car to car in a dialect Anna only half understood. Insurrection raged against British rule. Travel was safe for no *ferenghi*. Down the line a mob had destroyed the railroad bridge. That much she could make out from the tangle of native syllables. Outside, the night air was thick with soot and humidity. In the distance the engine chugged, its whistle giving off an occasional impotent wail. For weeks, rumors of native unrest had been spreading, but Josiah had taken no precautions. They were safe, he'd insisted, in the hands of God. Anna had believed the rumors, but the impetus that had fueled her solitary flight toward civilization, she now feared, must have been born of demon possession or of madness.

Gunfire cracked from somewhere down the railroad track, and Anna's heart responded with a tattoo of fear. Her only hope for safety was to reach Calcutta and find a packet ready to sail—a ship with a captain willing to take aboard an unescorted woman. A woman whose passage could only be paid with the healing skills she'd perfected during her decade of mission service—or with the gold ring she had yanked from her finger immediately upon boarding the train.

But the train did not move. The compartment was hot and dark. The pallet on which Anna sat smelled of rancid sweat, making her stomach rise. Oh, dear God, not sick again! She swallowed, hard. Cinders floating into the car through cracks in the wooden window frames lodged in her hair, in the folds of her shawl and blue calico skirt. The steam whistle sounded its long, lamenting wail. Still, the train did not move. Again, an exchange of gunfire. She jumped up from her berth and brittle specks scattered to the floor, crunching under her feet like bodies of hard-shell bugs. Through smudged windows Anna could see two species of flame: the sparks that rose from the engine down the curving track, and farther ahead, at the cusp of the horizon where the heavy blackness of the Indian mountain range met the lighter dark of the steamy night sky, a pillar of fire that rose and fell in sudden, ominous silence.

When I was at Mount Holyoke, Anna thought, *I still had breasts.*

She shuddered and threw herself back onto the pallet that served as both bed and bench. Surely she was going mad. Violence and destruction all around her. How could she entertain so vain a memory: her *breasts*! *It's not so much that you mind dying*, said the detached, ironic voice against which she had hurled so much anguished prayer during the past near-decade of missionary wifehood. *It's that you mind dying when you haven't even lived.*

"Oh, my God," Anna prayed, "help me! Help me! Just let me live, if only for a day …"

Her voice had grown louder with each sobbing word, until on the last it trailed off into an inarticulate wail. Heavy footsteps halted abruptly on the running board outside her door, and someone turned the iron handle. Anna had bolted the door upon entering, and it remained fast shut.

"Are you English, Madam?" asked an urgent voice in the masterful tones of the British ruling class. An officer? An East India Company agent?

"American," she responded, her heart pounding now with hope.

"Open the door," the voice commanded.

Anna rose and drew back the iron bolt, but as the carriage door swung open, she was stunned by the appearance of the man who stood in the doorway—a Bengali porter in filthy robes. Brown skin, black hair, dark eyes, the handsome wide cheekbones and sensuous mouth of the Indian native. But—a porter? This man spoke her language with the intonations of an upper-class Englishman.

The man in the doorway stared at her, incredulous, then entered the compartment, slamming the door behind him, leaning his weight against it, still staring. The night was dark, but a reflection from the flames danced through the window and illuminated his burnished skin. His startled eyes gleamed in the fitful light.

"Where are you going, Mrs. Roundtree?" the stranger asked. "Can it truly be that you travel alone?"

SIX

The morning following her fruitless visit to the Hudson Home, Anna awoke frantic. Miss Susan Parker had lied about her daughter, she knew, and she knew also that she had no resources whatsoever with which to force the mission worker into telling the truth. Had Miss Susan abandoned the child? Or sent her to the workhouse on Blackwell Island for the paupers and the demented to raise? Or, had she taken her to the East River and … drowned her?

At breakfast, Anna swigged down a cup of Mrs. Chapman's wretched coffee, grabbed up two unbuttered rolls, left the table precipitously, took up her bonnet from where she had placed it on the hall table, and headed out the door. Surely she would recognize Ashok's child anywhere. She knew the sidewalks of the bustling city well, and she would search them, one by one. But where should she begin? On the stoop she hesitated, looking first toward Broadway and then back toward Greenwich Street. Something akin to mania possessed her feet: they took off walking without her volition and with no direction in mind. She was perhaps a bit crazed, but she walked and walked and walked.

In the Five Points, after several fruitless hours of scrutinizing small faces, she stumbled across a troupe of swaggering young girls garbed in cast-off silks and taffetas that had begun life as garments far up the social scale. They sashayed through Paradise Square giggling and screeching, brushing against the men in their way. One dark-haired child, wearing red silk stockings of the kind favored by the fast set, fell behind the rest, hanging onto the arm of a leering sailor whose blue shirt was stiff with dirt. She couldn't have been more than twelve years old. She, in particular, caught Anna's eye—although the youngest of the pack, she had style and audacity. Still without bosom, she swished her hips like a seasoned street girl. A red-and-gold bodice topped her green velvet skirts, which were held high so she could flaunt her prized red stockings. While crimson toes protruded from broken silver slippers, she'd hung around her neck a pair of nearly respectable leather shoes held together by the laces—saved, perhaps, for good.

What if, Anna thought, staring at the flouncing girl, *what if my daughter has been abandoned to such a life?* She instinctively stepped out to waylay the child, but from amid the milling denizens of the Points, hustlers, loafers, sidewalk auctioneers, a woman's stern voice called out, "Patsy Moshier! Don't you dare!"

The girl's dark eyes opened wide, and she jumped back. The sailor took one look at the gray-clad Fury marching toward them from between a stale-beer dive and an old-clothes shop, and slunk away into the crowd. A skinny, pock-marked youth hooted. "Just saved yourself a good four bits, Davey, me lad. And most likely a dose of the clap, too."

"Patsy, you minx, what did I tell you about going with men!" The woman grabbed the girl by the arm. Anna gaped after the pair as Mrs. … yes … it was … Mrs. Ambrose … dragged Patsy in the direction of the Five Points Mission.

Upon returning to New York from India, Anna had determined to abandon pity. There, she had seen so much misery and cared for so many desperate people that she felt herself to have engaged in more than enough mercy for any one person's lifetime. Hundreds of destitute children roamed the Manhattan streets—New Yorkers seemed to brush them aside as nothing more than a nuisance. But this child, this one filthy—beautiful—girl, had revived her heart. Anna could no longer pass the others with averted eyes. She spent the remainder of the day seeking out such girls, feeding them at the street carts—oysters, roasted sweet potatoes, savory meat pies. Finally, when it grew too dark for safety, and the children disappeared into their hovels and hidey-holes, she turned her steps back toward the boarding house. She had obsessively scanned the faces of even the most pitiful infants, as well as—she couldn't help it—of the brutalized girls those infants would grow to become. She had seen no child who could possibly be her own.

"A nigger woman brought this for you before supper ..." Mrs. Chapman thrust an envelope at Anna. She wore a cotton dressing gown in a garish green print and her graying hair was screwed up in strips of old newspaper. "Uppity she was, calling at the front door the way she done. Didn't like it one bit when I made her take this thing round back as was only proper. She wanted to see you, and she weren't best pleased when I told her you'd bin gone most of the day and han't bothered to leave no word about when you'd be back."

Behind Mrs. Chapman, in the parlor, the widowed Mrs. Douglas wept over her dog-eared copy of *The Wide, Wide World*. Miss Higginson, an elderly schoolteacher, played "Home, Sweet Home" on the wheezy pump organ. Mr. Whittaker, a merchant's clerk, perused the latest *Police Gazette* by the light of a whale-oil lamp. The reek of its smoky wick mingled uneasily with the lingering smell of the supper cabbage.

Anna took the letter, mystified. Other than an occasional note or magazine publisher's bank draft, she never received mail. The landlady lingered in the vestibule, dampening a forefinger to wipe dust off a gilded oval frame. On the envelope, *Mrs. Anna Wheeler* was inscribed in black ink in a forthright, but unfamiliar, hand. The flap had been securely sealed with red wax. Anna was about to break the seal when Mrs. Chapman's presence gave her sudden pause. She slipped the unopened note, folded, into her left glove.

"Thank you, Mrs. Chapman," she said, a foot on the first step of the staircase. "Good night."

The lamplighter was just passing with his long pole, and wavering gaslight shone into Anna's window. She placed the envelope on the table by the bed and lit her candle with a brimstone match. Who knew her whereabouts and wished so urgently to communicate with her? She broke the envelope's seal and retrieved the folded page.

Mrs. Wheeler—

I understand that you are seeking a female child of dark complexion born at the Five Points Mission some two-and-a-half years ago. I may have information pertinent to your search. I shall be at home to you tomorrow afternoon.

Yours most sincerely,
Caroline Julia Slade
Lafayette Place.

A female child of dark complexion! Anna sat down, hard, on the rush-seated chair. This woman knew about her daughter! Who on earth was Caroline Julia Slade? The writing paper and the address were good—a woman of means, then. But how could Miss ... or Mrs. ... Slade possibly know about Anna's child?

Then she thought she understood, and a kind of fury came over her: Mrs. Ambrose must have told her! Mrs. Slade was probably yet another wealthy Christian matron wielding prayers and vegetable broth against poverty, disease, and desperation, the class of woman who sent a servant girl with an important message rather than deliver it herself, the sort of person whose pious pity for a fallen woman most likely would offer nothing to Anna but the taste of ashes in her mouth. Anna knew the type all too well. Crumbling the letter in her hand, she hurled it toward the cold stove—there was no way on God's earth that she would allow herself to be caught up in some condescending prayer circle of sugary benevolence!

Livid, she began unbuttoning the sweat-drenched black dress, popping off at least three of the small jet buttons, which rolled in the direction of the crumpled letter. Then she loosened the drawstring of her one petticoat, let the garment fall to her feet, unlaced and removed her well-worn corset, and stepped out of her drawers. Finally, pulling her long chemise over her head, she wrapped her unclothed body sarong style in the bright Kashmiri shawl her child's father had given her. She often slept thus; it was more comfortable than a nightgown—and as close as she could get to being with him.

Crimson and gold with indigo threads outlining the *boteh*, the traditional tree-of-life motif, the shawl was of a wool and weave so fine she could have, had she been so inclined, drawn it through a ring. Because she was not a shopper, Anna had no way of knowing how valuable it was, that such a hand-woven shawl imported to New York from India might sell for as much as two thousand dollars at the Marble Palace, as the elite Stewart's Mercantile was known. She treasured it, not for its monetary value, but for Ashok, for memory. When she left the room during the day, she would throw the shawl across her bed to welcome her back from the hard, uncaring city to warmth and color and life. When she sat alone, she removed her dress and corset, tucked one end of the shawl into the waist of her petticoat, and slanted the remainder over her chemise and shoulder like the *pallav* of a *sari*. Wearing it thus, one memorable night on a deserted tea estate in the high hills north of Calcutta, she had learned more of passion than she had ever before imagined possible.

But … *no* … abruptly, at the thought of Ashok, Anna sat up in bed. She had not told Margaret Ambrose that her baby was dark of skin; how could this Mrs. Slade possibly know? Had it been Susan Parker who'd sought her out? If so, why? She took a deep breath, stepped across the floor, and retrieved the crumpled letter by the stove, smoothing it out. Tomorrow afternoon, it said. Well, then, she would be on Mrs. Slade's doorstep at two o'clock sharp.

She blew out the lamp. *India Elizabeth*, she thought, warm and drowsy in the Kashmiri shawl. *I will name my daughter India Elizabeth*. The image of a dark child teased her into an exhausted sleep, vanishing into the distance with a coy backward glance.

SEVEN

The sun slanted into Anna's room from the east. Despite her eagerness, it was far too early to set out for Lafayette Street. She'd spend the morning writing more verses to give Mr. Larkin tomorrow. She laid out on her writing table the yellow notebook of inspirational images and the crimson-bound volume of ... what? ... earthier observations? From the first she plucked an image and deftly scratched out a poem.

The Grave

The dark house, the narrow house
That final home of clay,
To one who hopes for Paradise
Whose path is traced that way,
Is naught but a way-station,
A stop along the road,
A rest, and transfer, ticket punched,
To destination—God.

It was twaddle, but Mr. Larkin would like it—and pleasing Mr. Larkin was essential. Now, to craft another poem. Anna leafed further through the yellow book; nothing struck her fancy. She turned to the red book of city notes: a ragged hand-cut wooden cross fallen across a small grave in an uptown cemetery; the bell-man dumping rat carcasses off his cart into the river; a slaughterhouse spouting streams of blood into the gutters. Too raw, any of these, to stimulate the poignant little verses her publisher would favor. But write she must; to find India Elizabeth she would need money, and a great deal of it. Poeticizing was her only skill, and that tedious Mr. Larkin had shown her how profitable it could be.

She took up her pen again. Dipped it. Held it over the paper.

Nothing. Her mind was thicker than this morning's oatmeal. All she could think of was her daughter—should she write about India Elizabeth? No. Such an effort would surely break her heart.

In desperation, from a dresser drawer, secluded beneath two nightgowns, her third best chemise, and the newspaper that lined the drawer's bottom, she retrieved a third book, a limp black-covered, dog-eared volume: the Fatehgarh notebook in which she'd recorded so much beauty—and even more pain. Could she bear to peruse its contents? Her hand seemed to vibrate with memory on the shabby leather cover, and she recalled the day three years earlier when she'd slipped the book into her pocket and closed the door on her life at the mission. From the moment of fleeing that little mud-brick house to this very second, she had not once dared to open the ragged little volume.

The Fatehgarh Christian Mission sat on the west side of the Ganges seven hundred miles north of Calcutta. It was large, well-funded and ambitious, with five missionary families, the church and infirmary, the printing press, orphan asylum, schoolhouse, and Christian village, where native converts were secured from the evil influences of a heathen population. As much as possible, for their own comfort, the missionaries tried to keep their surroundings familiar and civilized, but in vain; they could do little about the house lizards that chased each other across walls and ceilings, the thieving black-faced monkeys that invaded kitchens, snatching up any food in sight, the constant stench of damped and smoldering fires, and the ungodly wail of temple chanting. Not for one moment were these transplanted Christians allowed to forget that they had been set down amid the alien corn.

Anna shared a whitewashed mud-brick bungalow with Josiah, but it had never, even in the early years, felt quite like home. Her days were spent either in the infirmary dispensing medicines and caring for the sick or in the mission office opening letters from home churches, drafting responses for Josiah to sign, and tallying up the donations, for donations there were, a steady stream of dimes and dollars from Sunday-School children and Ladies Benevolence Societies. Anna kept the accounts and held the keys to the safe. She oversaw the small orphanage. In the girls' school she taught English, needlework, knitting, and crocheting. When the native women called at the infirmary for bark powder or quinine, she halted her work and spoke with them at length, teaching—and, indeed, learning—the ways of healing. And this work was more than satisfying to her.

And Josiah? Finding all previous Bible translations in the native languages of the past hundred and fifty years of Indian Christian missions to be grossly inadequate, Josiah slaved, day and night, over a new and authoritative Bengali edition. He grappled with the original languages of the Bible, sometimes forgetting to eat or sleep, until all connotations of the Hebrew, Aramaic, or Greek had been considered, then rendered as literally as possible into the Indian tongue. Given his genius with languages, Josiah told Anna, this would surely be the most renowned translation of all time. And, Anna, for a long while, believed him.

But Anna also knew that, as surely as Josiah was a translator, she herself had *been* translated by her sojourn in India. She seemed somehow to have entered into the sacred book: the shepherds with their flocks; the women drawing water at the wells; the men grinding at the mills; the dusty roads lined with the blind, the lame, the leprous; the children clustering around her whenever she went out into the compound or the villages. The weather, too, was Biblical, hot and dry in season, with the scent of spices in the air. She loved the lilt of the languages, even when she could not understand their meanings; she took pleasure in the beauty of the people and their graceful ways; she thrilled at the bustling towns with their palanquins and wooden bullock carts, skinny cows wandering at will in the bazaars; she loved the chants and bells and drums of festivals in the temples; she could not get enough of the cardamom, turmeric, and saffron, the mangos and pomegranates.

Yet she learned well to keep her delight in all this to herself. Her body lost its luxuriant curves. With each miscarriage or stillbirth she grew thinner, more insubstantial. Nightly she petitioned the murky cloud-like image that served as her God, asking for acceptance of, and obedience to, Josiah's increasingly rigorous demands. And, in what quiet moments she had, she took out her small notebook and crafted the verses that had become her secret and defiant pleasure.

Now, in New York, she finally picked up the small black diary; it weighed almost nothing in her hand. Here she had noted the screams of wild peacocks, ten to a *neem*-tree bough; the pink-nosed mongoose, death to snakes; the lithe dancing girls with tinkling tambourines; the gemlike mosques and pagodas; the fire-lit face of the spice woman at her brazier: the exotic world in which her husband's calling had immersed her. Surely there must be something in this forgotten book she could use for a poem.

She breathed in deeply and turned back the cover. On the first page she had noted an Indian tree, nameless to her, whose blossoms blew white each morning, changed to pink as the day passed, and in the evening fell crimson from their boughs. Every morning, there they were again, baptismal white. Anna had told Josiah she thought they could be called "resurrection flowers." He'd frowned. "Do not," he said, "mistake some pagan arboreal happenstance for the one true Resurrection Tree—the Cross of Christ." For a preacher of Christ's parables, Josiah's habit of mind was surpassingly literal.

That first day in Fatehgarh she had cut a handful of the marvelous morning branches and placed them in an etched-glass vase, thinking to retain their snowy innocence, but by evening they, too, had fallen, crimson. Now, here in this New York room, looking out upon bustling Liberty Street, she supposed that she herself in India had been a cut branch in an etched-glass vase. There was, of course, a poem in that, but she could not write it. Josiah's ghost had killed the metaphor.

Oh, Josiah, where do you lie? You will not rest easy in an Oriental grave.

Just as Anna was about to turn to the second page of the battered India journal, Mrs. Chapman's bell rang for the noon meal. She sighed with relief and replaced the small book in its hiding place. Eventually she would confront the desolate midnight scrawling of her later missionary years, but at this moment she was grateful for the reprieve. She wiped her pen, surveyed the nib for signs of damage, sighed at the necessity of purchasing a new one. Her fingers were, as always, ink-stained, and she rubbed them with sand to whiten them. She would eat her dinner, then call at once upon this mysterious Mrs. Caroline Slade.

EIGHT

In the magnificent paneled hall of the Greek Revival mansion on Lafayette Place, Anna stepped gingerly across silken rugs. The housekeeper, a slender, tight-lipped, Negro woman in crisp gray poplin, vanished through a curtained doorway in search of her mistress. When a young woman, tall and arrow-straight with black hair and steady green eyes, appeared in response to the summons, Anna was startled. This was not at all the type of plump, devout, condescending matron she had expected. *Miss* Slade, the housekeeper had called her, not *Mrs*. Anna's courage faltered. Was it Miss Slade who unsettled her? Or was it the housekeeper, whose greeting had been taciturn, to say the least? Or was it the grand house itself, dimmed against the August heat, lavish with exotic objects, mysterious with tapestry-draped doorways?

Caroline Slade's gaze was bold and searching. She said, "You must be exceptionally warm, Mrs. Wheeler. Mrs. Fitch will bring us iced drinks in the shade garden."

Anna followed Miss Slade down a dark corridor to a wide oak door surmounted by a fanlight streaming muted light into the dim interior. Planted in foxglove, roses, and hydrangea, the luxuriant walled garden seemed as far as Eden from the muggy city surrounding it. Once they were seated at a wicker table under a spreading maple, Miss Slade looked Anna directly in the eye. "Mrs. Wheeler, I am not a person who cares for the mincing pruderies of polite society, so I will say at the start that it does not matter to me what you have done. When I heard your story, I vowed to assist you."

Anna sat perfectly still—she had told this woman no story. Who had? Why had Miss Slade summoned her to this magnificent house? What "assistance" was she offering?

Caroline Slade was attractive without the burden of beauty. She was too tall to be fashionable; her features, sharp, almost aquiline, were too prominent in a too-thin face. Nonetheless, her movements were graceful, and her mien disclosed character and intellect, the latter of which she made no effort to veil. She also seemed, Anna thought, to be possessed of enormous self-presence for one only in her early twenties.

In her dampish black silk, Anna envied Miss Slade's white muslin, loose and simple, ideal for the oppressive heat and humidity of a Manhattan summer. Then she chastised herself—how could she think about clothing when her child's very being was at stake?

Miss Slade gave Anna an odd sideways smile and leaned forward in her chair, just as the housekeeper entered the garden. Mrs. Fitch's eyes were large and dark, her skin the color of sugared cinnamon. On a bamboo tray she carried clinking glasses of lemonade and delicate stemmed dishes of a pale pink confection.

"Thank you, 'Bama," Anna's hostess said. "You must try the ice cream, Mrs. Wheeler. It was made up this morning from fresh country peaches."

Mrs. Fitch placed an etched glass dish at Anna's place. *Grudging*, Anna thought, that was the word for the housekeeper's attitude. But Anna hadn't sweltered all the way uptown to Lafayette Place to be browbeaten by a sullen servant, so she smiled her thanks and watched Mrs. Fitch turn back toward the house. Only when she'd seen her enter the back door and vanish from sight did she take a spoonful of the iced dessert. *Ambrosia*. Replacing the spoon on its china plate, she leaned slightly toward her hostess. "How is it, Miss Slade, you wish to help me?"

Her would-be benefactress rocked a lemonade glass restlessly from side to side. "Mrs. Wheeler," she said, "I will be frank with you. I am fortunate to have been born into wealth and to have been privately educated in Europe by a free-thinking and enlightened father. Among other things, I've learned the burdens and responsibilities that come with privilege, one of which is to assist the unfortunate."

Anna bridled: the *unfortunate*? Had she sunk so low as to become in Miss Slade's eyes one of that pitiable class? She sat up straighter and tightened her lips. "You are a charity worker?" she asked, with an air of dignity. "Like Mrs. Ambrose."

"Margaret Ambrose of the Five Points?" Caroline Slade's thin lips twitched as if she were amused. "Well, perhaps, but my goals are somewhat more ..." her smile again twisted to one side, "... *earthly* than hers."

Anna laughed. It was a rusty sound and surprised her—it had been so long since she'd found anything to be funny.

Caroline noted her response. "Don't misunderstand me," she went on. "Margaret Ambrose is sincere—even bold—in her desire to help the destitute, but she's limited in what she can do by her piety and her incessant urge to proselytize." She cast Anna a meaningful look. "While I, being neither pious nor precisely respectable, am free to help as I please." She cooled herself with a green and yellow silk fan.

A kind of intoxication came upon Anna, to hear a woman speak of freedom in such an unconventional manner, to hear anyone dismiss piety and respectability, the foundations of Josiah Roundtree's life philosophy, in such unequivocal terms. Miss Slade's words gave her a thrill of possibility. And it didn't hurt that she could feel, in her petticoat pocket, pressed against her thigh, the wad of bills Mr. Larkin had given her. *She* was not destitute. That, too, smelled of freedom.

"I had a friend at school, Miss Slade," she said, taking another spoonful of ice cream and sitting back in her cushioned wicker chair, "with whom I shared a great affinity. She was perfectly frank and perfectly free in her speech. You seem to be such a person. So I'll ask you directly, how is it you wish to help me?"

The sunlight in the garden began to wane, foretelling a change in the weather, but Anna hardly noticed.

The younger woman had pulled a needlepoint frame from a sewing basket by the table, and her attention momentarily was given to the square of needlework, rich with bold flowers in fantastic colors. "I'm active in a number of causes, most particularly the anti-slavery movement." She looked at her guest sideways, expressionless. Something that might have been said was not being said.

Anna didn't understand what Caroline's abolitionist affiliations had to do with her. She knew, of course, that slavery was evil, but, having lived so long in India, her awareness of the abolitionist movement was scant. She nodded at Caroline impatiently.

Her hostess fingered the stem of the ice-cream dish. "Among my interests is the welfare of the Negro children in this city."

"That is admirable, Miss Slade." She took up the luncheon napkin and pressed it against her ice-cool lips, wishing the woman would get to the point. "But what has it to do with me?"

Caroline gave her a searching look. "Bear with me—one person I have aided, although not a woman of color, is Mrs. Bridget O'Neill, a promising young midwife." The young woman gave a dry cough. "She has informed me of your loss of a child from the Five Points Mission."

Anna gasped, stunned into wordlessness. *Bridey*! Bridey had betrayed her! She felt her face redden. Then she squared her shoulders and returned Caroline Slade's bold gaze.

"So?" she replied, defying censure or pity.

"I think I might be able to help you. That is, if you desire to find the girl."

"Oh, yes," Anna cried, her shock overridden by a wild surge of hope.

Caroline leaned forward, a gleam in her intent green eyes. "You are certain? It is my understanding that your child is of mixed parentage. In a nation that sanctions the institution of African slavery it is not an enviable situation for a white woman to have given birth to a child of the African race." She sat back, chose cerise silk yarn, and began to thread a needle.

Anna gave her a steady look. "My daughter is indeed of mixed race, but she happens to be Indian."

Miss Slade's eyes shot wide open, and the bright thread between her fingers halted in its path toward the shiny needle. "Indian? Lenape, you mean? Or ... Algonquin? Mohawk?"

"Her father is from India."

Caroline Slade's expression grew fascinated. "India? You are certain?"

In spite of herself, Anna laughed. "Miss Slade, how could I possibly be mistaken? The child was conceived somewhere in the mountains north of Calcutta."

"Calcutta! Here I thought I was the worldly one, and I've yet to set foot on the Asian continent." She sat back in her chair, cerise thread dangling from her long fingers, and studied Anna. "Mrs. Wheeler ... Anna ... you are a most interesting woman."

No one had called Anna by her given name since she had left India. She searched her hostess's face for signs of condescension but found none. Was it possible Miss Slade could be a friend? "Not so interesting, I fear. I was ... married to a missionary who worked in the East India missions."

A breeze had picked up, ruffling the canopy of leaves above them. Anna felt a drop of rain on her arm, then another. She looked up. Dark clouds were blowing in from the west.

"Really?" The manner in which Miss Slade prolonged the word expressed her intense interest. "And, yet you ..." As a raindrop splashed her cheek, she glanced up at the threatening sky. "I would hear more," she said. "But at the moment I must tell you what I asked you here for. I am a Trustee of the Colored Orphan Asylum."

Of course—of course—there would be a colored orphanage separate from that for white orphans. This might be New York City, not, say, Charleston, but—like Miss Susan Parker—most people felt that the races should not mingle.

"The orphanage is uptown on Fifth Avenue," Miss Slade said, "at 43rd Street, a quiet and healthful neighborhood. Several hundred children are cared for there, mostly Negro, but a few Indians as well."

"Indians?" Anna was jolted to a sudden understanding: The *Colored* Orphan Asylum! Her heart had begun to race.

Caroline gave a wry laugh. "*Native* Indians, I mean, of course. Not East Indians. I'm sorry if I misled you."

"India Elizabeth would be as dark-skinned as any native child, and certainly as many Negroes. Susan Parker must have taken her there!" Anna pushed back her chair and jumped up. "I will go at once." Here was a miraculous gift, from Miss Caroline Slade, to be sure, but almost as if from on high. Surely at the Colored Orphan Asylum she was fated to find Ashok's child.

Caroline motioned Anna back to her seat. "Hear me out, Anna. I came to the self-same conclusion, which is why I asked you to call. Given your circumstances, I don't imagine you wish to show up on your own with such an ... an *outré* tale. As I often visit, to make certain everything is comfortably managed, I thought it would be best if we went together on a routine visit. Will you come with me tomorrow?"

Anna's heartbeat was so loud in her ears she couldn't be certain she'd heard Miss Slade aright. But nonetheless she responded immediately, "yes! Oh, yes!"

Her hostess inserted her still-threadless needle in the linen, and set the needlepoint aside. In the humidity her dark hair had begun to escape its rigorous braids, wispy curls softening her austere features. "Perhaps you will find your child in the nursery. Perhaps not. I will, in any case, tell no one of your situation."

Anna blinked back tears. "I cannot say how obliged I am." Thunder pealed in the distance.

Ignoring the words of gratitude, Caroline glanced up at the heavy clouds. She rang a silver bell that sat close at hand, its tone clear and penetrating.

Mrs. Fitch arrived so swiftly and quietly Anna was certain that the housekeeper had been hovering just beyond the rosebushes. Her gaze came to rest upon Anna, her eyes so knowing that Anna understood she had been listening to the entire conversation. She felt a sudden pang of anxiety. Had she, in the heady freedom of conversation with Caroline Slade, let loose her secret to be bandied about among bad-tempered servants?

That fear must have revealed itself in her expression. "Mrs. Fitch is to be trusted explicitly," Miss Slade said. "She would never betray a secret. Is that not true, Alabama?"

The dark woman nodded, her manner so inscrutable Anna was not soothed. And then she experienced an even-more intense anxiety: Caroline Slade's passionate intelligence perhaps did not bode well for comfortable acquaintance. She seemed like someone who might be inclined to act in a rash, impulsive manner. How did Anna know she could trust this intense young woman?

But, as she hastened across 4th Street to Broadway, she forgot her fears, galvanized by thoughts of India Elizabeth. Her daughter would be almost two-and-a-half now, a babbling, round-cheeked, dark-haired delight of a child. And, by the grace of God—and Caroline Slade—perhaps tomorrow Anna would hold her for the first time.

It wasn't until she was on the horse car downtown, drenched, wedged between a large German workman with the smell of sweat and beer on his coat and a thin woman in damp faded calico who coughed consumptively all the way to Canal Street, that she recalled again Mr. Larkin's summons to his office tomorrow. Well, Larkin & Bierce could wait until later in the day. She was galvanized by the possibility Caroline Slade had placed before her and could think no more of poetry.

It stormed all evening, and the damp air entering Anna's open window at midnight reeked of mud, horse piss, and the foul effluvia of brimming sewers. Each time she drifted into sleep, a cart or cab would rattle by, iron wheels screeching, weary driver cursing and cracking his whip, the poor sodden horse clopping heavy shoes over slippery cobbles. And, too, she could not rest for thinking of tomorrow's visit to the Colored Orphan Asylum.

When, after midnight, Anna had finally fallen into a restless doze, the trumpets and bells of a speeding fire engine awoke her rudely from a dream of jasmine. It was as if the sweet, heavy scent were there in the room with her, the glorious white blossoms of Bengal blooming in the corners, opening calyx and corolla, enticing her to reach out a languid hand and pluck a stem. Ashok, she thought, half-unconscious, Ashok. He seemed there in her narrow bed, his hand gentle, caressing her body. She caught her breath. Oh, how she missed him. Oh, how she yearned for his love!

Visions of India Elizabeth haunted her, a joyous child, brown and beautiful, playing in an Indian garden. Other, less happy, images supplanted these, her daughter suffering the machine-like regimentation of some soulless institution like Miss Susan Parker's. Or, worse, the girl brutalized, beaten, shivering in rags in some foul slum dwelling.

But never once did Anna Wheeler conceive of the even-more-dire fate that might well lie in wait, in that time and that place, for her dark-skinned child.

NINE

The haggard man in the shabby black frock coat, sadly soiled now after the long journey, disembarked as soon as the ship docked at South Street pier. Unencumbered by baggage except for a small Gladstone bag, he stepped from the gangplank to a broad, slippery quay, navigating between boxes, sacks, and barrels. The wharves bustled with early-morning life: a clan of German emigrants guarded a small mountain of well-corded chests; a group of wool-clad Englishmen stood at attention near a heap of large blue boxes; an Irish family clutched rope-tied bundles and all but danced in their excitement at being in America at last.

"Hacks! Cheap hacks!" A tattered boy clutched the traveler's sleeve, dragging him toward a ragged line of hansom cabs on Fulton Street. The man shook the child off. He stood still for a moment to orient himself, then strolled northward, past the shops of ship chandlers, sail-makers, and figurehead carvers. It was an overcast summer day, and the stench of filthy harbor water hovered damply above the streets, rankling in his nostrils after so many months of pure sea air. He chastised himself: A spiritual man must not find annoyance in the lesser indignities of the flesh. He strode past saloons and brothels, headed for a boarding house near Union Square that he recalled from a decade past, when he had last found himself a dweller in the City of New York.

TEN

At the last second before leaving her room the following morning, Anna grabbed up Ashok's vibrant shawl. The day would soon grow too warm to wear the shawl, but she could carry it over her arm. She wanted it with her—she *needed* it—for comfort, for her lover's phantom presence. Caroline's barouche pulled up just as Anna exited the boarding house. All the way up Fifth Avenue, this boulevard of sleek carriages and noisy omnibuses, she gaped at the changes in the once-rugged neighborhood. They passed large brownstone public buildings, elegant Italianate homes, great hotels, and soaring churches. Where were the old frame farmhouses with their ramshackle sheds, tethered goats and free-roaming hens? Where were the rickety, creaking farm wagons piled high with potatoes and winter squash?

Just beyond the massive stone walls of the Croton Reservoir, Caroline pointed abruptly to her left. "There's the asylum." The spacious brick building was enclosed within a high fence, its well-kept grounds with their tall trees and neatly tended gardens extending from 43rd to 45th Street. So this was the Colored Orphan Asylum? The barouche turned through tall iron gates and rumbled up a long lane.

Anna stole a glance at her companion. What was it about the plight of the unfortunate colored race that engaged such interest in Caroline Slade? Why, out of all the impoverished and disenfranchised peoples of the city, did she choose to care for those of African descent?

Impulsively she asked, "Just what is your relation to the Colored Orphan Asylum?"

The young woman waved a dismissive hand, her lace-edged sleeve falling back above the white net glove. "I am a patron. I give money. It is nothing."

Anna looked at the elegant young woman curiously. "Why are you so reluctant to acknowledge your philanthropy?"

Caroline gave a brittle laugh. "I must have some purpose in life, don't you think, something to keep me interested and alive. So I amuse myself by playing Lady Bountiful. Is that so very admirable?"

The idea of *amusing* oneself by aiding the poor was wholly alien to Anna's mind. She surprised herself by saying so and was further surprised when Caroline took her hand and squeezed it.

Anna shrugged. Miss Slade's motivations were not her affair. What did she know about the whims and fancies of the very rich? All she need concern herself with right now was the entrée this well-connected woman offered her to the orphanage.

They had come to a halt now, beneath a wide portico at the Asylum entrance. Off to one side, in the shade of a leafy elm, a dozen or so girls stopped skipping rope to wave at what was obviously a familiar carriage. Caroline smiled and waved back, but made no move to step down. "You asked me a question, Anna, and I will try to answer. It's not simply the Asylum I assist, but the colored people by and large, for even in New York they are in danger. A number of the city's Negro families have been here since the days of the Dutch, including established households and businesses, but not a single soul among them, prosperous or poor, is safe as long as the tentacles of slavery reach New York."

"Slavery? New York?" Anna sat bolt upright.

"Yes. Even now," her tone was acerbic, "in the enlightened year of 1860, Southern blackbirders—"

"Blackbirders?"

The horse nickered, restlessly, and Caroline held up a finger to the coachman who was waiting to help the ladies down. "Yes, Anna. Southern slave-hunters. They stalk and seize fugitives and return them to slavery. Not only do they have the full support of national law in so doing, they also operate with the complicity of city officials."

Some inchoate uneasiness worried at Anna's mind, more pressing than simple human outrage at what Caroline was telling her. She knew, of course, about the national Fugitive Slave Act that for the past decade had mandated fines—even imprisonment—for citizens who helped fugitive slaves on their journeys to Canada. Anna knew little, however, about the movement to abolish slavery. Josiah had always said we must obey the laws of the earthly powers because they had been ordained by God. She could almost hear his precise, preacherly tones announcing the citation: *Romans 13:1*. And, also, until recently, Anna had been so enslaved in spirit herself that she hadn't much thought about the enslavement of others.

"Sometimes," Caroline added, "these greedy bounty hunters even seize freeborn citizens of the city and sell them South. There's one blackbirder named Cracker Skaggs who's notorious for snatching up young girls like these." She pointed toward the skipping girls, who were now singing along with their game—*Doctor, Doctor. Call the doctor*— "That's just one reason for keeping them in the orphan asylum—to keep them safe."

"Oh, dear God," Anna said. "Blackbirders! You mean *kidnappers*!" Then she gasped. "My daughter! Is it possible she's been kidnapped into slavery?"

Caroline, jolted from her own train of thought, placed a hand on Anna's arm. "No. No. I certainly didn't mean to suggest any danger to your daughter. I'm sorry—I wasn't thinking."

"But it could be, right?" Anna's heart pounded with fear. "She'd be a beautiful brown child. The light-skinned girls, right? They sell the light-skinned girls to New Orleans and raise them to be … whores!"

"Now, Anna, that would be most unlikely, especially if it was that prudish spinster, Miss Susan Parker, who arranged for a placement." She jumped down from the carriage, refusing an assist from the waiting coachman. "We must think—where would Miss Parker take a brown-skinned baby?"

Anna, who had been restive during this entire discussion, took the coachman's offered hand and stepped out lightly onto the courtyard paving stones.

"If we're lucky, Anna," Caroline said, turning back to wait for her, "if the gods are on our side. If the wind is in our sails. If we're truly, truly fortunate—we'll find her here."

A large crewelwork of Noah's Ark hanging above the fireplace in the airy Asylum parlor showed the faces of the Noah family ranging from licorice black to chocolate brown to apple-pie tan to buttermilk white, all individual and mischievous. The animals, too, were rendered with artistry and humor: a leering camel in a top hat, a fat, canny tomcat in high boots, an elephant playing the bagpipes. Any child raised here, Anna thought, with a half-smile, would develop a richer imagination than one submitted to the Methodist rigor of Miss Parker's institution. So thin was the line between hope and despair that the elephant in particular, with its bright-blue Indian turban, raised her hopes of finding her Indian daughter here.

"Some of our children are true orphans," said the stout Quaker Matron in response to Anna's questions, "some, half-orphans whose mothers are out at service, some are runaways, and some are foundlings. We give them food, shelter, and a basic education, we train them for an occupation, and they go out to make of themselves whatever they can—in a white city, that is." The matron shrugged. "And," she replaced her teacup on its saucer, and turned her gaze toward Caroline, "whatever comfort they are now afforded is due in large part to the Christian benevolence of generous patrons such as Miss Slade."

Caroline jumped up abruptly from her straight-backed chair and waved away the matron's gratitude. Mrs. Dodge, however, would not be stopped. "She will deny it, Mrs. Wheeler, but Miss Slade is a beacon of God's loving light." She clasped her hands together, as if she were about to suggest a prayer of thanksgiving.

"Don't bother yourself, Mrs. Dodge, to show Mrs. Wheeler the premises," Caroline said as she hastened from the parlor. "I know my way around."

Anna followed her, once again aware of the young woman's emotional discomfort. Something was gnawing at Caroline Slade's … *what*? Her soul? Her conscience? Her heart?

What could it possibly be?

"No one need know your true objective in coming here," Caroline said. "So we will not visit the nursery first."

Anna tried to hold back her eagerness. It was not easy.

Children in the hallways greeted them politely, boys dressed for the summer in short pants and loose cotton jackets, girls in matching gingham dresses with white pinafores. Anna wanted to cuddle the younger children, to stroke their hair—but she didn't. In the vast, bustling kitchen, the air was rich with the enticing aroma of beef and vegetable stew, and bakers took brown loaves from massive ovens. Anna fidgeted with her bonnet strings.

In the noisy kindergarten, bright papers and toys were strewn everywhere. The older students, more subdued, studied at long benches and desks set against classroom walls. In the well-appointed infirmary, a white-haired black man carrying a doctor's bag nodded to them. He and Caroline began an interminable conversation. Anna paced the floor.

By the time they finally approached the large nursery that smelled so wonderfully of soap and talcum powder, Anna could hardly breathe.

"Mis' Slade," exclaimed a mulatto woman in a white cap and neat gray dress. "I's powerful glad to see you." A dozen or more small children tottered around her or played with wooden toys. Identical white metal cribs were lined up in long, neat rows. "Look, them cribs come!" The nursemaid waved toward the sparkling infant beds, and then turned to Anna. "If it wan't for Mis' Slade, them babies would be sleeping on old, broke-down mattresses. But, praise de Lawd, she—"

Caroline spoke abruptly. "That's enough, Betsy."

"It's God's honest truth," the nurse insisted.

"Betsy!" She seemed genuinely distressed. "Mrs. Wheeler would like to see the children."

Yes. Oh, yes: She would like to see the children. Surely here—in this kind and gentle place—she would find India Elizabeth. Anna followed Betsy through the rooms.

Babies slept under colorful tufted quilts, their cribs draped with white net canopies. Lively tots played with dolls, wooden puzzles, and pull toys. A nursery maid rocked an infant of about three weeks, feeding it milk from a bottle stoppered with a bit of chamois. Yet another played at ring-a-ring-of-rosies with a group of toddling girls.

She stared into the face of each girl. Some were too young, some too old. Some were too dark, some too light. A small brown girl, her hair neatly plaited and tied with crimson ribbons, caught her eye, galloping on a rocking horse with a comically determined expression. Her complexion was a deep tan, her eyes large and dark, her nose straight, incorrigible tendrils straggled onto her forehead. Anna stepped toward her. The child glanced over at Anna, her brown eyes radiating intelligence and curiosity. She smiled.

India Elizabeth! Anna's heart expanded like a morning glory at noon. She reached out and caressed the girl's cheek. At the stranger's familiarity, the child froze, her eyes wide. She jumped from the wooden horse, ran to Betsy, and buried her face in the nursemaid's apron.

A closer perusal revealed the girl was too old by at least half a year. Anna's heart shut like a midnight sunflower. By the end of her visit it seemed clear there was not a single child in this place who could possibly be her child—her child and Ashok's.

ELEVEN

Insensitive to Anna's grievous sense of loss, Caroline waved away the carriage, and began to walk south on Fifth Avenue in great strides. "Let me talk to Mrs. Fitch about where else Susan Parker might have taken your baby," she mused. "'Bama knows everyone in the colored community. Believe me, she'll know whom to ask." Then she seemed to brush the subject aside and began chattering about who lived in this marble mansion and who had paid how much for that elegant granite palace.

Anna, sweat rolling between her breasts, straggled after her. At 34th Street, she suddenly came face to face with a woman who stared at her intently: a small woman in a wilted, perspiration-stained black dress. Her old straw bonnet was crooked. Damp strands of hair fell down her forehead and over her ears. Then she recognized the Kashmiri shawl folded over the apparition's arm, and realized with a jolt that she was seeing herself, her reflection in a large plate-glass window. She looked, she thought, like a half-crazed, slovenly housemaid who'd pinched her mistress' priceless shawl.

They stopped for refreshment at a small tea garden near Madison Square, across from the magnificent Fifth Avenue Hotel. Caroline ordered iced Ceylon tea and sandwiches, but Anna had no appetite

"You may tell me it's none of my business, Anna," Caroline said, "but, I must admit, I am curious about your life story. I was going to ask you yesterday, but our time was cut short by that storm."

Anna knew she would have to tell Caroline about her years with Josiah, lest the young woman dream up a tale even more scandalous than was the reality. But how should she mention Ashok? Her reputation was already at the mercy of this new acquaintance. So she began, "I met my husband at Mount Holyoke Seminary—"

"Ah! I could tell you were an educated woman."

"Well, yes, educated, but so young, uninformed, and uncertain. And he was … glorious. So confident of … everything. Of his eternal salvation. Of his vocation in India missions. Of my call to be his helpmeet. It was as if he had a missive straight from Heaven." She took a lump of sugar from the bowl and dropped it into her glass.

Caroline peeled bread back from the top of an egg and mayonnaise sandwich, regarding it skeptically. Then she looked up at Anna. "And you were taken in by this … holy man? We women so often are."

Anna felt her spirit lighten; she was not alone in her folly. "I gave myself over to him completely. At first it was all an adventure, from sunny Calcutta Bay, to the lilting sound of the Hindustani language, to the beautiful faces of the Bengali children."

Caroline's eyes shone with fascination.

Anna took a sip of tea and returned the glass to its saucer. She reached out and stroked the petals of a wilting yellow rose in a blue glass vase on the table. She sighed. "But my India was not Josiah's. His was a land of damned souls and pagan savagery. He was—how shall I say it?—unyielding in his religious purposes."

Miss Slade leaned forward. "Did he mistreat you?"

Anna swallowed hard. "Well, you must understand that he had been taught all his life to believe in the 'God-given superiority of the male,' and he did believe it—with all sincerity."

Her companion widened her eyes in skepticism. "Did he mistreat you?"

"And, further, he genuinely believed in the innate inferiority of the female, who had been placed on earth to serve the male in all ways—"

"Like a dog—or horse!" Caroline scoffed. "Tell me! Did he *mistreat* you?"

Anna's shoulders sagged, and she sighed. Why did she feel it necessary to defend Josiah? "That drove me at last to leave him. But long before that … how can I say it? … his unshakable habits of mind wearied me."

"*Unshakable habits of mind*." The other woman rolled the words on her tongue as if they had flavor, as if she could taste them. "Indeed. So many gentlemen …" Caroline raised her eyebrows, "… are thus afflicted." She tilted her head and regarded Anna with curiosity. "So, he abused you, and he defrauded your heart?"

"Worse yet," Anna shot back, "he defrauded my soul." Hot tears threatened to spill. She grabbed up the embroidered tea napkin and hid her eyes behind it.

Caroline reached across the table and took her hand, but Anna pulled from her grasp.

"I don't know how long it was before I realized I was playing a false part," she said, "but I knew no other life. And I had no resources. Thousands of miles from home—where would I have gone?" She barely felt the thorn's stab as she plucked the fading yellow rose from the vase and breathed in its sweet scent.

"When I finally … left him," she continued, "it was not a considered decision. It felt like madness, like … what Josiah would have called 'demon possession.'"

Caroline laughed shortly. "*Self*-possession, most likely."

"Yes. *Self*-possession." Who would have known there was a word for what she had wanted all those unfree years?

"And then you met … the father of your child?" Caroline's eyes gleamed. This clearly was the part of the story she wished most to hear. "Do tell me about him."

"Ah, Ashok." Anna leaned back in her chair and breathed deeply, in and out. It seemed that she intended to trust Caroline.

India

1857

As the sound of gunfire drew closer to Anna's besieged train carriage, the dark man in the ragged robes grabbed her arm. Even given his insalubrious appearance, she knew he was not what he seemed. Indeed, she knew exactly who he was.

"Come, Mrs. Roundtree—the insurgents have captured the train. They are merciless to the *angrizi*." He pulled open the compartment door. "Jump!" And he pushed her. She hit the stony ground with an impact that knocked the air from her lungs, then heard him land with a Hindi curse a short distance away.

"Follow me," he whispered, grabbing her hand. And they ran, away from the shouts and the flames, away from the railroad that was her lifeline back to Calcutta and home. Ran into the thick, hot darkness. She had not uttered more than two words to him. Now they were fleeing together into the green Indian countryside.

His name was Ashok Johnston Montgomery, and Anna had met him two months earlier at the mission hospital. When the gentleman visitor entered the children's ward with Josiah, she had been changing the soiled bandage on a boy's ulcerated foot.

The visitor was Anglo-Indian, of middle height and healthy build, his skin the color of tea with cream. Wearing a white linen suit, immaculately tailored, and a fine white-embroidered waistcoat, he was one of those sons of British fathers and Indian mothers who were often highly placed in Indian society.

"Wife," Josiah now said, as obsequious as Anna had ever seen him, "this is Mr. Ashok Montgomery, a merchant from Farrukhabad. He takes a benevolent interest in our infirmary work." He waved a hand toward the row of children's cots. It was full afternoon and the breeze of the long *punkah* gave little relief from the unrelenting heat.

The stranger smiled, his teeth white in the brown face. He bowed, then took Anna's hand. It was soiled from the bandages, and she attempted to withdraw it from his grasp, but he held on nonetheless. "I am so grateful, Mrs. Roundtree," he said, "For the care you take of our village people." His voice was deep, with the clipped intonations of the English-educated Indian.

Anna's hand felt small and cool in Ashok Montgomery's clasp. Her husband cleared his throat, and she pulled back abruptly.

Just then, Nimrod Wentworth, a gangling young red-haired missionary, rushed into the bungalow. "J … Josiah, you are needed at the publishing house. There is a p … p … problem with the hand press." Nimrod never stammered except in Josiah's presence.

Josiah's tongue clicked in annoyance. "I *told* you …" Apologizing profusely, he followed Nimrod's tall, stooped frame out the door.

Anna, left in the spare, clean bungalow with its rows of cots and cribs, was surprised when Ashok Montgomery stayed by her side as if he were truly interested in her work. In silence she finished cleaning the small boy's putrid wound, treated it with a dressing of Manuka honey, unrolled a clean bandage and tied it on his foot.

Reaching into his coat pocket, the visitor pulled out a ginger nut and gave it to the thin boy, who regarded him solemnly as he shoved the confection in his mouth. "By the look of this wound," he said to Anna, "the child surely would have become lame—might even have lost his leg—without your help." He tickled the boy, who giggled, his teeth covered in brown cake.

As Mr. Montgomery was bending toward the child, Anna noted beneath his ear, in that soft, warm, recess just behind the lobe, a small blemish—a white splash on the tea color of his skin. Suddenly, it was all she could do to keep from reaching out with her forefinger to stroke this stranger's skin. What had come over her? She swallowed hard.

"Clearly, Madam," the man said, smiling at her again, "your Christianity is not merely a religion of pronouncements, as with some. It is in your hands and your heart, and …" He watched with close attention as she wiped the honey off her fingers, one at a time, with a clean handkerchief. "And … in your fingers."

Late that evening, Josiah strode into the parlor and tossed a bag of coins on the table. It landed with a thunk. "Our half-caste merchant is almost a Christian. He has sent ten-thousand *rupees* for the care of children in the infirmary."

"Ten-thousand *rupees*! Why, that's a small fortune!"

Josiah made a clucking noise with his tongue. "It is money that would have made a great difference in accelerating the publication of our new Bengali Bible. But, unfortunately, he specifies that every *rupee* should go for the children, and we must honor that request." Josiah looked at her sideways. "You have made quite an impression on Sahib

Ashok Montgomery." There was something acerbic in his tone, and she had never before heard him use the Indian honorific.

Now, as they fled into the mountains, Ashok told her that Indian soldiers in the British Army—the *Sepoys*—had revolted against British rule. The rebellion, he said, was directed against everything and everyone associated with the British. Like wildfire, rioting had overtaken the land. At Meerut, an enraged mob, furious at what they saw as British contempt for Indian religions, had massacred European and Indian Christians alike. Roaming bands of insurgents were burning army barracks and churches. Rioters, rumor said, had captured the city of Delhi. Not even respected Anglo-Indians were safe from the mob's fury. The British, he feared, would be equally barbarous in retaliation.

Anxious about the safety of his mother and his son, Ashok had been travelling by train to the family's tea estate in the hills north of Calcutta, taking on the guise of a native porter because he thought he would be safer. But now that tracks had been torn up and bridges destroyed, they had no recourse but to travel by foot.

The first day of their flight, Anna and Ashok followed the Ganges south, skirting ramshackle fishermen's villages where goats wandered freely and children played naked by the river banks. At one village, oddly deserted, with the cooking fires smoldering and the laundry spread out upon the grass to dry, they gathered mangos from a grove, and Anna's companion speared three trout from a stream that rushed down to meet the river. They grilled the fish over a fire, wrapped them in roti from the abandoned clay ovens, and headed off into the hills.

Scorched by the daytime sun, and unprotected from the chill night damps, they were exhausted. Ashok limped, rags wrapped around bare feet blistered by the stony ground. Anna, protected only by the meager cover of a battered straw bonnet, was nauseous and dizzy from the pounding rays of the sun. Of her possessions she'd kept nothing but her gold wedding ring, her ivory hairbrush, and the notebook secured in the pocket of her dress.

On the third day, Ashok abruptly halted and gazed with gravity at a cloud in the distant sky. Small and exceedingly dark, it appeared as a black, angry fist in the peaceful heavens. "Sandstorm." He breathed, rather than spoke, the word.

With the advent of the deadly storm, this brown stain devouring the earth, Anna felt a perverse thrill, one she could think of only as a kind of God-defiance. In her darkest moments she fancied this entire bloody revolt was punishment directed specifically at her by Josiah's God for having jettisoned the habit of safety that had structured her circumscribed life. Her husband's God was a God of retribution. Now this oncoming deluge of sand. …

Blindly she followed Ashok as, seeking shelter, he explored a sandstone outcropping in one of the surrounding hills. "Ah!" He motioned her to a gap in the rock that led into a small cavern. Once they'd squeezed inside, he turned and surveyed the narrow opening. "Your petticoat," he said, musingly. They needed something to construct a barrier from the oncoming sand.

"My *what?*"

"You do wear a petticoat?" It had gotten so dark she could scarcely see his face. "We need it."

Without a second's hesitation, she threw her skirts up over her shoulders, reached for the narrow cotton-tape ties at her waist, felt the undergarment slither to her ankles, shivered slightly, stepped out of it. The delicate, thrilling, shudder did not emanate from any degree of cold,

Ashok snatched up the underskirt, measured the length of cotton against the cavern's narrow mouth. "This might work," he said, skewering it on sharp protrusions in the rock face, weighting the hem with heavy stones to form a protective curtain. They retreated to a ragged nook far to the rear, where they huddled together in the darkness while wind howled and sand whipped at their meager curtained wall. All was heat and blindness and the roar of nature's storm. Was it not inevitable that, beyond terror and beyond hope, and given her reckless state of spirit, all caution would be swept away, that Anna would turn in all ways to Ashok?

This cave, here, with this man, was her only world. Together they had been stripped of everything by the storm. Except for touch, all her senses were departed—nothing could be known but the warmth of his body, the protection of his arms. "Ashok," she whispered, but in the howling of the storm she knew he could not hear. "Ashok," she said again ... into the din. Then she reached out and ran her hand across his rough, whiskered cheek. She felt him gasp, cover her hand with his own, and pull her close. She stroked his cheek, briefly felt his breath against her lips, which were gritty and covered with sand. Then it was mouth to mouth, breath to breath. Their whole little world of breath alone together centering the whirling wind. As the storm roared, the skies, and raging sands obliterated all reality outside the mouth of their sanctuary cave. She clung to him with increasing abandon as comfort turned to ecstasy. If death was imminent and Heaven naught but a myth, to what end deny themselves this surprising joy?

Never, in all her years with Josiah, had she imagined the possibility of such pleasure. Never had she conceived of bliss.

Anna told Caroline of the flight by train, the attack by native insurgents, of the weeks she had spent with Ashok, first in the hills, then at the remote tea plantation recuperating from a debilitating illness that had come upon her during their flight, then, briefly, at his family's magnificent town house in Calcutta.

Caroline Slade was enthralled. "And did you love him?"

"Love ... Ashok?" Her sigh was bottomless. "At first it was ... fascination, a type of madness. I was insane with fear, terrified of staying with Josiah, appalled at having left him. And the rebellion ... the danger. I thought we would die then and there. Ashok and I, we clung together."

The scent of the wilting yellow rose transported her in memory to Ashok's mountain home, which, when they finally arrived, they had found deserted by his family and protected only by two large male servants armed with the latest in Enfield rifles and a plump, fierce housekeeper with an English rolling pin. There, in that idyllic place, their love had been fulfilled over and over again, until it was time to return to Calcutta and civilization. Now, her feelings for her lover came back in a great rush, sweeping away further remnants of the numbness she'd built around herself since leaving India. With a hot shiver she relived for an instant the shared purpose and danger of their escape, his caring, the tenderness between them, the common sensibility they had discovered one in the other. She realized anew the power of their passion. She felt herself pale at the awareness of all she had lost in losing him.

"And *he* must have given you that exquisite shawl!" Caroline reached over and traced an indigo strand in the Kashmiri *boteh* motif. "Ever since you stepped outside the door of that shabby boarding-house this morning in all your splendor, I've been wondering how you came by it." Caroline Slade sighed; she was completely caught up in the tale. "I have never in my life heard a more romantic story. Why didn't you stay?"

A large white omnibus sidled up to a stop at the curb, and two women with market baskets alighted, chattering about the outrageous price of fish.

Anna brought herself back to the moment. "In India? With Ashok?" She sat up straight and folded her hands. "He wanted to buy me a house in Calcutta. To keep me there. I couldn't even think of it! A kept woman! Miss Slade, you have no notion. If you think American society is unforgiving, it is as nothing compared to the Hindu system. Every person's station is unalterably fixed, and any deviation evokes the deepest condemnation. I was a white woman—a *feringhi*."

Caroline was still starry-eyed with romance; Anna had not made herself sufficiently clear. "In addition, by deserting my husband, I had become a ... *pariah*." Another pause. "And I was ... with child—certain it was Josiah's.

"And it would have been worse for Ashok. He was a settled man with a thriving business and a well-connected family. His late wife had been a daughter of one of Calcutta's most revered families. Living with me he would have brought shame upon so many. And as for me ... You must understand that I did not know at that time that Josiah was dead. No, there was no possibility of remaining together. It was unthinkable."

"Shame?" Caroline ventured, "even in the exotic east?"

"Far more there than here. No he could not marry me, and I ... I would not be kept by him."

With a cambric handkerchief, Anna wiped a fine layer of perspiration from her forehead. A huge ice wagon lumbered by, leaving small scattered puddles in its wake. She followed it with her eyes until it was out of sight. Then her gaze was drawn to a small bookstore across the street, where shelves of second-hand books baked beneath the green-striped awning.

Bookstore.

Books.

Oh, dear God, Anna had forgotten about her appointment with Mr. Larkin—the publisher who'd promised to secure her fortune! She jumped up from her seat. "Miss Slade," she apologized. "I have just recalled an appointment—something … urgent. I must go at once." She turned toward the street.

"Anna!" Caroline called after her. "Wait just a moment."

Anna pivoted back. "What is it?"

"Two things. One, I am not Miss Slade to you. Do call me *Caroline*." She stood by the small table, embroidered napkin still in her hand, gazing hesitantly at her new friend.

"What else?" Anna was impatient to be on her way.

"Umm." Caroline brushed back curls of her crisp, dark hair. "Perhaps … perhaps if your meeting is indeed urgent … you should do something about … about your appearance?"

TWELVE

Anna left Caroline, sobered, recalling her unkempt appearance earlier reflected in that plate-glass window. Her friend was right; she must do something to improve her appearance. Mr. Larkin seemed the type of man who would equate feminine dishevelment with moral laxity. The packet of bills he'd given her was secured in her petticoat pocket. She felt quite giddy with the possibilities that the one-hundred dollars afforded her. She stepped to the curb and raised her arm—it was the first time in her life that Anna Wheeler had ever hailed a cab.

In a small cubicle off the second-floor Ladies Parlor of Stewart's Merchantile at Broadway and Chambers—the fabled Marble Palace—a seamstress stitched a new lace-edged collar and cuffs to Anna's weary black dress and hemmed a ready-made muslin petticoat to her length. While the girl was preoccupied with her meticulous stitches, Anna stood in chemise and drawers, her face washed, her hair decorous in new combs and snood, covertly studying her form in a full-length mirror: rounded breasts just visible above the cotton chemise and new corset, curve of hips disappearing into the crisp muslin drawers, neat ankles in new stockings.

She turned to one side to view her profile, unconsciously raising her hand to her breast: *So, this is how Ashok would have seen me*. For a moment fragments of memory stole her breath. Ashok: thoughts of whom she had buried beneath layers of numb grief. Now, her child—and his—alive!

"Madame, your gown is ready." The seamstress looked at Anna strangely, jarring her back to the present moment. Anna dropped her hand from her breast. Here she was, Anna Leonora Wheeler, engaged on the most vital mission of her life, immersed in the modern bustle of New York City with its tall buildings, energetic people—its Marble Palaces—and she was day-dreaming of mud-and-wattle villages baking beneath an uncivilized sun, and of ... of—

No! she chided herself. *Do not think of it. In the high green Asian mountains for one brief moment I ventured outside the ways of prudence; but here, in this city of Christian men and women, I must live with the consequences of that ... madness. If my child still breathes, I* will *find her. As for Ashok, he is of another time and place.*

"Have someone bring me a new lace bodice," she said to the seamstress, "of good quality ... with neck cut not quite so high as this," she gestured to the old one, "—yet still modest." She donned the bodice with her sponged and pressed black dress, tied the blue satin strings of a crisp new straw bonnet, and pulled on spotless white net gloves. One last glance in the mirror showed her a transformed woman, neat and respectable—a lady. She threw the bright shawl over her shoulders and set out to find the man who had paid for her new clothes, Mr. William Larkin, Publisher of Moral Literature for the People.

Mr. Larkin seemed delighted to see Anna—indeed, somewhat relieved. It was warm in the publishers' chamber, but nowhere near as oppressively hot as it had been in the street. Mere slits of afternoon sun penetrated the closed drapes of the floor-to-ceiling windows, picking out, seemingly at random, a marble bust of Shakespeare, one of Milton, and a portrait in somber tones of the publisher himself.

"Are you in a position at this time to oblige us with a dozen new poems so that we might take a book to press within the month?" Mr. Larkin ruffled though the pile of newsprint cuttings on his desk. "We've clipped sufficient of your poems from the newspapers to put together a slim volume of reprinted verses, but, of course, Larkin & Bierce would wish as well a handful of new poems, originals not yet put before the public. Is that not right, Mr. Bierce?" He slewed his eyes toward his partner

Mr. Bierce, a corpulent bearded individual in a yellow waist jacket and long black coat, nodded his assent. "For the freshness of the volume," he intoned, in an unfresh rumble of a voice. He stood behind Mr. Larkin, one handsomely booted foot resting upon a maroon leather footstool, his meaty hand braced against the back of his partner's sturdy chair, and mopped his perspiring forehead with a square of monogrammed linen.

A dozen poems? Within the month? Anna was almost too preoccupied with that challenge to notice the publishers' eagerness.

Her mind reeled. Then she recalled the small black notebook she'd pulled from her bureau drawer. She'd already written one new poem, and surely she could cull a few lines from those verses she had so compulsively penned during the long, sleepless missionary nights. "I will do my best to oblige," she replied.

"Splendid," Mr. Larkin said. "We shall take these ..." he ruffled through the cuttings on his desk with an acquisitive air, "to the printer this week. And we will expect the new verses by mid-September. Shall we say, by the fifteenth?"

She swallowed hard. "I will try."

"The book will then be manufactured for the Christmas trade, a most propitious timing."

Trade? How odd, Anna thought, to hear that word applied to lines originally meant only to relieve the pain in her heart.

Mr. Larkin drew out from his waistcoat pocket a watch with a rich gold chain fashioned to look like a serpent. He glanced at it and stood up. "I am delighted to welcome you, Mrs. Wheeler, to our little literary family here at Larkin & Bierce." He gave a slight bow to end the meeting.

Anna hesitated, then rose, smoothing her skirts. The publisher had said nothing about further recompense, which rather unsettled her. "Might I ask, Mr. Larkin, about our ... business arrangements?"

"Ah, yes, my dear lady." He hesitated and glanced at his partner before coming forward to take both her hands in his. His voice grew exceedingly smooth. "I should hope you understand that our goal here at Larkin &

Bierce goes far beyond that of commercial profit. We are engaged in an endeavor, as I am certain you understand, to disseminate moral beauty throughout this raw new nation. What draws me to your verses, Mrs. Wheeler," he said in silken tones, "is their innocence, their femininity, their joyous lilt, the trill of a pretty little warbler greeting the first rays of God's new dawn. Your poems, Madame, will do much to stem the tide of immorality that threatens to swamp the very soul of our reading public."

"Yes," she said, taking a breath so deep it strained her corset. "But what will you pay me?"

Mr. Larkin puckered his lips, then slid his gaze over to Mr. Bierce. He seemed set off-balance, as if Anna, in giving voice to the query, had violated some unspoken rule of decorum.

Mr. Bierce said, "Mrs. Wheeler, we are prepared to make you a most generous offer. Most generous indeed. Five hundred dollars for the copyrights to your verses." He smiled magnanimously. "And that is, of course, above and beyond the hundred dollars my partner has advanced you beforehand."

"Copyrights?" she faltered. "To my poems?" Five hundred dollars was a great deal of money, she knew, but she was out of her element when it came to handling business details. And it seemed somehow less than wise to sell ownership of her verses.

"To those poems that appear in our volume. That is all. We can let you have the cash this very day." The partners beamed at her with conscious beneficence. Mr. Bierce had some small morsel of vegetative matter caught between two upper teeth.

"Is that the usual arrangement?"

"You could be very comfortable on six hundred dollars," Mr. Larkin said.

"Yes. I do understand," Anna replied. "But is it customary for a poet to forfeit the copyright to her verses? I ask, you see, because I truly do not know."

"It is occasionally done." Mr. Larkin frowned, thick eyebrows gathering in the center. "And when I saw you in such … well … such constrained circumstances on Liberty Street—that squalid parlor, oh, my dear lady—I thought you might best be served by an immediate income."

Anna hesitated, and before she could speak again, Mr. Bierce slewed his eyes over to his partner and wrinkled his brow.

Mr. Larkin's gaze fixed intently on his colleague, as if attempting to read a message in a medium more complex than print. "Hmm," he uttered. Then he turned back to Anna, expression altered, still holding her hands in his paternalistic grasp. "It distresses us, Mrs. Wheeler, to see a respectable little lady like yourself bother her head with business matters. You have our assurances that you may safely leave your affairs in our hands."

Anna's gaze flickered back and forth from Mr. Larkin's thin face and puckered lips, to Mr. Bierce's fleshy visage, and a wave of hot feeling passed through her. Had she not spent half a lifetime piously and obediently suppressing even the slightest twinge of anger, she would more readily have recognized the emotion for what it was. Nonetheless, she pulled her hands abruptly from his loose grasp.

He cleared his throat, then continued in a dismissive manner, "Of course, if you wish to wait and see how the book sells, we can offer you instead a percentage agreement—say fifteen cents on each book—"

"On each copy that is sold?" She was in the process of donning her irreproachable new gloves, but now began pulling them off again without any consciousness of the activity.

"Yes."

"And I would retain the copyrights?" She folded the gloves, still unconsciously, and returned them to her reticule.

He nodded. "Of course, in that case there would be no money advanced before publication other than the one hundred dollars already paid, and no income from the books until they do sell. Indeed, you must understand, there is no guarantee that they *will* sell. ..."

Propelled by an agency that seemed to come from somewhere outside herself, she made rapid mental calculation. At fifteen cents a copy, she must sell four thousand volumes in order to match the publishers' offer. Was that too many to hope for? She recalled the publisher's earlier assurances. Still she was less than certain as she followed her instinct. "I believe, then, that I shall retain my rights in the poems and wait for my profits." She retrieved the gloves once again from her bag and strove for an air of aplomb. "I do thank you, gentlemen. When will you have the agreement drawn up for me to sign?"

Mr. Larkin fussed with his serpentine watch chain. "I should hope, dear lady, that you do indeed consider us gentlemen. As such, we seldom resort to written contractual agreements. Our word has always been sufficient for our authors."

"I see," Anna said. She would press them no further for fear of losing the opportunity to publish. Larkin & Bierce was a well-reputed company. Miss Susan Warner printed with them, and Miss Maria Cummins, too, she believed. She, herself, would prefer to have something on paper, but she knew so little about publishing practices. She supposed that she could trust to Mr. Larkin's honor. She could easily live on one-hundred dollars until well after Christmas and still have the much-needed resources with which to pursue her search for India Elizabeth.

The publishers ushered Anna from the office with gentlemanly bows. As the door closed behind her, she realized she had forgotten to ask just exactly when she might expect payment if the books did sell. She had opened the door a mere crack when she heard her name uttered in Mr. Larkin's reedy voice.

"Mrs. Wheeler seems a modest, respectable little lady." He chortled. "No danger of scandalous disclosures there, thank God."

"Not at all. Unlike some I could name." Mr. Bierce laughed. Then frowning, he mused, "Although, she's not quite as pliable as one might hope for." He pulled a tobacco pouch from his pants pocket. "Nonetheless, this should be a most profitable venture for Larkin & Bierce."

Hmm, Anna thought, *I must watch these gentlemen very carefully*.

Beneath the gilded American eagle brooding over the massive domed lobby of the Central Post Office on Nassau Street, Anna found a much-delayed check from the *Lady's Journal* in her postal box. Ten dollars—extremely welcome, but most likely the last payment for her work until money started coming in from Larkin & Bierce's sales of the books.

At the wide marble counter toward the rear of the building she purchased postage stamps. "Is there anything in General Delivery for me today, Mr. Barnaby?" she asked the wraithlike clerk. Occasionally editors made their initial contact simply by writing to her in care of the city Post Office. She always asked, just in case. And indeed today she had a feeling that something awaited her, an anticipatory lifting of the spirits. She could almost see the envelope.

The pale-haired clerk checked the alphabetized cubicles, bending with stiff knees to the W's. "No," he said, from his crouching position. "Nothing at all for you, today, Mrs. Wheeler."

So much for premonitions.

—

Calcutta, India
6 May1858

My Dear Mrs. Roundtree—

I am in receipt of your most welcome letter assuring me of your safe arrival in NewYork City, for which I am relieved and happy.

I write to extend my condolences on the death of your husband and of the other martyred missionaries during the massacre of so many souls at Cawnpore. Such a cruel and tragic chapter in the history of my country— I despair.

I am most distressed, Mrs. Roundtree, that in your aforementioned all-too-abbreviated missive to me, you neglected to include an address where I might reach you in New-York. Thusly, I address this to you through the headquarters of the Methodist Board of Foreign Missions of the United States, trusting that these gentlemen will kindly forward it to your possession.

My dear Madame, it is with treasured memories that I leave you, hoping for a response from you with all dispatch.

Your Servant,
Ashok Montgomery

New-York, August 28, 1858
RETURNED BY METHODIST BOARD OF FOREIGN MISSIONS
ADDRESSEE DECEASED

THIRTEEN

When the haggard, travel-worn man approached the house near Union Square, it was as he recalled from a decade earlier, plain, of somber brown, in a quiet, respectable street. Inquiring about the availability of a room, he found a new landlady, a godly Christian widow of comely appearance and modest dress. The smell of good roast beef pervaded the air. Tall glass-fronted parlor bookcases were filled with bound volumes of sermons by right-minded men of God; on the cabinet organ's music rack, he noted sheet music for "The Old Rugged Cross." A most amenable dwelling, indeed, propitious for his purpose. And thus he established himself quietly at Mrs. Etheridge's comfortable establishment, having no desire to meet old acquaintances or make new until he had completed the task laid upon his heart by an all-wise Master.

In his room by an open coal fire the new arrival passed his days scripting, with the Lord's assistance, the memoirs of his dire tribulations in the Far East, his near brush with bloody death, and the tragic loss at the hands of heathen devils of his dear, devoted, sanctified little wife. It should make a most engrossing tale for American readers, and he now felt strong enough to face the scrutiny. Indeed, all other witnesses—those who might not have understood the Lord's purposes as he did—were dead.

And, now, for the practicalities; he must find himself a godly Christian publisher.

FOURTEEN

When Anna had first returned to New York, she'd come across a book of thrilling poems at a second-hand bookstore. By a poet unknown to her, it was entitled *Leaves of Grass*, and many passages had enthralled her. *I am he* (she read, with total empathy) *that walks with the tender and growing night; / I call to the earth and sea half-held by the night. / / Press close bare-bosomed night! –Night of south winds! / Night of the large few stars! / ... Mad naked summer night*!

Never before had she conceived it possible to capture ... amatory experience ... in poetry. And, indeed, though thoroughly versed in the ways of lovemaking by Ashok, she herself could never aspire to be a poet of what Mr. Walt Whitman called "forbidden voices." Although, she did, of course, know those forbidden voices, had been hearing them all her life.

But, she was a popular poetess who wrote to earn a living; she could not afford to risk offending the delicate public sensibility. Not for her, she told herself, the wild indiscretions and torturous self-examinations of the true artist. The People's Muse was sufficient inspiration for her verses. And it paid; it was her livelihood. She could not venture even the slightest hint of indecorum.

She would write only what poems she knew she could sell to Larkin & Bierce. But how could she possibly come up with a dozen within a month? She hesitated. Did she dare use the unguarded lines she had written in India? No. Never.

But as soon as she wrapped herself comfortably in Ashok's shawl, his memory enfolded her. Covering the cherished wrap with a writer's smock against the inevitable ink stains, she began to write.

Simoom

As murk as midnight is the sky, sultry and still the air.
Dust flings death's veil around them, the lost and wandering pair.
She looks at him with frightened eye. He says, "We are together.
The only storms to kill us now will be of the heart—not weather."

So deep a darkness neither knew. They brave it, hand in hand,
Until, at last, deliverance viewed—the sun through floating sand.
The song of bird is heard again. Heav'n's air restored to earth.
And they who thought that they would die, now taste each other's breath.

Even as she wrote, she understood that this poem was not for Mr. Larkin. Although—she must say—she doubted that the poor man would recognize passion if he saw it. But, no, she could not risk discovery; she set the poem aside.

At the moment Anna could do nothing about finding her child. She must concentrate on her poetry. Caroline was going to ask Mrs. Fiske to make inquiries in the city's African community.

Leaving her desk only for a few fugitive hours of sleep and a snatched meal provided by Nancy, the Irish house girl, she wrote for the next two days straight. She wrote until her arm ached, her ink-stained fingers cramped around the scratchy steel-nib pen, and the words swam upon her retinas. Eventually she did find herself plundering the Indian notebooks—for monsoon, suttee, and creeping scorpion. For the savor of ginger, turmeric, and cardamom. For images of jasmine and languid evenings in the mountain air.

She wrote until she could write no longer. She had eleven completed poems. She made fair copies of these eleven, and then, in her exhaustion not quite as prudent as she should have been, she included the sandstorm verses with the rest. There. Twelve. Anna addressed the envelope to Larkin & Bierce, Publishers, Park Row, City, and carried it across Liberty Street to the Central Post Office.

She came home and slept for fifteen hours, awaking only when Mrs. Chapman sent Nancy up to see if her boarder was still alive.

When Anna finally reappeared at the boarding-house table, for Sunday dinner, she found an unexpected newcomer. Eben Garrett was a dark-haired, broad-shouldered young man in a shabby brown sack coat with ink stains on the pocket—not at all the type of faux-genteel boarder Mrs. Chapman favored. He introduced himself to the gathering as a writer for the newspapers and then lapsed into silence.

Anna helped herself to a soup of cabbage, carrots, and beans from a brown crockery tureen. It was hot and flavorful, leaving a sediment of half-cracked peppercorns at the bottom of her bowl. Nancy, dwarfed by her greasy apron, substituted plates for the bowls, and the main course was presented, great heaping basins of creamed cod and boiled potatoes; Mrs. Chapman served salt fish so often that the very window curtains reeked of it.

Anna paid little attention to the conversation until her ear caught a familiar name uttered in the quavering voice of Mrs. Douglas, a minister's widow who referred to her exalted status as such at least once every meal. "And in the Five Points slums, Mrs. Ambrose is a most indefatigable Bible Reader—"

Anna raised her head from contemplation of her plate. "Mrs. *Margaret* Ambrose?" she queried, unthinkingly.

All heads swiveled toward her; it was so seldom that she spoke. Miss Higginson, a schoolteacher, tittered nervously at the abruptness of her question.

"Yes, Margaret Ambrose of the Five Points Mission." Mrs. Douglas patted her lips with the cotton napkin and inclined her head toward Anna. "She's a fine handmaiden of the Lord."

"So I've heard," Anna said, engrossed in staring out the long dining-room window that framed a side-yard tableau of decayed flour barrels and deformed plane trees. A brick wall in dire need of whitewash blocked any more pleasing prospect from her sight.

"With the guidance of our Lord," Mrs. Douglas continued, "she visits the poor, reads them the gospel, urges them to learn the ways of self-denial and industry. The dear lady has even taken into her home Irish children from the streets, whom she essays to train in the teachings of Christ."

Mr. Whittaker, a merchant's clerk, spooned apple pudding onto a plate. "Might as well try to train the great ape in Mr. Barnum's menagerie. Them Micks is just naturally lazy, ignorant, and immoral."

"*Those*, not *them*," corrected Miss Higginson, the schoolteacher.

"*Those* Micks," Mr. Whittaker agreed. "It's bred in the bone."

"Even among the haunts of vice and crime," Mrs. Douglas insisted, "Christ's gospel transforms the most degraded soul."

"It's not their *souls* that need transformation. ..." The newcomer at the table spoke abruptly in a sardonic growl, capturing Anna's immediate interest. With his working-man's physique and shabby coat, his undisciplined mop of dark curls, this latest boarder looked like a farmer's son just off a stagecoach from some godforsaken New England town. But when he spoke, it became clear he was an educated man. "It's their stomachs. Starved wretches crowded together in vermin-infested slums like maggots in a cheese? You don't have a hope in hell of cramming any religion down their throats."

Mrs. Douglas's breath hissed inward through crooked teeth. "Cr. . . cr ... cramming? Down their throats? You poor, deluded man. To speak of the teachings of our Lord in such a manner—"

But Mr. Garrett laughed. "Lady, I write the police reports for Horace Greeley's *Tribune*. There's not a midnight in the Five Points you don't find half a dozen ragged starvelings rounded up by the police to be sent off to Blackwell's Island, or, even worse, some just-born infant's body floating by the docks because its wretched mother knows she can't feed it."

Anna paled at the image. Mr. Garrett glanced at her, briefly, then transferred his gaze back to the minister's widow. "Believe me, lady, 'suffer the little children,' don't cut any mustard on Little Water Street. The only do-gooder over there who's got the right idea is the Rebel Reverend, Pete Lyman."

Mrs. Douglas sputtered. "Peter Lyman is a Godless heretic. He's no true minister of the Lord."

"Godless?" The journalist laughed again. "Reverend Pete feeds the poor, he teaches them sewing, shoemaking, whatever they can work at to put a bite in their own mouths. He educates the kids. Reform is what he's after, not converts. Reform of the whole damn lopsided social system. And he doesn't give a … a fig for who they kneel down to. They can pray to Our Lady of Perpetual Bread for all he cares. Or to—"

"Or to Vishnu and Ram," Anna broke in, looking at him steadily. A dozen heads swiveled in her direction. It was as if she had spoken in a language never before heard by the human ear. *Vishnu? Ram?*

"Well, now …" Mr. Garrett narrowed his eyes at her, and raised a dark eyebrow. He exuded an attractive energy, she thought, compounded of physical magnetism and intellectual integrity.

She turned her eyes to the boarders gathered at the table. "Hindu deities," she explained.

This Eben Garrett was an interesting man, and, as soon as she could, she would speak with him privately. She wanted to know if the Reverend Peter Lyman ever took in abandoned babies. She'd feared that with her futile visits to the Hudson Home and the Colored Orphan Asylum, she'd exhausted the possibilities of finding India Elizabeth in this city, but now it sounded as if the good reverend might provide a further avenue of inquiry.

FIFTEEN

By the time Anna set out to visit Reverend Lyman in the Five Points on Monday morning, she'd thought better about speaking to Mr. Garrett. He seemed liberal-minded enough, but, on the other hand, his gray eyes were far too inquisitive. He was, after all, a writer for the newspapers; she must be careful that he not learn her true business with the good reverend.

In Paradise Square, a street evangelist preached to a small crowd of down-and-outers from his perch on an upended fish barrel. "For I will send into her pestilence," he shrilled, "and blood into her streets; and the wounded shall be judged in the midst of her by the sword upon her on every side; and they shall know that I *am* the Lord God." His words, the rude, jostling crowds, the beggars, the smells of unwashed bodies and overflowing sewer drains, all brought memories of Josiah's bazaar preaching in Farrukhabad. In Bengal, however, all had been overlain with the seductive spiced aromas emanating from the food stalls and the exotic scent of burning incense. Here the stench was raw. More honest, Anna thought, but less bearable. Here, as in India, the voice of the evangelist proclaimed eternal salvation to souls that had been damned from the moment of their conceptions to the earthly hell of want and fear. She did not pause to listen.

Then a strong hand grabbed her by the arm. "Ha! I thought so!"

She spun around as if pestilence itself had accosted her.

"You're the little lady who knows all about the Hindu gods!"

Oh! It was … Eben Garrett—who'd unknowingly started Anna on today's errand.

The journalist was grinning down at her. "What are you doing here in this hell-hole, anyhow? Slumming? I wouldn't have pegged you for one of those mission gals."

"Mr. Garrett," she said, looking pointedly at his ink-stained fingers on her arm. "Please unhand me."

Here on the street Eben Garrett seemed even larger and more rugged of stature than he'd appeared at the boarding house supper table. He seemed to radiate a type of unabashed masculine energy more at home on the streets than in Mrs. Chapman's boarding house. *Rude son of the soil*, her poetic Muse assessed him, but his speech was nothing if not educated and fluent.

He let go of her sleeve but kept his gaze on her face. "You know, I didn't recognize you at first. At Mrs. Chapman's table you looked just as plain as the rest of them, but I must say, out here in the light of day, you reward a longer scrutiny." He swept off his dusty derby hat in tribute.

She felt herself color. "Mr. Garrett, don't talk such nonsense." In his own way, he was a most attractive man, with his short dark curls plastered down on his forehead by the humid air. He wore a green-checked waistcoat, and his lapel buttonhole displayed a black-eyed susan.

"It's not nonsense, as I'm sure you must know." His half-smile seemed to lay as much claim to her as had his hand upon her arm. "But, in any case, what *are* you doing in the Five Points? It's no place for an unaccompanied lady."

"No one has offered me insult, Mr. Garrett." Now was a god-given opportunity, she realized with a thrill, to avail herself of the journalist's acquaintance with Reverend Peter Lyman. But how to prevent him from learning her true purpose here?

Anna's mind worked quickly. "I'm here because I'm concerned with the deplorable condition of the poor, Mr. Garrett." Even to herself she sounded sanctimonious, but there was no help for it. And, anyhow, it was true. "Especially of the children. At dinner you spoke of a minister, a Reverend … Peter Lyman, I believe … who concerns himself with the welfare of the destitute? I have come to offer my assistance with his endeavors."

"Have you, now? So there's more grit to you than to those canting hypocrites at old lady Chapman's table." A cabbage stump, thrown from a tenement window, came rolling to a stop at his feet. He kicked it neatly into the gutter, next to a pile of moldering potato parings and onion skins. "You'd like to meet the Rebel Reverend, would you? Well, you'll just have to wait. He's gone up to Westchester County—Dobbs Ferry, I think—setting up a new asylum for some of the waifs he's gathered in. Don't know how long he'll be gone. Listen, Mrs. ... it's Wheeler, right?"

Anna nodded.

"If you want, when the great man gets back, I'll take you to the House of Industry and give you a formal introduction."

Anna caught her breath. "Could you, Mr. Garrett? I would be most obliged."

"Sure thing," he said, and winked at her. "It's not every day I stumble across a little lady who knows all about Vishnu and Ram." When the clanging of fire bells and a sudden spiral of smoke to the east announced a fire somewhere in the direction of Hanover Square, he said a quick goodbye and took off at a run.

Anna did feel bad about misleading Mr. Garret; her true interest in the Reverend Peter Lyman, of course, was to learn if he knew anything about her daughter.

"Ah, so you've met me handsome boyo, Eben Garret—and her Highness, Queen Caroline. Well, then." Bridey O'Neill looked at Anna slantwise, and poured her a cup of tea from an earthenware pot sitting on the back of the coal stove in her dingy room. Anna had decided that, since she was already in the Five Points, she'd go visit Bridey O'Neill to whom she owed so very much.

Today the midwife wore a red bodice and multicolored petticoats, her sleeves pushed up above her elbows. She'd been frying onions, and the room reeked of them, while not a breeze stirred in the feverish air. There was a bowl of boiled potatoes on the crudely knocked-together kitchen table, but Anna couldn't see much else to eat in Bridey's room, aside from the bread loaf and slab of butter she herself had picked up at a German bakery. She would come back, she vowed, as soon as she could, with a basket of provisions for the midwife.

"Her Highness?" Anna responded. "You don't like Caroline Slade?" She squinted at a garish blue and red lithograph of the Virgin Mary that hung above the sagging bed.

"I didn't come to America to bow to the gentry, ye know." With the back of her hand Bridey pushed a lock of orange-red hair from her face. "She's been good to me, I'll say that for her, Lady High Muckety-Muck, but that don't mean I got to curtsy at her throne. Any road, it's not her help ye'll be wanting. It'll be that scamp, Eben's."

Eben? "And yours, of course." Anna cut a slice from the bread loaf and busied herself with buttering it. "Could I ask you to inquire in your neighborhood about … unclaimed babies?"

"Well, seein' as you been so good to me …" Bridey nodded toward the loaf on the table, and bit into the buttered slice Anna handed her. "Sure I'll ask around, Missus."

Anna was curious about the midwife's earlier words. "But tell me, Bridey. Why should I ask Mr. Garrett?" She took a tentative sip of the tea; it was tepid and over-stewed.

Bridey laughed. "Cause Eben knows everyone in the Five Points. And everything in the Five Points. If a nigger baby's gone missing—"

"Not a *nigger* baby," Anna interjected, "a *colored* baby."

Bridey shrugged. "A colored baby, then. He'll be able to tell ye everything about it, including the length of its drawing strings."

Anna's fingers drummed nervously on the well-scrubbed pine tabletop. She had set aside the thick ceramic mug. "I can't tell that man I have a … an illegitimate child—he's a reporter. If that story got in the newspaper, what a scandal it would make. And my publisher …" She could say no more, so terrible was the thought of what Mr. Larkin would do.

Bridey cocked her head. "'Tis a pity, then. Eben could be a real help to ye—even though he can be a bit of a rascal." She cleared her throat, as if she, herself, had reason to know. She took the final bite of bread, and, licking her buttery fingers one at a time, assessed Anna from head to toe. "It's looking fine, you are, Mrs. Wheeler. An' that's a new blue gown, is it?"

Anna glanced down at the light muslin. "Yes." She'd bought it yesterday from a Jewish merchant who sold second-hand clothing on the Bowery.

"I'll give ye one word of warning, then. If yer to spend any time a'tall with Eben Garrett," Bridey winked, "t'were good you kept your legs crossed tight."

Anna's eyes grew wide. A slow smile followed. "Ah, Bridey," she said, "you bad girl, you."

As Anna made her way back across Park Street, the evangelist on his fish barrel was still threatening eternal damnation. The dire words and the portentousness of his voice pulled her all too near to Josiah's ghost. She shuddered and quickened her steps.

SIXTEEN

He walked the streets of the city daily until he wore down the heels of his stout new boots. Each afternoon, he returned to Mrs. Etheridge's house and savored her plain New England dinners of roasted beef and oyster stew, so wholesome after a decade of spicy fare.

In everything, the wayfarer waited on his Master's pleasure. It was all there in his soul, all his Lord had given him to endure: his wife's vanishing just as the heathen uprising loosed its rivers of blood upon the People of God in India. His frantic search through the Mission grounds, where he had thought he and the other Christian workers secure in the Lord's protection. His dash to the river just as his comrades in Christ prepared to take to the boats in a last, desperate sail down the Ganges to what they thought would be the safety of the British garrison at Cawnpore. Where had she gone, his little wife? Had she woken early and set out walking in the cool of the morning, only to be taken by an advance guard of rebels; had she later escaped, only to find him gone, and herself lost, helpless, and alone? That latter possibility haunted his nightmares far more than the near-certainty of her instant, godly death. But, no—the people of India were everywhere blood-thirsty and devilish, and the murderous fiends had spared no one in their way.

He had tried, oh, how he had tried, to be teacher and preacher, helpmeet and friend and advisor, when, upon occasion, she, in her feminine weakness, threatened to go astray. Just has she had reached the apotheosis of obedient and unquestioning wifely silence, the heathen spirit arose in blood and fire, and the Lord visited him in His hot displeasure. And his little wife was lost, lost, her fate never to be known.

When he had first made his way back to Calcutta from the killing grounds at Cawnpore, he had been too greatly agitated by all he had suffered—his dear wife's loss, the long months of convalescence sequestered in a native village—to consider refuting the reports of his own death. All the other Fatehgarh missionaries had been killed, and his demise, too, had been presumed. But he had then upon his soul the memory of an incident that he'd feared could not bear scrutiny.

Once in Calcutta he'd taken a small house in a low quarter of town and kept his presence a secret. He'd used those months in the City of Palaces to reconcile through prayer his understanding of the circumstance that had saved his life. Oh, how at first he had wrestled with its bloody consequences, until his intelligence was near unhinged and he awoke each night screaming in a fevered sweat. Then, as his body healed, so also did his soul. He convinced himself that it was not his place to question the unerring hand of the God who had saved him. He had to believe in the absolute and certain power of God's will, else all his life's work was false.

Only when he felt himself once again to be right with the Lord, did he take ship for New York, purchase three quires of paper and begin to write, narrating the search for his sainted wife, the watery retreat to Cawnpore, then the murderous betrayal of the native fiends, and his hair-breadth escape as the Father of Miracles plucked him and him alone from certain death in the massacre.

SEVENTEEN

My dear lady, began the letter from Mr. Larkin, *I do not know where to begin. These new verses, so unanticipated in their content and style, quite took me aback. I had expected more of your spiritual effusions—and to receive these! My initial impulse was to return them, saying that they simply would not do. What can a sheltered lady such as yourself know of life in the steamy Orient? But then I reread the poems and became quite taken with your use of the exotic images. What a lush imagination you have, my dear. Sandstorms! Lotus blossoms! The deadly, slithering krait! I was transported. And, really, after all, there is nothing licentious in the verses, although their luxuriance at first gave me pause. Distributed judiciously among the others, these poems lend a certain piquancy to the whole. So, we have gone to print, with an editorial note as to the virtuous intent of the fair author, and the volume will be readied well before the holiday season.*

Yet, I feel I must warn you not to venture any further in the direction you have taken here. It is but a small step, after all, from the lush and alien to the merely sensual, indeed, even to a pernicious and morbid excitement. And, you must realize, my dear Mrs. Wheeler, how very dangerous a move that would be.

With all your best interests at heart,
William Larkin

> *P.S. You shall receive an invitation to a small literary soiree at the home of Mrs. Phoebe Derwent this Wednesday next. You will, of course, attend.*

Anna had received her editor's letter directly from the letter-carrier's hand as she left the boarding house for afternoon tea with Caroline at Taylor's Ice Cream Saloon on Broadway, and she had kept it in her glove, unopened, until she was settled at the restaurant table, staring in awe at the mirrored walls, the carved-and-gilded ceiling, the marble floors of the genteel ladies restaurant. She now frowned as she reread the line before Mr. Larkin's closing: "how very dangerous a move that would be." Was that a rebuke? A warning?

"What on earth is the matter?" Caroline Slade, in a green-and-white striped gown, glazed bonnet dangling from her hand by its green ribbons, strode up to Anna's table. Today Caroline's dark hair had been fashioned in ringlets, two of which hung down each cheek. "You look quite ... I don't know ... as if you'd just been bitten by a snake."

Anna folded the letter and slipped it back into the envelope. She laughed, but a bit shakily. "I feel that I have." Her companion's elegant appearance made Anna thankful for the new blue muslin.

Caroline sat on the dainty bentwood chair, no easy matter in her cage crinoline, and tipped her head inquisitively.

Anna raised the envelope from the table. "This is from my publisher."

"Publisher?" Caroline regarded Anna with astonishment.

"I may have told you about my child and ... something of my life in India." Anna found that she enjoyed startling Miss Caroline Slade. "But you don't know everything about me."

"Obviously not. Publisher? What have you written? An advice book? A sentimental novel?"

"Nothing so ambitious. I am a poet."

Caroline lost interest. "Oh. I never read poems. They're too ... airy for me." She beckoned to the waiter and placed an order without consulting Anna, then she took up the conversation again as if there had been no break. "What I like are novels. They've got the very heat of life in them—not 'I wandered lonely as a cloud, da dum, da dum, da dum, da dum.'" She drummed out the rhythm on the white-linen-covered tabletop.

Anna realized once again the essential disquiet of her new friend's character. Surrounded by the oriental magnificence of this fabulous eatery with its orange trees and splashing fountain, Caroline reminded her of a captive tiger she had once seen in a traveling Bengali menagerie, all energy and power with little scope for expression. In contrast, she, herself, she thought, was like some small mammal that went to ground and hunkered there until forced to defend its own.

The waiter set down a large silver tray of tea, sandwiches, berries, and ices. "Ah, yes," Caroline said, "I am famished." She took up a triangular chicken sandwich and studied Anna across the table. A wistful smile softened her patrician features. She gave a dry laugh. "I do so admire you."

"You do? Why on earth?" Anna poured a cup of *souchong* and sipped it black.

Caroline gazed at her over the gilded rim of her cup. "You have an enviable spirit. You may not be happy, but at least you know you're alive."

It had not always been so, but since … Ashok, and, especially, since the knowledge that she was a mother … yes indeed, she knew she was alive, vital in every cell. "And you do not?"

Caroline's expression became almost petulant. "It's all too easy. I'm heiress to a fortune whose origins are … Well, let us say that I've *earned* nothing. Whatever I want, I reach out my hand and take. While you. …" She ate the chicken sandwich in two bites and reached for another. "You, I think, have been refined in a kind of fire, some elemental need or even … desperation. It has made your life more … real than mine." A clergyman wearing a high clerical collar and an expression of professional cordiality slowed as he approached their table. Caroline ignored him, and he passed on by. "It has burnished your soul."

Once again she gave her short, dry laugh. "Or is it I who am now waxing poetical?"

Anna bit into a sweet strawberry. Uncomfortable with Caroline's romanticizing, she replied, "You help many people. You're helping me."

"And *such* money … Sometimes I despise myself." It was as if Anna's companion were lost in a conversation with herself.

Anna leaned forward and took Caroline's hands. "You hurt no one, Caroline, and do great good."

Her elegant friend looked down at the hands clasping hers. "Perhaps. But I would like to feel the depths of life I sense in you."

It was all Anna could do to keep from revealing her sudden irritation. "I must find my *child*." She gazed into Caroline's eyes, but found no hint of posturing there, simply a nameless melancholy. She sighed. "Caroline, don't sentimentalize me. From my youngest womanhood I've gone through the world in a haze of error, compounding one mistake with another, attempting to live as I *should*, rather than as I *might*. For a decade of marriage I lied, both to my husband and to my own soul."

Two fashionable women swept by in gowns of Marceline silk and crinolines so wide and stiff they disarranged the careful folds of the linen tablecloths. A waiter followed carrying a tray of sherry cobbler at shoulder height. Why, in this sumptuous establishment, surrounded by ladies of dainty appetite and exquisite *toilet*, did Anna feel so compelled to articulate her most ... improper failings? But the words tumbled out; there seemed no stopping them. "And then when I broke free for one ... luminous ... moment, what did I do? I scurried back to New York, only to sink myself anew in ... a kind of spiritual torpor. What ..." Anna reached for as emphatic a word as she could muster, "what ... cowardice!"

Anna still held Caroline's hands. Upon the word *cowardice*, she hit the table with them, hard, rattling the china. At the next table a lady in a white-straw chip hat with purple pansies leaned over and whispered to her companion. Anna realized she was making a spectacle of herself. She released Caroline, and concentrated on choosing another strawberry from her plate.

Caroline gaped at her and sat silent for a moment before she spoke in lowered tones. "Yes, I understand. As I said—the heat of life. Its passion and sorrow, too. Have you thought at all about writing your experiences in a novel?"

Anna choked on the berry. The mere possibility of such public exposure appalled her. "Nothing could be further from my intention," she said, as she recovered her voice. "I cannot emphasize that strongly enough."

Caroline gave one of her rare smiles and took a *petit-four* from the plate. "Why, pray tell, is your publisher like a snake?" She raised the little cake to her lips.

"Oh." Anna paused, startled by the change of subject. "A snake? That was most likely an overstatement. It's just that his letter began smoothly enough, but ended with something of a sting." She told her friend about the Indian poems and Mr. Larkin's misgivings. "He fears I am in danger of giving in to 'a pernicious and morbid excitement.'"

Caroline glanced at Anna with another little smile. "Now poems such as those I *do* want to read."

"Someday … when they are printed … you may read them. But I should have been more … judicious …" she borrowed her publisher's own word, "in what I sent to Mr. Larkin."

"William Larkin?" Caroline scowled. "I think I know the man. He has a pursed-up little mouth, as if he were born sucking on a pickled lime."

"That is unkind, Caroline." Anna touched her lips with the damask napkin. Then she laughed. "But so very accurate. I should not say this, but when I first saw him I thought how …" She hesitated.

"Yes?" Caroline encouraged her.

To no one else would she even have considered speaking so plainly, but she leaned over the table and whispered. "How very … *unkissable* he was."

Caroline let out a great snort, and, taken aback by this unseemly eruption in such a genteel establishment, they laughed together.

EIGHTEEN

Each day he arose at sunrise, read the Bible and engaged in prayer, wrestling with the angel of the Lord until Mrs. Etheridge's colored boy tapped on his door announcing breakfast. His daily after-breakfast constitutional, which he conducted in every weather, took him all over the city. He walked the streets south to the Battery with its neat plots of grass and graveled walks, and as far north as the newly excavated trenches for city streets to be numbered in the seventies.

But he was most at home in the streets of the Five Points, where the refuse of all nations swarmed, hopelessly damned in their ignorance and sin. Africans still dwelled in and around Cow Bay, though after the influx of Irish most had moved to more salubrious neighborhoods. Germans lived on Centre and Elizabeth Streets. Jews on Baxter or on Mott. The Irish, everywhere.

Evangelization efforts in this place were sorely lacking, he perceived; he had seen only one or two preachers in the streets. When he completed the God-appointed labor of the book he was writing, he would make himself known once again to those members of the righteous who now thought him asleep in the Bosom of the Lord. He had been hesitant thus far to reveal himself as a survivor of the Uprising, of the brutal massacres at Cawnpore; the attention he could expect at such a revelation would consume the time and sap the strength he needed to carry out the Will of God. Once the charge was accomplished—once he had justified in writing his Father's mercy to ... him alone ... when such a multitude of godly souls had perished—once the book was published, then he would approach former acquaintances and once again bring his glowing zeal for the Savior to bear upon the salvation of the lost and damned inhabitants of New York City.

He was particularly interested in establishing relations with two dear sisters-in-Christ he knew only through letters. Mrs. Margaret Ambrose and her co-worker, Miss Susan Parker, had over the years been among the most faithful supporters of the Fatehgarh Mission, sending contributions regularly, at times as much as ten dollars a month. He had never failed to reply in gratitude, sharing with them by letter some small news of his work of conversion inside the ramparts of heathenism. But he would wait until the Lord Jesus Himself had written *finis* to the tale of his beloved servant's mission work. Then, and only then, would he introduce himself at the Five-Points Mission.

NINETEEN

With cries of delight the following afternoon Bridey O'Neill began unpacking the napkin-covered basket of foodstuffs Anna had brought—a ham, a round Irish cheese just off the boat, half a dozen peaches, a small tub of farm-fresh eggs, a butter cake, another loaf of bread. When there was a sudden, urgent knock on Bridey's door, Anna went to answer it.

The gaunt, squinting girl who stood outside Bridey's door seemed eerily familiar to her. With a sudden uncanny shiver, Anna recognized her as Crazy Sal, the half-lunatic with whom she'd shared a room during her miserable sojourn at the Five-Points Mission. Anna shuddered again. *Pray God she won't know me. The last thing I need is for Sal to go blabbing to the ladies at the Mission that she found me with the midwife who delivered my child.*

But the girl ignored Anna, intent on getting her message across to Bridey. "Missus Ambrose sez yer to deliver a nigger baby over in Cow Bay." The raddled woman scowled. "The darky midwife can't be found nowhere. Yer to follow me. Hurry!"

Bridey wiped her hands on a greasy rag, covered the ham with a towel, gave it a longing backwards glance, and grabbed her midwife's bag.

"I'll come, too," Anna said. Here was an unlooked-for opportunity. Helping deliver a child in the colored neighborhood of Cow Bay, she could ask questions about brown-skinned babies without attracting too much notice.

"You, Mrs. Wheeler?" Bridey stopped and stared.

"Yes, of course. I'm a trained midwife. I delivered babies in India."

"In *India?*" Bridey, rolling her sleeves down, cast Anna a look of disbelief. "Yer jokin' me!"

Anna shook her head. "Hundreds of babies. Maybe a thousand."

Bridey stood with her hands on her hips, then she gave a half-incredulous snort. "Well, then, ye might as well come along. Guess twat's made the same over there as it is here."

Following Sal to the muddy *cul de sac* that was Cow Bay, Anna and Bridey were directed toward a sprawling, derelict building known citywide as the Dead End. The tall windows were smashed, the roofline sagged, the wide chimney leaned precariously. Anna and Bridey hastened up the outside steps, keeping well to the edges so their feet wouldn't breach the rotten wood at the center. Inside, the building reeked of humanity's every lower function.

In a dark attic room, its only light a sputtering candle, they found the young mother in full labor. Bridey motioned Anna toward the makeshift bed, a heap of straw, in one corner. She, herself, grabbed a warped bucket lying in a corner and pounded down the stairs to the street pump. The baby came at once, and, thankfully, without incident. By the time Bridey returned with the water, the new-born squirmed, naked and unwashed, in Anna's hands, and the chamber smelled of the peculiar liver-like scent of fresh placenta.

She dampened her handkerchief in the pump water and warmed it between her palms before washing the mucus from the baby's nostrils and mouth. As she bathed him, she noted how pale his skin was compared to his mother's black-coffee tones. It had been her experience in India that babies darkened as they got older, but the disparity here was striking. Anna knew that many white masters made free with the enslaved women at their mercy. She sighed. But this healthy, beautiful baby, no matter how he was conceived, looked to her like a newborn prince of the world.

Lacking a flannel to wrap him in, Anna swaddled the mewling infant in lengths torn from her petticoat. Then, while Bridey examined the young woman for possible tearing of the birth passages or signs of hemorrhage, she put him to the mother's breast, where he took hold eagerly.

"You done got a drink a water for me?" wheezed a voice from a dark corner. Anna started; she'd been so preoccupied with the birth that, in the flickering darkness of the derelict attic, she hadn't seen the elderly Negro woman huddled there, her head and shoulders wrapped in a ragged blanket. Anna scrubbed her own hands before she dipped water from the pail and bent over the woman. Immediately she recognized the fetid odor of infection; the old woman's right leg was swollen and discolored. *Uh, oh*, Anna thought, and tore the remainder of her petticoat into bandages.

"Word is, Cracker Skaggs's back in town," Bridey informed Anna as they navigated the muddy lane leading back to the street. It was twilight, and Anna was anxious to get to the safety of Broadway, five blocks away, before dark. Indeed, even as they passed two loafers leering at them from in front of a raucous stale beer dive, she could hear Broadway's roar and clatter in the near distance. It sounded like safety.

"Cracker Skaggs?" Anna had heard the name somewhere, and Bridey's doomsday tone boded no good about that ill-named fellow. "Who's he?"

"A god-damned black-birder, that's who. The worst of 'em all. Weeks go by, and he don't show his face in the city. Then, alluva sudden, he's here, snatches up five or six colored kids, and hops ship for Charleston afore anyone's the wiser." Bridey blew her nose on a worn handkerchief she'd pulled from her sleeve. "Tell ya the truth, I'm feared that's what happened to Pansy, the darky midwife. No other reason for her not to leave word where she can be found." She jerked her head back toward the Dead End. "And them back there's runaways. Bet my Irish boots on it."

As she stepped gingerly from cobblestone to cobblestone, it took Anna a moment to focus. "Oh, you mean … the two women? They're fugitive slaves, you mean?"

"Uh huh. Stopping on their way to Canada. He'll be after them, for sure—that pretty gal and the half-white baby. They'll bring a fat reward. That old one though, don't look like she can take another step, let alone run from no goddamn slave-catcher." She kicked a browning apple core into the gutter.

Black-birders. Slave-catchers. Anna thought of her daughter, and fear once more jolted her. Caroline had said that India Elizabeth was in no danger from slavers, but how on earth could she possibly know?

To Anna, helpless and hopeless as Josiah had made her feel, the movement to abolish slavery had, until now, been an abstraction, like the women's rights movement, all high-toned rhetoric and posters pasted on the walls. She'd felt that she had no place in either. And over the past days she'd been so narrowly focused on finding India Elizabeth, that she hadn't paid any attention to the escalating clamor over slavery. But, now! Now!

The two women she and Bridey had helped today … that beautiful child … they were not figures on a Fugitive Wanted poster. They were warm, living human beings, weren't they? She would help them! She would banish Josiah's ghost, all his *Thou shalts* and *Thou shalt nots*!

"I'll come back and see these people again tomorrow," she told Bridey. "The mother and baby will be fine, but, like you, I've got grave concerns about that older woman."

And, indeed, grave concerns about her beloved, helpless, daughter. Cracker Skaggs? Slave-catchers in this city? Oh, dear God, please help them all.

Anna said goodbye to Bridey in front of her building, but before she'd gone more than a half block in the direction of Centre Street, the Irish woman ran back down the steps and out onto the darkened street. "Missus," she yelled, and Anna stopped, swiveling around.

"I've something for ye by way of saying thanks." She pressed a cool metal object into Anna's hand. "For the food … and for the help with the baby."

"Bridey, you don't need to—"

"I ain't one for taking charity, ye know, Missus. I pay my debts. This'll mebbe bring ye good fortune."

Half-wrapped in a corner torn from the *Sun*, the object was a silver crucifix on a thin chain, tarnished and worn. The limp, tortured body hanging from the cross made Anna shudder. "Bridey, I can't take this." And, indeed, she didn't want the ugly thing. But Bridey insisted, so she smiled at the Irish woman, slipped the chain over her head and let the crucifix fall inside her bodice.

"Thank you, Bridey," she said, managing not to cringe at the feel of it against her skin.

When she got safely back to the boarding house, Anna gave the tarnished crucifix to Nancy, Mrs. Chapman's scrawny maid of all work, who accepted it with clamorous delight.

The following afternoon, returning to Cow Bay with a crock of applesauce, a roast chicken and a set of infant garments, Anna found the Negro women and child gone, and the room occupied by a family of six just off the boat from County Cork.

An unwelcome image struck her, a drawling thug from the South in a waistcoat and a broad-brimmed planter's hat. Anna felt a deep uneasiness for the three desperate strangers who'd previously found shelter in this attic. No one in the house seemed to know where they were.

And no one seemed to care.

TWENTY

The invitation from Mrs. Phoebe Derwent, beautifully inscribed on deckle-edged stationery, came two days later. It read: "*I am pleased to invite you to a small, informal literary gathering Wednesday evening next, at my home on Gramercy Park. Having seen your lovely Indian verses—I trust you won't mind that Will Larkin has shared the manuscripts with me—I find that I desire to know you.*"

In her dreary room, that overcast late-summer afternoon, Anna dropped the note on her writing table, jumped from her chair, began to pace the room. She'd forgotten Mr. Larkin's mention of this gathering. His insistence that she attend. But, how could she show herself in literary society? If she were to run into someone at Mrs. Derwent's who recognized her, someone, say, like Mrs. Ambrose, who knew she'd given birth to a child under suspect conditions, she would be thrown into social and literary perdition. Yes, it was her talent that had bought her entrée into such a cultured circle as Mrs. Derwent's, but it was her reputation as a chaste and respectable woman that would keep her there. No reputable literary house would publish the poems of a fallen woman, no matter how accomplished.

How ironic! Her unblemished character would provide the means allowing her to search for her daughter, but, on the other hand, the very fact of India Elizabeth's existence belied the spotlessness of that character and would render her in society's censorious eyes a mere voluptuary. How could Anna risk attending this genteel Gramercy Park gathering?

She could not, that was for certain.

It might have been ten minutes or it might have been an hour before she grabbed up the Kasmiri shawl, throwing it over her head and shoulders. She would talk to Caroline. Surely her friend would know how Anna could gracefully decline the invitation. She clasped the shawl under her chin, took up her umbrella, and went out into the mist.

The fog had turned into a filthy drizzle, and walking down the Broadway sidewalk under her wide black umbrella, Anna passed hundreds of her fellow New Yorkers, shawl-covered housewives, arms loaded with string-tied packages, dyspeptic clerks in gloves and galoshes, two literary-looking ladies under blue umbrellas, deep in conversation. What would they think, these people in the streets, if they could see into her heart? Perhaps they could, some of them, those who'd themselves violated society's laws. Surely there must be fellow sinners among this crowd of bland-faced men brushing past her in their green greatcoats, these fashionable ladies in their bell-shaped skirts. And surely, she feared, surely among the guests at Mrs. Derwent's soiree, those literary men and women whose experience of life was brighter, deeper, less cautious than that of the ordinary run of people in the streets, her iniquity would be … recognized? … comprehended? … known?

Sympathized with?

Condemned?

Anna bustled into Caroline's parlor in a state of panic. Waving Mrs. Derwent's invitation at her friend, she croaked, "I can't. I simply … can't …"

Caroline set aside her needlepoint frame, plucked the missive from Anna's hand and read it. Then she glanced up with one of her infrequent smiles. "But, Anna, my friend, you must. You simply *must*. You're at the beginning of a literary career—you have to meet people who will be interested in your work, whether to read it or to publish it."

When 'Bama Fitch brought a tea tray to the cozy private parlor where they sat, she gave Anna a sharp, enigmatic look that almost seemed to pin her in her brocaded chair. Then she turned and left the room, quietly closing the door behind her. Despite the heat, Anna shivered.

Filling Anna's teacup, Caroline said, "Now, where were we? Oh, yes. *I* could afford to refuse an invitation like that. I'm known everywhere for bad manners and invited in spite of them." She paused, then gave a little laugh. "Or, perhaps, because of them. But you … well, there will be poets, editors and writers of all stamps." She mimicked a high-pitched faux-genteel voice. "Some gray-bearded poet will read his latest effusions, an illustrious tenor will render an aria from 'Norma,' and a supper of curried chicken, lobster croquettes, and champagne will be served at precisely ten o'clock." Anna laughed, and Caroline's voice dipped back into its usual alto range. "Oh, it will be tedious, but these are the people who will be most useful to you in your career. Really, Anna, you must attend."

"But, Caroline," she played with the fringe of a red-and-gold-silk Chinese pillow, "I'm terrified."

"Terrified? For goodness sake, of what?"

She replied without having to think at all. "Of being seen, of being noticed, of being … judged. Most of all I'm terrified of being exposed as a … you know … sinner."

Caroline threw back her head and laughed. "Nonsense," she said. "There will be so many there steeped in their private iniquities—even if you wore a scarlet letter, like Mr. Hawthorne's Hester, no one would dare to say a word."

She paused, then picked up the needlepoint frame, shook a needle from a silver needle case, and threaded it with a flamboyant emerald-colored silk. "Including me. Anna, may I speak frankly?" Without waiting for a reply, Caroline rushed on, lowering her voice. "You did not think *me* a virgin, did you? Well, disabuse yourself. When I lived in France, I had a very skilled tutor in the ways of sexual passion." She glanced up briefly before taking the first stitch in a fantastical crewel-work vine.

Anna's eyes widened. Nothing in their growing friendship had prepared her for such a conversation. She knew about sexual love, of course, about *making* love, but she had no experience at all in actually *talking* about it.

"In New York, however," Caroline went on, almost immediately setting her needlework aside, "I find myself lonely and restless. Oh, let me just say it—my unconventional ways seem to have frightened away the timid gentlemen of Gotham." She skewed her eyes at Anna. "You, I think, know whereof I speak?"

Anna simply nodded.

"And, then, of course, there's our hostess, herself. I've known Phoebe Derwent forever. I've called her Aunt Phoebe since I was twelve. She and my father were ... well, let me say, they were very discreet." She raised her eyebrows, knowingly.

"Re-e-e-aly?" Anna's head was spinning. How had she managed to remain so naïve? But, nonetheless, she felt uncomfortable about attending the gathering. From a mahogany side table, she picked up a turquoise-silk Chinese fan, opened it, shut it, and lay it back down. "But ... in such august company I would be rendered speechless."

"Rubbish! I'll be there to speak for you."

"You have an invitation?" Anna clapped her hands in delight.

"Well, no. But I don't need one. Oh, Aunt Phoebe pretends to disapprove of me, the way I racket around the city all on my own, my refusal to marry—she's obliged to, circulating as she does in such very respectable circles. But I make the good Mrs. Derwent laugh, and her door is always open to me."

Anna's relief vanished as soon as she felt it. She paled. The most powerful objection of all had raised its ugly head. "Oh, but Caroline ..." she gasped, "I have absolutely nothing to wear!"

As Alabama Fitch passed the iron-picket fence of Manhattan's Zion African Methodist Episcopal Church at Leonard and Church Streets, she could hear the ardent Hallelujahs. She knew the preacher and the congregation well, but on this misty autumnal afternoon, worship was not her intention. Although the law allowed a colored woman to ride the street cars, custom made it always less than comfortable, and this evening she did not wish to draw the attention of hostile passengers. So, although the way was long and her market basket heavy, she walked to her destination, passing a high gray fence that had been plastered all over with political posters supporting presidential candidates, chief among them a gawky-looking fellow named Abraham Lincoln. 'Bama gave him a brief glance. Caroline had high hopes for this broadminded westerner, but, as neither she nor 'Bama could vote, their support made no difference.

A half-block up from the church, 'Bama turned in at the wooden gate of a stout brick house and knocked for admission. A thin man opened the low front door, gray eyes in a light-brown face venturing a quick glance up and down the street. She was not surprised by the nervous vigilance, not given the furtive, frightened sojourners to whom this house was accustomed.

"Sister Fitch," the man said. "Your presence is always a blessing." His mouth twitched involuntarily. "No matter what the circumstance."

"Mrs. Washington no better?" she asked.

He shook his head, his expression grim.

The smell of starch and boiled soap greeted her as she entered into a spacious whitewashed kitchen with a low ceiling. She sat on a maple bench by the worktable and opened her basket, taking out first an earthenware pan of the beef custard so nourishing for an invalid, then a large parcel of Ceylon tea wrapped in a cone of coarse straw paper, and, finally, a soft calico patchwork dog with a jaunty red satin bow. "And how is our little one today?" she asked.

TWENTY-ONE

"My dear …" Mrs. Phoebe Derwent, fashionable in black glace silk, her skirts covered with infinitesimal flounces, glided up to Anna. "I must tell you how very much pleasure your poems have given me. Those lovely verses with the Indian settings transported me back to my youth. I spent six months in Munnar, you know, in the hill country with my late husband."

Caroline came up behind them. "Aunt Phoebe was married to his Lordship Arthur Derwent of the renowned Derwent's East India tea company," she broke in, "until, that is, he was eaten by a Bengal tiger on their wedding journey. Have you no greeting for me, Aunt Phoebe?"

Mrs. Derwent kissed Caroline on both cheeks. "So, you are here, too, you bad girl. Miss Wheeler, don't believe a word of it." She adjusted the wide lace sleeve-edging that fell over her plump hand. "Arthur was no lord, just a simple English tea merchant. And he died of nothing more dramatic than malaria."

"Simple." Caroline coughed, gazing around pointedly at the elaborate surroundings. The room was high and commodious, its walls covered in pale-peach silk embossed in silver with floral wreaths, its vaulted ceiling frescoed with a depiction of Psyche and Cupid in the palace of the gods.

Mrs. Derwent made a shooing motion at Caroline, who sailed off, laughing. Then she turned a wide chased-silver bracelet on her wrist, as if it were some exotic talisman. "Now, Miss Wheeler, your poem about the sandstorm …" She raised a thin eyebrow suggestively. It was disconcerting, Anna found, to be asked in person about her poems, when to date those verses had been relegated to the distance and impersonality of print. But Caroline had convinced her she must get used to appearing in public; without the income from her poems, she could never hope to make a home for India Elizabeth

When Mrs. Derwent had finished gushing over the India poems, she introduced Anna to two women who sat engrossed in conversation on a hexagonal Turkish ottoman in the center of the large parlor. The older was plump, with a head full of graying curls and a satirical gleam in her eyes, dressed in black silk, simply cut. The younger was dark-haired and angular, wearing a gold crape gown.

"Mrs. Parton. Mrs. Stoddard," Anna's hostess said. "Let me present Miss Anna Wheeler, whose volume of exquisite verses will soon be brought before the public by Larkin & Bierce."

The older woman gave a practiced smile; she seemed to expect to be recognized. Mrs. Derwent continued, "You will doubtless know Mrs. Sara Parton, the popular author, by her *nom de plume*, Fanny Fern. And this is Mrs. Elizabeth Stoddard, the wife of Richard Stoddard, the poet of the moment." She nodded toward an adjoining room. Through a wide arch they could see a dark-bearded man standing between tall candles on ebony stands reading to a scanty audience. "Mrs. Stoddard also writes," she concluded.

Elizabeth Stoddard tightened her lips at this relegation to an ancillary status.

Just last week at Astor Place, Anna had seen Fanny Fern's books stacked high in a bookstore window. The lady was celebrated—or infamous, depending on who was doing the judging, but *Ruth Hall*, her best-selling novel, had erased the stigma of scandal and rescued her from poverty. Well, if Mrs. Parton could survive public scandal, Anna mused ...

When the popular author indicated the seat between herself and Mrs. Stoddard, Anna sat, her unaccustomed hoop skirt flying up at an alarming tilt to reveal a brief glimpse of white frills.

"Careful," Mrs. Parton warned, with a wicked grin, as Anna adjusted the offending garment, "you'll send the more delicate gentlemen into swoons."

Anna gave a slow smile. With Sara Parton in the room, the evening showed signs of becoming pleasurable.

Elizabeth Stoddard gazed at Anna out of slitated eyes. "Speaking of the more delicate gentlemen, is it true you will publish with William Larkin?"

"Yes."

The two ladies exchanged freighted glances. Then Mrs. Parton patted Anna's hand in a consoling fashion. "Never fear, my dear, Larkin & Bierce is a respectable house."

Never fear? Anna immediately became fearful.

Mrs. Stoddard's thin lips curved in a withering smile. "Most respectable," she said.

Anna felt as if some little drama were being played out at her expense. She glanced from one lady to the other.

"But?. . ." she ventured.

It was the desired reaction, inviting disclosure.

"*But*," Mrs. Parton patted her gold-gray curls, "they are, it is all too true, so *very* respectable. William Larkin will touch nothing that has even the slightest whiff of the carnal world upon it. The poor man doesn't quite approve of Shakespeare, and there are parts of the Old Testament that render him exceedingly uneasy." She winked. "Fortunately for him, Edward Bierce has his eye first and foremost on the cash. There is, you must be aware, quite a profitable market in good books."

"*Good* books," Mrs. Stoddard elaborated, with a twist of her thin lips, "more so than good *books*. I assume your verses are of the pious kind, Mrs. Wheeler?" And without waiting for a response, she continued, "coin of the realm for Larkin & Bierce. You should do well."

In her mouth the word "pious" acquired a venomous tone, and Anna felt a shiver pass through her.

"On the other hand, those of us," Mrs. Stoddard continued, "who write about, shall we say, that forest of the heart where the human passions roam do not find ourselves enriched in monetary terms." She rose in a graceful swirl of crinoline. "I wish you the best of luck with your publishing career. But do beware Mr. Larkin's delicate eye." She sailed toward the back parlor, where her poet husband had just finished reading.

"Forgive Elizabeth, dear," Mrs. Parton said. "As she is too sensual a poet for the respectable press and too accomplished for the gutter press, she does poorly in placing her poems. When you joined us, we were bemoaning the pusillanimous timidity of New York publishers."

"Mrs. Parton ..." Anna found her voice. "I know nothing of publishers and their houses—or of poets and their factions. I write my verses and the magazines take them. I earn just sufficient to keep body and soul together."

Fanny Fern's gray curls bounced as she nodded. "Believe me, I more than understand. But, if it is not overly bold on my part, let me offer some advice that will allow you to do far more than that."

"Oh, yes." Anna sat back on the hexagonal ottoman, anchoring her skirts with both hands.

"We live at a moment," Mrs. Parton said, "when it is possible for a woman with the gift of language to capture the ear of the public and, consequently, enrich herself greatly. Books and newspapers are transported across the country on the wings of steam—or, if I may speak more prosaically—by railroad car and steam packet. All an authoress must do is speak directly to the heart of Woman, and she may do extremely well. Never before has the cottage widow in Michigan or the lonely miner's wife north of San Francisco been able to read, within weeks, the latest novel or magazine from the New York presses. Now, I don't talk about men as readers—they have all gone West simply to make money. But the women are starving for stories and verses."

"Is that so?" Anna breathed. She leaned forward again, mindless of her hoops.

"Oh, yes, my dear. My editor Mr. Bonner tells me that when he took over the *Ledger* a handful of years ago, they circulated only twenty-five hundred of each issue. He now ships 400,000 a week across the nation. I am here to testify that there is money to be made in abundance by the canny writer." She gazed steadily at Anna from knowing eyes. "I tell you this because I have heard of Mr. Larkin's business practices, and fear he will omit to let you know just exactly how much profit you are worth to him."

Anna's spirits, which had risen wildly, suddenly plunged. "What have you heard?"

"Well, my dear—" Just then a bearded man in a crimson-embroidered waistcoat and a swallow-tailed coat approached. Sara Parton broke off and arose in a swoosh of taffeta. "Here, let me introduce you to Mr. Bonner. Robert, may I present Miss Anna Wheeler, a coming poet, I am told."

Surprisingly, Mr. Bonner had heard of Anna. "Oh, yes, Miss Wheeler, I've seen a copy of one of your Indian poems." His voice held remnants of an Irish lilt. "Most elegant. Would you have anything for me, dear lady?"

Anna's head was spinning. Within one brief conversation, she had been snubbed as a pious versifier, set on the path to wealth, warned against her publisher, and approached by a rich and famous editor. No small wonder that she found herself both elated and alarmed. She experienced the oddest sense of having become two different souls inhabiting the same body, the timid writer of inoffensive verses and, emerging as from a cocoon, a bolder, more self-confident literary woman. Then she felt the newer Anna smile. "Certainly, Mr. Bonner. I would be most honored to have you read my work."

Robert Bonner flicked a card into Anna's hand. "I must listen to my Fanny Fern. She brings me nothing but good fortune. Excuse us now, please. We have some business to conduct." He took Mrs. Parton by the elbow and steered her across the room.

Before Anna could do more than take a single step away from the ottoman, Mr. Larkin's reedy voice was in her ear. "I regret leaving you to such questionable company, but before I was aware of your arrival, that shameless Fanny Fern already had you in her clutches."

Anna squeaked, "yes, I was just now introduced to Mrs. Parton." Suddenly, Mr. Bonner's polite invitation to submit her poems seemed nothing more than pie-in-the-sky. Mr. Larkin, at least, was cash in the hand, and she desperately needed the money. Perhaps someday she would be able to write for Mr. Bonner, to stretch herself and try something new. Perhaps someday, she thought wistfully, she might attempt something with—how had Mrs. Parton put it?—with a whiff of the carnal world upon it. For Mr. Larkin, as she had been made aware by his cautionary letter about her Indian lines, she had taken honesty of expression just about as far as she could.

Beyond her editor's narrow shoulder, Anna saw Caroline raise a stemmed glass to her, as if in ironic toast to her conversation with the tight-lipped publisher.

"And, Miss Wheeler," William Larkin continued. "I do hope I was mistaken, but I thought I saw you arrive in the company of Miss Caroline Slade." He gave her a narrow appraisal.

"Miss Slade was kind enough to bring me here in her carriage," she replied cautiously.

"Oh, no, no, no." His papery hands flew in agitation, as if they were startled butterflies. "I understand you are new to our society, so I feel I must warn you. Caroline Slade is not at all the type of woman with whom it is wise for you to associate. Not at all."

Anna smoothed down her skirts. She was torn between loyalty and self-interest. "I have found Miss Slade to be most gracious—"

"My dear ..." Anna was tired of having her hands clasped by Mr. Larkin, but she dared not pull them away. "There is, with Caroline Slade, a most regrettable immodesty of manner and a tendency to interject herself in situations no true woman would deign even to acknowledge. And her family ... well! Indeed, allow me to escort you home in my conveyance, rather than subject you further to such dubious company."

All of Caroline's kindness came rushing back to Anna. She took a deep breath. "Your solicitude is most gratifying, Mr. Larkin, but I shall not trouble you." Her heart was pounding at this act of daring. "Ah, I see my hostess by the conservatory. I most go speak with her. Good evening, Mr. Larkin."

Anna returned home as she had come, with Caroline.

That night, as she drifted off to sleep in the lumpy bed at Mrs. Chapman's house, an image came to her mind: her verses, linked together like railroad cars, steaming across the nation carrying the precious freight of one small, dark-eyed girl riding into a safe and joyous future. But, just ahead on the single track, around a hairpin bend, came the wail of a heavy engine speeding at full throttle toward them.

TWENTY-TWO

On Broadway the next afternoon, weaving through a crush of lady shoppers and men of business, Anna found herself suddenly standing stock still in front of Appleton Bookseller's large show window at Leonard Street. Featured was a display of the books of Mrs. E.D.E.N. Southworth, whose novels Anna had read serialized in the New York *Ledger*. Many people had chastised the author for venturing beyond correct taste and good judgment, but Anna had burned precious lamp oil late into the night, mesmerized by the trials and tribulations of the author's plucky, but virtuous, heroines.

Books were a luxury for Anna. She owned only four, a much-read three-volume edition of *Jane Eyre* and a blue cloth-covered copy of Mrs. Browning's poems, both of which she had found at second-hand booksellers at Nassau Street, a falling-apart dime copy of *Charlotte Temple* she had rescued from a gutter, and her treasured edition of *Leaves of Grass*. Her other reading was in the newspapers, or in magazines she perused at free reading rooms.

Enticed by Appleton's blended perfume of paper, ink, leather and glue, she entered the shop. Floor-to-ceiling bookshelves were crammed with books, and brightly colored volumes were piled high on long tables: cookery books, histories, sermons, novels, missionary memoirs. Anna turned from the memoirs with a shudder to the rows of brightly covered novels. So many books; perhaps she could purchase just one. … No, she would satisfy herself simply with having looked.

And having touched. She took down a copy of Lydia Sigourney's poems from a shelf, ran a finger over the gilded cover, the gold-mottled endpapers. How beautiful it was. She found it almost impossible to believe her own book would be here, that other shoppers would take her volume in their hands, other readers would enter into her world, feel her feelings, think her thoughts. She, Anna Wheeler, was an author. Her book would soon be displayed in this very shop. The thought caused her to suck in her breath. Passing the tables by the show window, she snatched up a copy of Mrs. Southworth's *The Curse of Clifton* and carried it over to the clerk at the counter.

Stepping out of the shop with her impulsive purchase added to her other parcels, she felt an energy radiating into her, as if it were through the soles of her boots in their contact with the sidewalk paving. At the corner of Catherine Lane, with its mint sellers, buttermilk stands, and hot corn vendors, she purchased a paper cone of grapes and popped one in her mouth. For a moment she felt totally mindful of all around her: the deep, rich hue of the fruit, the stark lettering of the signs on the buildings, the rank smell of the gutters, the cries of the vendors, the bold aspirations of the people. For a moment she saw herself not as an isolated being, but as part of the teeming multitudes of this great city. For a moment, in spite of her fears for India Elizabeth, she felt herself almost giddy with life.

Not far away, a one-eared pig staggered drunkenly into the man's leg, spewing a thin boozy vomit over his respectable new wool-gabardine trousers—filthy swine had been gorging on discarded mash behind some stinking East River brewery. He kicked the beast, and it lurched down Worth Street, squealing. He passed a coffin warehouse with sawdust on the street and the sound of hammering. Ragged gray towels hung from a rusting fence that surrounded the corner grog-grocery. Slop pails tilted against the back-door steps of squat, sagging wooden houses. He turned a corner and there stood the Five Points Mission, clean, foursquare, and brick-solid, a monument to the demands of the immortal spirit.

He stood a moment and considered. Then he pivoted on his heel. It was not yet quite time to open his heart to the ladies of the mission.

TWENTY-THREE

The New-York Tribune, Thursday, September 7, 1860

The body of an elderly Negro woman was found floating in the East River yesterday morning by two boys fishing for stripers at Peck's Slip. She was shabbily dressed, with one leg heavily bandaged. The coroner estimates that the corpus had been in the river for over a week.

Anna, reading this item in the newspaper, felt an immense sadness come over her. No doubt about it—this must be the old woman from the Cow Bay attic. The woman who had asked her for a drink of water.

"Yeah? Well. It's too bad, but there ain't nothin' we coulda done about it." Bridey rubbed her dough-covered hands on a cotton flour sack, as in the distance bells at the Church of the Transfiguration chimed the half hour. "Could be blackbirders caught up with them. I told you, didn't I, for someone like Cracker Skaggs the mother and baby would fetch a good bounty, but the old one wouldn't be worth the trouble of taking back South. 'Tis evil, it is—that whole damn slavery system, but, like I said, there ain't nothin' we coulda done."

Anna knew that Bridey was simply being realistic, but her heart went out to the old woman. And to the new mother. And to the baby, who would live out his life in bondage—here in the United States of America, the world's Beacon of Liberty! Finally she was beginning to understand Caroline's fury at the nation's tolerance of human bondage, her passion for the well-being of New York's African people.

But what for Anna was closer to home, more agonizing: *Blackbirders*! Bridey's words had confirmed her own premonitions. Slave-hunters. Dear God, if these cruel slavers were to catch sight of brown-skinned India Elizabeth they would surely snatch her up.

Indeed, might they not already have done so?

Bridey poured tea into her only mug and handed it to Anna. She gazed off past the bread trough with its dough now set to rise and out her one small filthy window.

"Mebee some people are doin' somethin' about this god-damned slavery," she mumbled, almost under her breath, "and mebee I know what it is, but I ain't at liberty to tell you nuthin'."

For more than a week following Mrs. Derwent's literary evening, Anna heard nothing from Caroline. But this particular afternoon she urgently needed to talk to her friend; she'd received a note from William Larkin that had left her shaken. "*Dear Miss Wheeler, I remain disturbed by your ill-advised friendship with Miss Caroline Slade. Ask Miss Slade, if you would, the source of her ungodly fortune. If she has the grace to be truthful, you will not like what you hear.*"

Her publisher's note distressed Anna, and she decided to show it to Caroline—not that she doubted her friend, but she wanted some insight into Mr. Larkin's motivation for trying to quash their acquaintance.

A coal fire crackled in the fireplace grate of Caroline's small withdrawing parlor. Anthracite, Anna thought, with its clean burn and light sulfuric smell, not Mrs. Chapman's cheap, smutty Liverpool coal that begrimed Anna's hands and blackened her walls. What would it be like to live in a well-run home like this, she wondered, everything orderly and comfortable? She pictured herself seated on the hearthrug with a dark-haired child dressed in white and smelling of rosewater. They'd be playing with a wooden Noah's Ark, lining the animals up two by two. Elephants first. Then tigers. Then monkeys. She could hear the child's delighted laughter—

From somewhere in the back of the house, the real house, not Anna's castle in the air, came the cry of a baby. A real baby. Then a door slammed, and the cry was cut off, and all was silent once more. Must be the child of a servant, Anna thought.

She'd been waiting at least twenty minutes. Oddly enough, after Anna had pulled the doorbell over and over, it was not Mrs. Fitch who'd finally answered the door, as usual, but a skittish young Negro girl wearing multiple braids and a vast white apron. She'd ushered Anna into the parlor. "They be busy, now," she said, breathless. "But Miss Caroline say you wait."

So she waited. A substantial mahogany clock ticked on the marble mantle, flanked by two large Chinese vases glazed in red and gold. The pagodas rising up the sides of steep painted hills were not quite Indian temples, but close enough that Anna could almost capture the scent of jasmine in her memory.

Another door slammed, more faintly, perhaps one leading from the kitchen courtyard where deliveries were made. This was not the quiet, well-ordered domestic atmosphere Anna was used to at Caroline's, the swift arrival of her hostess, the welcoming cups of tea. Today even the yellow roses in the crystal vase seemed neglected; three brown-edged petals had fallen onto the polished table top. There was an air in the house as of ordinary life somehow … suspended.

Another five minutes ticked away on the mantle clock. Clearly Caroline was occupied with something more important than a visit. Anna had poems to write; she would wait no longer.

Rising from the sofa, she pinned her shawl tight against the nippy breeze, tied the strings of her bonnet, and took up her gloves. In the entrance hall, her hand was on the brass door-knob when she heard a footstep behind her.

"Anna! Wait!" Caroline's voice.

She pivoted, to find her friend entering through the plush door draperies, wearing a blue-striped cotton day dress. "Anna," she said, in a low, intense voice, "would you please come with me?"

In her arms she cradled a blanket-wrapped baby.

The kitchen air was moist with the rich odor of chicken broth and the yeasty scent of rising bread. A colored woman was slumped in a cushioned rocker by the fireplace, and 'Bama Fitch, seated at a small table, fed her spoonsful of soup. The stranger's matted hair hung over her face, and she took the soup almost like an automaton, seemingly insensible to her surroundings.

From where she fed the young woman, 'Bama glanced over at Anna, her expression inscrutable. Anna was puzzled. "What's happening here?"

Caroline spoke in her lowest tones as she and Anna sat at the long worktable. "You trusted me with your secret, Anna, and now I will trust you with mine. 'Bama and I, we're ... well, we're agents ... on the Underground Railroad."

"But—that's against the law!" As soon as Anna said it, 'Bama skewed her eyes toward her, scornful. Anna was instantly ashamed.

Her friend looked at her with a straight, green gaze. "There's law, Anna, and then there's Law. I thought you, at least, would know the difference."

"Umm huh!" 'Bama breathed.

"But, you could be arrested, Caroline. God only knows how long you might spend in jail! According to federal law these people are property!"

Caroline turned back the flannel that covered the baby's face, smiled down at him, then placed him in Anna's arms. "Is his freedom not worth it?"

"Yes, but—" She too looked into the child's face. A handsome, light-skinned newborn, he looked like ... he looked like ... like ... a prince of the world! Anna gaped, inspected him at length, astonished, and then stared over at the mother, asleep now by the fire. 'Bama Fitch brushed back the tangles of hair that hid the woman's face. "Oh," Anna said, recognizing her. "Oh!" It was the woman whose baby she'd helped deliver in the Cow Bay attic.

By the time they had the fugitives sequestered in the long, narrow attic compartment that served as a hiding place, it was dark. A low-burning whale-oil lamp cast shadows on the wide maple bed where the mother and baby slept. Caroline placed her hand on a carved finial of an elaborate mahogany wardrobe and turned it. She parted a row of heavy coats, and Anna saw the set of narrow steps that led downward to a door accessing the stable.

A flame leapt up in the massive kitchen fireplace as Caroline and Anna sat down to a cold supper at the kitchen table. "Tomorrow morning they'll be on a steamboat north," Caroline said. "'Bama will conduct them as far as Albany, and give them over to the care of a Quaker family on State Street."

Anna shook her head in disbelief. "What has led you to take such risks?"

Caroline looked over at Anna, her expression sober. "You truly do not know?"

Anna fingered the thick curved handle of her blue crockery cup and shook her head.

Caroline bit her lower lip. "I thought everyone in the city knew the shameful source of my, ah, prosperity. And I *am* ashamed, but what can I do? Shall I give up everything? The money? The house? The properties? Shall I go to work as a factory operative and die of consumption in a cellar room? Shall I turn Catholic and enter a nunnery? I'm not suited, I think, for either."

"What?" Anna sat forward on her seat. "What on earth has you so chastened?"

"Oh, Anna—I hope you will not despise me." Caroline's eyes were opaque with feeling. "I could not bear to lose your respect."

"Caroline!" She leaned forward and clasped her friend's hands. "I love and admire you—look at all you have done for me."

Caroline swallowed. "I make amends in any way that presents itself to me—but it never seems to be enough."

Had Caroline stolen from the poor? Had she committed murder? Had she— "Tell me!"

Anna's friend would not meet her gaze. "My great grandfather, Obediah Slade, was a ship's owner from Liverpool. He came to Long Island almost two-hundred years ago and set up housekeeping in grand style in Oyster Bay. He prospered and built many ships." She took a deep breath, as if steeling herself for the words to follow. "He was an importer of molasses and a distiller of rum—and, oh, yes, most lucratively, a trader in African slaves.

"Now you know." She pulled her hands free. "Are you still my friend?"

Anna smiled slowly. Yes, Caroline was still her friend. Now, more than ever. The young woman's confession about the source of her fortune explained a great deal: her passion for the abolition of slavery; her interest in the orphans of the Asylum; her offer to help Anna find her dark-skinned child. And, especially, it explained her relationship with 'Bama Fitch.

"But look what you do with it all, Caroline." She gestured upward, toward the attic. "You take that filthy money and turn great evil into great good."

Caroline laughed bitterly. "Don't make the mistake of thinking me noble, Anna. And … here's something you must understand—Alabama Fitch is my blood cousin."

"No!" Anna rocked back in her sturdy kitchen chair.

"Oh, yes. She doesn't want that embarrassment made public any more than I do, but 'Bama Fitch is the daughter of my great-uncle. My grandfather's brother, Enoch, set up a second family with her mother, Naomi, while Naomi was still enslaved. Everyone knew it; no one acknowledged it.

"And he did right by his children, settled upon his sons a small ship chandlery, and bought his daughter a house. But I—we both, 'Bama and I—feel strongly that I owe far more than that."

Anna set aside her plate of ham and bread. She still couldn't quite comprehend that the two women were cousins. Did that somehow explain why 'Bama Fitch so disliked her? Was she jealous of Caroline's friendship with Anna?

"You are a courageous lady, Caroline," Anna said, "a risk-taker, and so is Mrs. Fitch."

"Hah! Look who's talking!" The customary self-assurance had returned to Caroline's words.

Anna could eat no more. She folded her red-checked napkin and laid it on the table before her. She rose, ready to head home for the night. "What do you mean?" she asked.

"Who fled an abusive husband? Who escaped a bloody rebellion? Who engaged in a forbidden love? Who travelled alone from India? Who searches for a child born both outside the law and outside custom?" Caroline picked up a chicken leg from her plate, took a bite, chewed. When she set it down, she said, "Anna, I merely break a human law, while you, and justly so, defy what is considered to be a divine commandment. Just who is the risk-taker here? Hmm?"

TWENTY-FOUR

Northwest Provinces, India
1857

From Greenland's icy mountains,
From India's coral strand . . .
They call us to deliver
Their land from error's chain.

The Missionary Hymn (1819)

"Renounce, oh, heathen sinner, renounce your idols and your filthy gods." The Reverend Josiah Roundtree pitched his voice so low that the congregants in their long robes and thin veils breathed more shallowly and inclined their heads forward to make certain they heard every word over the chatter of the monkeys in an enormous *neem* tree just outside the church's open door. And then he spoke even lower. "Come to Jesus who alone through his abiding mercy can save you."

Anna Wheeler Roundtree watched a pair of small green lizards scamper across the wall next to the pew. They were fast and light on their feet. What color green? Not New-England grass-green, for sure. A flickering evanescent green, more like green fire, like a ripe lime split in sunlight or the heart of an emerald flashing in the fierce Bengali noon. *A green and wayward flame*. Her fingers itched for her pen. *Green and wayward*. She yearned to write those words in the small black-covered notebook, the secret book in which she composed her secret verses. But not now. Not here in Josiah's church.

The afternoon heat was torrid, and, even in her thinnest cotton gown with its loosened corset and a mere two petticoats, Anna felt feverish. Tendrils of light-brown hair escaped the confines of her black net snood, curling damply around her ears, softening her thin features, and lending an illusion of youth to a face marked by twenty-six years of worldly trials. Indian women knew how to dress for their climate—she envied them the light muslin draperies. Meena, a convert, sat beside her in a flowing yellow sari with an orange border. Her foot, next to Anna's buttoned boot, was shoeless, slim and brown and beautiful.

High atop the whitewashed sanctuary walls, sparrows twittered in the church's eaves. A large *punkah* fan creaked overhead, back and forth. The tiny *punkah wallah*, in his ragged loincloth, sat cross-legged in the aisle, pulling mechanically at the hemp rope that moved the fan. From the open door a rich scent of bougainvillea wafted over Anna, over the scrawny near-naked boy, over Meena—even over Josiah, who had banned flowers from the church as an odoriferous distraction from the sweet truth of God's Word. The notebook concealed in her petticoat pocket pressed damp against her thigh.

"Lost! So lost—to burn forever in a hell of darkness." Josiah sighed. Meena shuddered. So, for all the wrong reasons, did Anna.

The previous midnight, a thin man in a sarong had come limping into the infirmary of the Fatehgarh Mission, a pitch-soaked torch smoking in one hand, a small child gasping over his shoulder. Anna was alone. "A little devil flew up and seized my daughter," he cried. "It is burning her with fire. Will you help, Memsahib? Will you cast it off?" From the village outside the mission compound came the monotonous pounding of drums and the eerie wailing of incantations to the gods.

The cholera had been raging all that week, two hundred people in the province dying every day. Anna, with the native nurses and other mission wives, had been run ragged cooling fevered bodies with wet clothes, mopping up vomit, brewing black catechu to staunch the deadly diarrhea. Now here was little Harini, fevered, twisted with cramps, screaming for water. Her thin legs spasmed. The stench of watery bowels was almost unbearable.

Anna dripped laudanum down the girl's throat, then tried her with camphor, opium and cayenne. When Harini sank into prostration, her skin cold and clammy, Anna packed the bed with warm bricks and rubbed her twitching legs. Just as the first mango-tinted rays of morning penetrated the windows of the mission infirmary Anna's small patient took a last shuddering breath and died.

Over the tea tray at breakfast, she could still hear Harini's parents wailing by Mother Ganges, to whom at dawn they had committed their daughter's ravaged body wrapped in coarse-woven cloth. Never, in Manhattan's Five Points or here in India, had Anna become inured to the death of a child.

"Why?" she cried to her husband. "Why does the Lord allow such anguish! The child was innocent. If God is indeed a God of Love, wouldn't He—"

And Josiah, in his customary manner, pressed his finger against her lips. "Hush, my little wife. Enough of this. The painful dispensation of providence which God sees fit to inflict is not ours to question."

Anna had married Josiah understanding that it was her wifely duty to defer to him in all things. For many years, faithful at his side, she had practiced spousal obedience. Of late, however, the habit of submission had become more difficult. She found herself restless, and growing increasingly so. The tip of her tongue was sore with biting back her words. Now her thoughts spoke themselves. "I *do* question! I do! Harini was a sweet child. She came to Sunday School. Why should she not have lived?"

An expression Anna knew all too well came over Josiah's face; she had so many shortcomings as a missionary's wife, and her husband felt them with such profound regret. She was dreamy and uncertain, and far too fond of the world. He was as sharp and purposeful as a knife. Try as she might she could not live up to his desire for a helpmeet immersed wholly in the mission of Christian evangelism. The work of conversion did not go as Josiah had expected; the native people clung to their mistaken beliefs and abhorrent ways. And Anna did nothing to bring the Word to the heathen, he reminded her gently. Nursing them as she did through dysentery, hepatitis, and cholera would save only their bodies, never their souls. Delivering their babies only brought more lost souls into this wicked world. Caring for the orphans in the asylum set no child's foot on the narrow path of righteousness.

But Anna loved the people and they were fond of her, and in that tropic clime she felt her soul expand like a silent blossom.

Indeed, Anna's husband observed her deficiencies with far more pain than she felt them herself. She was not what he had intended a wife to be, and over the years he had devised ingenious and excruciating methods by which to correct her. He spoke of such chastisement variously as *tender mortifications of the flesh* or as *necessary rectifications of the spirit*. Now, at the breakfast table, running a finger over the buttercup cross-stitched on her linen napkin, she sensed what was about to happen.

"It pains me to say this, Mrs. Roundtree, but your soul has once again demonstrated itself as sadly in need of discipline." Josiah flicked a finger toward her arm. "You know what to do."

Anna cringed, but habitual obedience conquered protest. Holding out her arm, she unbuttoned the wristband of her loose dotted-swiss sleeve. Josiah watched intently as she turned the flimsy fabric over, so that her wrist was fully exposed, then her pale lower arm, then her inner elbow, then she folded it up again and again, until the sleeve reached her shoulder. Running his fingers slowly up her tender inner arm, he reached the soft, sensitive area of her outer breast. Then, gazing directly into her eyes, he took hold of a small piece of delicate flesh, twisted it tightly between his thumb and forefinger, and pinched long and hard.

I can bear this, she told herself, attempting to master the searing pain. Her teeth were clenched against any wayward sob. A surprising variety of unchristian thoughts assailed her.

"And," he continued, as he released her, "in all pious constancy I cannot feel sorry for that child. Is she not better off dead than to grow up in such heathenism?"

Later that morning, shifting in the sanctuary pew with the busy green lizard skittering about, Anna adjusted the thin lace scarf that covered her shoulders. *Better off dead. Better off dead.* It ran through her head like a child's sing-song hymn chorus. No child is better off dead; that much her heart understood.

Anna dabbed droplets of perspiration from her upper lip as she considered the man in the pulpit. The decade in India had darkened his skin and lightened his hair to an even more angelic hue, which in no way had spoiled his beauty. She herself, however, had gone from a well-rounded, rosy girl to a thin, pale woman she no longer recognized in the looking-glass. As her husband sermonized, she kept her eyes dutifully upon him. Black dye from the high-neck wool waistcoat had diffused itself once again into his white clerical collar; yet another thing about which he would not be pleased.

How could he, she wondered idly, speak in the same hushed tones about depraved appetites, imperious passions, and hellfire, then, without drawing another breath, about God's abiding mercy? It was a question she had never before articulated, even to herself.

"In the beginning was the Word," Josiah now pronounced from the pulpit, "and the Word was with God, and the Word was God." For the first time the poetry of the familiar phrase failed to comfort Anna. Her family, farmers on a modest scale, had owned but one book—the Holy Bible. She'd read it until the binding shredded and the cadences seeped into her very soul. Its rhythms, its images, the lovely King James idiom, were all as much an essential part of who she was as were the body and blood of the communion sacrament. "In Him was life," Josiah now breathed, "and the life was the light of men."

In Him was Life. Anna sat next to Meena, the newly devout convert. Her fingers itched to reach out and stroke the pretty leaf-embroidered border of Meena's sari, green silk stitched upon orange. She fingered instead the notebook hidden in her petticoat, then folded her hands in her lap. Green silk on orange—tongues of verdant flame. From outside came the familiar tweet and trill of a bird, one she knew was small and green, but for which she had no name. And with the sure and certain note of that green song, something akin to a miracle came to pass in

Anna's soul: In the breathless air, between one pass of the *punkah* and the next, a green lizard jumped from the wall and flickered across the toe of Anna's buttoned boot, and it was as if all things changed, as if she had woken with a start from a long, cold New England dream to find herself here in the midst of a life so fecund it spoke not in print on Josiah's page, but in the scent of bougainvillea, in birdsong.

She shuddered, cold and hot at the same moment. She felt momentarily lifted out of her body.

A lifetime's doctrine drained from her as wine might spill from a cast-off communion cup, only to be replaced by a new revelation. *Life! Here! Life! Now! Life!*

She had heard of Christians who had lost their faith; now, in "the twinkling of an eye," as the Bible said, something equally cataclysmic had happened to her. She felt as if she'd been stunned by a celestial hammer. It was all she could do to keep herself seated in the pew, all she could do to keep from shouting out: *Life. Here. Life. Now. Life.*

It was as if her mind had leapt beyond its education and entered a larger sphere. As if she hadn't lost *faith*, but had simply been liberated from icy *dogma*. As if finally she knew what she'd been born to know: life was not simply some anxious, sin-fraught anteroom to salvation or damnation; existence was *itself* salvation, warm and bright, throbbing with energy.

In that moment, after years of numb obedience, she decided to leave Josiah and the dry, closed universe of his world.

TWENTY-FIVE

What though the spicy breezes
Blow soft o'er Ceylon's isle ...
The heathen in his blindness
Bows down to wood and stone.

The Missionary Hymn

The service having ended with the final strains of "*O'er the gloomy hills of darkness*," Anna stood in the church doorway looking out across the mission compound, her thin perspiration-soaked dress clinging to her limbs, her soul in a state of tumult. That unholy revelation during Josiah's sermon—she could not think of it as anything but an epiphany—had staggered her. What did it mean? *Life! Here! Life! Now!* Behind her was the empty sanctuary, darkened by rolled-down bamboo shades. The punkah was motionless now, and the teak pews in their orderly rows were shadowed.

Behind her lay the darkened church. Before her lay India, or at least the small portion of it claimed by the Fatehgarh Christian Mission to the Heathen, a sun-drenched compound designed on the model of a New England village. Gazing around at the familiar clipped privet hedges, well-tended beds of cauliflower and green peas, and, of course, the beloved English roses in their terra-cotta pots—larger, but far less fragrant than the crimson Indian roses that blossomed on low-growing shrubs—Anna noticed a group of native children playing a game with sticks and coconut shells. They ran, jumped, shrieked with laughter, and Anna smiled. A wanton thought assailed her; if she could go home, she might be as free and as happy as these children. She meant *go home alone*, of course.

To go home she would have to get herself to Calcutta. Then she laughed dryly to herself: between here and Calcutta was little but impassable jungle. No white woman could travel that by herself. And, even once in the great City of Palaces, she would have no money to take ship to New York.

Continuing to look out across the compound, Anna saw the door of the bungalow she shared with Josiah open, and a feeling of dark oppression came over her. Josiah emerged, and she eased back into the shadow of the church doorway, as if he might catch sight of her and intuit her wayward thoughts. But he did not look up. His attention was all on the work toward which he trudged, and he followed the mud-brick path that led to the mission's publishing house, his hair blazing gold in the sun. While Anna's daily care of the native people had transformed her, Josiah's spirit had shrunk from the people and adhered to the word—not to the Word of God as it was lived in the world, but to the letter of that word as it was printed on the page. Watching him climb the publishing-house steps with his measured pace and disappear through the door, she envisioned him now moving diligently toward his desk, where he would spend interminable hours bent over his manuscripts, struggling with the native languages. For him, India had become less about saving souls and more about translation, preaching, and printing the Christian Bible in Bengali, Hindustani, Telugu.

Perversely now, as the door closed behind her husband, she suddenly missed the young man she had married and had loved so very much, the man who was all afire for the lost and suffering people of the world. She yearned for that time when she had felt herself to be of one heart with Josiah, when she had told him everything. But, that time had passed long ago. This, this … awakening … this *thing* that had happened in the dim, quiet sanctuary behind her, she knew she could breathe no word of this, for the Reverend Josiah Roundtree would pronounce his wife either insane or lost—forever lost—to Heaven. "*Kendee, memsahib? Kendee?*" The children with the coconuts had spotted her and now stomped around her in a circle, laughing. Chathan, a round-faced boy of seven whom she had helped deliver, played at snatching her reticule.

Anna smiled at him—how could she not?—and held the handbag high, teasing him. The boy jumped for it, his brown body agile as a mongoose on the prowl. She laughed, then opened the drawstring and took out a paper sack of candy. This was a familiar game, and the children clamored around her, giggling, pulling at her skirts. Anna selected a single peppermint humbug, held it up, studied it, said *hmmm*, and made as if to put the piece of candy back into the bag.

"*Kendee, kendee*," Chathan cried.

"Ohhhh," Anna said, as if she had made a great discovery, "you *want* one." She popped the striped candy into Chathan's mouth and pretended to put the bag back into her reticule. The other children cried out in protest, and Anna, once more feigning surprise, placed a humbug in each child's beseeching hand.

"Anna," called a woman's voice from the path behind them, "do you have one left for me?"

Lucy Markham always made Anna smile. Perhaps it was the fair, curly hair that surrounded her dimpled face like a pale cloud. Or the scent of rosewater that clung to her blue dimity dress. Or perhaps the sheer goodwill of Lucy's character was infectious. Certainly Anna would never think of contaminating that innocent spirit with her own abrupt discontent.

"Sorry," Anna replied, "no sweets left, but I can give you Chathan." She made a mock grab toward the boy, and he dodged her, shrieking with excitement.

Suddenly, from halfway across the compound came a true shriek, an agonized and drawn-out scream. Both women turned toward it. A twelve-year-old girl had gone into labor before dawn, and Anna had rightly feared a long and difficult delivery for one so young.

"Kaila?" As she asked, Anna noticed a patch of damp appear at her friend's bosom. Her own nipple reacted with a ghost twinge.

All Anna had were ghost babies. Ghost babies and ghost milk.

Lucy nodded. "She'll deliver any moment. I came for you." She pulled her light cotton shawl over her breast.

The girl's scream came again, like that of a soul crying out in agony from the bowels of hell. Anna knew the tenor of that scream; her attentions were needed, and at once. "I'll go now," she said, shooing the children away. "And, Lucy, you get on home to your own baby." She hurried past the schoolhouse toward the infirmary, miniature sandstorms swirling around her already sand-caked boots.

And, for a brief moment, she forgot about the whirlwind in her heart.

As she eased the howling boy from his mother's womb, tears rolled down Anna's cheeks—after so many deliveries, the tears were not from emotion, but from the corrosive fumes of red chilies and camphor burning in a copper brazier to ward off the evil eye. Rather than squatting on the ground, as was the local custom, the young mother lay on a cot, which made the delivery easier for Anna. Gently massaging the girl's abdomen with *ghee* to encourage the placenta's delivery, she sighed with relief. Both mother and infant would live. Anna wasn't so certain about herself; one moment she felt giddy with life, the next as if she could howl louder than this sturdy new boy-child. She poured water over her hands to cleanse them, watching as the baby's grandmother placed a mixture of *ghee*, honey, and curds on his lips—the first taste of life. The boy scowled at the sensation and all three women laughed—the young mother, the grandmother, the midwife-*memsahib*: this new child did not yet know what to make of sweetness.

Anna walked home that night through the cool, lush evening air, leaving the baby and young mother in the care of the joyous grandmother. Tall bamboo branches that bordered the mango grove swayed dark and feathery in the flood of moonlight, and the simple mission buildings, too, were illuminated as with a beacon. Suddenly and ludicrously an image of Josiah in the pulpit pressed upon her mind's eye—Josiah that afternoon pious and sweating in his black woolen suit. *Pious*—what an odd word. Alone in the bright night, she whispered it—*pious*. Suddenly in her mouth the word had the taste and texture of overripe pear.

But she must not be so hard on Josiah. She, herself, had not been innocent of fault in their marriage; she had lacked courage. It had taken years for her to admit to herself that Josiah preferred his lost heathen multitudes in the abstract to these insistently individual dark people, people with bodies and faces and stories and names. When she sensed him shrinking from the abundance of life that so endeared India to her, she had ceased confiding in him, had taken refuge in rote obedience. That, she now understood, had been an act of cowardice, a sin of omission. Perhaps, Anna thought, she had owed it to her husband all along to speak openly, to speak the truth. Perhaps she owed it to him now. But what would that truth be? What could she say to him now that would not arouse his wrath? What part of her truth would be acceptable to him?

She wanted to go home; that was it. She was homesick. Homesickness was no sin. Mission workers were supposed to take a furlough every five years, and she and Josiah had been almost twice that time in the field without one. They were long overdue. Yes, she'd petition Josiah to go home on furlough. And, then ...

"What did you say, wife?" Josiah sanded and blotted his manuscript page, wiped the pen nib and laid the pen aside. Over his writing desk hung a large chromolithograph of a white-robed Jesus preaching to multitudes that covered the steep hillside well beyond the solid carved black oak of the picture frame. He spent a great deal of time at that desk as well as at the one in the publishing house. "Letters from India," his monthly column in the *Missionary Advocate*, had earned him a church-wide fame at home in the American states. It had also the satisfactory consequence of eliciting those very welcome dimes and dollars.

Now he responded distractedly to Anna's only half-heard comment as he closed his Bible and snuffed out the wick of the smoky whale-oil lamp suspended from a rafter over the parlor table. The lamp's illuminated halo of gnats and moths dispersed instantly. The only light remaining in the parlor was that diffused through the woven curtain that veiled the bedroom door.

"I said, Josiah, that I very much wish to go home." She removed her net snood, struggling to keep her voice calm, keep her words from sounding hysterical, like the desperate plea she felt them to be. She released her hair, tangled now and dusty, from its confining pins, shook out the thick brown tresses and reached for the ivory-handled hairbrush she had brought with her from the bedroom. *One stroke. Two strokes. Three* ... The brush was a present from a wealthy Indo-European matron, who, although not a Christian, was a generous supporter of the mission orphanage. Josiah said it was extravagant and inappropriate, over-luxuriant as were many Indian gifts to the missionaries. Anna treasured it for its sheer Oriental beauty, sculpted ivory engraved with the image of a peacock in gold.

She knew through experience that there never was, in Josiah's rigorous—even harried—schedule of prayer, preaching and translation, a favorable time to discuss with him her own, inconsequential, concerns, but this night she had steeled herself and determined to try. She chose her moment carefully, after their late supper of buffalo milk, *chapatees*, and bananas, after he had completed his monthly column, and just before his evening prayers when he should feel himself approaching close to God.

"Hmmuh?" He waved the letter in the cool night air to dry the ink completely, before folding it and placing it under a brass elephant paperweight. "Go home?"

"Yes," she said, "we are long overdue for a furlough." Anna left off the brushing, her hair falling over her shoulders now, curling about her face. Standing between Anna and the available light from the bedroom door, Josiah was a looming shadow whose expression she could not see, let alone read. Then he moved to take her chin in his hand. He was, she saw with a sinking heart, in an amatory mood. He turned toward the light, and she could tell that he had interpreted her ardent declaration as a mere feminine whim.

"My dear, sweet, wife" he replied with patient forbearance, "you know better than that. There is a new printing press on its way. I cannot leave. We must print the Hindustani testament immediately, then the Telugu translation." He stroked her cheek. "And the Bengali is not yet completed. It will be at least two years before we can even think of it. Now, to bed, little wife, to bed."

And she, not knowing what else to do, went to bed and lay quiet and dutiful in a clean white cotton nightdress, as was her godly role, while Josiah satisfied his masculine needs.

Mosquitoes droned all that night, disrupting Anna's sleep with their hollow, tormenting whine. Restless beneath the netting, she could not keep her mind still. For the first time she was angry about the use Josiah made of her body, offering release to him, but to her nothing, not even children who lived. Then anger grew about his casual refusal of her heartfelt request to return home. So. So, her husband would not be persuaded to grant even as reasonable a request as a well-deserved furlough. So.

So. What if she *did* go home without him?

A wave of guilt swept over her at the thought, and, lying next to her husband, she shivered in their bed. How could she even think of doing that to Josiah? He was not as strong in his spirit as he assumed; what would he do without her? She knew that with her marriage she had taken on the responsibility of being his helpmeet in all things. How could he live without his wife? Oh, at times her heart had risen up against his narrow righteousness, but until this moment she'd always been able to tamp her anger down; she'd had a lifetime of discipline in suppressing her essential self. But now she felt as if her heart had been transformed, as if it had grown wings. Her *soul* had grown wings and she felt it beating against the cage of Josiah's strict expectations.

She walked through the following days like an automaton. Slowly her heart hardened against her husband; she felt its new weight, solid and smooth and cold, as if it were composed of jade. Her body did what needs must be done; her mind was obsessed with but one question: *How can I get away?*

TWENTY-SIX

Shall we, whose souls are lighted
With wisdom from on high,
Shall we to those benighted
The lamp of life deny?

The Missionary Hymn

They had come to Fatehgarh up the Ganges on a clumsy barge-like *budgerow* during the hottest season. One side of the boat had been kept dark and cool by large bamboo shades upon which servants continuously threw river water, and Anna had huddled there on a bamboo chaise day and night. It had been a tedious and unsanitary voyage, and, with her first pregnancy, she had been sick the entire way. The river would be one way for her to get to Calcutta, she now realized, except that she had no money to hire boat and boatmen.

In the years since their arrival at the mission, a railroad had been built, but the nearest depot was at Agra, hours away by bullock cart. She could not travel those perilous roads on foot, alone, and no one from the mission would accompany her there if it were contrary to Josiah's wishes.

And it would be.

In any case, there remained the same consideration: her lack of money for the train fare.

But if she could get to Calcutta, once there she could teach in a school to earn money for the ship passage to … where? London? New York? … But, no, Josiah could find her too easily in Calcutta; most of the English schools were church-run, and someone would be sure to inform him. Perhaps she could use her maiden name and take a position as a governess for some wealthy Anglo-Indian family. …

But all this fretting was premature; first she had to get to Calcutta. She could no longer remain with Josiah; it would be but a charade of marriage. A charade of life. The person Anna had been all those years might well have been able to resist this new restlessness and keep her feet on the narrow path; the person she was becoming clamored: *You must go, Anna. You must go.*

That evening Anna was once again in her nightdress. She took the ivory hairbrush once again to her hair. *One. Two.* …

"So," Josiah continued with his unheeded after-dinner instructions, "you will have much work to do to expand the services of the infirmary. You must begin at once."

Her heart was the weight of a well-stone. "Josiah, I must speak to you plainly. I will not be continuing with the infirmary. I wish to leave India. For good."

"Not this again, Anna." He took the brush from her and set it down. "You know we cannot think of a furlough at this point. I've told you why. The Lord has pressing business for me to undertake. I've told you that, as well."

She retrieved the ivory brush and held it between them. She breathed in as deeply as she could, then let it out in a rush: "Then I shall leave without you."

The tilt of Josiah's head was one of benevolent puzzlement. "Without me? But, wife, how would you manage the voyage alone?"

"You do not understand me, Josiah. Let me be very clear—I wish to leave you."

"Leave? Leave *me?*" There was a moment of blank incomprehension. Then his face went bloodless, his lips, white as paper. He grasped her arm above the elbow and tightened his fingers, as if he thought she would bolt that moment.

She stepped back, pulling away from his grip. "You have your mission. I have nothing." Even as she said it, she realized this wasn't quite true. She had the women and children of the village. She would miss them. Even with this new opportunity for the infirmary ... No. It simply wasn't enough.

He dropped his hands. "Nothing? Your husband's devoted love is nothing? Our Lord's mission of salvation to the benighted heathen—nothing? Translation of the Holy Scripture— Hold out your arm!"

"No!" Some irresistible power of defiance overtook her, seeming, oddly enough, to emanate from the gold-engraved ivory weight of the brush in her hand, jolting through her body, galvanizing her spirit, goading her into recklessness. "You see, Josiah, I no longer believe—"

"*No longer believe?*" Josiah fixed her with those steady pale eyes that had always until now vanquished her slightest self-assertion. "As if the Lord had not planned from the very foundations of eternity for you to serve faithfully as my helpmeet in this heathen place! No longer believe?"

She stared back at him. What punishment would he insist on for this, the unforgivable sin? What humiliation?

But, no, Anna was to suffer neither the standard small torment nor the usual minor shame. She would not escape that easily. With a great blow from the back of his hand Josiah Roundtree slammed his wife into the whitewashed wall. The hairbrush flew out of her hand and across the room. Her brain reeling, her ears ringing, she slid down to the packed earth floor, bones in her jaw and skull crackling back into place. He raised his hand again, and she crossed her arms before her face to protect against another blow. She breathed in deeply. A swirl of dried dirt from the floor coated her tongue and filled her nostrils. She was a dust eater, a dust breather. Was this the ignominious manner in which her life would end? Dust unto dust. Helpless to move, she slumped into herself and looked up at her husband through a crimson haze.

And he, he loomed over her in his black ministerial garb, his eyes mere slits of blue, staring not at her but at his red and swelling hand as if somehow he had sprouted a new, mysteriously autonomous appendage and had no idea where it had come from. Never before had Josiah struck her, not actually *struck* her, but now his hand seemed to hover halfway to another blow before, with a visible effort, he controlled himself and brought the one hand back to the other in an attitude of prayer. Posed thus for sacred petition, he returned his gaze to her. If a look could have weight and substance, his righteous regard would have flattened her to a mere shadow on the packed-earth floor. Then his expression darkened, the shadow that was Anna seeming to rise and cross his face, and he was upon her bodily, throwing himself forward so that his full weight stunned her.

She struggled beneath him. "No, Josiah, no!" she cried, but he was deaf to her pleas. He grabbed her shoulder, digging his fingers in. With a strong hand and straight arm he pressed her down, the full strength of his body holding her there immobile against the hard mud floor, his free hand fumbling with the hem of her nightdress. She screamed, and he gripped the nightdress at the neck, ripping it down the full length, tearing it away from her body. She shrieked and kicked at his shins. Abruptly, he transferred the restraining hand, jabbing ruthless fingers into the flesh of her thigh. She bit his arm where she could reach it, but he seemed to feel no pain, intent now on scrabbling with his trouser buttons. When he entered her, she endured, despite the tearing that she felt and felt again. The agony went on and on. And then he was done, rising abruptly, as if he could not bear the feel of her. "Our Father," he said, looming above her, arranging his clothing for the sake of decency. His eyes were open and hard upon her. "I lay this woman before you in all her iniquity. Redeem her, Lord, from sin. Restore her to the proper submission of the true Christian wife, and return her, Lord, cleansed, to my faithful loving side. Amen."

When he raised his hand again, Anna cringed, but he did not strike her. Instead he swiped a brusque finger across her chin and raised it, bloodied, to where she could see and contemplate the consequences of her desires. "Surely, wife," he whispered, "the evil one has unhinged your intelligence and corrupted your immortal soul." He grabbed his Bible from the table and, clasping it to his chest, stalked out onto the tropic darkness, without once looking back.

"I only wanted to go home," she said to no one but the night. "All I wanted was to go back home." Anna wept as she had never wept before. She wept until the oil in the bedroom lamp had burned itself out and midnight conquered the little mud house. Then, still sagging against the wall, she felt her sobs abate. A kind of apocalyptic clarity engulfed her, a vision as clear as her epiphany in the church. What, upon her first sight of the angelic Josiah Roundtree in that Mount Holyoke parlor, had seemed the will of God, now appeared to Anna to be a cruel trick of fate. She had lived a misbegotten life. She had been seduced, yes, by Josiah's beauty and piety—but even more so, by a glorious, all-encompassing, myth of selfless Christian womanhood. Entranced by Josiah's golden allure, she had mistaken the romance of righteous obedience for an affinity of the heart, she had confounded the lie of the perfect womanly woman for the truth of her own being.

In the darkness, her thoughts drifted. The delicate scent of oleander perfumed the air. What if she had not loved flowers? What if she had never gathered those peonies from the Mount Holyoke flowerbeds? What if she had never carried them to the seminary's parlor?

Somewhere outside a peacock screamed. Anna could see nothing, but it was as if the bird were with her in the night, iridescent, its harsh cry the music of her defrauded heart.

If she had never met Josiah, what would her life be now? Might she have gone West as a schoolteacher, as had so many of her classmates, to bring Woman's saving influence to the raw and brawling American frontier? She could imagine herself, a beloved educator, dispensing sums and civilization to the eager youth of the Dakotas. But, no, she'd had enough of noble work for any lifetime, enough of sacrifice. A new, more enticing, vision arose: Anna in a silk gown composing sonnets by firelight as lazy snowflakes drifted past the window panes. What if, following her passion for verse, she had gone to New York City not as a mission trainee, but as a poet? An American Mrs. Barrett Browning? Yes, such a life might well have been hers. In such a life she would still have breasts.

The peacock squawked again.

Through the open door of the mission house she could see a beautiful Indian sky, so studded with the sparkling eternal stars that eventually it reassured her and soothed her, right there, flat out on the packed earth floor, into sleep. A hymn tune began ringing in her dreaming brain:

Rock of ages, cleft for me,
Let me hide myself in thee;
Let the water and the blood,
From thy wounded side which flowed,
Be of sin the double cure—
Save from wrath and make me pure.

A hand grasping her shoulder startled Anna. *Josiah!* She opened her eyes. Day had dawned. She was lying in a blood/mud slurry that had coagulated on the parlor floor.

A wizened village woman with the black mouth and red teeth of the habitual betel chewer hunkered at her side, frowning down at her with an air of horrified concern.

"Lallia," Anna said. There was no one else on earth she would rather have seen.

You are in danger, Memsahib." The village healer jumped up from her squatting position. "You must leave this place at once." Silver bangles on her wrists and ankles clanged together, sounding like miniature alarm bells.

"Oh, no, Lallia. No." Anna sat up half-way, then leaned against the wall; the sudden movement had made her dizzy. When words came, they were choked and raspy. "It was just that I made Reverend Roundtree very angry. He will not do it again." Even as she spoke, she knew it was not true.

The woman reached down and probed Anna's bruised jaw with inquiring fingers. Her hands and arms were encircled with rows of tribal tattoos. Although Lallia's touch was gentle, Anna winced. The healer frowned, and the lines of blue-green dots tattooed above her eyebrows formed a birdlike V. "Memsahib, I do not speak of Reverend Sahib. It is the warning of the drums I bring you. They speak of blood and fury against the *ferenghi*. Guns and death are on their way. You have once saved my life, I wish now to save yours. Come, you and the others, you must leave at once for Calcutta, where the British armies will keep you safe."

When Anna first met Lallia, head woman of the local village, *tum-drums* had throbbed in the distance and lamentations had sounded on the cool night air. In defiance of the temple priests, Lallia's family had brought her to the mission infirmary suffering from a deadly bout of dysentery. Even after Vaskar, Lallia's son, conceded that his mother would not survive, Anna continued to administer a decotation of bilberry root in hopes of easing the bloody flux. Moths circled the overhead lantern, their fluttering wings causing a confusion in the light. When Josiah entered the infirmary to see why Anna was so late, he ordered her to cease her futile ministrations and come to bed, but she persisted nonetheless, dispensing drop after tedious drop of the medicine.

Then Lallia groaned. Vaskar jerked awake where he squatted by the cot. The sick woman's eyes flickered and opened. *Water*, she said. To the villagers clustered around the open doorway Vaskar shouted out, *acharaj kam hai*! It's a miracle!

After that, the villagers could not do enough for Anna.

A month or so later, Anna entered the kitchen early one morning to find Lallia standing in the doorway clutching an object wrapped loosely in a banana leaf.

"A gift for you," the healer said. Her black hair was freshly slicked with oil, the *bindi* on her forehead newly refreshed with vermilion. She wore a red sari and a necklace of silver coins. Other women, also in their finery, appeared in the doorway behind her.

Anna recognized that this was a ceremonial occasion. With a grave smile of thanks, she accepted the offering.

"This talisman—certain it is," Lallia went on, "to drive away the evil spirits that snatched your baby at his birth."

Anna's heart clenched and her smile vanished, but, mindful of the somberness of the occasion, she pulled back the corners of the large leaf. As she gaped at the vile object within, she kept her horror silent;

the gift was a polished monkey skull. She could not take her eyes off of it; a mesmerizing force seemed to exude from the hollow eye-sockets, as if they called to her to fall into their darkness. This was a power new to Anna, one that held frightful possibilities. Her skin shivered as if it had a life beyond her volition. Early on that April morning, the air was as cool as a New England summer, but it seemed almost as if she could already hear the monotonous noontime calling of the barbets and the brain-fever birds. She felt herself suddenly heated, in as much of a sweat as if she stood bareheaded in the furnace-hot midday sun.

"When the next baby is born, place monkey god close by his hammock. He will bring good health and best of fortune to your child." Lallia bowed to her, hands pressed together.

Anna shuddered. Then she recovered her composure, thanked Lallia profusely, offered her a crystalized-sugar basket that had been sent at Christmas from mission headquarters in Calcutta, and gave small cakes to the village women.

The very next morning, before the sun grew too hot for walking, she took the skull to the far edge of the mango grove that bordered the mission and threw the horrid orb as far as she could out into the jungle.

That had been during their first year in India.

Now: *Guns and death are on their way*. From where she sat slumped on the parlor floor, Anna could see through the open door the whitewashed bungalows and neat hedges of the mission compound. In this first light of dawn all was as peaceful as ever. It was impossible to imagine violence where they had worked so hard to establish shelter and healing. "But, Lallia," she protested, "we are perfectly safe. In all our years here there has been no trouble. Among the missionaries we have five strong men to protect us. Should there be unrest, the men of the Christian village will surely remain loyal, and British detachments are all around. I do not see what could possibly happen."

I must tell Josiah, she thought. In spite of her protests, she half-believed Lallia's dire warnings. But she could imagine her husband's response. *The hysterical inventions of a heathen harlot,* he would scoff, *intended to drive us from our divinely-ordained mission of salvation in this place*. But she must tell him, nonetheless.

What if Lallia truly did have ways of knowing beyond the ken of Christians?

The woman grunted. She looked as if she understood even more than she was telling. "The drums speak of blood. I do not wish it to be yours." She stood and reached out a hand to help Anna from the floor. For a woman of her age she was wiry and strong. "Come, let me treat your injury."

Anna brooded silently as Lallia bathed her wounds, applying an astringent oil of turmeric and an ointment made from the opium poppy. "Your son, Vaskar," she asked in an offhand manner when the healer had finished, "he owns a bullock cart, am I right? Does he ever travel as far as Agra?"

Anna's husband came home at midday, grim and silent. She knew this dark mood, which had come upon him numerous times over the years and which nothing of her doing could ever ameliorate.

"Josiah, I must speak to you," Anna said, despite his lowering mien, and she told him of Lallia's warning.

He cut her off with a glare. "Consorting with heathen? What filthy road does Satan lead you down?"

She did not ask him where he had spent the previous night.

He did not tell her.

The following morning as they left for church Josiah barked at her to bring the sermon notes from his desk. It was all she could do to refrain from shredding the pages and hurling them into the cooking fire.

TWENTY-SEVEN

Salvation!—O Salvation!
The joyful sound proclaim,
Till earth's remotest nation
Has learned Messiah's name.

The Missionary Hymn

"I wish not to frighten the women and children, Reverend Roundtree," said a man's voice from the outer room of the mission office. He spoke in the clipped Anglo-Indian accent of the upper classes. Ashok Montgomery, Anna thought, the merchant who had recently donated so much money to the mission infirmary. "But I felt I must come and warn you," he continued. "Truly I do not know how much longer it will be safe for missionaries and their families to remain here. There are rumors on all sides that—"

"What?" Anna had been in the inner room, opening envelopes from stateside supporters. She jumped up from her work and ran to the door. "What is it you say?"

"Mrs. Roundtree!" He spun around at the sound of her voice. "I did not mean for you to hear me." Once again he was dressed in a white linen suit, but his jacket was unbuttoned and his cravat disordered. His dark hair, so sleekly combed the last time she'd seen him, now fell in curls over his forehead and around his ears.

"But you must tell me." She was thinking of Lallia's warning: *blood and fury.*

Mr. Montgomery glanced at Josiah, who shrugged. He turned to her. "Madame, the Indian *sepoys* have rioted—and they have their reasons. Insensitive orders from their British commanders—*stupid* orders—have set off a religious furor among the Indian soldiers, both Mohammadan and Hindu. They fear a forced conversion to Christianity and have rebelled against the British army at Meerut. Even now they march on to Delhi. But, lady, do not fear. Here in this place, we are far from the powder keg of their anger—there is no imminent danger."

"Has there been … bloodshed?" *Blood and fury.*

"Well, yes, Madam. I am afraid so."

"Against …*ferenghi?*" *Guns and death*: Lallia's voice was shrill in her ears.

"Yes, I fear so. Horrendous bloodshed. They have slaughtered many Europeans, spared not even women and children."

She swiveled to her husband. "Josiah! What did I tell you?"

"Anna," he said, drawing out her name in warning.

"But, Josiah, Lallia was right. Mr. Montgomery says—"

"Silence, Wife!" In the superior manner of one man to another, he addressed the visitor over Anna's head. "My wife is of … excitable temperament," Josiah said. "It would be best to speak of this no further. It would not do," he slewed his eyes toward her, his visage darkening, "to … to disorder Mrs. Roundtree's reason."

The visitor glanced at her; his eyes widened.

Josiah continued. "Now, I must speak with my fellow missionaries about this news." In the doorway he turned back to Anna and held up a monitory finger. "Contain yourself," he warned, then walked away.

Anna's teeth ground together in fury. She feared the sound was audible.

Ashok Montgomery hastened to reassure her. "But, Madam, surely the King's troops will restore order when the rebels reach the British cantonment at Delhi. You will be perfectly safe here."

She looked him directly in the eye. "My husband exaggerates, sir. There is nothing … excitable … about me. Nothing at all. News has already reached me about the troubles. Pray tell, be honest with me."

His eyes meeting hers now, were somber. "Seeing you work with the children has already assured me, Mrs. Roundtree, that it is not you who are … excitable." He reached out and ran his own fingers lightly over Anna's bruised jaw.

"*Uhh*." Startled, she who had already noted the Eurasian racial mix, the fine clothes, the high social status—plus that compelling little white flowerlike blemish tucked behind his earlobe—abruptly saw the man. His eyes held her: a rich dark intelligent brown. She inhaled sharply. This stocky, seemingly stolid stranger was concerned about her. And the way he looked at her, as if he knew her.

And as if he knew she knew he knew her.

The air in the room, though tropical, seemed suddenly invigorating, as if a fresh breeze had blown through from some utopian land where men and women were free to speak together. She felt a most extraordinary impulse to say to this unknown man, take me away from here. To plead with him, take me anywhere, but take me away from here. She was burning with this urge, but a lifetime of propriety dampened her words.

What would he think of her, this respectable merchant? He must be a family man, with a home and a wife and children. Her dealings with Anglo-Indians had shown them to be wary of scandal, more prudent than the British, more British even than the British in temperament and behavior. This honorable-looking man would risk no estrangement from respectable society in order to accede to the anxious whims of an excitable missionary wife. Why should he? And was she so desperate that she needs must throw herself upon the mercies of a most unlikely stranger?

Before Mr. Montgomery could say more about the rebellion, Josiah returned. "We thank you for your concern, kind sir, but I have spoken to my fellow missionaries, and we agree, leaving Fatehgarh on the basis of a few wild rumors is out of the question. So much prayer and labor—and money, too—has gone into our work here that we cannot think of abandoning it. Why the publishing house alone is worth fifty thousand rupees! No, sir, it is unthinkable. We will stay—and defend the mission if necessary. For my part, I am ready to be cut into pieces rather than to flee this place."

"But, Josiah—" Anna wailed.

"Silence!" He turned on her, his words clipped and angry. "We shall stand our ground in the Lord and shelter in the covert of His wings. There we shall find protection."

Anna watched Mr. Montgomery depart the mission compound riding a fine gray Arabian stallion and accompanied by two mounted servants. She was sick with anxiety about Josiah's pious obstinacy and the peril into which it might well lead them. Lead *her*. *Horrendous bloodshed*, the visitor had said, sparing not even women or children. But her emotions were unsettled almost as much by the compelling Anglo-Indian merchant himself as about the ominous rumors he reported. She found herself wishing she had snatched up her straw bonnet and leapt onto the horse behind him.

"I beg you, Josiah, do not go into the bazaar today." The Reverend Lionel Crosby stood by the mission gate in his black clerical garb, wringing his hands like a character in some low melodrama. His usually pale lips were this morning utterly bloodless. "Amidst all this unrest, we do not know what danger will face Christians in the city." The branches of the wide-spreading banyan at the gate were heavy with the weight of multitudinous doves, whose loud never-ceasing moans sounded like village women keening for their dead.

Erma, Lionel's wife, sneezed, then gave a nervous laugh, raspy like a nutmeg grater. The air was full of the perfume of yellow-flowered jasmine. When a ripe mango fell from a nearby tree, Erma started, then sneezed again. Once again came the grating laugh.

Josiah slapped at the leg of his dark trousers, raising a puff of dust. "This is my usual day for bazaar preaching," he said, his jaw set in determination. "I will allow no native rabble to turn me from the Lord's purpose."

The multitudes of conversions Josiah had envisioned when in New York had never materialized in India. Converts had come by the handfuls, rather than by the hordes: orphans taken in from the wayside; "rice converts" who came to the mission for gifts of food. And, of course, there were others, sincerely gripped by the Christian message. But Josiah's heroic vision did not come to pass; he had foreseen redeemed souls by the thousands, not by the ones and twos, not in yearly accretions of a few dozens. But he never gave up. And he never said that it disheartened him, but Anna knew that it did. Now, like a good wife, she stood by his side in a white dress, white gloves, and her straw bonnet with the blue ribbon, dressed to accompany him, as usual, to the bazaar in Farrukhabad.

She was terrified.

Lucy Markham stepped up, her cloud of fair hair haloing her rosy face. "At least, Josiah, allow Anna to remain at the mission this one morning." Two blond children clung to Lucy's skirts. In her arms she held an orphaned Indian baby. "I could use her help with the little ones in the asylum."

A closed expression came over Josiah's face. He took Anna's arm firmly; it was a message to remain mute. "I am sorry to have to tell you this, my dear Mrs. Markham, but Mrs. Roundtree suffers lately from a nervous disorder. I am … concerned about her reason. I fear what she will do once out of my sight. Anna goes where I go." He squeezed his wife's arm again.

Yet another bruise, would have been her thought if she had been thinking about anything other than *blood and fury*.

Lucy, Anna's one true friend at the mission, looked at Anna askance, her pretty face puzzled. Her lips formed the silent words, *is it so*?

Anna shook her head, *No*. Josiah led her toward the mission wagon. It was not the over-strong scent of jasmine that gave her such a vicious headache.

The cruel noonday sun glinted off something bright and silver at the far edge of the bazaar. In the middle of the busy spice market, Anna squinted and turned to look, catching a fleeting glimpse of a bayonet-fitted rifle in the hands of a red-coated *sepoy* soldier wearing the distinctive black hat. She gasped, then cried, "Josiah, look!"

"What is it?" He was occupied with choosing a place to preach, somewhere with at least a modicum of shade, but not far from the bazaar's bustling central square.

"A *sepoy*! With a gun!"

Josiah paled. "Where?"

"There!" She pointed to the spot where she had seen the native soldier, near the stall of a toy vendor selling hollow paper elephants. Josiah turned to look.

The man had vanished.

"I see nothing," Josiah replied. "You fret too much, Wife. And, besides, didn't Mr. Montgomery say that the rebellion would be contained at Delhi? The *sepoys* here are loyal to the King." With a sweep of his hand, Josiah indicated the vast marketplace. "See, all is quiet."

Indeed it was. Too quiet. Most days, vendors would be shrieking their wares, beggars pleading for *bakeesh*, and snake charmers piping their serpentine tunes. Today, the coconut and mango stalls were stocked with wares, and trout still damp from the stream were wrapped in banana leaves and laid out on the fishmongers' counters, but except for the occasional carriage rumbling by and a hand cart squeaking its passage, the torrent of sound had hushed at the arrival of the black-clad *ferenghi* with his holy book.

Josiah seemed not to notice.

He opened his Hindi translation of the Book of John and began to read from it in sonorous tones. Essence of tumeric and cardomen flavored the air. This day his Bible-reading attracted more boys than usual, several *karanchie* drivers, a small mob of bearers, two pariah dogs, a goat-herder with a bleating kid, and a pensive looking Brahman of middle age in a white robe. All but the goat were silent. Following a clear strong rendition of "The Missionary Hymn," Josiah preached briefly on the Ruinous Nature of Idolatry.

The bald-headed Brahman *pandit* stepped forward. "Reverend Sahib," he said, speaking in careful, scholarly English, "do you not think it presumptuous to speak of bringing religion to a land where a metaphysics of the most sublime order has preexisted your own civilization by centuries? Where arts and literature flourished when your own ancestors roamed the forests naked?" All eyes turned toward the learned man. A caged parrot squawked. A rice salesman drifted over to join the listeners. Next came a prosperous-looking Moslem gem merchant. Two market women in muslin saris hung on the fringes of the growing crowd. One of the bearers shouted out raucous words that Anna did not understand, and the crowd burst into hoots and laughter. Anna's husband stood speechless for a moment. The motley assembly jeered. The small congregation was becoming something very close to a restless mob, and Anna, for the first time since she had come to India, truly began to fear for her life.

Suddenly she gave a little screech. Two red-coated *sepoys* had pushed their way through the crowd. In their scarlet jackets with bayonet-tipped Enfield rifles at their sides they were tall and commanding, clearly in control of whatever would occur next. With scowling faces they positioned themselves one on each side of the missionary couple. Time seemed suspended; Anna thought, *anything might happen now*. Flames flared up from a cook fire by a curry stall. The parrot squawked again, and the small goat bleated. A *chapatti* maker ceased patting his small loaves into shape over the flame. Anna could not take her eyes off the rifles. Would she die here, in this alien city, at the shiny steel points of those bayonets? Or were these particular *sepoys* still loyal to the crown? Ashok Montgomery's words echoed in Anna's mind: *horrendous bloodshed*. Was her death waiting on the sun-glinting point of that honed steel shaft? She could see Josiah's lips moving in prayer, and she trembled and stopped breathing. Then the taller of the two men spoke to the other, and both soldiers pointed their guns.

They pointed their guns, but not at the missionaries. Rather they aimed them at the crowd. Anna breathed again. The tall soldier shouted an order, and the mob's jeers became a sullen murmur. The *sepoy* shouted again, and the boys were the first to run, fleet as mongooses on their bare brown feet. Vendors ambled back to their stalls. The *chapatti* maker speedily rolled his thin loaves. The white-robed Brahmin spoke to the soldiers, but so quietly that Anna could not hear the words. Then he, too, left, and they were alone with the native *sepoys*, or as alone as it was possible to be in a still-bustling marketplace.

Josiah turned to the tall soldier. "In the name of the Lord Jesus Christ, my savior, I thank you," he said.

The man, a handsome Bengali with elaborate side-whiskers, promptly spat at his feet. The other soldier, a darker man with a well-groomed mustache, laughed harshly, stepped up closer and spat in his face.

"Oh," Anna cried. "Oh, no."

Josiah stood paralyzed, crimson with humiliation.

With military precision, the soldiers came to attention, spun on their heels and marched off.

In horror, Anna stared at her husband, the soldier's spittle running down his cheek. She pulled a handkerchief from her reticule, but before she could reach him, he'd wiped his face with his coat sleeve. Then he grabbed her arm, twisting it in the process, and yanked her toward the mission wagon. "We have no divine obligation to stand still for the diabolical blasphemy of God-hating men," he hissed. They jolted home in the wagon past endless banyan trees and troupes of gray-haired monkeys sporting in mango groves. Neither spoke a word to the other.

That night, after much effort, he finally turned away from her in bed, incapable of completing the manly act.

One afternoon, soon after that, Anna slipped off to Lallia's split-bamboo hut in the native village. Sitting on a stool next to the fire, piles of fodder and neat stacks of dried dung behind her, she asked again about Vaskar and his bullock cart. It was peaceful here, drinking coconut milk and eating a proffered banana. She and Lallia talked in a broken, rambling, sun-drenched manner, of men and women, birth and death, and the best way to bake the delicious thin, buttery cakes called *purees*. It was a meandering conversation that felt like a moment in some eternal discourse—as well as like a farewell.

The first wisps of a papaya-colored dawn were edging the black horizon. Anna arose silently and dressed for her usual early-morning constitutional. But today she slipped her small black notebook into one petticoat pocket, and her beautiful ivory hairbrush into the other. The cherished possessions hung heavy against her thighs, bumping as she walked. Around her neck she hung an empty linen drawstring pouch that dangled by a cord between her breasts. Then she dressed in one of her better cotton gowns—not her best, for what if Josiah should suddenly awake? The dress was blue with a simple white collar, and around her shoulders she threw an inexpensive orange and blue printed shawl, for the air was morning brisk. Under the mosquito netting, Josiah turned in the bed and mumbled.

Anna stopped still. She neither moved nor breathed. Her husband pulled the pillow over his head and drifted back to sleep. Anna breathed.

In the kitchen she grabbed a loaf of *naan* and wrapped it around a slice of sheep's cheese. On a hook in the parlor hung a brass ring with three keys. She reached for it, hesitated, then snatched down the ring. One key clanged against the others. Again she ceased moving. Interminable seconds passed until she breathed again: No sound from the bedroom.

As she left her home for the last time, its door swooshed shut behind her. She took a deep breath and glanced around at the familiar mission bungalows surrounded by well-tended flowers of both hemispheres, the potted roses, the oleander bushes with their delicately scented pink and white blossoms, the pale-yellow jasmine. The air was delicious with the fragrance of dawn. It was still too early for anyone to be about. She turned her step toward the mission office.

The brass key-ring in her hand, Anna entered the inner room. She selected a key. Between her thumb and forefinger it felt heavy and hot. *I cannot do this*, she thought. *I simply cannot*. If she hurried back to the bungalow she could return the key ring to its hook before Josiah awoke. She pictured herself preparing his breakfast, drinking tea with him, kneeling with him for the morning prayers. She groaned, and the key burned in her fingers. With little agency on her part, it seemed to insert itself into the lock of the mission safe, then twist. The safe door swung open.

Something brushed against her foot. She swallowed a scream. It was Gus, the mongoose tamed by the missionaries to keep down snakes.

In the dim light, Anna peered into the safe. Mr. Montgomery's bag of golden rupees was on the bottom shelf where she herself had placed it. She dipped into the soft goatskin bag and grabbed a handful of the heavy gold coins, which she then let fall into the pouch hanging from a cord around her neck. The rest she left for whoever took over the infirmary work after her. She sighed and pulled the drawstring tight. First an apostate, now a thief.

Somehow she felt Ashok Montgomery wouldn't mind.

Vaskar and his bullock cart awaited her just outside the compound gate.

TWENTY-EIGHT

Waft, waft, ye winds, his story,
And, yon, ye waters, roll,
Till, like a sea of glory,
It spreads from pole to pole:

The Missionary Hymn

After an interminable journey through the jungle, Vaskar had gotten her to Agra. Anna, exhausted and nauseous from the jolting voyage, recuperated at a quiet guest house and arranged for the purchase of a modest wardrobe at an inconspicuous ladies' shop. Then, after a three-day wait for the train, she'd installed herself in a private carriage and was safely on her way to Calcutta. When the train first chuffed from the depot into the teeming, noisy city, she'd been greatly relieved. The main roads had then been alive with strings of burdened camels and long files of pack elephants. Then the train had steamed from the marble-templed city into open countryside, where men and women naked to the waist toiled in grain and poppy fields. All was as expected.

But on this, her second day of travel, Anna knew something was amiss. Indians were a gregarious, busy, communal and noisy people; however, all afternoon she'd been jolting along in her narrow compartment without seeing a soul in the countryside. The train cars cut through oddly deserted fields, skirting small, empty villages with cooking fires that still smoldered. Where had the people gone?

Secluded behind a locked door in her solitary compartment, she'd spoken to no one since the train attendant had tapped on her door with breakfast. Sick with the swaying carriage and the sooty air, she'd refused the meal. Then, at the engine's stops for water, not a single peddler had rapped insistently at the carriage windows to offer tea or honey cakes. Nor had her attendant arrived, as expected, with tiffin. Anna was hungry and frightened, but as long as the train kept moving she could do nothing; the outside footboards upon which the trainmen balanced expertly with their trays and trunks were far too narrow for her to traverse. Something was more than wrong; she knew it. But the train rode steadily along, now through a tall forest-like stand of bamboo, now into a patch of cleared land next to a wide, dusty road.

A riderless bull elephant stumbled into sight, its teak *howdah* shattered and sagging on half-severed straps down the animal's massive side. The silken canopy was shredded, the silver-embossed railing half-detached and trailing through the dirt. The train slowed, creeping along on screeching iron rails. What had happened to the *howdah* and its passengers? What had happened to the animal's *mahout*?

Blood and fury. Guns and death.

Then, rounding a long, sweeping bend and coming up to a central crossroad she saw in the disordered dirt of the thoroughfare signs of massive flight. Wagons and carriages and carts: their wheels had all too recently thundered across this road heading toward the south. Elephants there had been, too, their dung still steaming. But all was lonely and silent now, the air, unnaturally still, a sense of menace almost palpable.

Blood and fury. Guns and death: Lallia's prediction had come to pass.

Oh, Anna thought, she had delayed too long in leaving Fatehgarh. This looked as if refugees were fleeing from the carnage of which Mr. Montgomery had warned. If only Josiah had listened to him, they might have been lodged now, safe, in Calcutta. Had this violence reached the mission? Was Lucy safe? Were her children?

The train sped up with a lurch, as if the engineer had suddenly thrown on shovelfuls of coal. After a mile or so, the tracks skirled away from the road, but not before revealing undeniable signs of violent skirmish—blood in the dust, jumbled prints of boots and of bare feet, a lady's trunk, smashed open, skirt hoops and chemises strewn all around. A child's shoe lay on its side in the center of the road, a small, white kidskin slipper with blue satin ties, a girl's shoe—gory with blood. When the train tracks drew near the river, she began to see the bodies, men and women, European and Indian alike, bloated and floating down the river, where they had been thrown. One child of about five years old had been dragged out of the river by dogs, who were ripping the small body to pieces. Anna screamed upon seeing this horror and threw herself down on the train pallet, burying her face in it until they were far beyond the scene of carnage.

Nightfall was sudden as the train sped back briefly into the jungle, then out into a mountain-enclosed valley. After an immeasurable time, Anna fell into a muddled sleep, only to jerk awake when, from somewhere down the track came a sudden crack of gunfire, then another, then a volley of shots. Heavy steps traversed the train's footboards, and porters shouted. A mob had destroyed a railroad bridge directly ahead. Inside the compartment, the air was thick with humidity and horror. Anna jumped up from her berth and brittle specks of soot scattered to the floor. And then the train jolted to an abrupt halt. Anna staggered, righted herself.

In the distance the engine chugged to no effect. The steam whistle sounded once again, a long, lamenting cry. Still the train did not move. Shouts in the distance. The howl of the mob. A line of torches advancing. Anna would die here, on this train, at the hands of a people she had worked so hard to heal.

"Oh, my God," Anna prayed aloud. "Send me to hell—I don't care. Just let me live. . . ." Her sobbing voice trailed off into an inarticulate wail. Footsteps halted abruptly on the boards outside her door, and someone tried to turn the handle of the bolted door. It remained fast shut.

"Are you English, Madam?" asked an urgent voice.

"American," she responded, her heart now hoping.

"Open the door," the voice commanded.

And thus it was that Ashok Montgomery stood there, outlined against the lurid light, aghast at the sight of her.

TWENTY-NINE

New York
1860

“Anna!” It was Caroline’s voice. “Anna, let me in. I have momentous news.” Anna flew to the door of her room and turned the key. Caroline, wearing a walking dress of dark blue faille, practically fell into the shabby chamber. She came to a halt, glancing around: the sickly green calico window curtains; the framed print of a stage coach yellowing under cracked glass; dresses and petticoats hanging from hooks in the ceiling. “*This* is how you live? Oh, Anna, why didn’t you tell me? I would have found you some place more … salubrious.” She shivered in the chill, smoky, atmosphere of the room; it was an overcast late-September Sunday.corpus

Anna’s pride stung, she grabbed a handful of coal from her bucket and threw it into the stove. The fire flared up and glowed with an angry eye. “I’m no charity case, Caroline. I care for myself well enough.” True, upon leaving the Five Points Mission, Anna had burrowed here, invisible and unknown among the city’s hundred thousands, insensible to her surroundings. This room was not her home; it was simply the place where she stayed. She had forfeited her right to anything called a home—or so she had thought at the time. “Why have you come?” she asked, still miffed.

Caroline placed a gloved hand on Anna's arm. "'Bama knows where your daughter is."

Alabama Fitch met them on the sidewalk in front of Saint Paul's Chapel. "Miss Susan Parker brought me your baby the day it was born," she said. "She lied to me, said the mother was a Negro and had abandoned the girl. Could I find someone who wanted her? If not, she'd take the baby directly to the Colored Orphan Asylum."

Anna staggered against the chapel's wrought-iron fence. Broadway's throngs jostled past her. "That … That …" Her vocabulary was inadequate to express her fury. "That … damnable … old *cat*!" she sputtered.

'Bama, her face expressionless, continued her tale. "I saw a dark baby, so I found her a dark family. It's true she didn't look like any colored baby I ever knew, but the people coming up from the south nowadays are very different in appearance than they used to be.

"Leticia and John Washington had just lost their little Euphemia. Letty said your daughter was God's blessing, to replace her own girl."

Anna grabbed 'Bama's arm. It was all she could do to keep from screeching at her. "When you heard my story, you knew the baby was mine. Why didn't you tell me?"

'Bama shrugged. "It would've broken Leticia's heart. She loved that child. And, anyhow …" she tightened her lips, "… you, you were … are … a white woman. We take care of our own."

Anna felt her face grow hot, felt the blood simmer in her veins. "But she's not *your own*. She's *mine*! *I'm* her mother!"

'Bama looked down at Anna's hand on her arm. "You're hurting me," she said, fussing with her disordered paisley shawl.

"Anna!" Caroline spoke sharply. "Let go of her!"

Anna swiveled toward her friend. "Did *you* know about this?"

"I knew nothing until 'Bama told me this morning." Caroline swished her skirt out of the way of a small, muddy dog.

"But you said you would ask her." Anna recalled their conversation after the visit to the Colored Orphan Asylum. "Remember that? You said you would ask Mrs. Fitch where Miss Parker would take a colored baby!"

"I *did* ask her. She said she didn't know." Caroline shrugged. "'Bama Fitch is her own woman. She doesn't have to answer to me."

Anna pivoted toward Alabama Fitch, speechless.

"Mrs. Wheeler," 'Bama continued, "by the time you showed up, it was too late. They were a family." She looked out across Broadway, continuing to avoid Anna's fierce glare. A boy passed, sucking on a stick of striped candy. A gray cat stretched out, scratching at the trunk of a newly planted tree. Then 'Bama looked directly at Anna. Her gaze was flat, like a mortared wall. "You hate me, don't you?"

"*Hate* you? ..." Anna felt an emotion so powerful it almost consumed her: heat and cold at the same time—a chill burning her heart. If she allowed this passion to overcome her, what might she do? It frightened her.

But was it *hate*? "I'm angry, Mrs. Fitch. If you want the truth, I feel that I could ... *strike* you. But, *hate*? No. I know what hate is. I feel nothing that deadly for you. Especially now that you ..." Anna ran a trembling hand over her face, then let out a deep breath. "Why *now*, Mrs. Fitch? Why are you taking me to her *now*?"

"Leticia got sick." 'Bama's expression was pained. "My friend. Some kind of wasting disease." She adjusted a green glass hatpin. "She passed on last week. Who's going to care for the girl, now, I asked myself. You see, John ... well, John's a good man, but he's got other things on his mind. He goes ... South a lot. And, now, with war talk rumbling through the newspapers, the work will be more urgent than ever."

"Oh," Anna replied. "He's a ...?"

"Conductor," Caroline clarified. "He poses as a slave, goes right onto the plantations—"

"Shush!" From under straight lashes, 'Bama gave her cousin a warning look, then addressed Anna. "And, besides, now I know you, I know you'll give the child a good life. So I had a long talk with John." She gave a weary shrug. "Sometimes there's no one right thing to do." With a dark, direct gaze at Anna, 'Bama Fitch said, "I'll take you to her. It's not far. We can walk."

It was about ten blocks—a city half-mile—to the house on Church Street where India Elizabeth had lived since a few short hours after her birth. Anna's entire being was focused on stepping quickly along behind Alabama Fitch, one foot before the other. She envisioned the meeting: a small dark-eyed child turning from her doll with a joyous welcoming smile.

The distance was nothing to Anna, who walked everywhere to save the two-cent cost of the horse cars, but today the streets themselves conspired to keep her from her destination. At the great Y intersection of Fulton and Broadway, a team pulling a dray cart of full-grown hogs bolted in front of her, the cart overturned, and two dozen filthy pigs fled their captivity. Between the rampaging swine and the rearing horses, traffic in the intersection came to a total standstill. With 'Bama now breathing heavily behind her, Anna spun on her heel and detoured west, leaving the chaos and the swine stink behind.

Reaching the relative quiet of Church Street, she halted on the sidewalk to scrape pig dung off the sole of one shoe with a stick. At the corner of Chambers Street, where an old hip-roofed Dutch house was being pulled down, two-hundred-years-worth of dust roiled the air, and 'Bama succumbed to a coughing fit so severe she had to stop and catch her breath. Anna shifted from foot to foot, frantic to be moving on, but broken stones and splintered boards from the old house were heaped everywhere, driving them off the sidewalk almost into the path of a red-and-yellow omnibus pulled by six lathered horses.

When a space in the street traffic opened up, Anna gathered her skirts, stepped into the gap and hastened across the street. They paused for 'Bama to catch her breath again, this time in front of the African Methodist Episcopal church at Leonard Street, where singing, stomping, and clapping echoed the wild pounding in Anna's ears: *There is a balm in Gilead / To make the wounded whole. / There is a balm in Gilead / To heal the sin-sick soul.* A shout rose from the congregation: *Yes, dear Lord, yes there is.*

A steady wind blew straight at them from the west with a touch of river dampness. 'Bama pulled her shawl tighter and pointed out a squat brick house a half-block up from the church. "See that place? That's where your girl lives."

Anna gasped, her eyes riveted to the comfortable little house. The front door was hung in black crape; black curtains covered the windows.

'Bama continued, "It's hard for John to give Gracie up, but he promised he'd have her ready for you when we get there." They began walking toward the house. "Then, by the time we get her back to Lafayette Place, Caroline will have purchased new clothes and things—"

"She's not Gracie. She's India Elizabeth—"

'Bama tightened her lips. "She knows herself as Gracie. The child misses her mother a great deal, but she's still small, she should—"

"But I'm—"

"Her mother. Yes. But she doesn't know that." She pushed open the low iron gate.

Anna's daughter. Just behind that door. Her India Elizabeth. Ashok's child. Anna's emotions were volatile today. Ten minutes earlier she'd been hot with fury; now she felt light, as if she were gliding inches above the packed-dirt path.

"Oh, Miss Fitch—Gracie gone." The tall brown man with gray eyes stood in the doorway, looking frantic. Although he seemed unconscious of the action, one long-fingered hand rubbed along his jaw line, back and forth, back and forth. "I bin looking all over the neighborhood."

Anna felt the blood leave her heart. Someone gave a strangled moan. It was Anna herself.

'Bama gasped. "What do you mean, *gone*?"

"I had to go out this morning," John said, "Lany Croke be watching her. . ."

"Daniel's girl? The one with the hare lip?" 'Bama's expression was unreadable.

"Yes, that her. She none too bright, but she got a good heart. She have Gracie out on the porch, rocking in that swan seat I made. She say lots of people walkin' by, but she don't think nothin' 'bout them. Then she have to go out … to the necessary house. She tell Gracie, you stay right here. When she come back, Gracie gone." His eyes filled suddenly with tears. "My little Gracie," he said. "Oh, Lordy, my little girl." He paused and swallowed hard. When he spoke again, a deep anger mingled with the grief. "I jus' know it be a blackbirder, see a likely child, snatch her up. Down South they likes they girls light-skinned."

Anna went numb as a stone, following 'Bama and Mr. Washington into the neat little house, as if she were a Barnum's automaton, the Mechanical Woman. The child's absence was everywhere she looked: the swan rocker on the porch was empty; in the front room a red ball sat abandoned on the hearth; a calico patchwork dog peered out from beneath the treadle of a dusty loom. She wanted to cry, but her eyes were empty. Then on the mantle Anna saw an intricately worked gold daguerreotype frame. In two bounds she was across the room. A small girl in a ruffled white muslin dress sat propped against a pillow on a paisley-shawl-draped table. Of medium complexion, she had a white satin ribbon threaded through glossy curls and tied in a neat bow. She appeared well-cared for, but her eyes were closed and her mouth was sad.

Feeling came flooding back. "India Elizabeth!" Anna snatched the portrait and stared at it: the first glimpse ever in this mortal world of her only child's face.

"No." John Washington took the hinged frame from Anna and regarded it soberly. "This be Euphemia, our own girl." He turned the image toward Anna once again. "She look so natural here you can't hardly tell she be … gone."

Anna dropped into the nearest chair. "The child in this picture is *dead?*"

"We had no likeness of her," John said, "and Letty want a memorial portrait." He rubbed his ear. "And now she gone, too. My Letty."

"Oh." Anna's heart was divided: pity and fury at war. Trusted with the precious charge, this stranger had lost her child. And, too, she had been doubly thwarted: not only had her daughter been snatched from within her very grasp, but the image she'd thought was India, turned out to be a portrait of someone else's heartache.

Then, abruptly, John Washington's words sank in, and a horrific image consumed her: India Elizabeth, older now, trembling on some Southern auction block, pawed over by lascivious men. The tears came in floods, the sobs in great gasps. Never in her life had Anna wept like this. She collapsed against a table, knocking over a blue pottery vase filled with asters. She would have fallen if 'Bama hadn't guided her into a chair. India Elizabeth seemed like nothing so much as a chimera, a will-of-the-wisp appearing faintly before her and then evaporating into the ether. Each time Anna thought the child might be within her reach, each time she thought to realize her presence, her daughter vanished into the depths of whatever nightmare was to mire her fate—and Anna's hopes—once again.

John stood in the doorway, watching her in shared grief. Abruptly he turned and left the room. When he entered again, he was carrying an almost identically framed daguerreotype in his lean brown hand. He held it out to Anna. "Now this, this be Gracie," he said. "We took her likeness on her first birthday. Didn't want Death sneaking up on us again.

"But, oh, my Lettie. I knows she be so mad at me, I lose little Grace. ..."

The gold frame was warm from John's hand. Anna could hardly believe that here at last was India. Another small girl in another white muslin dress, the child regarded the camera gravely, but the daguerreotypist had caught a dancing light of mischief in her eyes. Anna was so thirsty for this intoxicating image—her daughter!—she practically drank it in. India Elizabeth was lighter than she had expected, with curly hair, Ashok's great dark eyes, and a face very much like her own.

"That be for you," John said. "Take it." She could tell by the pain in his eyes how much the gesture cost him.

She left John Washington's house clutching India's portrait. He and 'Bama were deep in consultation about how to plumb the colored community for news of slave hunters in the city, for sightings of little Gracie. Anna left because there was nothing else she could do. It was all over; her child would be sold into slavery. She knew it.

THIRTY

Anna retreated to her room at Mrs. Chapman's house. The weave of the stiff drugget covering the front stairs created an almost insurmountable friction as she dragged her feet from one step to another. She sat on the lumpy bed, removing the Kashmiri shawl, folding it over and over: Oh, how she had failed Ashok, allowing his child to be snatched from under her very fingertips! She placed the daguerreotype on top of the bundled shawl, clasped it to her breast and cradled it there. Overcome by another wild storm of tears, she wept herself into a state of exhausted despair.

Why hadn't she remained with Ashok? Had she done so, their lost daughter would now be secure, loved and cared for. Instead India Elizabeth had been thrust out of the womb into God only knew what kinds of peril. And that peril was Anna's fault; she had lacked the courage to follow her heart.

Once the Mutiny had been subdued, she and Ashok had traveled to Calcutta from his family's mountain tea estate. His parents welcomed her, this widow of a martyred clergyman who herself had been snatched from certain death, and they offered her refuge in their elegant home. She was welcome, she knew, but she also knew that she must prepare within a reasonable time for her homeward voyage, or her residence might prove awkward for Ashok.

They stood together one cool evening on a wide verandah suffused with the over-sweet scent of jasmine and bougainvillea. In the violet sunset haze, Ashok, unusually silent, pressed a ring of keys into Anna's hand. "What are these?" she asked, frowning at the keys that flickered brightly in the light of a burning *flambeau*.

"They are keys to our new house," he replied. "I purchased it today. You will stay with me, my dearest heart? We will make a home for ourselves. Please say yes. I cannot bear to lose you." The yearning in his dark eyes was almost impossible to resist.

But Anna, perforce, had already made clandestine plans for her return to New York. Oh, yes, three years later she was to give Caroline a list of insurmountable barriers that had necessitated her departure from Calcutta: shame for herself; social stigma for Ashok; the certain displeasure of his mother's family. That's what she had told Ashok. And herself. But, had she consented to remain, they would have found a way. They would not have been the only lovers in Calcutta whose passion crossed the strict barriers of ethnicity and culture. Indeed, were not Ashok's own parents—his British father and Bengali mother—evidence of that more liberal love?

But the truth was that Anna had struggled for weeks with a secret knowledge, the unwelcome awareness of a new life growing in her womb. She'd been certain the child she carried was Josiah's—the result of that vicious rape the night she'd announced she was leaving him. She could not foist the child of rape, blond and pale and bloodless (as she imagined it—despising Josiah as she had come to despise him) upon the man she loved. Why had she not considered the possibility of Ashok being the father? In truth, she had no certain way of calculating her fertile days—her monthlies had been off-and-on over the past year or so. Looking back, she'd thought for certain that the nausea and weakness she'd experienced during her flight, before she'd met Ashok on the train, had been morning sickness. Oh, if only Ashok could have been her child's father … But, no, the dates were off … the signs were wrong … the heavens had cursed them. It could not be.

So she stood there on that Indian verandah, breathing in the luxuriant scent of exotic flowers and studying the ring of keys that emblemized Ashok's love. She did not feel she could tell him she was pregnant with Josiah's child.

"Oh, my dear heart," she said, looking up into his dark, pained, eyes, allowing the keys to fall back into his hand, resting her cheek against his. "I cannot remain. My dearest love, I must go home."

And now, here in New York, she had lost Ashok's child for the second time. After the night of bitter tears that had followed her visit to the small, neat Church Street home of India Elizabeth's infancy, Anna grew calm again, too calm. She felt strangely as if she no longer had a heart. In its place had come something cold and metallic. Something it would not do to touch or prod. Something explosive.

For days on end she stood back from the friends—it surprised her to realize she had so many friends—who continued in her stead to search for India. 'Bama Fitch and John Washington kept an eye on all comings and goings in the Negro community. Caroline's abolitionist associates were, as always, attuned to the possible presence of slave catchers in the city. Nothing. Suspicions were that the child had fallen into the clutches of Cracker Skaggs or someone of his ilk. But no amount of inquiry could locate that scoundrel anywhere in the city. The consensus was that the little girl must, immediately upon her abduction, have been taken to the South to be sold.

Twice Anna dressed herself for a walk through the city streets in search of India, but turned back halfway down the stairs. To what end should she walk? The child had vanished utterly. Her friends grew increasingly concerned as she continued to withdraw—withdraw from them, withdraw from life. For Anna, this time constituted a dormancy of the heart. She was suspended in loss; hope, anticipation, need, and desire were as distant as a continent beyond a thousand seas. She was without sensation or volition. If 'Bama had not brought her soups and custards, she would not have eaten. If Caroline had not supplied her with clean clothing, she would have huddled in the Kashmiri shawl night and day. Eben Garrett, alarmed by her absence from the table, sought her out in her room, and she sent him away without even a pretense of an explanation. His notes she returned unread by way of Nancy O'Brien, who still wore the crucifix Anna had given her, so tarnished now that the body on the cross was nothing more than a blackish bulge.

Anna seemed able to do nothing but stare at the small figure in the daguerreotype. Her daughter sat up straight and gazed frankly at the camera. There was so much trust and intelligence in the child's great dark eyes that Anna was both heartened and dismayed: heartened by the love in which the girl's infancy had been immersed; dismayed at the potential for spiritual destruction if she had indeed fallen into the hands of slavers. The remainder of her countenance was that of any infant, the rounded cheek, the rosebud mouth, the sweet little nubbin nose. . . But, lost. So lost. It did not cease to mesmerize her: the play of light and silver on a copper plate, and, behold, an image of the unattainable.

Then one afternoon Nancy pounded on her door, and everything changed. "Mail for you, Mrs. Wheeler."

Mail? Anna opened the door to find the house girl offering three letters and a small package tightly bound with twine. "Mrs. Chapman says I shouldn't bring these up to yez. If ye wanted them bad 'nuff, ye could come down and get 'em yerself."

A pinprick of interest pierced Anna's apathy. She snatched the mail and began sorting through the pieces. Bridey went on, "That package there been on the mail table for at least a week. The others come yesterday and today. When the old cow went out to Jefferson Market after dinner, I grabbed them up."

"Thank you, Nancy. Thank you so much!" Anna wrapped herself in Ashok's shawl and curled up on her lumpy bed. The package was from Mr. Larkin. One letter was from George Putnam, Publishers, another from Mrs. Phoebe Derwent at Gramercy Park. The last letter was postmarked Philadelphia. She turned it over; no return address. She was acquainted with no one there, so its sender was a mystery to her.

But she turned first to Mr. Larkin's package. Her heart was beginning to flutter in anticipation. Could it be? Was it possible? It was still only October, and he had spoken of publication for the Christmas trade.

With numb fingers Anna struggled to undo the knots. There: One. Two. But the next was hopelessly tangled. She sacrificed the twine, severing it with scissors from her sewing box. The heavy brown paper opened, as if of its own will, and fell away, disclosing a thin deep-red volume elegantly gilded with jasmine blossoms on its cover and spine.

"Oh!" She stared, enraptured: the book was beautiful, the paper prime rag stock, the page edges gilded. In bright gold letters, the title read *Poems, Sacred and Sentimental*, by Anna Wheeler. She traced the gilded letters with a trembling finger. Her hands as she opened the book and studied the title page were less than steady. Once again—and for all time—*Poems* by Anna Wheeler, New York, Larkin & Bierce, 1860. This might be, she supposed, as close to immortality as she would ever come.

She leafed through the gold-edged pages, entranced by her own verses, now printed together for the very first time.

From the first poem:

The rose of Oriental clime
In crimson cluster grows.
The dusky foot that treads the path
Is softer than the rose. …

She turned a page, and then another. When she had sated herself with the book, she set it carefully on her writing desk, gave it a final pat, and turned to the enclosed letter.

My Dear Mrs. Wheeler,

I send a copy of your Poems, and am pleased to be in a position to tell you that the books are selling nicely.

Yours, etc.

"Selling nicely." She spoke the words aloud; they sounded so well. "Selling nicely." She leafed through the pages and shook the brown wrapping paper. No payment accompanied the book. How soon, she wondered, could she expect to receive further remuneration from Larkin & Pierce. If she was to continue her search for India, she would need far more money than she had left from Mr. Larkin's initial one-hundred dollars. "Selling nicely," he'd written. So she assumed that the publisher would soon be forwarding the percentage she had been promised from the sales of her book. The amount should be substantial.

She turned to her other mail.

The note from Mrs. Derwent was inscribed in purple ink on lavender paper.

> *My Dear Mrs.Wheeler,*
> *How lovely it was to meet you at my little party. I would be most grateful for your presence next Wednesday evening at my monthly literary evening.*
> *Yours Truly,*

Anna felt her heart tighten with anxiety once again. But ... yes. Certainly she would attend Mrs. Derwent's upcoming salon. It was difficult, but she must get herself back into the literary world.

The letter from Mr. George Putnam, one of the premiere publishers of the city, expressed his enjoyment of her verses, and continued:

> *I would be most gratified if you would submit any further book manuscripts to me for consideration of publication by George Putnam and Co. I believe I could make such publication well worth your while.*

Anna was pleased to find her hand still steady as she returned this request to its envelope and laid it on the table beside the book. Perhaps she need not be always solely dependent on the good will of Mr. William Larkin. She would write more poems tomorrow, and the next day and the next, these for Mr. Putnam.

Then she turned to the last letter, the one from Philadelphia. Frowning, she studied the laid-linen envelope. Suddenly she was flooded with speculation: could this be news about India Elizabeth? Had her daughter perhaps been taken to that city? She slit the envelope and removed the folded letter.

It was not about India.

> *My Dear Miss Wheeler—*
> *It has been my great privilege to read your splendid lines. I make so bold as to request that you consider serving as*

Contributing Editor for the Ladies Book for the upcoming year. You will not find the duties onerous, merely the use of your name on our masthead and the publication of perhaps three or four of your verses. We would be most grateful for your assent.

The signature was that of Sarah Josepha Hale, the editor of *Godey's Ladies Book*.

A sheet of paper fluttered to the floor. Bending to retrieve it, Anna found herself in possession of a bank draft for five-hundred dollars. She began to feel empowered. She began to feel like going on.

"Oh, Caroline, my fortune is made." Anna waved the bank draft in her friend's face. She'd practically sprinted uptown to share the good tidings with her confidante, and—not least—show her the book of poems. A candid friendship was growing between the two women, so unlike each other in character and circumstance.

Caroline, lounging on a wicker divan in her comfortable drawing room, a crimson shawl draped over her shoulders, set the *Atlantic Monthly* aside and exclaimed over Anna's book—its beauty, the quality of the paper, the crispness of the print. "And some of these poems are actually quite good," she said. "Even I can tell, and, as you are aware, I don't like poetry."

Anna snorted. She didn't know whether she should be grateful for Caroline's unknowledgeable opinion, or whether her feelings should be bruised.

In either case, it didn't matter, as long as editors seemed willing to pay well for her verses. For once—five-hundred dollars in hand—she rested easy in the knowledge that her quest for India was not over, that wherever it took her, she would have the means to go.

"Caroline," she said, "you do understand what this means, don't you? Now I will find my child, because I will have the means to scour the earth for her."

"I'm pleased for you, Anna," Caroline responded, still leafing through the book. "Although, I must say, five-hundred dollars is scarcely a fortune. I know two or three ladies who would spend that much on a ball gown. Nonetheless, it bodes well for future earnings. You can make yourself more comfortable—leave that horrid boarding house; find a more congenial lodging. Perhaps you could buy a little house—"

"Oh, no," Anna replied, "No. I will stay as I am until I find India Elizabeth. I don't at all care about my own comfort, only about her safety. I must find her—give her a safe, happy life, an education, a home ... all the things a mother's love hopes for. I must manage my income prudently. If it takes every cent of Mrs. Hale's largesse, I will rescue that child." She swallowed. "Or I will learn her fate."

Almost euphoric on her trek home through the crowded afternoon streets, she decided as she passed by her bank that she'd write a poem or two for Mrs. Hale before she accepted the *Godey's* offer and redeemed the bank draft. She'd like to enclose the poems with her letter as a show of good faith.

Once back in her room, she sharpened a new nib, and fitted it to her pen. She must write, and write she would. No longer out of loneliness or personal insight or sheer joy in the play of the language; rather because she must enhance her funds. It should be easy. All she had to do was choose some pretty words—*bud*, perhaps, and *blossom*, *rivulet* and *ribband*, *sacrament* and *shrine*--and put them all together in some pretty manner, reassure the readers of the ladies magazines that God was indeed in his heaven and Home was the heart of the world. That was all she had to do. Over the tools of her trade she had complete mastery: sonnets and villanelles, couplets and quatrains, blank verse and rime royale. She could write of sleigh bells and fresh-fallen snow, of brisk April mornings with the lilac in half-bud, of a child's handprint evanescent on a misted windowpane.

But, no. No. Words refused to come. Each time she sat down to compose a poem, a great ... zero ... came over her imagination. A cloud of nothingness. A frozen blankness in her brain where the language used to flow.

Anna had lost her Muse.

The man turned the brass doorknob and entered into the publishing offices on Park Row. Not ready to declare himself alive to the public world, he had attributed authorship of his memoir solely to "A Survivor of the Massacre at Cawnpore." The rusty-haired, frock-coated clerk standing behind the tall desk in the outer room was scrawny and dyspeptic, and he took the string-tied manuscript with a less-than-sympathetic air. His demeanor implied weeks and months, cobwebs and mouse droppings, and an indifferent outcome.

Nonetheless, as the publisher's minion bowed him out of the wide front door, he had no anxiety about the success of his memoir. It was a compelling tale. The Lord was with him in the telling of it. He would hear in God's good time from Mr. William Larkin, publisher of moral literature for the people.

THIRTY-ONE

Five days after receiving the copy of her book, and still afflicted with an inability to compose anything for the *Ladies Book*, Anna had not yet responded to the *Godey's* editor or cashed her check. Indeed, she was afraid to do so—what if her Muse had vanished forever?

Returning to the boarding house one brisk afternoon from a walk to the Post Office, Anna found on Mrs. Chapman's hall table an engraved envelope from Larkin & Bierce Publishers. Her spirits rose—it must be a payment. Her funds were increasing. Shifting her red knitted gloves from her cold right hand to her cold left hand, she swooped the envelope up and took it to her room. Inside she found a bank check for one-hundred dollars.

Well ... good. ... She peered into the envelope again. Nothing else. No explanatory letter, and no accounting of the number of volumes sold. What exactly was this payment? Still an advance against future profits? Or did it reflect the number of books already sold? If the latter, was this the true amount of money to be earned by a book "selling nicely," as Mr. Larkin himself had said? Or might there be more to come? She needed to know.

Anna had become increasingly concerned by the lack of any further communication from her publisher after that first advance payment of one-hundred dollars. Now here was a second hundred. Certainly she had earned more than that. The generosity of Mrs. Hale had led her to consider that perhaps her poems were worth more than Larkin & Bierce had yet acknowledged. Caroline had informed her that the book was selling like hotcakes, that all the ladies were finding Anna's romantic poems to be "deliciously exotic."

Despite Mr. Larkin's attitude of paternal benevolence, his assurances that all would be familial and friendly, she'd come to realize how naïve she'd been not to insist on a contract in writing. William Larkin had offered her economic salvation, yes, indeed, but without a regular accounting of books sold and moneys earned how was she to know he was treating her honestly. That steamy August day in his office she'd been raw and untested, such a ninny, but how to go about rectifying her error? She was actually beginning to feel quite sick about it.

Should she approach her publishers in person? She tried to imagine such a confrontation: her vocabulary was replete with poeticisms, yes, but she feared that business terms and legal words would drop from her mouth like toads. The scene would end with Mr. Larkin taking both her hands in his and assuring "the little lady" that she could rely on him.

Shortly thereafter, over a boardinghouse dinner of stewed mutton and turnips, Anna looked up from the lumps of gray gristle lurking in the bottom of her bowl, and Eben Garrett caught her eye. He smiled. She smiled back, then studied the young man intently. His face was plain and honest, his conversation witty, knowledgeable and intelligent. He seemed to be a compassionate fellow. And certainly he would be knowledgeable about the literary world. She decided to trust him.

"Mr. Garrett," she'd said, taking him to one side in the front hall after dinner. "Might I ask your advice on a business matter?"

"A *business* matter?" He paused, his expression closed, then he shrugged and winked at her. "O.K. Go ahead. Shoot." Slipping a cigar from his coat pocket and lighting it, he considerately blew the first stream of smoke back over his shoulder, away from his companion's face. "Though I warn you, if it's about … money, I don't have a heck of a lot of experience."

"But you do know the world of books," Anna had said, "and perhaps you can give me some sound advice."

So, she was to meet Eben Garrett the following morning at Buttercake John's Coffee Saloon, in one of the few brick houses left on Broadway near Bowling Green. At ten, she descended a short flight of worn stone steps from the foot pavement. An old Dutch stove faced in blue-and-white tile greeted her, heating the chamber to a welcoming warmth. Not so welcome were the stares of workmen in donkey jackets and junior clerks in much-brushed broadcloth coats with large iron keys attached to their belts. This was an establishment unaccustomed to being patronized by women of such a clearly respectable stamp as Anna, in her blue wool cloak and sober gray bonnet. Ignoring the gawkers, she settled herself at a table in the cold light that flooded in from a row of high windows and beckoned to the waiter. When a large stoneware cup of steaming coffee arrived, she sipped quietly and waited for Eben Garrett.

Finally, he rushed in, mist soaking his hair, which lay in flat curls plastered against his skull. "I'm famished," he said, raising a hand to summon the waiter. "A plate of buttered biscuits, please." Then, yanking off a pair of rugged leather gloves and winking at her, he said, "So, Miss Anna, unless you've taken a sudden passion for my manly shoulders and beautiful brown eyes, I'll bet this … assignation … really *is* about your book."

"Of course it is!" she huffed. "What did you think?"

"Who knows what I might have thought." He raised his eyebrows suggestively and gave his wolf's grin.

Anna frowned.

"O.K! O.K!" He plunked himself down onto the sturdy oak chair. "My mistake! So—business, is it? I hear your effusions are selling like hotcakes."

The grinding of a coffee mill released the aroma of beans fresh from South American packet boats docked a few short blocks away. Anna breathed in, then out—an irresistible elixir. "Yes. Hotcakes. That's exactly what Caroline said."

"Caroline?" he asked, with an air of studied casualness. "Is that the lady who's come to visit you a few times lately?"

Anna was startled by the sudden change of subject. "You don't mean Bridey O'Neal?"

"No. I know Bridey—of course I know Bridey." His words had an air of circumspection. "The other woman—tall, skinny, unruly dark hair. And, you know—unbuxom. Not a pretty little lady like you. A looker, though. Dresses well—has a real air about her."

Anna stared at him: *unbuxom*? No man had ever before referred to a woman's bosom in her presence. Well, except for Ashok. She doubted that the word *buxom* had even been in Josiah's lexicon.

Had she become the type of woman with whom men felt they need not guard their tongues? she wondered. Strangely, the thought thrilled her.

"Oh, you must mean Caroline Slade."

"Caroline Slade? Is that who she is? Certainly I've heard of Miss Slade—who hasn't? And *you* know her? Hmm."

Then Eben rushed on, all business this time. "So, I'm not surprised you need advice—Larkin & Bierce have a reputation for cutting corners with their authors. How much have they paid you so far?"

She told him.

"Two hundred dollars! Why, that's highway robbery!"

"It's not that I'm mercenary—" But her feet *were* wet and cold in her old, leaky boots. Surely she deserved a warm new pair. Was that mercenary?

"Hey, you don't have to tell me. You wouldn't be at Old Lady Chapman's if you weren't living from hand to mouth. Believe me, I know all about it. It ain't much fun."

The waiter delivered three flaky, soft biscuits dripping with butter. Eben snatched one and pushed the plate over to Anna.

She didn't feel like eating. Instead she told him of Mr. Larkin's reluctance to offer her a contract putting their dealings on a business basis. "Now I must pay the man a visit and demand an accounting of monies due. Can you tell me how to approach him? What my rights are? How I should phrase my case?"

Eben brushed crumbs from his mouth with the back of his hand, and sat back in his chair. "That louse!" His eyes narrowed. "Even I can do some basic math—two-hundred dollars!" He took on a concentrated look, and, after a couple of moments, sat up and grinned at her.

"No. Let me handle this. You going there in person is just going to elicit more of the same smarmy gobbledygook you got the last time. Let's see what I can do." He winked again. "The power of the press, you know."

"Oh, no." She gasped. In no way did she wish to see her situation in print.

He leaned forward and covered her hand with his. "Don't worry, little lady. I won't betray you. It's just that sometimes I don't actually have to use that power—it's enough simply to threaten it. Leave everything to good old Uncle Eben." Patting her hand, he released it and reached for the biscuit plate. "And if after all my persuasion, you don't see considerable improvement in your receipts, we're going to have to find you an attorney-at-law."

"No! Not a lawyer!" She couldn't bear her situation being brought into the public courts.

Eben's second biscuit went the way of the first, with much butter and honey. Then, his tongue flickering out to lick his lips, he tipped his head with another lightning-fast change of subject. "So, since you, yourself, seem to have no interest in ... ahem ... me and my manly charms, would you perhaps give ... Miss Slade ... my most respectful greetings?"

She smiled at him. Having addressed her business worries, she took a deep sigh and released them. For now. Then she reached for the third biscuit before Eben could grab it. She studied him in the flood of morning light: the dark curls, the physical vitality, the vibrant intelligence. "You know, I think she might be happy to receive ... your most respectful greetings."

That night, deep into her sleep, she dreamt that she was riding into battle on Don Quixote's donkey, wrapped only in the lush Kashmiri shawl. A lone fife was playing "Onward, Christian Soldiers!" Riding to meet her came a formidable opponent on an ebony stallion, an upright pillar of a man, seven-feet tall in his narrow black suit, shining boots, and tall top hat. She was alone on the field, while he was backed by ranked battalions of similarly mounted comrades, their numbers disappearing into the far distance. For weapon, Anna carried a cheap, wobbly pen, its blunted nib dripping ink. While he, he—*he* was armed, like every member of his troops, with a gleaming military bow and arrow of strange but intricate design.

Charge!, Anna cried, her frail pen rampant, digging her bare heels into the donkey's boney ribs.

Charge!, cried her magnificent opponent, spurring his dark steed forward while taking sure aim with his strange, sinister weapon. The beautiful shawl in which Anna was wrapped suddenly turned to cold blazing fire—luminous green, blue, coral, gold! She was transformed with power! Only at the final second—just before she wiped him off the face of the earth with one sure inky swipe of her pen—did Anna recognize her opponent and his weapon: He was Mr. William Larkin—and the weapon he wielded was a lethal forged-steel dollar sign!

She woke up laughing, and laughed until she cried.

THIRTY-TWO

The ladies swirled to the Jenny Lind Polka, bright fuchsia and gold blurs against the stark black-and-white evening dress of the gentlemen. The music swirled, too, piano and concertina in energetic rhythm. Anna had concealed herself in a small niche just off Mrs. Derwent's ballroom, from which she was watching the dancers when a short young man in immaculate evening clothes entered. The intruder smiled at her with plump lips beneath an elegantly branching moustache. "Might I be so importunate as to introduce myself, Mrs. Wheeler?"

Anna nodded. She did so hope that this *importunate* stranger wasn't about to ask her to dance.

He bowed deeply. "I am, Mrs. Wheeler, yours most truly, Elliot B. Cliff—no doubt you've heard my name?—columnist for several papers in the city, with a special interest in book news and literary personages."

It was the word "personages" that gave Anna pause. "People" or "persons" she would have simply glided over. But "personages" suggested a public visibility that offered immediate cause for alarm. She instinctively shuddered at the thought. Someone was certain to recognize her as the woman who'd been searching the less reputable neighborhoods of the city for a child of color. Oh, why hadn't she had the sense to publish under a *nom de plume*? At first all she'd wanted in publishing her verses was the five or ten dollars each poem would bring. All she wanted now that the book had appeared was to make a living for herself and her child—and first, of course, to find her child. To be a *personage* had never been her goal.

She studied Mr. Cliff, a dandy wearing a white cravat and embroidered satin waist-coat with his exquisitely tailored evening coat. His brown hair was long, slicked back from a low forehead, and his sleek moustache attempted to compensate for a most unmasculine pebble of a nose. He smelled of a musky eau de cologne.

"And you, yourself, Mrs. Wheeler," he continued, "have in a short period of time become just such a personage—"

Anna cringed, but he seemed to take no notice.

"—just such a personage as is of the highest interest to my discerning readers. A poetess who has burst upon the New York literary world from absolutely nowhere. A modest little lady whose sedate, spiritual verses in the local papers gave no advance indication of the sensuous and exotic imagination that would conceive such poems as 'Frangipani,' 'Night Thoughts at Calcutta,' and 'The Sandstorm.'" He leaned forward, just a little too close. "Where have you come from, Mrs. Wheeler? Where have you been? That is what my readers wish to know." His breath smelled of peppermint.

She paled, but he was too enamored of his own eloquence to await an answer.

He sat back again, a forefinger at his lips. "I am, Mrs. Wheeler, intrigued. And when Elliot B. Cliff is intrigued, his readers will be intrigued. And when Elliot B. Cliff's readers are intrigued, they will buy an author's books in undreamed of quantities. Mrs. Wheeler, how would you like a profile of your life and career in the January *Harper's Monthly* magazine?" From somewhere a little gold pencil had appeared, and he twirled it between his thumb and forefinger. "With an engraved likeness by the city's most renowned portraitist?"

The recessed niche in which Anna sat was hung with fantastical gilded cages five feet tall containing dozens of green-and-yellow parakeets Mrs. Derwent had brought back from India. Anna pitied these caged birds, recalling the small Indian parrots that had flitted free from tamarind tree to banyan tree. Indeed, at the moment, she experienced a particular sympathy, feeling like a captive bird herself, tightly corseted, pearls hanging heavy around her neck, confined in the cage of hoops and crinoline beneath her borrowed tissue-of-gold ball gown, her hair crimped by Caroline's curling iron.

The music played. The birds twittered. Anna nodded and smiled. It was a gracious smile, she hoped. Indeed, she was afraid that said gracious smile might have become permanently engraved upon her face this evening, precluding ever again any expression of genuine pleasure.

She rid herself finally of the journalist by pleading a most ladylike reluctance to appear personally anywhere other than her proper sphere of home and the sympathetic society to be found in such salons as Mrs. Derwent's. He went away, trailing his musky scent behind him, but he departed reluctantly. Anna breathed a sigh of relief. For the moment, she felt safe, but she feared she had not seen the last of Mr. Elliot B. Cliff.

THIRTY-THREE

Later that night, moonlight shone through the gap in the curtains of Anna's room and glinted on the tissue-of-gold ball-gown that now hung lifelessly from two pegs set into a rafter. Caroline's string of pearls was tucked with care inside Anna's pillowcase to be guarded by her sleeping head. But Anna wasn't asleep. Though she'd left Mrs. Derwent's party well before midnight, she was so over-excited by the unaccustomed music, conversation, rich food and drink, that she felt as if her very brain were dancing the Jenny Lind Polka.

Then Anna heard something. A scratching. Not mice, no. That was different—more random. This was a deliberate scratching—on the door of her room. She sat bolt upright. Her first—and ludicrous—thought was that Elliot B. Cliff had followed her home and was trying to enter her room! Then a deep, familiar, voice whispered, "Anna, it's Eben Garrett. Let me in."

Eben? Surely he didn't think ... But, throwing the Kashmiri shawl over her nightgown, she pulled back the bolt. Eben Garrett slid into the room in his overcoat and scarf, the autumn mist damp upon his curly hair. "Mrs. Wheeler," he said, easing the door shut behind him. He ran a hand through his hair, and water dripped onto the short shoulder cape of his green wool overcoat.

"What do you want?" Anna shivered. "Is it about Mr. Larkin?"

His expression was unreadable. "Larkin? No. Haven't managed to track that slippery eel down. But, listen, here's the deal—Reverend Pete is back in town. And he wants to see you."

"Me?" She pulled the shawl more tightly around her, and the moonlight brought a transformative shimmer to its tropic hues—it seemed to glow now lime-green, now coral, now the amethyst of an Indian autumn twilight.

"At the House of Industry. Right away."

Now? Anna was baffled. How did the rebel Reverend even know about her?

Eben stared at her for a moment in an enigmatic silence. Then, "He says, it's about your ... child."

The tall gas lamp in the center of the Five Points slum cast a strong light over the notorious area. From its radiating circle of illumination, crooked streets and mud-thick paths wound into sinister darkness. Anna knew that, as far as New York City was concerned, she was venturing into the center of hell. But Eben Garrett's watchful eyes, streetwise swagger, and extensive acquaintance in the Five Points marked him as someone to be reckoned with. The carved Malacca cane he swung as if he were a dandy seemed to readily part the occasional lurking sidewalk cluster of loose women and ne'er-do-well men; Anna suspected something in the nature of a sword concealed in the seemingly foppish item.

As they hastened toward the House of Industry, Eben said, "You know, of course, that I'm not a man of faith." He tipped his derby hat to an orange-calico clad young woman with a pockmarked face who simpered at him and curtseyed. "But if anyone on earth could make me a Christian, it would be Pete Lyman."

"Why is that?" Passing a rowdy oyster house, they picked their way around shells shucked hours earlier, fetid now with the stink of spoiled fish. Then, before they'd escaped that odiferous zone, the reek of a tannery assailed them. Anna pulled out a handkerchief and held it to her nose. The autumn chill, also, kept the vile stench from choking her, and the long, second-hand wool *paletot* she'd purchased for winter wear kept her from shivering to death, as she would have in her shawl.

"The good reverend doesn't preach conversion—he advocates social transformation," Eben continued. "So, first he feeds and clothes the poor, then he teaches the pathetic wretches work-skills and remunerative crafts, so they can pull themselves out of the gutters, earn their own livings—"

"Reverend Lyman is a reformer, then, not a missionary?"

"I'd call him a street Christian." With the tip of his cane, Eben lifted a soiled red rag from the pavement and flung it into an alley. "When he first started his children's school, the little gutter rats stank so much the teachers couldn't stand it. So he built bathing rooms, got them clean clothes and shoes. But the need is great in this city, and he's only one man." He tossed a penny to a snotty-nosed girl in ragged skirts slumped in the doorway of a shuttered old-clothes shop. She caught the coin on the fly.

Anna couldn't bear looking at even one more street child; would such a life become her daughter's fate? *India Elizabeth*, she thought. *Reverend Lyman knows something about India Elizabeth*. She picked up the pace.

Eben went on. "The ladies of the Five-Point Mission call the man a heretic—he's more concerned with the earthly well-being of sinners, you see, than he is with their eternal salvation."

Josiah, too, would have called him a heretic, Anna thought, and walked even faster.

The Reverend Peter Lyman met them at the open front door of the House of Industry just as a steeple clock struck two a.m. A wedge of lamplight sliced out into the darkness, revealing streets that had been swept clear of rags and horse droppings. Rev. Pete was tall with thinning yellow hair. Wire-rimmed spectacles lent him the appearance of a stern schoolmaster. In the flickering gaslight, the gray eyes behind the glasses were kind.

"Come, Mrs. Wheeler," he said, gesturing toward an inner door. His library was a cluttered room with dingy windows, and Anna perched on a well-worn, blue wing chair, so tense she could scarcely breathe.

"You, too, Garrett," he said. "But—" Reverend Lyman removed his glasses and fixed Eben with a look so strict it would have slammed shut the gates of Hell. "But this is not for print. Right?"

Eben nodded.

"What is it, Reverend," Anna said. "Tell me—before I go mad."

"Of course, Mrs. Wheeler." Peter Lyman stared at his steepled fingers. "I've heard on the grapevine that you have a child who has recently been kidnapped. I know the circumstances of her birth and the color of her skin—"

Anna jumped up. "Do you know where she is?"

He looked concerned. "I'm sorry, no." He rose from his desk chair and began to pace the worn rug. "But—and this must not go any further than this room—I'm active in a network of people who do our best to help enslaved people on their way north, to freedom."

"The Underground—"

He held up a hand to stop her. "Say nothing. We risk so much. Even murderous retaliation from Southern thugs. Needless to say, I keep my eye very closely on comings and goings in the city." He removed his steel-rimmed spectacles and rubbed his eyes. Before he replaced them, Anna noted inflamed indentations each side of his nose where the bridge of the glasses rested. "Today I heard that a certain Cracker Skaggs has recently taken ship for Charleston—"

Cracker Skaggs!

Eben Garrett blurted out, "I know the man—short and muscular, a cheap dandy in flashy clothes. Quick to temper—"

"Yes, the very one. With a tonsure of red hair fast turning white, and a face that makes me think Mr. Darwin's theories might well be correct."

"Hah!" Eben's brusque laugh baffled Anna. *Who was Mr. Darwin?*

"The man," Reverend Lyman continued, "wouldn't be leaving New York without having his bounty payment assured when he gets back to the Carolinas. He travels with a low female accomplice. And they have with them a small brown girl, two years old. …"

"I must go to Charleston." Anna stumbled over Caroline's threshold, her feet half-frozen in their old, cracked shoes. Despite the lateness of the hour, light streamed out onto the cobblestones of Lafayette Place from between maroon drapery panels.

"Charleston?" Caroline, still garbed in garnet silk, pondered the word. Then she repeated it, in a higher tone, in two distinct syllables: *Charles*-ton? She threw open the door to admit her friend, and Eben Garrett, who'd accompanied Anna through the darkened streets, materialized out of the shadows to follow her inside.

Caroline's eyes widened when she saw him. "Oh!"

"Charmed," the journalist drawled, his eyes fixed on her: the dark curling hair, the slim form, the bright, jewel-like dress.

If Anna had not been so intent on her mission, she would have seen—or, perhaps, *felt*—Caroline's quickening of interest. But she was shivering so hard after their long trek from the Five Points that she'd scarcely been able to pull the doorbell, let along decipher the nuances of her friend's attention.

And, besides, she hadn't traversed the deep-night city streets in the interests simply of making introductions.

In the small parlor a coal stove radiated steady heat. An oval table in the center of the room held a lamp with a perforated porcelain screen casting images of the constellations upon the walls. Anna tossed her dark-blue *paletot* onto a rosewood table and pulled a plum-colored slipper chair as close to the stove as she could without scorching her hem. Eben perched, large and awkward, on the edge of a saffron-colored divan. "Caroline, this is Eben Garrett," she announced, in a perfunctory manner, the niceties forgotten.

"Ah," Caroline mused, studying him openly, "so *this* is the gentleman who sent me his greeting from Buttercake John's?"

Before Eben could reply, Anna deflected further introduction, beginning an impassioned account of the Reverend Lyman's story about the slave-catcher and the little dark-skinned girl. "So, you see, Caro, I must go to Charleston at once—before that brute sells the child. And, you being so well-traveled, I'm here to ask your advice about planning my trip."

Caroline stared at her in a mixture of horror and awe. "Charleston? By yourself? But you can't!" Eben forgotten, she jumped up and began prowling the cozy room back and forth. "I know that wicked city, and I would no more let an innocent like you loose there than I would ... put a kitten in the dog pound."

Eben's gaze followed Caroline as she moved, as if he were a python hypnotized by a snake-charmer. "Hah!" His laugh caught both women's attention. He shook his head. "Sorry, but that was just such an apt analogy."

Anna scowled at him. "Don't worry about me, Mr. Garrett. I managed Calcutta—I can certainly handle Charleston."

Caro stopped in front of Anna, placing both hands on her friend's upper arms. "I'm not making myself clear, Anna. What I meant to say is that you'll have more than my *advice*. You'll have my company."

She jumped up from her seat by the stove, cold feet forgotten. "Oh, would you come? *Would* you? I'd be so grateful."

"We'll go by ship," Caroline said, already busy with plans. "It's better than that filthy railroad."

Eben Garrett frowned at them, abruptly holding up a hand. His tone was admonitory as he said, "Ladies—"

"What?" Caroline rounded on him sharply. "You think we shouldn't go? You think we're not up to it?" Her voice was turning to acid. "You think—"

He allowed his hand to drop lightly on her forearm. "I think—if you go, you'd better leave at once."

She shook his hand off. "Why's that? Hurricane weather? You think because we're women, we're afraid of a storm or two?"

Anna's head was whipping from one to the other.

Eben laughed heartily. "God, no, lady! I can't imagine you being afraid of anything—not even a tiger in the jungle! But what I *am* thinking about is the election. If Lincoln wins—and he will, mark my words—there's no telling what will happen in Charleston. They *will* secede! We don't know when, but they've promised. It's not just braggadocio. A couple of Yankees in their midst could become the enemy pretty damn quick. You might not have such an easy time getting out of town."

Caroline looked at him soberly. She took a deep breath. "You're right, of course, Mr. Garrett. When is Election Day?"

"November 7."

She turned to Anna. "Leave everything to me. We'll embark with the next direct sailing. I think we can safely give ourselves two weeks in Charleston. Then out before the end of October. What do you say?"

"Oh, Caro, how can I thank you?"

"You can thank me by saying absolutely nothing to anyone here in the city about our plans. As you know, many Manhattanites openly advocate support for the South."

"Oh!" Anna was not shocked. She'd simply found it convenient to forget that much of the city's wealth came from trade with the southern states.

"Oh, *yes*. Haven't you been paying attention? Even as we speak, slave ships are fitted up in, and set out from, New York harbors, to the profit of ship owners, bankers, insurers and other upright, church-going men. Our manufacturers spin cheap Southern cotton on their looms. Our merchants sell inexpensive fabrics in their shops. Our bakers buy cheap Cuban sugar for their cakes. Our—" She plopped onto an ottoman, skirts flying. "Oh, I am so in need of doing something against slavery! This will be a small step—to rescue one child. And it will be such an adventure!"

Anna didn't notice Eben's stillness, his fascination, but Caroline did, and she narrowed her eyes in his direction. "And, Mr. Garrett," she said, smiling, "I will be at home tomorrow afternoon at two. If you care to call, you will most likely find yourself quite welcome."

The following day, Anna went one last time before the voyage to retrieve her mail from the Central Post Office. In her box in the lobby she found an envelope engraved with the return address of the *New York Ledger*. It contained a check signed by the editor, Mr. Bonner, for a poem she'd sent him. Twenty dollars. It would be her last income until she returned to New York, and the last payment for her poems until more money started coming in from Larkin & Bierce's sales of the books. She'd suggested to Eben that he wait for her return from Charleston before he approached the publisher. As always the thought of Mr. Larkin made her feel a bit queasy, as if she'd eaten a rotten egg—raw. She hadn't yet cashed the Godey's check, which was now sequestered in the false bottom of her new oak travel desk. That, too, could wait until she returned to New York.

At the wide marble counter Anna purchased postage stamps. "Is there anything in General Delivery for me today, Mr. Bartleby?" She always asked, just in case; occasionally editors made their first contact by writing to her in care of the city Post Office. The pale-haired clerk checked the alphabetized cubicles, bending with stiff knees to the W's. "No," he said, from his crouching position. "Nothing at all for you, today, Mrs. Wheeler."

But if Anna Wheeler had thought to ask for mail under her married name of Mrs. Anna Roundtree, this is what she would have found waiting:

Calcutta
22 September 1858

Mrs. Anna Roundtree
General Delivery
New-York City, United States of America

Dear Mrs. Roundtree,

My lady, where are you? I should not have allowed you to travel alone—you were not well. The fear torments me—once you returned to America did you succumb to mortal illness? Who would know to tell me?

In that one all-too-brusque letter you sent, you did not say if you would be well and prosper. You did not say if you remember me with any of the respectful affection I bring to the memory of you. You did not say if you would wish to see me again

If you by any fate or fortune receive this letter, please—oh, please—allay my fears.

Your friend,
Ashok Montgomery

Post Scriptum: You did not say if you would stay in New-York. I write to you in care of the city postal service there, as previous communication has been returned by the Foreign Mission Society, who informed me that you had perished with the rest at Cawnpore, which I knew not to be true.

Hold for Caller
General Delivery
New-York Central Post Office
Nassau Street

Once back on Broadway, she pulled her skirts around her, raised them to her ankles for freedom of movement, and followed a surge of pedestrians into a breech in the traffic, crossing with no more incident than an unpleasant jostling by a pink sow with two half-grown piglets. It was suppertime and the sun was declining in the west. Despite the crowds, the city had an air of momentary quiet. Broadway dandies and fashionable ladies had retired to dress for dinner, giving way to tired laborers hastening home to humbler repasts.

Then she heard a newsboy cry, *Trouble in the South*! The headline—*South Carolinians Increase Agitation for Independent Confederation of States*—struck her with a sudden chill. In departing for Charleston now, did she and Caroline sail directly into peril equivalent to India's Great Mutiny of 1857? Everywhere Anna turned, would rebellion and violence be close to hand? This nation would never let its southern states withdraw from the Union, would it? Not without war. Would there be bloody insurrection in America as there had been in the Indian provinces? Did strife and violence and, yes, further bloodshed lie ahead for her? Here in the land of her birth, the land where she intended to raise her child, the land of the free?

THIRTY-FOUR

The buildings on the stretch of Broadway the returned missionary walked were high and ornate, painted everywhere with business signs, testimony to the deity of Commerce that seemed to have successfully proselytized the entire city since his previous sojourn here: *Hatter*; *Looking Glasses*; *Imported Laces*; *Tobacconist*.

A sooty drizzle hung in the air. He pushed his way past well-dressed shoppers under their black umbrellas, a pack of dogs rooting in a barrel of restaurant refuse, and a newsboy whistling some godless Negro melody. Here was Appleton's magnificent bookstore, new to this neighborhood since his last residence in the city, the building four stories tall and fashioned with marble columns like a temple. A temple of learning, he trusted, rather than yet another temple of Mammon.

Always a bookish man, he succumbed to the temptation. The window displayed light literature, he saw with disgust, the class of novels that fed into the morbid appetites and sickly sentiments of fashionable readers: heart-rending separations, improbable coincidences, sudden reversals of fortune. But surely Appleton's carried more substantial reading material, as well, volumes of sermons and theological expositions. Perhaps, he thought with an intensified interest, they also sold memoirs of missionary life. He had not yet heard from Larkin & Bierce about publishing his recollections and was suddenly curious to see how many narratives of missionary life were already on the shelves. Bounding up the bookstore steps, he entered open doors.

Although outside it was foggy and cold, here all was warmth and light, the gas jets flaring, an unseen furnace churning out an almost excessive heat. Searching the bookshelves, he found many memoirs of mission workers: from Burma, China, the Indian Territories of America, and, of course, several from East India. As he took from the shelf a volume by the sainted Adoniram Judson, a clerk brushed past him with a stack of books piled high in his arms. Their uniform bright covers attested that they were fresh from the printer. The bookseller began to lay them in attractive stacks on a nearby table.

The browser's eye brushed casually over the new books: *Poems: Sacred and Sentimental*, by Anna Wheeler. *Anna Wheeler*, his late, sainted wife's maiden name—such a coincidence! Intrigued, he set down the memoir and picked up one of the volumes of verse. Dear Anna had always been fond of poetry; sharing a name, however common, with a published poet would have pleased her. He opened the book of poems: Larkin & Bierce, Publishers. Hmm. Would the verse they published live up to their credo, Publishers of Moral Literature for the People? He began to read.

After the third poem set in the torrid climes of India—the overlush blooms of the temple tree; the *nautch* girls dancing, with their lewd braceleted ankles—his gaze removed from the page and settled upon some distant nowhere only he could see. When five minutes had passed—or was it half an hour?—his mind returned him from a whirlwind of appalled speculation back to the present moment and the present place: Appleton's Bookshop, New York City, in the autumn of the year of our Lord eighteen hundred and sixty.

This could be no coincidence. Only his wife could bear both this name and the oriental knowledge revealed in these verses.

My God, he thought, can it be? *She must be still alive.*

He kept to his room for several days in a species of wonderment, stunned by the revelation that his wife had survived the bloody killing fields of Indian rebellion. Praise the Good Lord who had protected them both from being cut down at the hands of murderous heathens! The missionary's own tribulations, Providence willing, would soon be published widely, for the edification of the people of this nation. But what was

Anna's story? What wondrous deliverance had God devised for poor, helpless Anna? Anna who had so relied on he, himself, for guidance and direction? Anna's tale, he was certain, would be one of meek piety and prayer, she having fallen in, most likely, providentially, with stronger Christian brothers and sisters who had led the way to delivery.

But how was he to find her? Reluctant to approach the Messrs. Larkin and Bierce in search of her address, lest they find his tale unsettling and hesitate to acquire his memoirs, he thought instead about the Ladies of the Mission who had supported his foreign endeavors so very generously. Leaving the boarding house, he set his course for the Five Points. At Park Street he turned up the front walk to the Five Points Mission. He could do worse than nurture a connection with Mrs. Margaret Ambrose and Miss Susan Parker, as intimates, of course, in the family of the Lord.

And these dear Sisters-in-Christ would know all the members of God's flock in this urban pasture. They would surely be acquainted with Anna. Astonished to find him alive, they would welcome him with all due Christian effusion and would be eager to direct him to the domicile of his dear, meek, trusting wife.

THIRTY-FIVE

Anna's first ocean voyage—to India with Josiah—had been an adventure. The person she had been, the woman who had given her heart into her husband's hands, numb and obedient, was no more. Now Anna's heart was a different organ, its pulses deep, angry and determined. If this girl kidnapped to Charleston was indeed her daughter, she felt powerfully as if she would die—even kill—before she let her child be sold into slavery. No, this voyage to slave country was no adventure—it was a sacred quest.

When Anna had last taken ship, homebound from India, her cabin was nothing more than a small closet with a cramped crib of a bed and a porthole no bigger than her face. For this voyage to the South, Caroline had booked them a spacious stateroom with wide windows near the stern of the ship. Now, from the stateroom's divan as she waited for the ship to put out to sea, Anna had a prime view of the filthy water around the East River docks, which swam with broken hogsheads and barrel slats. The docks themselves were in a great hullaballoo. Shouting cartmen and porters shifted mountains of chests, boxes, and portmanteaux. Hens and turkeys squawked as they were loaded aboard in crates. The ship bobbed and swayed.

Caroline appeared suddenly in the cabin doorway. She held a straw leghorn hat in one hand, and a newspaper in the other. Her face was flushed.

"Did you tear yourself away from Mr. Garrett in time for him to disembark?" Anna teased. Since she'd met the handsome journalist a week earlier, Caroline had spent every spare moment of time with him.

But the younger woman didn't respond. Instead, she threw herself down on the broad divan, waving the paper at her friend. "Oh, Anna, we must be mad to go to Charleston right now. Election fervor is so high down there—Eben says the city is a nest of secessionist firebrands."

The mournful horn sounded for departure. The ship creaked and groaned as the anchor was hauled in. Reaching for the newspaper, Anna scanned the pages. "'*Lincoln's party*,'" she read, quoting a reprinted editorial from a Charleston paper, "'*is a sectional, Anti-Slavery organization based on hostility to the institutions of the South. Men of the South! will you suffer that yoke to be fastened upon your necks and still claim to be men and freemen?*'

"Those politicians!" she continued, glancing up at Caroline. "They don't understand the bloody consequences fighting words can have." Then the ship lurched and jolted away from the dock. Anna, jolted along with it, knew all too well the passions and consequences of rebellion; in India she'd had bloody insurrection tattooed on her very soul. After a long moment, she continued, "It will end in bullets and swords, no doubt. In blood running like a river. In bodies being torn apart by dogs."

She rose from her chair and looked out the broad window at the distance beginning to widen, pale-green, between them and the tall, familiar wood and brick mercantile buildings of Manhattan's downtown. "This is not a safe venture."

"No, it's not," Caroline agreed, running the red and black silk of her shawl's fringe through nervous fingers. "Are you frightened?"

Anna turned back to her friend. It was the first time she'd heard doubt in Caroline's voice. "Of course I am. Are you?"

She shrugged. "It doesn't matter. Our plans are made, and the ship is under sail. No turning back now." The wealthy and fashionable Miss Slade and her meek companion, Miss Wheeler, were to arrive at Charleston in the grand manner, set up at the best hotel, court slaveholders until Caroline was invited to their homes. Once there, they were to watch and listen and wait. Help would come from an unexpected quarter.

Miss Angelina Grimke, a self-exiled native of Charleston, and one of Caroline's vast acquaintance among abolitionists, had arranged for that help.

"Miss Grimke says that, as Northerners, we will be under constant surveillance, even now on board ship." Caroline arose and began to pace the stateroom, skirts swishing. "Let's go up on deck and practice playing our parts as Southern sympathizers. If we don't get that right, we place our lives in jeopardy.

"And for God's sake, Anna, take off that superb shawl! You're supposed to be my paid companion—you can't flaunt yourself around our enemies in priceless Asian fabrics!"

Before dinner, the two women strolled the wide deck wrapped lightly against the breeze of the coming night, Anna wearing a plain blue mantle. With steam in the engines and wind in the sails, the vessel settled into a steady hum and began to pick up speed. A well-dressed couple approached them, shadowed by a Negro serving maid. The lady, wearing a rich plum silk gown studied them with narrowed eyes, then smiled, reassured by Caroline's regal bearing and peacock-blue Worth dinner gown. The gentleman swept off his wide planter's hat and gave the deep bow of the cavalier. Caroline returned the smile. Anna cast her gaze downward, as was proper to her position. They passed an elderly man in a white linen coat, who stood at the rail smoking a thick Cuban cigar, half obscured in a cloud of odiferous haze. Caroline lowered her voice, and said, "As you see, even now we're in the company of our Southern cousins."

Eventually, they settled at the far rail of the afterdeck, watching the wake behind the ship spill over in a continuous froth of white foam.

After some contemplation, Anna said, "Caroline, this trip is a quixotic venture on your part. For me, the reason for venturing into slave country is clear. But you go into danger with nothing personal at stake."

Caroline abruptly switched her gaze from the water to Anna. She spoke sharply. "Oh, I would say I have something personal at stake—blood guilt, if nothing else." Anna winced at the fierceness of her words. Her friend paused for a moment, adjusting one of the ivory combs holding back her dark hair, crisp and curly in the sea-damp air. Then she shrugged and placed a gloved hand on Anna's arm in apology. "And, besides, life holds worse dangers than going unprotected into slave territory." Her mouth pursed. "For instance, I'm genuinely terrified of suffocating to death in the cotton batting of polite society."

Anna laughed, thinking of Eben Garrett. "No danger of that, I fear."

That night, after the chambermaid had turned down their beds, unlaced their corsets, and departed, Caroline returned to the subject of Miss Grimke. "Fortunately," Caroline continued, "Angelina has given me more than warnings about the dangers of Charleston. Today, as we said our goodbyes at the dock, she also gave me the name of someone who knows everything that happens in all communities of the city. Someone who's committed to liberating slaves."

"Who?" Anna ran the ivory hairbrush she'd brought from Calcutta through her waist-length hair. "Tell me."

But Caroline went on without answering. "Angelina said if your daughter is indeed in Charleston, this woman can find her. She has helped many on their way to freedom. So trusted and well-placed is she in that city, that no one ever suspects her. If that Skaggs beast has brought the girl there, Angelina says, her confidante will secure the child for us."

Anna jumped up from the dressing table, and the hairbrush fell to the polished floor with a loud clunk. "Who *is* this woman?"

"Oh, didn't I say?" Caroline slipped under the bed's silk and down coverlet, snuggling in for the night. "She's a slave in the household of one of the wealthiest plantation holders in the Carolinas. Her name is Mammy Lydia."

Once in the sitting room of their suite in the Charleston Hotel, Caroline pulled off her gloves and threw her shawl over the back of the silk-upholstered divan. She wore a smart straw chapeau with three long blue feathers drooping languidly down the back. Plucking out hatpins, she tossed the delicate hat onto a rosewood table. "Well, Anna, what do you think so far of our reception in Charleston?"

Anna placed her bonnet next to Caroline's hat. "As soon as you told the manager you wished to hire the hotel's premiere suite whatever the cost, one might have thought you were Queen Victoria, herself."

Her friend's laugh rang out. "Yes, that caused quite a flurry. Word will soon be out all over the city that Miss Slade, the well-traveled cosmopolitan, spares no expense in securing what she wants. And the letter of introduction from Miss Harriet Lane won't hurt."

Anna shifted on the sofa—a new corset was pinching her ribs. "Why Miss Lane, of all ladies? You know other, more socially prominent, women."

Caroline threw herself on the divan. "As President James Buchanan's niece, she's the White House's First Lady. Many Charlestonians hope President Buchanan can still be encouraged to annex Cuba as slave territory. So—"

A knock on the door, and a dark man in hotel livery entered with a refreshment tray. As he arranged peaches in a bowl, then poured minted tea into crystal tumblers over shards of ice, the women chatted idly about Charleston's beauty.

When he'd left, Caroline's generous tip in his pocket, she continued, "The ladies of the city will be most gracious to the wealthy Miss Slade, if only to see which of the latest European fashions she's wearing, the gentlemen will be courtly and hospitable, trusting that she has influence with her great friend, Miss Lane. We'll be invited everywhere. But, what we need most, Angelina told me, is an invitation to the Vaughn household on Colleton Square. That's where we'll find Mammy Lydia."

THIRTY-SIX

Charleston reminded Anna of Calcutta: intense, steamy heat; dark people in fantastic garb; the mingled scents of mud, salt air, rich blossoms, and exotic spices, all overlain with the stench of human and animal waste. She found herself fascinated by the black and brown people in the streets: the men, strong and well-muscled, working as blacksmiths, iron mongers, carpenters, shipbuilders; the women, fish and vegetable vendors in bright-colored head clothes, singing out their morning wares in long-drawn melodic calls. And the children, the children were everywhere. Anna couldn't keep her eyes off them. She fingered the gold-framed daguerreotype in her reticule. If India Elizabeth were indeed in Charleston, she would someday be on the street—like this curly-headed child in the homespun shift offering melon slices to passers-by from her woven-grass tray, like this older girl of perhaps ten balancing a basket of sweet potatoes on her head.

"The children appear well-fed and decently clothed." She and Caroline were being served oranges and iced milk in a public garden. Although they were seated in the shade of a flourishing live oak, Anna felt herself to be covered with perspiration.

"Valuable property, well maintained," Caroline replied. "We are not seeing the worst of it."

"The worst of Charleston?"

"The worst of *slavery*. In the cities slaves are somewhat protected by the closeness of the houses—no one wants the reputation of abusing his people. But out on those plantations, with no neighbors watching … We cannot imagine." She sipped her milk, then leaned over the table to speak even more confidentially. "But there *is* a darker side to this city, and we will find it. When we return North, we can testify first-hand to anyone who still has doubts about the true nature of slavery."

"What do you have in mind?" October, and it was still high summer. Anna brushed the thin film of perspiration from her upper lip. Her fingertips smelled of oranges.

"We'll begin by taking a walking tour of the city. We'll stroll at a leisurely pace, without a guide, of course, because he would merely show us the pleasant areas. We are two ladies on our own. We will lose our way. All innocently we will turn down the wrong street, or the wrong lane, or the wrong alley, and …"

"And, we will see what we will see," Anna concluded.

As it turned out, they didn't have to go off the beaten path. Passing down Chalmers Street in the very heart of the city, they found themselves facing a flourishing slave market under a long, low shed at the rear of a four-story brick double tenement building. Forty or so Negroes awaited sale there, some huddled together in the shade, some pacing back and forth. One thin young man particularly caught Anna's eye, his back festering with dozens of unhealed welts from a severe flogging. She recoiled from the scene, her instinct causing her to turn away. Caroline placed a hand on her arm. They came to a full halt near a large rice warehouse. Their faces already shaded by parasols, Anna and Caroline sequestered themselves in the deep shadow of the building. No other ladies were present.

One small boy about five years old had attached himself to the slave keeper, clutching the man's dirty homespun coat and following him down the line of slaves on exhibit, from one to the next. He was sold first. "A tolerable likely lad, sold only because his mammy run away and left him behind. He's a good boy. Obedient. Never been whipped. Look him over, gentlemen. Your full black African, but bright as can be. Now, I paid six hundred dollars for this prime boy and ask six-fifty to start. Six-fifty? Who's got six-fifty? Over there, the gentleman with the white hat. Now, I want seven hundred. Who's got seven hundred?" The boy went for seven hundred and fifty dollars to a distinguished-looking gray-haired man leaning against a maroon cabriolet.

A young girl was offered next. There was a general murmuring and shuffling of feet when she was led to the block. Her complexion was so light she would have passed without remark on the streets of Manhattan. Her hair was a lustrous brown and hung in neat curls. She was respectably clothed in a cream-colored muslin gown with a white neck cloth.

"All right, gentlemen, what am I bid for this likely girl? Brought up in all respects like a lady. Sold for no fault of her own, only for her master's want of money. She can embroider, play piano, dance a quadrille as nice as you please."

He ran his eyes around the crowd and, seeing, as he thought, no ladies present, raised one bushy eyebrow and got to the point. "Now, gentlemen, this here is extra-handsome goods, and I expect to get an extra-handsome price for her. You ain't gonna find many such prime fancy pieces this side of New Orleans. Show your neck, Jenny," he ordered, pulling off the fine linen handkerchief that covered the shoulders of her dress. The girl was trembling. He pulled open the drawstring and yanked down her bodice, cupping one small breast in his hand.

Anna ceased breathing. She could feel Caroline go rigid. The terrified Jenny began to sob. The auctioneer gave the girl a shake. "Don't take on so, girl. Everyone's gonna be real nice to you. Now, gentlemen, ain't that as sweet a bust as you have ever seen? No surplus flesh. …" He ran his other hand down the girl's body, letting it linger briefly at her private areas. The girl let out a wail. "Firm as a ripe peach. And I mean all the way, gentlemen. Fourteen years old, and I've got a doctor's certificate saying she ain't never been touched. How much am I bid, gentlemen?"

Anna lunged forward, her instinct to put a halt to the wickedness perpetrated upon this helpless child. Caroline gripped her hand tightly and cast her an admonitory glare: *We can do nothing here.*

A fat man spat his tobacco wad into the dust and bid eight hundred dollars. An elderly man with a bone-pale complexion and the countenance of a white-haired Biblical patriarch, accompanied by a short, burly, red-headed fellow wearing a bright green coat over a check waistcoat, came up to the platform and looked the girl over more closely.

He queried his flashy companion, grunted, opened the girl's mouth and examined her teeth. He ran his hands over her body. He took his time. "Fifteen hundred dollars," he said at last.

"Sold," grunted the auctioneer.

A hoot went up from somewhere in the small crowd of slave-buyers. The new owner's expression remained impassive. He and his advisor entered the imposing arched door of the slave mart to take care of the paper work that would make him Jenny's master.

On the journey to Charleston Anna had been concerned only with her own child's fate, but the living presence of the sons and daughters, mothers and fathers, she saw here today abruptly expanded her sympathies. She felt as if a blindfold had been let drop from her eyes. From now on she, like Caroline, would actively oppose this godless system of slavery, even if it meant breaking every single law of the land.

Anna was shaking. She pulled Caroline away down an alley. "And this," she hissed, when they had emerged onto Queen Street, "is what they call a Christian land."

THIRTY-SEVEN

Caroline's letters of introduction opened the right door. It wasn't long before an invitation was offered to the Vaughan's home. In Colleton Square a double flight of stone steps led up to the wide flagstone porch and massive mahogany front doors of the large, airy house where they were greeted by a liveried butler. Edwin and Isabel Vaughan met them in the spacious drawing room on the second floor. Mr. Vaughan, an urbane and gentlemanly planter impeccably garbed in a white frock coat and embroidered vest, was in his late thirties and handsome in the English manner, fair-haired and fine-featured, with a pronounced widow's peak, bright blue eyes under bushy eyebrows, and a neatly cropped goatee. Isabel Vaughan was slight and twittery, dressed in light-green striped muslin with three tiers of ruffles to the wide skirt. A discreet application of pearl-powder had turned her pasty complexion soft and velvety, so she was the only person at dinner whose brow was not coated with a thin sheen of perspiration.

Regaling them with her wit and elegance, Caroline charmed the Vaughans and their dinner guests with stories of European travels and accounts of conversations with celebrated writers. Anna, in her role as lady's companion, was silent and observant. A footman in dark-green livery kept the glasses filled with wine from the crystal decanters on the sideboard. Gray-clad slaves served the courses. Two dark-complexioned girls of eight or nine years, neatly clad in white cotton, waved long-handled fans of peacock feathers to keep the flies from the dinner table. The servants moved about the room, removing plates and filling glasses, as silent, omnipresent, and unremarked as the very paper upon the walls.

"Miss Slade, am I to understand that you are a close acquaintance of President Buchanan's niece, Miss Harriet Lane?" Edwin Vaughan asked. They had reached the final courses of cakes and fruit.

"Why, yes. I have known Miss Lane since our years together at school."

Anna knew that Caroline had never darkened the door of anything as plebian as a school.

But Mr. Vaughan was too single-minded to question anything. "I ask, because I presume to hope that you might use your influence with Miss Lane in the interests of a passionate and righteous cause of mine. Now, it may be too late, since the election is fast upon us, but do ask her to remind her uncle that he owes his Presidency to support from the South, having several years ago drafted the initial manifesto to annex Cuba as slaveholding territory. He now seems to have forgotten us in favor of those fanatical Free-Soilers and abolitionists. I implore you—suggest to Miss Lane that her uncle yet has time to influence the annexation of Cuba, which, as a slaveholding state, would more than balance out the tragedy of Kansas having gone free-soil."

Caroline allowed her expression to sober as she developed her role of Southern sympathizer. "Certainly I will plead your cause with dear Harriet." She accepted a small cake from a silver basket proffered by one of the women. "Clearly," she went on, "the robust economy and civilized culture of the South are dependent upon the system of benevolent slavery." She nibbled an edge of the little cake. "And—I must say that during my sojourn here I have seen nothing to convince me that the Negro race would survive without the benevolent oversight of its white masters."

Anna admired Caroline's skill at mimicking the half-regretful manner with which these enslavers of human beings spoke about their burdens as "protectors of the colored folk."

Coffee in a porcelain cup appeared at Anna's place. The serving woman offered sugar from silver tongs. Her fingers were long, tan and slender. The cuff of her sleeve was white and crisp.

Edward Vaughan pressed the damask napkin to his lips, then he sat back in his broad-armed chair. "Few of your Northern compatriots are open to the Southern way of life, dear lady. Without the peculiar institution of slavery, both white and black would perish in this place. For the white man, the climate renders excess of any kind dangerous. Why, in the full heat of the dog days, a night spent on the rice plantation would mean certain death to me. But the Negro is born acclimated to the heat. He suffers nothing."

"Further," interjected the Reverend Pringle, seated next to Anna, "slavery is a mercy granted to the African by a benevolent God, a moral system designed for the protection and Christianization of a primitive people." The serving woman appeared at his shoulder with the sugar dish and tongs. He held up three fingers. *Father, Son and Holy Ghost*, Anna thought irreverently. The woman added three sugar lumps to his cup.

"It cannot be easy for you," Caroline said, her open, concerned glance sweeping the table. Her voice was low and feminine, her tone compassionate.

Edwin Vaughan nodded. "Dear lady," he said, "you have no idea what a heavy obligation the good Lord has placed upon the slaveholder's shoulders. It is only the protection of the master that keeps the darky happy and productive. Take Suzy here," he gestured at the younger of the two serving women, a slight girl with a freckled complexion. She was wiping a china cup with a white linen cloth. "She is happy with us. Are you not, Suzy?"

"Yes, Massa, ver happy." She poured coffee with a steady hand.

Her master sipped the fragrant brew. "You see. She has our lifelong care and protection. If she were free, she would not be so well off. Would you, Suzy?"

"No, sir, Massa." She poured another cup.

Caroline's voice had softened almost imperceptibly in converse with their hosts; her vowels had broadened. "I can tell by the obvious contentment of your servants," she continued, "that this magnificent home of yours (*yo-ah's*) is run not only efficiently, but compassionately as well. I should like to witness how all is managed." Her eyes widened as she turned her admiring gaze to Isabel Vaughan. "Is it not a most trying occupation for a lady, running such a distinguished home?" What they wanted was an invitation to tour the entire Vaughan establishment, including the slave quarters, in hopes of making connection with Mammy Lydia.

The mistress of the house lowered her gaze modestly. "I do my best to care for my people in sympathy and kindness."

A tinkling crash was heard near the sideboard. The young serving woman stared at the shattered remains of a porcelain cup on the polished floor.

"Suzy," Mrs. Vaughan couldn't keep a brittle edge out of her voice. "That was the Limoges."

Suzy's complexion had turned ashen. "I's sorry, Missus. It jes' jump out of my hands."

Isobel Vaughan scowled, her fine brows contracting, her tightened lips opening in preparation for a stronger reprimand, but an admonitory glance from her husband kept her silent. It was the first unharmonious moment of this visit to the Vaughan household.

Anna watched Suzy as she swept up the porcelain shards and carried them off. The girl's hands were shaking.

The master of the house touched Caroline's arm lightly. "And, so, Miss Slade," he said, in a jovial tone, "truly, you wish to see the workings of the Southern home? While we gentlemen enjoy some fine Havana cigars, I'm certain Mrs. Vaughan will be happy to show you through our humble abode."

"She look jes' like her mammy, that Rosetta," a low voice spoke in Anna's ear, "only whiter." The last words were freighted with meaning.

Anna turned. A spare Negro woman with piercing eyes and a long nose stood right behind her in the doorway of the nursery. "Are you Mammy Lydia?" Anna asked.

Mrs. Vaughan's tour had taken them through both the public and the private rooms: the vaulted drawing room with its beautiful Axminster carpet; the comfortable and well-stocked library. Upstairs they saw the bedchambers still furnished for the warm months with Japanese matting, chintz counterpanes, and light net curtains. Pink and yellow roses in glass bowls graced every polished surface.

In the hallway, a chambermaid with an armful of folded baby linen stood back against the wall as they passed. Two small slave boys accompanied her, one carrying a basket of oranges and bananas, the other a bowl of sugared pecans.

"Oh, might we visit the nursery?" Caroline enthused. "I am so anxious to make the acquaintance of your precious children."

The Vaughan children were indeed "precious." Two pink-cheeked girls wore satin-sashed dresses, and satin ribbons graced the curls that clustered around their seraphic faces. In the airy nursery Caroline went into paroxysms of admiration, cuddling the pretty girls, peeling oranges for them, teasing them with pecan confections. When a wail from the nursing baby in the adjacent chamber took Isabel momentarily from the room, Caroline trailed after her hostess.

But Anna—Anna stood transfixed by the sight of a small dark child sitting alone in a corner of the nursery, lining up a half-dozen wooden farmyard animals with great concentration.

It was then that she heard the dark woman's voice.

"Yes, I be Lydia," she answered Anna's question. Mammy Lydia wore a white linen head cloth and a well-washed blue muslin dress, and she bore an air of great knowing. Anna didn't doubt for a moment that, through some intricate network of Miss Grimke's acquaintances, Lydia was fully informed of exactly who she and Caroline were and what they had come to Charleston for.

"Miz Wheeler," Lydia whispered, "Miss 'Lina tole me you be concerned about a girl stole from New York by slavers."

Anna nodded, staring at the child in front of her. She was little more than two years old, with a bronzed complexion and unruly dark curls pulled back from a pronounced widow's peak. Could she be India Elizabeth? But ... Anna took a closer look; something told her ... maybe not.

"I won't be foolin' you none," Lydia said. "This girl here ain't who you be lookin' for."

"What?" Anna hadn't realized she was holding her breath until she exhaled sharply and sank down onto a green satin slipper chair, still entranced by the tot in front of her.

"No. An' after I get Miss Lina's message, I look everywhere in the city. I don't believe your little gal come here."

"But—"

Lydia held up a slim hand. "Now, listen to me quick—Mis'ress be right back. This girl be Rosetta Burden, and I be thinking that the best thing for her, poor child, be you take her back North. So she don't go the way of her momma." Lydia coughed. "She be too young yet, but won' be long 'fore Massa after her, too, she such a pretty little thing."

"Oh," Anna breathed, shifting from the low chair to her knees beside the child. "She's beautiful."

Lydia cleared her throat.

Anna paid no attention, reaching out a tentative hand to stroke the dark girl's silky head.

Isabel Vaughan's voice suddenly grated in Anna's ear. "She doesn't look as much like a monkey as do the other pickaninnies." There was a twist of emotion in her words difficult to identify.

Anna started, angered by the crude image. Mammy Lydia vanished into the adjacent room where a wet nurse fed the Vaughan infant.

Isobel went on, oblivious. "This little minx is called Rosie. Believe it or not," she said, turning to Caroline, who'd come up behind her, "she was born in your city. One of our best girls, inflamed by some meddling abolitionist, ran away, even though she was ... in an interesting condition." Her tone was again ambiguous. "They're like children you know, the darkies. They'll believe anything anyone tells them. Eventually we traced Mandy to New York, and Mr. Vaughan ... sent someone after her." The twist of emotion intensified; she seemed aggrieved, perhaps bitter. "For her own good, you know. Her family has been with us for three generations. We feel a responsibility."

"Of course," Caroline assured her. "Of course."

Isobel babbled on. "The girl was simply not equipped for independent life, as the slave hunter learned when he found her on her deathbed in a low house in the worst quarter of your city." Isobel Vaughan shrugged vaguely. "So he brought little Rosie home with him. She sleeps with Mammy." The slave mistress indicated a pallet on the floor by the door to the sleeping chamber.

Caroline didn't look at Anna, but they were both galvanized by this information. That "someone" Mr. Vaughan had sent to New York was most likely the notorious slave catcher, Cracker Skaggs. *This* was the girl he'd abducted

Anna studied the beautiful child again. The tight, unruly curls, the golden skin, the bright blue eyes. Blue eyes! Indeed, she looked nothing like Ashok, and so very much like Mr. Vaughan.

They had followed the wrong child.

THIRTY-EIGHT

"She may be the girl the Skaggs brute took from New York, but she is not my daughter." The opulent hotel drawing room, twilit, now seemed filled with silence. Anna felt as if she had been bled dry, so great was the disappointment of her heart.

"No, she resembles her father quite closely," Caroline said.

"Mr. Vaughan? I thought so, too." The rich food and hot weather had caused Anna's feet to swell uncomfortably in her new calfskin shoes. She sat on the window seat and untied the laces.

There followed a moment of meditative quiet, which Caroline, standing in the tall window, toying with the drapery fringe and looking down upon picturesque Meeting Street, broke. "You say Lydia wants us to take Rosetta back to New York?" Preoccupied, she seemed to see nothing of the women in bright calico who walked side by side balancing baskets of laundered clothing upon their heads.

Anna kicked off one shoe, then the other. "It's not that she *wants* us to—she *expects* us to. I wouldn't be surprised to receive a message from her at any moment."

"Vaughn may well have fathered the girl," Caroline mused, "and she may belong to him by law, but he has no moral claim to her. He doesn't even acknowledge her."

"Nor does his wife," Caroline said. "Obviously Isabel Vaughan knows the child's paternity, and hates her. Her volatile temperament will make life in that house hell for Rosetta."

"As will her father's licentious nature. Once Rosetta is grown, she won't be safe at Colleton Square."

Caroline cringed, and an expression of utter determination crossed her face. She opened her mouth to speak.

But Anna raised a hand to stay the words. *She* would make the proposal. "We came to Charleston to restore a child to liberty—we simply didn't know that this was the one." She felt resolution strengthen her spirit. "No matter what, Caroline, we have been given this child to save, and save her we will."

"Yes!" Caroline said, nodding. "We must save Rosetta Burden." Then she gave a wry laugh. "But, how? It's one thing to conceive a rescue based on high moral principle—but it's very different to actually devise and carry out a plan. If we were in New York, I'd have people to turn to, but what can we do, here, in a strange city?

"We'll rely on Mammy Lydia—this is her territory." Anna suspected just from that one brief encounter with Lydia that she was a person who could make things happen.

She rose to gaze out the window down to the now-quiet street. Once returned to New York she would begin again her search for India Elizabeth; meanwhile she and Caroline had a child close at hand to rescue.

Suddenly she was struck with the enormity of what they were setting out to do. If caught in the North while abetting the escape of a slave, they would be fined, perhaps even imprisoned. Here in Carolina, where chattel slavery propelled the economy, a more private retribution might easily be enacted against them. In the inflamed passion of betrayal, might not Mr. Vaughan seek deadly revenge?

Nonetheless Anna was determined. "Yes," she said. "We will take Rosetta back to New York—it's the right thing to do." She gathered up her bonnet and shoes and opened the door to her bedroom. "Oh!" she exclaimed, startled. Their chambermaid, a slight girl of sixteen or so, was engaged in smoothing the wrinkles from Anna's silk evening dress, and doing so with a far more officious busy-ness than the task would seem to warrant.

"Evenin', Missus," the maid said, with an obsequious smile. "I be done directly."

Anna gasped. "Thank you, Sarah," she said, closing the door and turning back to the sitting room. She glanced at her friend. "Do you think Sarah overheard us?" she mouthed.

Caroline spread her hands and shrugged, but her expression was grave.

Lydia sought out Anna that night.

"Hsst. Hsst."

Anna was deep in a dream about returning to New York by overland stage with a multitude of errant children. It was well after midnight, and she had been asleep for hours.

"Hsst. Miz Wheeler."

Anna opened her eyes to a flickering light that played upon fantastical features, casting sharp cheek bones into high relief above shaded hollows. Large, dark eyes shone into hers with fixed purpose. Then Lydia let drop the slide on the dark-lantern.

Anna pushed herself to a seated position, abruptly awake. "Let me get Miss Slade, and we'll tell you what we intend to do."

"No!" Lydia held up a hand. "No, I be talkin' jes' to you. They ain't nothin' fine ladies *can* do. People be all the time lookin' at them." The glow of gaslight from outside the window revealed nothing more than a dark outline among the shadows. Along with her voice, a mingled scent of soap and starch, tinged with lilac, was the strongest sensory evidence of Lydia's presence. "You jes' be getting yourselves ready to sail. Real soon. I fix it. I be knowin' people. I be makin' everythin' happen." She had the air of a woman who was used to managing the affairs of others. "This what we be plannin'. We gon' have four, five runaways that day, get they slave-hunters hoppin' like someone open a sack o' baby rabbits. Rosie be jes one of many gone. Then, well, we gettin' rumors started 'bout some big ab'litionist raid 'bout to begin, and nobody goan' care about little Rosie after that. Nobody even think 'bout comin' after you."

Lydia's plan was that Anna and Caroline should book passage to New York, then let her know through Sarah, the chambermaid, the name of their ship and the sailing date. They should not attempt to get in touch with Lydia again. They would not see her or hear from her until she delivered Rosetta to them.

The moment Lydia was gone Anna woke Caroline and told her about the visitation. Indeed it had felt like a visitation. They sat awake in the chilled night air planning their small part in the rescue.

THIRTY-NINE

When Anna entered the hotel's dining salon the following morning, the commodious room was peopled largely with gentlemen breakfasting on ham and fish, sweet potatoes and hominy while reading the newspapers or conducting business affairs. The few ladies present were resident at the hotel, either accompanied by their husbands or chatting together in pairs. Slave waiters took the orders and delivered the food, carrying the heavy silver trays with an easy grace. The air smelled of coffee, chewing tobacco, and broiled trout. It was the epitome of civilization, based on the traffic in human beings, who were bought and sold in this room in the same businesslike manner as hundredweights of cotton, sugar, or rice.

While they waited for their breakfast, the women sipped coffee and perused the Charleston newspapers.

Caroline attempted to cheer Anna by reading choice tidbits to her from the paper. "You will be happy to know that ladies may now purchase nets for the hair with little tassels already affixed to the side. And that the Zouave jacket will continue to be worn by fashionable ladies this autumn."

"Hmm," said Anna, who did not know—or care—what a Zouave jacket was. Her reading was of a weightier sort. "The editors of the *Mercury*," she whispered, "openly endorse disunion. Listen, Caroline, they quote from 'The Declaration of Independence' to justify secession. First they bring up the promise of 'Life, Liberty and the pursuit of Happiness,' and then they go on to quote, 'Whenever any Form of Government becomes destructive of these ends, it is the Right of the People to alter or to abolish it, and to institute new Government.'"

Caroline, leaning over the table to hear Anna's hushed words, responded, "don't I recall some few little words in there about *all men being created equal?*"

"Of course." A waiter set the breakfast plate in front of Anna, and she took up her fork, stirring the soft-boiled egg into the rice.

"Interesting editorial strategy, I'd say. What's actually at issue is the vicious and inhumane enslavement of fellow human beings, but these fire-eating Southrons twist it so that the enslavers themselves are guaranteed the constitutional right to deprive the others of their constitutional rights. Oh, Anna, and these madmen are intent on war."

War! That word spoken in this company horrified Anna. She scanned the room to see if anyone had heard. Her gaze ended up meeting the open leer of a broad, green-coated man, who, upon meeting her eye, tipped his slouch hat at her and smirked in admiration. His hair was red. His teeth were brown from chewing tobacco. Anna dropped her eyes in seeming genteel modesty.

She'd recognized him instantly! This was the man from whom that elderly slaveholder had taken advice when purchasing the girl, Jenny, at auction. Anna was glad to have the space of half the dining salon between them; his countenance, she thought, was almost bestial.

From somewhere deep in her memory, Reverend Lyman's words echoed: "a face that makes me think Mr. Darwin's theories might well be correct." Eben Garrett had later explained what the good Reverend meant by speaking of "Mr. Darwin's theories." Could it be? Could this be … *Cracker Skaggs*! It was all she could do not to gasp aloud. Not only did he have the countenance of a brute, but, also, he gave off an aura of feral appetites. This was the bounty hunter who had brought Rosetta to Charleston!

"Ha!" Caroline said, setting down her cup with a clatter. She glanced briefly at Anna without noticing her distress. "You are in the Charleston newspaper."

Anna did gasp then. The square of maize bread she had just buttered crumbled in nerveless fingers. "How can it be? What do they say I have done?"

"Done? Why, you have written poems." She passed the large news sheet over the table. There in the left-hand column under a headline, "3 Poems by Miss Wheeler," were printed "The Cowbell," "Misty Morning," and "A Violet."

"Oh, my," Anna exclaimed. "Mr. Greeley published these verses last spring in the *Tribune*. The Charleston editors must have clipped them from the New York papers to reprint. And, look, here at the bottom they announce the book Mr. Larkin has released."

Caroline retrieved the newspaper. "'*Poems, Sacred and Sentimental*, by Miss Anna Wheeler, available now, for the Christmas trade.'

"So," she laughed, "Miss Wheeler, you are famous, printed in the southern states as well as in the North. You'll soon be in the poet's pantheon with Mr. Longfellow."

Anna demurred modestly. She read the printed poems as if they had been composed by a different person, so foreign to her now did their pretty verses seem.

When they rose to leave, Anna wished to point out to Caroline the brutish man she suspected of being Cracker Skaggs, but a white-jacketed waiter was cleaning brass ashtrays on the empty table at which the slave-hunter had sat.

During their sojourn in Charleston, Anna had written nothing except a letter to Mr. Larkin explaining that she had been called away from New York and would inform him of her return. One rainy afternoon, recalling the necessity of supporting herself, she'd taken out her lap desk, set it on a table in the window light, and prepared to write. While Caroline engrossed herself in Miss George Eliot's *Adam Bede*, Anna mixed ink from the packet of powder and sharpened the nib of her pen. Then she sat and stared at the blank page. She thought about what would sell. She thought about what editors would like. She attempted verses about oleander and bougainvillea. She attempted verses about dark women gliding along cobbled streets balancing baskets of fruit and sugarcane. All her pen could summon up, however, was the memory of a frightened young girl being offered for sale on a Charleston auction block. There was nothing in the least poetical about that image, yet she could not rid her mind of it. She wrote the tale in prose and in unsparing detail. When she had finished, she folded the sheets of paper and tucked them away in a hidden drawer of the travel desk. She could not bear to look at them again.

The Charleston Battery on Sunday afternoon was crowded with well-dressed families passing the interval between church services and dinner by strolling on the promenade. A brisk breeze blew in off the water, providing an autumn respite from the brutal heat and whipping the Union flags flying proud over Fort Sumpter. Caroline, trailed by Anna, nodded to her Charleston acquaintances, twirled her silk parasol, cooed at babies in their wicker carriages, and laughed at the antics of boys driving two-wheel goat carts in and out among the pedestrians. When Edwin and Isabel Vaughan came into view, their daughters dressed identically in a seraphic blue that intensified the color of their eyes, Caroline paused to greet them.

Anna, waiting two steps behind, as was proper, felt someone's gaze upon her. She looked up. Mammy Lydia was engaged in re-tying the older girl's satin hair-bow, but her eyes were on Anna, dark and bold and knowing. Over the child's head, she stared at Anna for a full ten seconds, an eternity for a slave to look directly upon a strange white woman. Then, as she gave a final unnecessary twist to the limp blue satin, she nodded, almost imperceptibly. Each women resumed a modest downcast gaze, but something essential had been communicated. Anna knew that all had been arranged.

At five a.m. on the day of their departure, the drum that called the slaves to work began its relentless pounding. The women were awake and dressed, ready for an early sailing. Sarah had alerted them to expect the arrival of a gentleman's carriage just past dawn. Driven by a groom in blue livery and accompanied by an ox-drawn cart, it came as the first rays of sun illuminated the east-facing roofs of the city. The baggage was loaded into the cart. Caroline and Anna were handed into the carriage.

All was done in silence. The conveyances pulled quietly away from the hotel's elegant portico. During the entire procedure the travelers saw not a single white face, except for each other's.

While the cart drove straight down Meeting Street toward the docks, the brougham made an abrupt turn onto Queen Street, then another, past a sagging gate. Here the road was marshy sand, the houses were ramshackle and small, and the air smelled of brine and sewage. The wooden shanty at which they stopped leaned forebodingly into the lane, its windows shuttered tight against the fetid atmosphere. Before the carriage had come to a complete halt, however, the door of the little house opened and Lydia was there, wearing a red calico head cloth and holding the hand of a sleepy boy in a neat blue linen suit and a small felt hat. She led him to the carriage.

"You be goin' with the nice ladies, Roe," she said. "They be good to you." The child clung to Lydia's skirt, wisps of short, dark hair escaping from the narrow-brimmed hat, big blue eyes confused and wary.

Anna took from the folds of the Kashmiri shawl she had finally dared to don as she was now leaving Charleston, a little wooden elephant she had purchased in New York. She held it out. "This is for you, Roe," she said in a soft tone. "Come and get it, sweetheart."

The child's eyes fixed on the toy, then glanced up at Lydia.

"Go with the ladies, honey," she urged. "They take the best care of you." She hugged the child and lifted him onto the seat. Roe reached for the elephant. His hat fell off. Lydia kissed the curly pate, then replaced the hat. "The Lord bless you, li'l honey," she whispered.

Roe snuggled into Anna's side, fascinated by the toy.

"I'll do my best to get word to you, Lydia," Caroline said in hushed tones. "It may take a considerable time, but, never fear, you'll hear from me." Lydia waved them off. The driver clucked to the horses, and the carriage jolted away.

Looking back in the murky light of the advancing dawn, Anna thought she saw tears run down the dark woman's cheeks.

The voyage home took three days and three nights. It was a stormy passage, and they had good reason to keep to their stateroom. Undressing Rosie for bed that first night, Anna found hanging from a woven cord around the child's neck a little drawstring bag made from a scrap of white flannel. "Caroline, look at this," she said. She could feel small objects inside the bag. Twigs? Pebbles? Bones?

"Hmm." Caroline said. "No. Leave it, Anna. Don't open it. I think it's what they call a conjure bag. 'Bama Fitch will know what to do with it."

FORTY

"Down south they call it *ju-ju*," 'Bama Fitch said, in response to Anna's question. "It's magic—to keep the child safe—or so they say." Sitting upright on an ottoman by the tall windows that looked out onto quiet Lafayette Place, 'Bama crocheted a child's pelisse in fine white silk worsted, her hook flashing back and forth with practiced speed. "But I'm an educated woman, and I don't believe in any of that nonsense." Rosie sat on the oriental carpet at 'Bama's feet, cropped hair brushed to a silky sheen and curling softly. The little girl's coffee-colored face was plump and dimpled, and her blue eyes shone like this morning's newly washed sky.

"*Ju ju* works something like a spell," Caroline added. "Objects have spiritual power—trees, stones ... bones."

"Or not." 'Bama slewed her eyes at her cousin. "It's a tradition that supposedly comes down from Africa through the ancestors. Particular objects are said to hold particular powers. Take the bag Rosie was wearing—it smells of roses—."

Caroline interrupted, "Roses mean Love. The *ju ju* was put on Rosie by someone who loves her."

"Mammy Lydia," Anna said, and glanced over at the little girl. "But, she's not wearing it now." Had 'Bama, with her modern ideas, somehow *un*blessed the child?

"I hung it over the door to her room," 'Bama said, lips twisted. "The thing should keep her as safe there as anywhere."

Rosie had made herself at home. The front drawing room was strewn with tiny camisoles and petticoats. A miniature straw bonnet decorated one of the finials of the brass fire screen as she played contentedly with an unclothed doll. She, herself, was doll-like in a short blue merino dress and kid boots. Despite the stormy weather since their return from Charleston, someone, most certainly 'Bama, had managed to get to the shops and outfit her.

At first 'Bama's ease in the drawing room had surprised Anna, who had previously known her only as housekeeper, but *servant* must simply be the role Caroline's cousin played when admitting people other than intimates to their home. Now Anna studied the slender, serious woman who wore a nicely made gray wool dress with fashionable black satin piping at the collar and cuffs. She and Caroline seemed at home together, cousins indeed—including the squabbles. Caroline, of course, had inherited the family name and the money, as well as the privileges of the white race. Where did that leave 'Bama? While Caroline lounged on the divan, plucking hothouse grapes from a bunch in a cut-glass bowl, 'Bama's eyes were on her work, her quick hands moving back and forth in the window light as the small crocheted garment grew. Rosetta bounced back and forth between the two women, as if she had two new mothers.

"So," Caroline said, "as you see, we are quite the little family here." She reached out to Rosetta and fussed with the blue satin bow of her sash. She smoothed the unruly curls. She took the girl's chin in her hand and studied her face. Then she rose, released the child, shaking the wrinkles from her own wool-grenadine skirts, moved to the window overlooking the street, and held aside the maroon velvet drapery so she could look out. "Tell me, Anna, what will you do now to find your own daughter?"

Anna sighed. "I scarcely know where to turn next."

Except for Rosie's prattle, it was quiet in the room. Caroline said, "Perhaps we should take another look at the Colored Orphan Asylum."

Anna's heart felt like a stone; she couldn't bear another futile visit to the Asylum. "Surely it would be sufficient simply to ask whether or not there are new admissions since we were there." A set of porcelain figures sat on the bone-inlaid table beside Anna. She shifted the shepherdess a little closer to the sheep. "I don't want my heart to be broken again."

Caroline turned back to the room. "Well, yes. You're right, of course. A short note would suffice. I'll make the inquiry."

'Bama glanced over at Anna, and gave a short nod, as if she had been considering something and had come to a decision. "Miss Wheeler," she said, "I think Caro and I should tell you what we've been thinking about for Rosetta."

Caroline opened her mouth as if to intervene, then closed it abruptly and turned her gaze back to the child, her eyes shining.

"The first thing," 'Bama continued, "is that Caro will make Rosie her ward—we think that would be the safest legal status for the child. We'll hire a nursery maid now, and when she's older, a governess."

Caroline broke in, "Then, if she wishes further education, we'll send her to Oberlin College in Ohio. You've heard of that school, right? They admit both women and Negroes."

Anna was flabbergasted at the boldness of their plans. But if anyone in Manhattan's elite society would have the effrontery to take a colored child into her home as a ward, it could only be Caroline Eleanor Slade. There seemed a species of social insolence in the move that would gratify the heiress's renegade sensibilities.

"Now, the other thing is—" 'Bama continued, "we've also been discussing another project, something that would eventually benefit our own little sweetheart, but would go far beyond her." She smiled at the child cuddled half-asleep now in her arms, thumb in mouth. Then she looked directly at Anna. "I thought you should know that much, Mrs. Wheeler. But we're not ready at the moment to tell you anything more about it." Her tone was decisive.

Anna opened her mouth to protest, but Caroline held up a hand. "Be satisfied, my friend. If it does come to fruition, you'll hear about it before anyone else. At the moment this is between me and ..." she smiled at her cousin. ". . . my family."

Leaving Caroline's on this cold November day, Anna shuddered in the brisk wind. Alabama Fitch had certainly surprised her. This previously silent, enigmatic woman had shown herself to be intriguingly bold. Well, why wouldn't she be? Anna's assumptions had heretofore been biased by the role 'Bama played as Caroline's subordinate ... and, she had to admit, by faulty notions about the African race.

But what on earth kind of project could the two unlikely cousins have in mind?

FORTY-ONE

The first snow of the season had fallen, and Anna walked cautiously east on Liberty Street toward the Central Post Office. In the pocket of her cloak she carried a letter politely declining to serve as a Contributing Editor to the *Ladies Book*. She was in greater need than ever of the *Godey's* money, but she now well understood that life had rendered her incapable of ever again composing the fragile and accommodating verses—the truly *feminine* verses—for which Sarah Josepha Hale was delighted to pay so handsomely.

The day was still early when she left Mrs. Chapman's, and the sidewalks had been little trodden. With few sleighs or carts yet about, the streets, too, had kept their fresh, white aspect. The occasional muffled clop of horses' hooves in the snow, the *whish* of the fresh-waxed sleigh runners, the jangling bells of winter harnesses, added an almost festive music to the air, music foreign to her mood.

In spite of Anna's efforts to keep to the cleared center of the sidewalk, her feet in their light shoes soon became damp and cold, sliding precariously on the slope of the hill approaching Broadway. Once on the thoroughfare, she halted at the show window of a shop whose awning advertised BOOTS AND SHOES. A pretty pair of buttoned boots, black kid with a neat fur cuff and thick cork soles, caught her eye. *Winter is fast upon us*, said the voice of reason in her mind: *you need walking boots*. An opposing voice countered: *integrity demands that you return the money to Mrs. Hale; you must accustom yourself to wet feet until Mr. Larkin pays you*. But she still did not know for certain when that would be.

It wasn't too late. The envelope with *Godey's* uncashed bank draft and her letter of refusal still resided in the inner pocket of her wool cloak. All she had to do was turn around and head back to her room. All she had to do was sit down at the cherrywood desk, sharpen a new nib and fit it to her pen, take out a sheet from the ream of English laid paper she had purchased at the stationers on Park Row in a moment of affluence. All she had to do was—write.

For a long moment she stood irresolute, her feet icy. Then she entered the shop. Sighing, she purchased the well-made boots and wore them out onto the sidewalk—so warm and comfortable. Mr. Larkin would pay her eventually, and it wouldn't do to die of pneumonia beforehand.

At the large post office a crew of Irishmen was busy shoveling the street. She braved their racy banter and pushed open the heavy door. She handed her letter to the familiar wraithlike clerk at the wide marble counter, paid the postage, and watched him toss the envelope with the five-hundred-dollar bank draft into the bin for out-of-city mail as carelessly as if it contained nothing of any value whatsoever.

"Anything else I can do for you today, Mrs. Wheeler?" the pale clerk asked while Anna stood as if rooted to the polished granite floor staring at the bin into which her prosperity had vanished.

"Is there anything for me in General Delivery?" she asked.

He shuffled back to the alphabetized boxes and bent down to the W's. Sorting through a multitude of envelopes, he came up empty handed. "No," he replied, lugubriously. "Nothing at all for you in General Delivery, Mrs. Wheeler."

Calcutta
6 March 1859

Mrs. Anna Roundtree
General Delivery
New-York City
United States of America

My Anna,

I think of you incessantly, of the distance between us.

Yesterday I took my best horse, Milton, through those hills we traveled together, but in all that wilderness the cave in which we sheltered was not to be discovered. What folly! Did I think I would find you there?

Do you remember Milton? The chestnut? You rode him once, in a fit of giddy glee—and fell. And then you laughed at my distress, and kissed my tears away.

Are you to be discovered anywhere in all this wilderness of a world. I wish you would write to me and let me know if you still live. My heart is anguished—I fear so for you.

Your despairing Ashok

Hold for Caller
General Delivery
New-York Central Post Office
Nassau Street

FORTY-TWO

Yet another soiree at Mrs. Derwent's, her third, and Anna felt almost ... self-satisfied—a most unusual state of affairs for her. All evening her hostess had been steering the New York literati her way. And these writers, it seemed, had read her poems: Rufus Griswold, the editor; Anne Lynch Botta, the literary hostess; Miss Alice Cary, the poet; even, at one giddy moment, the novelist Mrs. Emma Southworth, whose novel *The Curse of Clifton* Anna had purchased at Appletons and thoroughly enjoyed.

Having bathed in the praise of such celebrated writers, Anna was for a moment glad to be alone in the curtained recess so she could luxuriate in her success. Surely she had reached a visibility among the city's literary lions where further success was solidly assured. Why, Mrs. Southworth, herself, had said that Anna's poems "near-shimmered in their exotic brilliance."

So she sat half hidden behind the velvet curtain exulting in memories of praise and daydreaming of a steady, profitable career that would allow her to undertake further search for her daughter. Caroline had proposed hiring a private inquiry agent. Eben had suggested advertisements in the papers. Anna, herself, had thought of visiting the slave states again, if it was safe. Charleston certainly, perhaps Atlanta, maybe even New Orleans. Perhaps a futile endeavor, but for the first time in her life, she felt secure and in charge of her own destiny.

When she heard voices once again approaching, she turned with her prepared smile to greet whomever her hostess might bring next. The lady with Mrs. Derwent was modestly but elegantly dressed in dove-colored tulle with little ornamentation except for a string of lustrous matched pearls. Her white hair was confined low at the back of her neck in a lace-banded silver net. Her appearance proclaimed her to be a kind and benevolent person. Nonetheless, the mere sight of her made Anna's blood run cold.

"Margaret, my dear," the hostess said to her companion, "let me introduce you to the toast of the town, Miss Wheeler, our newly celebrated poetess. Miss Wheeler, this lady is a great benefactor to the poor of our city, Mrs. Margaret Ambrose."

Anna stared at Mrs. Ambrose. She felt herself pale. Mrs. Ambrose had probed her once before with that uncanny gaze. Mrs. Ambrose had held Anna's hands and prayed with her over the state of her soul. And no doubt Mrs. Ambrose had learned from Miss Susan Parker, her subordinate, that Anna had given birth to a child of dark complexion.

Margaret Ambrose squinted at Anna, and paused for a long moment. An exquisitely complicated series of expressions crossed her countenance: recollection, evaluation, judgment, condemnation—icy outrage. "I know exactly who you are," she said, measuring each word. "Why, your poor, dear, sainted husband. … And you have the temerity—" Deliberately she turned her back on Anna, cutting her dead. "Phoebe," she said to Mrs. Derwent, "Dear Phoebe. I fear you are greatly mistaken in your patronage of this … this … woman. I must speak with you privately. At once."

In a swirl of gray tulle she pivoted away from Anna, pulling the reluctant Mrs. Derwent with her into the festive crowd.

Left alone, Anna scanned the lively company. Mr. Larkin was just entering the room, drawing on his evening gloves. The pious novelist, Miss Susan Warner, sat in a plain gown next to her equally plain sister, Anna. Wearing a black silk gown with three tiers to the skirt, Mrs. Stowe, the author of *Uncle Tom's Cabin*, held forth at the center of an admiring crowd. Mr. Elliot B. Cliff, restlessly tapping the toe of one shiny boot, searched the room in quest of yet another literary personage to accost.

Evading the journalist, Anna excused her way through the gathering, heading for the cloakroom to reclaim her bonnet and mantle.

Mrs. Ambrose would tell everyone what she knew—or what she thought she knew: Miss Anna Wheeler, newly celebrated devotional poetess, was one and the same as the debauched Mrs. Anna Wheeler who had come to her in suspicious circumstances seeking news of her child's birth at the Five Points Mission. Anna might as well depart of her own volition, with dignity, before she was asked to leave. Never again would Mrs. Derwent welcome Anna with her generous hospitality. Never again would William Larkin ...

Anna's two lives had collided. Anna Wheeler the popular inspirational poet from now on would be known as Anna Wheeler, mother of a bastard darky child. Of this company, only Elliot B. Cliff would ever again wish to speak to her.

She did not, at that moment, think to ask herself how Mrs. Ambrose could know anything at all about Anna's "poor, dear, sainted husband."

FORTY-THREE

At Mrs. Chapman's breakfast table the next morning, a letter awaited Anna. She stared at the envelope for a long moment before slipping it into her waistband; it was addressed in Mr. Larkin's neat Spenserian hand. Then she inhaled deeply and let the breath out in a sigh that must have been audible to everyone in the room. The air smelled of onions, sausage, and burnt coffee. Nancy, the serving girl, was ill this morning, and their landlady was, as she growled over and over, "run off her feet because of that lazy Irish slut."

Tea and a half-bowl of oatmeal mush topped with bluish milk made up Anna's meal, and even that light repast sat uneasily upon her stomach.

"Are you quite well this morning?" Mrs. Douglas, the minister's widow, asked. She wore a white lawn breakfast cap edged with fine crochet-work. "You look positively nauseous."

"Yes," echoed Miss Higginson, the schoolteacher, her lank hair confined to a black net snood, "positively nauseous."

"A temporary indisposition, ladies." She folded her napkin. "Excuse me, please."

Sitting in her room, at her desk, she stared out at the denuded branches of the maple. A wan cold light washed the worn brick façade of the four-story residence across the street. She gave another of her bone-deep sighs and slit open the envelope. The note read:

Mrs. Wheeler—

Word has come to me of scandalous—indeed unthinkable—behavior on your part. I must see you at my place of business by half-past ten this morning to discuss the future of our association. Do not be late!

William Larkin, Publisher

Anna *was* late. She was exceeding late. Indeed, she surprised herself by deciding not to go to Mr. Larkin's office at all, even though her concerns about money were excruciating. In spite of steadfast efforts at frugality, her cash was vanishing faster than ever she would have believed possible. Had she been a fool to return the five-hundred dollars to Mrs. Hale?

But, then, there was the matter of integrity. Her note almost wrote itself:

Mr. Larkin—

Your discourteous tone dissuades me from any expectation of civil treatment by Larkin & Bierce. Therefore I see no purpose in attending you at your office at half-past ten—or ever.

Please send to me post-haste a full accounting of books sold and monies due me to date. I will expect a full remittance by bank order at the conclusion of this business week. Except for future monies earned by this edition of Poems, Sacred & Sentimental, *consider our business relationship terminated.*

Anna Wheeler (Miss)

Given Mr. Larkin's parsimoniousness, Anna expected no return from her ultimatum, but it had felt so very good to write it. Before she could waver, she dispatched the note to Larkin & Bierce by the hands of Mrs. Chapman's kitchen boy. But a far different missive received minutes after the boy's departure drove all thoughts of Mr. Larkin from her mind and sent her scurrying down the stairs and across Liberty Street to Broadway.

Mrs. Wheeler—

The note read: *I have ill news. That snake, Elliot Cliff, will today publish an item in the so-called 'literary' notices of*

> *the* Sun *alleging grave impropriety on your part. Be prepared. I hope I may be able to be of help to you. At ten o'clock this a.m you will find me once again at Buttercake John's. Your Friend and Admirer.*
>
> *Eben Garrett*

She'd felt stunned by his news, "pole-axed," as Caroline might have said in one of her more emphatic moments. But upon reflection Anna knew that she should not be surprised. The previous evening at Mrs. Derwent's, Elliot B. Cliff had been present when Margaret Ambrose made the connection between Mrs. Anna Wheeler, supplicant at the Five-Points Mission, and the Miss Anna Wheeler of burgeoning literary fame. And, of course, Mr. Cliff would have jumped at the story; he had already made it clear that Anna's life was one of public interest. Now, with today's issue of the New York *Sun*, he would make her a figure of public notoriety.

But, the knowledge of her impending disgrace had somehow liberated her, she realized, sitting there once again at Buttercake John's with the coffee cup as hot between her hands as her heart was within her chest. Losing her reputation, what more would she have to lose? Except when she had left Josiah, she'd never before known such a sense of freedom. But that had been different. Then she had run. Now she would stay—and fight.

Above her in the window she could see the feet of pedestrians hurrying by. A pair of stout black leather boots like those favored by Josiah passed. She shuddered. Then three pair of dainty, well-made kid shoes. Girlish laughter filtered even through the thick, grated window glass. Behind them followed two pair of small, bare feet, one limping badly. This was not an unfamiliar sight, but she sighed.

She could always live by her pen, she thought, no matter the circumstances of reputation, no matter the lack of the dollars that had come to flow her way so unexpectedly. She could take a pen-name. She could write for the penny press. She could—

Anna was jolted out of her meditations by a stout clerk in a burgundy overcoat who stopped at her table to remark upon the rosiness of her cheeks. Leering, he showed a mouthful of crooked teeth. "I'd be happy to treat such a pretty little lady as you to a plate of buttered biscuits," he offered.

Anna settled upon the bold clerk an icy stare that seemed to slice right through his swagger. What could one rude man do to her at ten o'clock in the morning at a coffee house in lower Broadway? She would survive his prurient interest as she would survive Mr. Larkin's ire. Her refusal to kowtow to the publisher had made her bold. Even though it went against all her womanly training, she would do whatever she had to do against him in order to assert her rights to the earnings of her pen.

"Was that lout bothering you?" Eben asked, staring after the departing man. The journalist's nose and chin were red with the cold, and he carried upon his plaid wool overcoat and fur Cossack hat the fresh scent and temperature of frigid air.

"It's of no matter," she said, her attention focused on the copy of the *Sun* tucked under the journalist's arm.

Stuffing his heavy leather gloves into his coat pockets, he handed the paper to Anna. "Hot off the press," he said. "Literally. I grabbed one from the folding room at the *Sun* office." The short item was on the fifth page.

An Impious Poet?

It seems that Miss Anna Wheeler, she of the pious verses currently garnering rapturous literary notice, has not herself led such an exemplary life as her poems would lead trusting readers to believe. At Mrs. Phoebe Derwent's exclusive literary salon last evening, a source of unimpeachable veracity announced that this modest-appearing lady poet has secreted in her past a scandalous liaison leading to the existence of a child of exotic hue. What should respectable readers make of the seeming disparity between the poetess's impeccable words and her less than impeccable life?

"It will be on the street within the hour, I'm afraid," Mr. Garrett said, leaning over the table toward her.

The German waiter brought him a cup of steaming coffee. With a clank of knife against crockery, he set down a plate of fat bread rolls and a pot of blackberry jam. "Here you are, Mr. Garrett—like you ordered."

Without taking his eyes off Anna, the journalist nodded his thanks, immediately spreading jam on a roll with a wide-bladed knife. He bit off a large mouthful and chewed lustily. "That Elly Cliff gives us writers for the newspapers a bad name. An honest journalist gathers facts and evidence, but Cliff works with gossip and innuendo—anything to pick up ten or fifteen dollars from one of the dailies. I'm afraid, as long as he thinks there is a story, he will not leave you alone."

Anna folded the paper and shoved it back over the table toward him. Seeing the actual article, knowing it would soon be circulating on the streets, had chastened her mood of social defiance. "Mr. Garrett—Eben, I thank you for your kindness in giving me advance warning. Now I shall not be caught unprepared by whatever scandal is to come." She choked down a gulp and worked to recover her previous resolve.

He laughed. "Think of this, sweet lady: You may yet benefit from Mr. Elliot B. Cliff's treachery. Nothing is necessary but to attach to any book the merest suspicion of immorality and the public will plunk their money down as if to see the two-headed boy in Mr. Barnum's museum. The only thing is going to be how to squeeze the cash out of that old skinflint Larkin."

"I'm beginning to fear it won't be possible."

Eben shrugged. "Listen, there's one thing I can do for sure. I'll puff your poems in a review in the *Tribune's* next literary column. Mr. Greeley will go for it. He's read your poems, and he no more likes to see a woman of literary ability slandered in the public eye than I do." He stubbed out his cigar on the bread-roll plate and gazed at her assessingly. "At least he liked the ones about India. I'm afraid he said the others were the usual 'female sauzle'—only better written than most. But he told me your Indian poems made him wish passionately to go east as well as west. You can't get much higher praise than that from old Horace."

The sun was high in the sky when they emerged onto Broadway. A beam glinting off a neighboring skylight dazzled Anna. Tipping his hat to her, Eben strode away in the direction of Nassau Street. She had turned to walk north toward Mrs. Chapman's when a newsboy with a bundle of papers jostled her in his hurry to achieve the prime corner of Broadway and Bowling Green. She saw the masthead of the *Sun* and froze in place. "I must be strong," she thought, inhaling deeply. She shuddered, anticipating the notoriety awaiting her. For a long moment her exhaled breath hovered white in the sooty air.

FORTY-FOUR

When she rounded the corner of Greenwich and Liberty, a large closed carriage waited before Mrs. Chapman's house with a driver in a triple cape upon the box, shivering in spite of his glowing foot-stove. Anna knew by the solidity and respectability of such a conveyance in this modest neighborhood that it must belong to William Larkin. She had thought that with her refusal to wait upon him this morning, she had seen the last of her publisher. But, no, it seemed not.

Mr. Larkin, in a dark-blue greatcoat, climbed down from the carriage. She expected righteous indignation, but, to her surprise, he came toward her with his hands out beseechingly. "Mrs. Wheeler, surely after all I have done for you, I deserve better than that curt note I received this morning."

Her feet were cold from the long walk, and her nose felt frosted at the tip. An express wagon pulled by a mismatched pair rumbled toward the Hudson River docks, empty now of whatever its freight had been. The sound of iron shoe against cobblestone was clear and bell-like in the frigid atmosphere. She nodded at Mr. Larkin, astonished by his conciliatory words, not trusting herself to speak.

Not a muscle moved in the mask of the publisher's thin face. "All I wished in summoning you this morning was to tell you to pay no attention to that impertinence about to be published in the *Sun*. With my patronage and my irreproachable reputation we will together weather this insupportable attack on your good name."

Anna tried not to show her incredulity. Eben Garrett's words echoed in her mind: *the public will plunk its money down*. Yes, if there was one thing Mr. Larkin knew, it was money. A deep cold anger suffused her: In the interests of preserving womanly decorum she had spent her life submitting to men like Josiah and Mr. Larkin. And what had it gotten her? Nothing but virtue and poverty. When she spoke now, it was that anger speaking, a far better advocate of her self-interest than feminine modesty had ever been.

"Ah, Mr. Larkin, are publishers indeed the natural allies of authors? I have yet to find it so. I have received from you, I believe, two-hundred dollars in all. Yet my books, it is said, sell in the tens of thousands. Why so small a return to the author?"

A muscle twitched by Mr. Larkin's eye, and he squared his shoulders. "You malign my business practices?"

"I merely ask a question. Mr. Larkin, I must leave you. It is cold out here on the street, and my dinner is waiting." She had no appetite whatsoever. "Have you come to deliver a bank check?"

He sputtered something about not yet having done the accounting, about the quarterly payment system, about …

As she started up the steps away from him, Anna spoke over her shoulder. "I wish not to see you again, Mr. Larkin, unless you have my monies in hand."

He seemed not to fathom how deliberate and absolute was her rejection of him. "This to me? After I came and found you in this sordid boarding house. After I established you in literary society." He was speaking as if she were a creature of his own making. "After I risked so much capital on a completely unknown writer. And, now … Oh, Mrs. Wheeler, my dear lady, I do worry excessively about your good name."

"My good name is my own business." The high drama of the words made her feel like a character in a play: the outraged heroine, perhaps, or the imperious *grande dame*.

He flushed as rage broke through his paternalistic mien. "Mrs. Wheeler, I yet have the power to withdraw your book from the market."

She pulled the door key from her muff. "Do so if you wish. I still hold the copyrights, if you recall, and may find another publisher. Now … my dinner, Mr. Larkin. I will send my man of business to call upon you." She barely knew what a man of business was, but she would ask Eben Garrett to recommend someone. Or, perhaps he, himself … She swept through the front door of Mrs. Chapman's establishment as if she were a merchant ship at full sail.

William Larkin raised his voice to a most indecorous level. "Mrs. Wheeler, beware of making an enemy of me. I am all that stands between you and literary perdition."

But she had, she feared, already done so.

The air in Mrs. Chapman's front hall smelled of rancid lamb fat. The landlady stood at the bottom of the stairs, her fat cheeks quivering. "Well, well, Mrs. Wheeler, I must say, now you have men waiting outside for you, sending their coachmen in after you! Well, I declare. If that don't beat all. When you was first here, you was a mouse. Never went nowhere. Never said nothing to nobody. Never was no trouble. Then letters and packages started coming for you day and night. And callers of all stamps! And that sleazy Eben Garrett! Well, I thought, so the quiet little mouse is a poet. No harm in that. At least it pays her room and board. But, this!" She shook a copy of the *Sun* at Anna. "This is the last straw. I ain't having no lewd woman in my respectable house." She thrust out her arm and pointed to the stairs. "Get upstairs, you hussy, and get up there now—and start packing. I want you out of my house. You got thirty minutes."

Anna stood, flabbergasted. She had not thought sufficiently far ahead to anticipate her landlady's response. But, of course, Mrs. Chapman was just the sort of reader to whom the *Sun* pandered: dull of mind and eager for the sensational. "But, but …" she sputtered, at a loss for how to respond. "But … I am paid through the week," she said, ludicrously.

"Humph," Mrs. Chapman replied, turning on a rundown heel and marching through the hall toward the kitchen. The sound of a chair creaking drew Anna's attention to the parlor. Mrs. Douglas and Mrs. Higginson were hovering just behind the door curtains. The former's fascinated gaze quickly dropped to the needlework in her hands. Adelaide Higginson ruffled through the pages of a *Gleason's Illustrated* snatched up from a pie-crust table. Within seconds the landlady was back with a handful of coins which she flung at Anna. "There! There's your three days' room and board. Now pack up and get out!"

At the sight of her landlady's almost comic fury, Anna did not know whether to laugh or to cry. She thought of turning and walking out of the house, but then she remembered Ashok's shawl. On this cold day she had worn her warm blue cloak with the fur trim, and had left her shawl covering the bed. Edith Chapman was perfectly capable of confiscating the precious talisman. She could not bear to lose it—or the small travel desk in which she had stored so much of her writing and her small remaining store of cash. Leaving the coins where they had fallen on the faded Brussels carpet, she turned instead to the stairs.

Twenty minutes later Anna stood on the sidewalk next to her small heap of possessions with the sound of Mrs. Chapman's slamming door still ringing in her ears. Like some shop girl of suspect morals, like some impecunious drunkard, she had been summarily evicted from the only home she could call her own. A wagon full of beer kegs passed northward, then a grungy white horse pulling a two-wheeled coal cart. The horse raised its tail leaving a steaming pile of dung in the street. The bright sky of the morning had clouded over and it looked fair to snow and snow heavily. Anna did not know where to turn. Should she go to Caroline's? But she wished to be dependent on no one. She raised her hand to summon the hansom cab that had just turned the corner. She still didn't know whether to laugh or cry.

FORTY-FIVE

Miss Susan Parker's disclosure to him (and to an appalled Mrs. Ambrose) of his wife's unnatural and perfidious betrayal of her marriage vows resulting in the birth of a dark-skinned bastard had so distressed him as to spur the desire for righteous chastisement. He had taken the necessary steps to obtain for himself that which was necessary, and then had written to Anna at her boarding house with compelling reason to return to her rightful place at her husband's side. He had delivered the missive by hand, along with an inspirational book, placing both in the questionable hands of a slovenly Irish house girl.

He had asked the Mission ladies to keep his wife's disgrace to themselves. It did not serve his purposes to make her infamy public; she was, after all, in the eyes of the Lord—and of society—still his wife. And, in truth, he did not wish Messieurs Larkin & Bierce—or, indeed, anyone else—to know of his shame.

But he would not sit passively by and wait for her to respond. He intended, in the guise of an anonymous concerned reader, to write to all the editors who had published her verses and warn them against patronizing a woman with such an infamous past. Once her literary income had disappeared, she would be destitute and would have no resort but to return to his bed and board. All he wanted was the wife God had given him—or, as he now knew, with whom God had cursed him. All he wanted was the opportunity to bring her ... no ...to *discipline* her ... back to virtue.

FORTY-SIX

At the lively Merchant's Hotel on Courtlandt Street, Anna found welcome anonymity. Her room was comfortable and the fare far better than anything to be found at Mrs. Chapman's: salt cod served only at breakfast. The peripatetic residents, travelers for the most part immersed in their own mercantile and political purposes, paid no attention to a small, meek, soberly dressed woman who came downstairs only for meals. Her few friends knew where she was; that was all that mattered. And she'd been fortunate in her timing. The very day of her disgrace, the news flashed north from Washington—Mr. Abraham Lincoln had won the presidency, and in the Southern states sabers were rattling ominously. The city's newspapers were preoccupied with the possibility—indeed, the probability—of Southern secession. The scandal about Anna's illicit child flickered for a week or two in the gossip sheets and then died down for lack of fuel, its subject having vanished. Indeed, weeks later, when the remains of a drowning victim were pulled from the Hudson River, the *Sun* speculated that it was she, that the Impious Poetess, once having her sins found out, had ended her scandalous life.

Hoping that India Elizabeth was still somewhere in the city, Anna took long solitary walks through the winter streets wearing a thick green veil. Every child she saw, no matter how unlikely or impossible, Anna searched for her daughter in that child's face: the seraphic, well-blanketed babies pushed by nursemaids in their shaded wicker carriages; the plainly dressed but well-cared-for children of colored maids and butlers on Fifth Avenue; the scabrous tots huddled under rags in cellar doorways.

Anna was sane, although her impulse may not have been. She knew how slight the possibilities were of finding India Elizabeth in this manner, but she was compelled to try. So every day she walked, each day taking a different route. As a consequence, she learned to know intimately this city where India Elizabeth had vanished, its people, the din and hubbub, the odors, the texture of its life—the curve of its stones beneath her shoes. She watched everything, and listened to everything, and sniffed the air. And she jotted everything down, filling notebook after notebook with written images and rough-drawn pencil sketches.

One day her explorations would concentrate on nearby Washington Market. Washington Market, the dense, raucous crowds in the vast, columned space; the hucksters with their distinctive cries, "fish, fish, liiiive fish"; the hotel-keeper's minions, rushing to their wagons with the best cuts of beef, venison, wild turkeys fresh in from the Erie railroad cars. And always the odors, smells of both the rotten and the sweet. And always, always, the reek of fish.

Another day she would venture further, up Broadway to Fourteenth, the first of the true uptown streets, perfectly straight from river to river. From the Hudson railroad tracks, she traveled east past Union Square to the great architectural iron works at Avenue C on the East River. At the Square, surrounded by well-designed freestone houses inhabited by the best families, she stopped to watch children rolling hoops and jumping rope inside the high railings, beside the majestic fountain. And, always, it seemed, an aroma of rich meat roasting with gravy for some fortunate family's leisurely four o'clock dinner.

In the Five Points, she pushed her way through streets crowded with women haggling at the vegetable carts, neatly garbed German hausfraus with straw baskets and Irish mothers with three or four children hanging onto their ragged skirts. A butcher boy in a bloody smock hoisted a side of beef from a three-wheel cart. The auctioneer at a sidewalk furniture sale stood on a barrel-top crying out the virtues of a battered rosewood parlor table.

The East River waterfront, an unbroken line of ships, their jibs projecting over the cobbled wharf and immigrants swarming off the packets from Liverpool and London. There she saw the waterfront dollymops with their short skirts, red-topped boots, and bells affixed to their ankles. A girl in a greasy dress and soiled petticoat sidling up to a stranger, saying, "won't you come home with me, my dear."

Anna didn't want to even consider the situation of children born from these unions.

In the blocks behind the Broadway hotels there were no children on the streets. Here were the female boarding houses on Church Street, with their elegant quiet fronts, the gentlemen calling all day and night. The perfume of jasmine and magnolia wafting forth as doors opened, trailing ermine-wrapped women as they passed.

One late afternoon with the sun gone early dark over the winter meridian, she was halted by the lure of various dusty curios in the cobwebbed plate glass of a pawnbroker's in a narrow lane off Chatham Square. Amid a miscellany of both useful and useless objects—a kaleidoscope, a hunting horn, a large ivory hourglass, its circular top carved in rosettes, a chunk of ambergris—she saw nestled what looked at first to be an ivory ball, but proved upon closer inspection to feature empty eye sockets and gaping jaw. As gaslight from the streetlamp shone on the polished pate, Anna was suffused by an eerie chill, and the empty eyes compelled her: it was a monkey skull. This curio reminded her of the talisman the village headwoman had given her in Fatehgarh. She stood and studied the grotesque thing for quite some time, experiencing a hazy regret for having thrown away Lallia's well-meant token. Slowly she turned her steps homeward.

The following noon, when she returned to Chatham Square, she was unable to locate the winding, narrow lane upon which the shop had been situated.

And, then one February morning, footsore, Anna woke up to the tap tap of small, mean snowflakes on her windowpane. Something had altered; Anna didn't know precisely what. She was stronger. It was as if steel had entered her soul as solid as that framing Manhattan's great new buildings. That day she ceased walking and, in her clean, comfortable fourth-floor hotel room, she began to write again.

She sat down at the cherry-wood desk, and the lines that emerged from her pen she did not recognize as poems. They were not rhymed. Their meter was neither iambic nor trochaic nor spondaic. The words flowed; they came out cold and bright, obdurate and angry.

Thirty long years, and countless spinning centuries,
Gabriel shining by the bedside,
The fear of being smothered in his wings.
It seems there was a birth
And swaddling clothes
Being bound, or binding,
Shepherds with uncomprehending eyes,
A star and no lack of wise men.
But that was endless cycles of stars ago.
For this nativity I am alone.

Anna recognized a new genius to her work, but these were not pieces for Mr. Larkin or for *Godey's Ladies Book*. They were neither inspirational nor comforting. They were poems for herself, and she kept them to herself, hiding the fragments of verse away in the secret compartment of the travel desk.

Anna Wheeler the poetess, it seemed, was no more. No more the bright lyrical effusions to God's grace and goodness in a beautiful world. No more the odes to an innocent childhood that floated like a bubble above the cares of life. No more, even, the sensuous evocations of dazzling, sun-drenched Indian days and star-studded Indian nights. Anna was in need of money, and, quite by happenstance, she found herself a new literary market.

Opening her travel desk that chill February, she found the sketch she had written in Charleston about the auction of the young girl, Jenny, at the slave market. On Eben's advice, she took it to Horace Greeley, who peered at her above gold-rimmed spectacles, paid her fifty dollars and printed the sketch in the very next issue of the *Tribune* under the byline of *A New-York Lady in the South*.

Mr. Greeley asked for more sketches of real life. She wrote about the Reverend Peter Lyman, street Christian; about the new white iron cots at the Colored Orphan Asylum; about a fugitive slave giving birth in a Cow Bay attic room.

Mr. Greeley offered her a regular column: *Life as It Is, by a New-York Lady*. She was to expand her scope, so she turned to her notebooks, wrote about the complacent burgher at Union Square, rotund, slightly out of breath, summoning a horse car with an imperious kid-gloved hand; wrote about the vegetable man at Washington Market, the clatter of his quick, sharp knife; wrote about the girl in Paradise Square raising her flounced skirts to reveal neat ankles in red silk stockings. No one suspected the *New-York Lady* of being Anna Wheeler, disgraced and vanished poetess, their styles and subjects being so irreconcilably different. She put her earnings in a Wall Street bank. For the moment she was not in need of William Larkin's still-unrendered payment; she would obtain that eventually—even if she had to go to court. From the moment city steel had entered her soul, Anna Wheeler ceased to be hampered by ladylike reticence. From now on she would demand what was rightfully hers.

And, still, she was saving all her money for that trip to cities in the South. Perhaps she could find Elizabeth in Savannah. Or Memphis. Or New Orleans. Or …

Calcutta
17 January 1860

Mrs. Anna Roundtree
General Delivery
New-York City
United States of America

Oh My Anna! I must write from the heart, and the devil take the consequences. Why did you leave me? You knew I loved you! I told you so—perhaps too many times. I lie awake nights berating myself for allowing you to go. Did I frighten you with my ardor?

I was stunned by your decision—and your decisiveness. Was I too harsh with you in my dismay?

In the quiet tea hills I thought you would be mine forever, but among the clamorous streets of Calcutta, I lost you. Was it the sight of white faces among the brown? Did you recall your native race and long for home? For purity? I would not think it of you. Could anything be more pure than love? You did love me. You said so! That sweet face of yours—it does not tell a lie. Do you remember that day in the sandstorm? How you reached out to touch me, your fingers like a butterfly upon my face? Your touch was so light, but it bound me. Binds me still.

Why did you go? Why did I let you go?

Your Ashok

Hold for Caller
General Delivery
New-York Central Post Office
Nassau Street

FORTY-SEVEN

Caroline and Anna entered Pfaff's Saloon's cellar room at four in the afternoon, but it would have been neither darker nor smokier had they come at midnight. Eben Garrett sat at a long center table deep in conversation with a robust gray-bearded man wearing a working-man's blouse and rough trousers. With a thrill Anna recognized the poet, Walt Whitman. She stopped dead just across the threshold, catching the hem of her dress in the closing door.

The room was a sort of cave beneath the pavement, with a counter, a small table under the window, the long table in the center, and for seating, a few chairs and some barrels. On this heavily overcast mid-winter afternoon, the light from the too-widely-spaced gas jets was enhanced by filthy oil lamps hung from the rafters on bent, rusty nails. The reek of the lamps mingled with heady odors of coffee, spirits, and cigars to create a thick smoky fug almost palpable in the stale air. They had come to meet Eben, who'd sent a boy with a message—he had something for Anna, something she would want to see at once.

The journalist glanced over at Mr. Whitman, then nodded toward them. The poet's frank gaze traveled between Anna and Caroline, then settled on the former. He rose and held out his hand. "Young Garrett said you'd be here, Miss Anna Wheeler. I've read your poems, and I wanted to meet you. Come, sit next to me." He pulled out a chair. He, himself, was seated on a barrel.

"Really? You've read my poems?" She studied Mr. Whitman openly. In spite of his rough dress and free-wheeling manner, his eyes were gentle and quiet.

From a pocket in his short brown coat, the poet took a folded newspaper and handed it to her. The *Saturday Press*. She glanced questioningly at him, and he reached over to unfold the thin paper. The front page carried one of his long poems in two columns, but he didn't stop there. He opened to the third page and pointed to a headline in small type: *A Review of the Poems of Miss Anna Wheeler, by Walter Whitman*.

"Oh," Anna said. "Oh, my." And she began to read: *Setting aside, of course, the merely pretty and pious in Miss Wheeler's insipid religious verse, we recognize in her secular writings the true hunger of the heart and body. Those poems of India so piquant in their passionate sensual honesty. . . .*

Anna blushed, grateful for the dimness of the room. "Mr. Whitman, I had not intended to reveal 'hunger of the heart and body.'" She glanced up at him and laughed uncertainly. "And certainly not 'passionate sensual honesty.'" She took a deep breath. "But for you to praise my poems in print gives me ... gratification above all things." She paused. "Most unladylike, I know."

He laughed. "All I can say, Miss Wheeler, is that your Oriental verses gave this old reprobate a good deal of pleasure. My best advice to you is never again to write anything 'ladylike.' Just follow the instincts of your heart. They're pretty damn sound, I'd say." Someone slapped a tankard of ale in front of her. She pushed it away. She did not need the alcoholic drink, the poet's words were so intoxicating.

Mr. Whitman left shortly thereafter. Anna, recovering from the excitement of his presence, ordered coffee and a German pancake.

A burst of laughter from the other end of the table caught her attention. She looked up to find Caroline drinking from her own tankard, intent in frank enjoyment of the others at the long table. Flushed and loquacious, hands flying and tendrils of hair curling around her face, she laughed at their racy wit and teased them with bold sallies of her own.

The ladies here, Anna noted, spoke as readily as the men and seemed equally as opinionated, venturing forth on even the most risqué topics. They were dressed with great flair. One, small with waterfall curls and beautiful dark eyes, wore a fitted jacket of black velvet and blood-red roses in her hair. The other lady, plainer and more animated, had thrown a dashing wool cloak in a large red plaid carelessly over the back of her chair. Actresses, probably; ladies of the stage were known to frequent Pfaffs. Caroline seemed right at home. No one here—except Anna and Eben—knew of her fortune or social standing, and it looked as if she thrived on the anonymous bonhomie.

When Eben Garrett had finished his eggs and sausages, he moved down the table and seated himself on Mr. Whitman's vacated barrel. He spoke quietly to Anna. "As promised, I visited old man Larkin on your behalf. I have two communications from him." He placed a bank draft and a sealed envelope in her hand.

In the smoky light Anna squinted at the check. "Another hundred dollars," she said. She would put it directly in the bank. Even though she had the additional expense of living in a hotel, her nest egg was growing nicely.

Eben threw back his head and laughed so heartily he attracted the attention of all at the table. Winking at her, Anna's companion lowered his voice. "Perhaps you need spectacles, sweet lady. Look again."

She raised the slip of paper at an angle to the soot-stained lamp above her. "Oh, my," she said. She had missed the third zero; Mr. Larkin's remittance was for a thousand dollars. A *thousand* dollars! She felt a catch in her breathing. With money like this she could buy a small house, make a home ready for India Elizabeth.

"The envelope contains an account sheet and a letter. I waited while he wrote it. Anna, you've got that poor devil in a hell of a bind! He finds your Indian poems terribly improper and you yourself scandalous, but your books are raking in cash hand over fist, and he has gone to a fifth printing. By the time I was through speculating about what it might do to his reputation to be exposed in the newspapers as a publisher who cheats his authors—"

"You threatened him on my behalf?"

"Yep."

"W … well," she stumbled over the word, "I don't know what to say."

"Say, thank you." He grinned.

"Thank you." She stared once again at the bank draft.

"But, best be prepared. When I left him, old Larkin was in a rip-snorting bear of a mood." The journalist tapped the envelope in Anna's hand. "So I am not at all sanguine about the contents of this letter. However, there is more money to be had where this comes from, so perhaps you will not mind so much Larkin's fulminations."

FORTY-EIGHT

Distressed beyond Christian forbearance and spurred by the desire for honorable chastisement, he had left that letter for Anna at her boarding house—Miss Susan Parker had known the address—directing her to return to her husband's side if she ever in this life wanted to see her child again.

Weeks went by and she did not respond. Outrage simmered. Such aberrant disobedience! He would no longer sit passively by and wait for her to respond. He took from his desk the cautionary letter he'd drafted to her editors and revised it for mailing.

Living unknown as he did in this city, Josiah Roundtree had had no previous reason to visit the Post Office, but now he needed a quantity of postage stamps. Broadway was so dirty with ash-fouled slush as to dissuade all but the most determined pedestrians. Since crossing Chambers Street, he had seen no one—only three filthy children, their feet wrapped in rags, plucking out half-burned coals from the ash-box behind a shuttered bake house. He turned east, grateful to the Lord for the provision of his own stout, double-soled leather boots. The sidewalks were no cleaner here, even though the run-down brick buildings he recalled from a decade past had been replaced by elegant marble-faced commercial mansions. As he approached Nassau Street, he slid on a hidden ice slick and wrenched his shoulder grabbing hold of an iron spike, part of a building's perimeter fence.

Along with the postage stamps, the wraith-like clerk at the Post Office counter returned to him a jumble of coins. Josiah turned to leave; then a thought struck him and he turned back. "Might there be anything in General Delivery for the Reverend Josiah Pierce Roundtree," he asked, quite certain there would not be. By most of his acquaintances, he was, after all, still believed to be dead.

While the clerk scuffed his broken shoes across the wide back-counter floor and squatted down arthritically to reach the R boxes, Josiah glanced around the almost empty vestibule. A rough sailor counted out bills for a postal money order. A modest-appearing woman in a blue cape inscribed an address on a dainty envelope. A boy carried a string-tied box toward the counter, a small brown dog trailing him. The clock on the wall of the Cedar Street side read 4:17.

"Mrs. Anna Roundtree? Is that your wife?" the clerk asked in his whispery voice. "A letter for her has just arrived." And he handed over a crisp envelope.

Josiah gasped and took it, his eyes riveted to the smeared postmark. *Calcutta.*

He tore the letter open, then and there, and read:

5 September 1860

Mrs. Anna Roundtree
General Delivery
New-York City
United States of America
My Sweet Darling,

I have written many letters to you, but know not whether you have received any. Do you ignore me? I ask myself. Or are you cut off by mischance from my missives? Do you live under some other name? Have you perhaps forgotten me? Have you married again? Are you, indeed, still alive?

I feel that I write to a ghost. As if the continents that divide us are those between the living and the dead. But even ghosts have habitations. I would pass into death, if must be, to find you. All other continents I have the means to cross alive.

Therefore, I sail for America next month on HMS Provenance. With good seas, I should arrive at Manhattan in April. I cannot live with this unknowing. I must attempt to find you—or learn your fate.

Will you receive this letter?

Will you be at the docks to meet me?

I love you,
Your Ashok

Hold for Caller
General Delivery
New-York Central Post Office
Nassau Street

FORTY-NINE

Anna held her merino skirt high as she clambered up the steps of the northbound omnibus on her way to Lafayette Place. It had snowed heavily during the night and was still snowing, but the driver wrapped in his oilskin cape and heavy drab overcoat seemed not to mind. "Broadway—right up," he called, as if the drift-clogged thoroughfare provided no more of a challenge than the puddle or two of an April shower. If Anna had still been writing poems, she would have said that the streets were blanketed with jeweled ermine, but now the pretty image didn't even occur to her.

Few passengers had braved the weather, and the straw strewn across the floor of the car was as clean and smelled as sweet as if it had just come from the barn. She'd scarcely gotten herself settled on the bench, shaking off the snow melting into her woolen hem, when a young voice piped, "An' if it ain't Mrs. Wheeler? And us all thinking ye wuz surely dead!" Anna, startled, raised her eyes. A girl of perhaps fourteen, in a skimpy shawl and overlarge India-rubber men's boots goggled at her from across the aisle.

"Nancy O'Brien," Anna said. It was indeed Mrs. Chapman's maid of all work, this scrawny bareheaded child with her dripping nose and fingers red from chillbains. "Are you all right? You look so cold."

The girl ran her sleeve across her nose. "An' ain't I used to it? That old hoor of a landlady don't pay enough t' keep me more than half-alive." She stuck her hands in her armpits for warmth and looked down at herself. "I'm that ragged even a beggar wouldn't rake me up from the gutter."

The horse-car stopped in front of a cigar store at the corner of Fulton Street, and three workmen with tin lunch kettles climbed on. The car jolted up again, passing Barnum's Museum, flags drooping now, heavy with snow. Open sleighs raced by in both directions, bells jangling, their muffled-up drivers laying on the whips and whooping at the speed. Otherwise the 'bus had the wide pristine thoroughfare almost to itself.

"Here, take these." Anna pulled off her gray knit gloves. "I've got another pair at home."

The girl quickly donned the gloves. "Ain't they nice?" She held her hands out to admire them, flexing her newly warm fingers. "I'll be thankin' ye for these all winter, I will," she said. Then she looked up at Anna. "I still got that holy crucifix ye give me, too. An', Missus, ain't I got something for you in return."

"You do?"

"I been holdin' on t' it ever since you walked out so sudden without leavin' no address." She grinned. "Oh, didn't we all laugh when you set that ol' hoor up by her heels the way you done. She was spittin' mad, madder than Ol' Nick himself. Thought you'd beg an' plead t' be allowed to stay, she did. Never guessed you'd be out of there in ten minutes with Micky Dolan carrying down that nice little desk of yours. Then ye took off in a cab, like Queen Victoria herself! Ol' Lady Chapman was fit t' be tied!"

Anna laughed. "Good," she said. "I'm glad. She's a mean, small-minded, unchristian woman, and I'm truly sorry you must work for her. But what is it you have for me?"

Nancy held her gloved hands out again, turning them around so she could view them from all angles. "The ol' lady set me to cleanin' your room soon's you left. I went to pullin' out the wash-stand to mop behind it, and wasn't there a package there all wrapped up in brown paper. A man brung it and I'd took it up an hour or so before ye stalked outta there like ye wuz Lady High Muckety Muck. Guess it got knocked down when ye wuz packing, so I snatched it up and hid it in my apron, but I didn't know where you wuz, did I? I kept it fer ye 'cause you was always so nice t'me. Tell me where you're staying, an' I'll fetch it t' ye."

They were passing Stewart's Marble Palace now. A crew of Irishmen were out shoveling the sidewalks, but the snow was being blown back as fast as they got rid of it. Anna had no idea what the package might be. Something from her publisher, maybe, that she had overlooked in her distress. In any case, she didn't want anyone from Mrs. Chapman's—aside from Eben—to know she was at the Merchant's. "Can you get away after dinner today and bring it to me? I'll buy you a good supper—oyster stew at that oyster saloon on Dey Street."

"Oyster stew? Oooeee! That'll beat the scraps Ol' Lady Chapman feeds us in the kitchen. I ain't had nothin' fer breakfast t'day but a cold potato. Oh," she jumped up, "Duane Street. Here's me stop. I can be there, say, around lamplighting time." She handed her copper coins to the driver through the hole in the car's roof, he slackened the rope that kept the door closed, and she jumped the steps. With the agility of a cat, she landed upright on the street, snow spilling over the tops of her ungainly boots.

Anna was on her way to Caroline's, and all the way up to Astor Place, she wondered about the package Nancy had, who it was from, what was in it, how she had overlooked it. She began to feel the cold bite into her bare fingers; it was her turn now to tuck her hands into her armpits. A ragged woman bent beneath her load of firewood, broken boards and old timbers from a demolished building, was crossing Broadway, and the car slowed to let her pass. Plodding like a packhorse, she turned down Anthony Street toward the Five Points. Anna sighed at the thought of the grim hovel awaiting the poor woman, and that so very close to the grandeur and prosperity of this magnificent stretch of Broadway. But now, absent its shoppers, Broadway was like a deserted landscape in one of those new-fashioned stereoscope boxes: the windows of Appleton's bookstore drifted over with snow; the white marble front of the St. Nicholas Hotel at Broome almost invisible in the whirling flakes; Niblo's Garden, a white blur on the right. The undistinguished building which housed Pfaff's Saloon was just above Bleecker, but she didn't even catch a glimpse of it.

At Astor Place, when she got down from the omnibus, she narrowly missed being knocked head over heels by a young uptown dandy racing past in a shiny sleigh with a pair of fast horses. He was going so fast the ends of his long scarf stood straight out behind him. As she approached Caroline's house, Anna concentrated on remaining upright and avoiding the worst of the drifts.

"What should girls read?" Caroline asked, as Anna entered the library.

"Everything," Anna replied. A log fire crackled in the library's massive stone fireplace, and she went to the hearth and held her reddened hands out past the hand-painted fire screen. Behind her, she could hear Caroline taking books from shelves and slapping them down on the long carved mahogany table where 'Bama sat. "What are you doing?"

"Emerson," Caroline said, "of course. And Carlyle. Browning. Tennyson. Lowell. Barrett ..." *Slap. Slap. Slap.*

Caro sat down at a curved escritoire and tapped her fingers restlessly on the green felt of its open leaf. "You remember, don't you, that 'Bama and I were considering a ... project?"

"Yes." Although many weeks had passed, Anna had heard nothing more about it.

"Well, this is it," 'Bama cut in. "A bold project, if I say so myself. We're going to open a boarding school—an academy—for colored girls."

"How wonderful!" Anna cried.

"Yes. Isn't it?" the older woman replied. "At first we'll take in promising girls from the Colored Orphan Asylum. Most of them go out into service, now, when they come of age, say fourteen, but many have it within themselves to do so much more—"

"Yes," Caro interrupted. "'Bama will be Head of School. We'll provide comprehensive education in science and liberal studies. When finished, the girls can go to college, if they want—we'll find places for them and pay their expenses."

"With Mr. Lincoln's administration coming into Washington," 'Bama said, "things should soon be very different. We'll need all the educated women we can find."

"I've already written to the faculty at Oberlin College," Caroline added, "about supplying us with graduates for teachers, ladies both colored and white. I'll endow the school in perpetuity. This, we think, would be the most fitting use for my misbegotten fortune."

Anna was thrilled. "What a difference it will make in so many lives!"

Caroline nodded. "That's the purpose. And the family mansion in Oyster Bay is large enough to be the school building. We'll begin renovation in the spring and hope to start classes by this time next year."

Anna shook her head in wonderment at the daring of her friends' vision. "Oh, ladies," she said, "that is absolutely splendid! What can I do to help?"

Caroline clapped her hands. "We were hoping you'd ask! For now, we need help compiling the list of books to be purchased for the school's library. So, I ask again: What *should* girls read?" Caroline's gold pen was poised over a sheet of fine paper.

"Everything," Anna repeated, thinking of her own good education at Mount Holyoke Seminary, and of the many books she had devoured at Manhattan's free reading rooms since she'd returned from India. "Novels by the Bronte sisters, George Eliot, Mrs. Stowe; Mrs. Gaskell; the philosophical writings of Mr. Alcott, Mr. Thoreau's journals from Walden Pond. And, of course, Mr. Whitman's poems. I can make up a comprehensive list."

'Bama, lips twisted, gave her a sidelong look. "Frederick Douglass's slave narrative, Olaudah Equiano's autobiography." She had a stack of books in front of her on the table, her own possessions, it seemed, and was turning them over, one by one. They looked well-read. "The poems of Mrs. Phillis Wheatley," she continued. "David Walker's 'Appeal to the Colored Citizens.' *The Narrative of Sojourner Truth* and her speeches, which Mrs. Frances Gage has written down. And many, many more by Negro writers." She looked up from her pile. "Then there are the marvelous sermons of Mrs. Julia Pell, if they've been written down anywhere. Mrs. Harriet Jacobs has written vividly in the *Tribune* of her experiences as a slave in North Carolina—I believe she has a book in preparation."

Aside from Mr. Douglass, whom she had seen in Broadway one day walking boldly between two white women, Anna had heard of none of these colored writers. She reached out for 'Bama's books and picked up the first that came to hand: Frances Harper, *Poems on Miscellaneous Subjects*.

In a stack of magazines, she found *Freedom's Journal* and the *Anglo-African*. Anna felt chastened, as 'Bama had clearly intended she should be, by her own presumption of being thoroughly and authoritatively well-read.

Caroline was writing as fast as she could. Now she handed the sheet of paper over to her cousin. "Correct my spelling on these, will you, 'Bama? And perhaps the Colored Ladies Literary Society can add to the list. Now, Anna," she said, sliding more paper across the table. "You make your list—and include your own poems, of course. The girls will love them—especially, I imagine, the Indian ones. And I have a compilation here that Eben gave me—Theodore Parker, Henry Ward Beecher, Miss Margaret Fuller—poor Miss Fuller who drowned so tragically with her husband and baby just off of Fire Island—Orestes Brownson, Nathaniel Hawthorne, William Gilmore Sims, Alexis de Tocqueville. Mrs. Lydia Child. Miss Sedgwick. It goes on and on. Shakespeare, of course, and Chaucer, and Milton. Eben, too, says the girls should read Mr. Whitman. That a good jolt of pure natural 'American blab' will be good for them after their pious education at the Orphan Asylum." She laughed, savoring the journalist's turn of phrase.

So, now, Caroline had taken to quoting Eben Garrett's advice. She was still seeing a great deal of the journalist. Anna wondered, not for the first time, just what their intentions were.

Anna left Lafayette Place in good time to meet Nancy at the oyster saloon by dusk. The streets had been salted, then churned into a muddy mess by the trampling of horses, and the traffic had assumed its usual cacophony of wheels, hooves, and the coarse shouts of drivers. She went first to the ready-made shops in Baxter Street to buy a parcel of things for Nancy; it seemed only right to trade one package for another.

The lamplighter had just passed with his ladder and tall pole, and Nancy, shifting from one foot to the other, was waiting for Anna in the circle of wavering light from the oyster saloon's painted lamps. She looked, if possible, even colder and more ragged than she had that morning. Anna said, "This is for you," and handed over the bulky string-tied bundle.

Nancy tore open the heavy brown paper and a pair of sturdy new shoes tumbled onto the sidewalk. "Holy Mary, Mother of God!" She clasped them to her scrawny chest as if she'd just give birth to unexpected, but wondrous, children, then threw her arms around Anna, granting her, even in the crisp open air, a whiff of unwashed garments and rancid onion. It was all she could do to refrain from pulling out her lavender-drenched handkerchief.

"There's more." Anna pulled a warm flannel wrap from the package, following it with a red wool hood. The servant girl snatched up the warm hood and draped it over her head, tying the strings with shaking hands.

"It's a good woman, you are, Mrs. Wheeler," she said, "an' if I had the doin' of it, I'd name ye for a saint."

Anna laughed. "Nonsense. Put your new wrapper on, Nancy, and let's go get our supper."

This subterranean eating house was a respectable establishment, as its location suggested, and the men savoring raw oysters at the long bar paid Anna and Nancy no insult. A black waiter in a long apron nodded them toward the brightly lit dining chamber beyond the noisy barroom. From an adjacent kitchen, came the clatter of pottery, the banging of pots, and the rich, buttery odor of stewed oysters. Anna ordered two dishes of the succulent bivalves and a pot of tea.

From a long table across the room arose a roar of masculine laughter. The stolid German woman seated across from Anna and Nancy scowled at the raucous group gathered around a long table. They were burly men, and young, in the loose yoked shirts and round hats of workers: omnibus drivers and cartmen, puffing on cigars and guffawing at each-others' witticisms.

Nancy, having devoured her fat sweet oysters with great appetite, tucked into a slab of apple pie. Only when finished with that, did she seem to notice the tableful of strapping young men, and then she was transfixed by them.

Anna laughed. "Nancy, be careful. You'll lose your eyes if you pop them any further out of your head!"

The housemaid looked abashed, eyes skewed suddenly down and fingers tightly twined. "Ye can't take me nowhere," she said, looking back up at Anna, "but what I make a great fool of meself. But ye must understand, Miss, I ain't seen so many pretty boyos in one place ever in me life."

She delved into a capacious pocket, pulled forth a string-tied parcel wrapped in brown paper, and handed it over. "And here I am, forgettin' what I come for."

Anna inspected the package. Her name, and only her name, was written on it in thick, penciled block letters. Hand delivered, then. She felt it. A book, she thought. She'd open it later; the multitude of tight knots in the string would require some attention.

FIFTY

Full of good food and feeling the warm afterglow of a good deed, Anna returned to her room at the Merchant's Hotel. She took off her warm cloak, shook it to remove the street grit from its hem, and hung it in the oak wardrobe. The chambermaid had been in to close the curtains and turn down the bed. Anna sat in the upholstered chair by the window with the small package and attempted to untie the string. After five minutes and a broken finger nail she resorted to scissors from her sewing kit. Finally the brown paper fell back revealing a black-covered book, *The Good Wife*, by the Rev. Adrian Burroughs. Anna stared at it, not making any sense of this ... this ... what? Gift? Offering? Admonition? An advice book, it seemed, but nothing she had ordered—or even *wanted*. She paged through it, mystified, and a cream-colored envelope fell out, an envelope addressed to Mrs. Anna Wheeler Roundtree. Her blood ran cold.

The handwriting was Josiah's. It was dated four months earlier.

October 1860

Wife—

The Lord, in his omniscience, has led me to his faithful handmaidens, Mrs. Margaret Ambrose and Miss Susan Parker, longtime correspondents and supporters of our Mission in Fatehgarh. Although it pained them exquisitely to do so, they made me aware of the shameful birth to you—my wife!—of a dark-skinned bastard!

Oh, Anna, what am I to think? Were you savagely defiled by one of the Satan's spawn who have wreaked such havoc upon God's work in India? Or you are a woman of no moral character whatsoever? Could I have been so defrauded in my long devotion to you? My little wife, I do not know which caused me more pain—the thought that you had been violated by mutineers or the fear that, weak in your woman's spirit, you had succumbed to a heathen's wiles. Oh, Anna! Can you imagine the hell it was for me? To be forced to wish you ravished rather than lost in sin!

As your husband and as a devout man with a single object in life, to honor God and his teachings, I know myself to be responsible both to you and to this ... whelp ... of yours, to whom I am in law and conscience, but clearly not in actuality, father. Concerned with the salvation of the child's soul, Miss Parker had recently taken steps to secure custody of the unlawful brat from the godless home where it had been residing and to oversee its care at the Hudson Home. The Lord thus determined my course of action—to salvage it for Our Redeemer's fold.

Thus, I now have your child.

If you are of penitent spirit and wish to return to your wifely duties and submit yourself once again to me, as our Lord commands, you will find your whelp now with me at the boarding house of Mrs. Helen Etheridge in Fourteenth Street. I propose, in all Christian obligation to take both you and your misbegotten child under my benevolent protection. If I do not hear from you ...

But that does not bear thinking of.

Your Husband,

The Reverend Josiah Pierce Roundtree

Josiah was alive! That in itself rendered Anna near insensible with shock. But she was transfixed with horror by the knowledge that he had her daughter. She shuddered as she re-read the letter. Even to save the child, could she spend the rest of her years with this smug, joyless tyrant? But, oh, oh, she must, or poor, tempest-tossed India Elizabeth would be lost to her forever?

But … could she? No, she must calm herself and think. Would the law indeed consider Josiah, as Anna's husband, to be India's lawful father? Everyone knew of notorious instances, reported at length in the newspapers, of fathers refusing estranged wives access to their children—and being supported by the courts. She could not bear the thought: her beloved, long-sought daughter—the precious child of Ashok—to be brought up by this … wooden-hearted, sanctimonious bully! Wasn't it enough that Anna had poisoned her own life by devoting her youth to Josiah Roundtree? But her daughter—? No. No! The daguerreotype case made a small golden click as she opened it to gaze helpless once more at her daughter's innocent face.

This letter had been dated months ago, but she had never known Josiah to be less than implacable once he had determined upon a course of action. Why hadn't she heard from him since? She glanced around her comfortable hotel room, a hot-house rose gracing a crystal vase on the table next to her, a fire crackling in the small hearth. Of course! He did not know where to find her! And he could not possibly know that this missive had been delayed in reaching her.

She must go to him! And—now! Anna could hardly button her boots, pull on her gloves, each loop, each finger presenting a unique and hopeless quandary. It took her, it seemed, a year—a century—to prepare herself once again to go out into the inhospitable nighttime streets.

As Anna left the hotel, she heard a church bell chime ten. She hurried past shuttered shops and past a still-lighted apothecary's with its show-window jars gleaming in crimson, blue, and green. On Broadway, no cabs would stop for an unaccompanied woman at this time of night. Finally she secured one by stepping boldly from behind a chest-high sidewalk drift into its path and forcing the driver to rein in hard on his horses. Half-asleep, reeking of cheap spirits and even cheaper Long Island cigars, he was reluctant to take her up, but her offer to pay triple the fare secured her a ride to Fourteenth Street.

The house she sought was two blocks to the east of Union Square, a large unornamented four-story brick painted in somber gray. Ah—this was the same house in which she and Josiah had passed the year of their mission training. In the light of the street lamp, Anna threw open the gate of the low wrought-iron fence and charged up the steps to the front door. Every vestige of snow had been shoveled from walkway and granite steps, and the latter were scrupulously gritted with fine sand.

Behind drawn curtains, lights had been dimmed for the evening. She pulled the bell handle. When there was no immediate response, she pulled it twice more. Seconds passed, and Anna began pounding on the door. It flew open and a colored boy, perhaps twelve years of age, stood buttoning up a white cotton shirt and staring at her. Behind him a handsome woman in a blue dressing gown hastened down a mahogany staircase, frowning. At past ten o'clock in the evening, it was unheard of for a respectable boarding house to receive visitors. But when Anna asked for the Reverend Josiah Roundtree, she was admitted in from the cold.

The landlady said, yes, the good reverend and the little girl had been there at the boarding house. Her breath smelled of peppermint humbug. When she spoke, the sweet scent suffused each word. He'd handed the child over into the care of the housemaids, she said. They'd been much troubled with her; from the beginning she'd been neither happy nor well-behaved.

"That's the difficulty with attempting to rescue a waif from the streets." Mrs. Etheridge said. She had not cared to invite Anna into her parlor, and now, as they stood in the drafty hall, she pulled together more tightly the bodice of her wool dressing gown. Wax pansies wilted under a glass dome on the hall mantle. "That degraded class of people is from birth simply incapable of learning civilized behavior. Especially the darkies."

"From the streets?" Anna stripped off her gloves, finger by finger, so she could grasp the closed daguerreotype case in the pocket of her cape.

"Yes, Reverend Roundtree found that little girl abandoned on the sidewalk in Cow Bay, he said, a lewd and insalubrious neighborhood. He is a saintly, goodhearted man, so of course her plight distressed him."

Mrs. Etheridge reached up to straighten a gold-framed crewel-work motto hanging on the wall. In fastidiously stitched letters it read, *What is Home Without a Mother?*

"Is this the child?" With trembling hands, Anna showed the portrait of India Elizabeth.

"Yes." The landlady screwed up her round, prim face. "But how did you—"

Anna cut her off with a sharp gesture. "Is she … well?"

"She's *well*—but she's not well-tempered. Little Prudence was nothing but a source of upset in this household—obstinate ways, incessant fits of temper."

"Prudence? Her name is—"

"Prudence. He said since she had to be called something, it might as well be edifying. Who knows if she even had had a name on the streets. But I must say, the Christian name did nothing to make a Christian out of that imp. I was not in the least distressed when one day, after a fortnight of trouble, Reverend Roundtree left with the child and came back alone."

Anna's heart went cold. "Where," she ventured, "did the Reverend Roundtree take little … Prudence?"

Mrs. Etheridge shrugged most inelegantly. "Probably back to the street where he found her."

Anna cringed, but the woman went on. "I didn't ask—I was only too glad to be rid of her."

Biting her lower lip, Anna asked, "And where might I find Reverend Roundtree?"

The landlady frowned. "I don't know. It was odd. He stayed here all the autumn and winter with no word of leaving, then about a week ago he came home from the Post Office in a great rush with a letter clenched in his fist. Said God was calling him back to the mission field. He seemed almost beside himself, not ecstatic the way I would think someone would who'd had a divine call. Packed up his steamer trunk and hailed a cab. Wouldn't even tell me where to forward his mail."

Suddenly she seemed to register Anna's distress. She frowned. "But why do you want to know?"

"The mission field?" Horrific possibilities unrolled before Anna's eyes like some appalling scroll of Revelation. "Where? Where in the mission field?"

Mrs. Etheridge looked askance at her increasingly distraught visitor. As a sign of dismissal, she took up the kerosene lamp from the half-moon hall table and turned toward the front door. "Burma, was it? Or Ceylon? No. No. It was India. He said he was going to India—and he was taking that little colored girl with him."

When Anna returned to the hotel from her desperate visit to Josiah's boarding house, the desk clerk handed her a city-post-marked letter along with her key. "Shortly after you went out, Madam, a Mr. Garrett came in and left this for you. He said to tell you, Bridey found it on the hall table when she got home from dinner. She thought he might know where to find you."

Anna knew the handwriting. She held the missive tight in a sweaty fist until she'd climbed the two flights of stairs, opened her room door, bolted the door behind her, sunk down into a small blue-upholstered chair. Then she pried off the green wax monogram stamp—*JPR*—opened the sheet of foolscap, and read:

> *Wife—*
>
> *I am on my way to the South Street docks to take ship with your bastard child for the country where the heathen brat was spawned. I thought you dead, you know, that you had died a martyr's holy death, and I mourned you with all my wounded heart. Then, returning, with my widower's melancholy, to New-York, I was rudely disabused, informed by a Christian friend that you had sought refuge at the Five-Points Mission, pregnant with a bastard child. A child of the native complexion, as it turned out! Think of my horror and my shame!*
>
> *When Miss Parker, my righteous friend, first learned that you sought the child, she recovered it from its habitation, lest you find it there. Could you want more evidence of God's providence? She did not at that moment have any idea that you were*

my wife! Yet when I sought her out and told her my piteous story, and that you published as Anna Wheeler, she, with saddened heart informed me of your perfidy. As I told you in the letter I left at your boarding house months ago, the letter that you did not deign to answer, *I recovered the girl from her in hopes that I might persuade you to return to me, as the law requires. It soon became clear that you would not respond to my plea, and I decided to place her in some rigorous educational institution for the colored where she would be taught the ways of virtue, modesty, piety, and service to others.*

But worse was yet to come! By the merest happenstance—or by the Grace of God!—I intercepted, last week, your seducer's letter. *Mr. Ashok Mongomery! That half-caste hypocrite who had led me to believe he was a friend of the mission!!! Oh what heartache! My wife could give that idolater a child—but none for me!*

He dares write of love—the black licentious brute! God has led me to understand that I must confront this heathen seducer face to face and fling his betrayal in his teeth! As a godly man, I will right the wrong that has been done both to my honor and to my race! Your brat is the embodiment of his sin—and yours!—and I will thrust her into his filthy hands. He shall be the one to determine her fate—whether she will be raised in soul-killing pagan luxury or thrown out into the streets with the other beggar bastards. In either case her fate shall be sealed. By the time you receive this missive, she will be gone forever from New-York—and from any hope of Christian salvation. Along with her perfidious mother and father, the little imp will be doomed to hellfire for eternity!

Your Deceived Husband,
The Rev. Josiah Pierce Roundtree

FIFTY-ONE

After waking, half-stunned by nightmares in which she dreamed about ravenous crows snatching up babies laid out in rows as if they were grown in neat New-England cabbage beds, Anna left her hotel for Caroline's house well before the breakfast hour. She had come to feel that she had only one choice; for the sake of her child, she must return to her marriage. The law was the law. A married woman, she was legally a *feme covert*—her legal identity was subsumed under her husband's. Upon Anna's marriage, her person and everything she possessed had become Josiah's. She remembered that well. If the law now said her child belonged to Josiah—if there was any possibility of that—she could not leave her alone in his hands.

As she hastened through hushed streets toward Lafayette Place, sunlight shone straight across Broadway from the east, turning plate glass windows to gold. A big white omnibus sidled up to the curbstone, and a clerk with a ring of jangling keys stepped down, tipping his hat at her. Near City Hall a man with a paste pot and long-handled brush slapped up a Barnum's American Museum poster on a tall wooden-slat fence and the pungent wheat-paste odor made Anna sneeze. A newly awakened pig slowed her as it dashed furiously toward its feast of eggshells, potato parings, onion skins—garbage flung from home kitchens into the side-street gutters.

Between sips of steaming coffee at Caroline's breakfast table, Anna showed her friend the fateful letters. "In my worst nightmares I couldn't have imagined a more malign twist of fate than that ... that *man* would return from the dead." A great gulping sob escaped her.

"Just what is it he wants?" Caroline asked, Josiah's second letter dangling from her hand.

"He wants his wife back," Anna said, in the flat tones of the hopeless. "Not *me*, you understand, but *His Wife*. And so you see. . . I must return—"

"Bah!" Caroline slapped the missive down on the table. "Don't be a ninny. If you go to India, it will be on your terms, not his! You have the means to do it, and I will help in any way I can."

Startled, Anna sputtered, "B-b-but the law says—"

"Nonsense! The laws of this state changed, oh, about a decade ago—don't you remember? The Married Woman's Property Act."

Anna shrugged. No—she didn't recall this. Or she'd never heard. "We didn't get many issues of the *New York Tribune* in Fatehgarh, India."

"Well, in 'forty-eight our noble male legislators, those Lords of the Universe up in Albany, deigned to pass a law that allows women the rights to property. Your lack of knowledge is just what the Very Reverend Mr. Roundhead—"

"Roundtree," Anna corrected, automatically.

Caroline shrugged. "—what that vicious man wants. He wants you to think he has legal rights to your daughter because that's the only way he can control you. But, now, whatever women bring into a marriage with them, whatever they earn, whatever is gifted to them—they *own* it. Legally." Caroline took an absentminded sip from her coffee. "About your child—and nobody, seeing her, could possibly think she was Josiah Roundtree's—there would be no question in a New York courtroom of who should have custody."

"But she isn't in New York! He's taken her off to India!"

"So? She's an American citizen. The British Raj will respect that and help you retrieve her."

Someone laughed—a harsh sound. Anna and Caroline swiveled to stare. 'Bama stood in the doorway, holding Rosie, the child still in her rumpled nightclothes, thumb in her mouth, head on "Bama's shoulder. How long had they been there?

"I'm sorry—that was rude," 'Bama said. "But it's just that . . ." she stopped for a moment to kiss Rosie on top of her tousled curls ". . . hearing you speak so confidently of the law—even as far away as India—allowing you to reclaim a child based on her citizenship. . . . Well, I think about this poor, sweet imp, conceived here and born here—right here in the United States of America. But *Rosie* is not an American citizen. No law exists that can reclaim *her*." 'Bama's eyes sparked. "Except back into slavery!"

Anna opened her mouth to speak. But 'Bama held up a weary hand. "Enough for now." She handed the child to Caroline and sat down at the table. "May I read your husband's letters, Mrs. Wheeler?" When she had finished, she looked over at Anna. "Mrs. Wheeler, you may not want to hear this from me, but I'll say it—you are not thinking straight. *I* am a colored woman—it might be possible in this nation for someone to claim the right of ownership over me and my child—although I would fight it tooth and nail, body and soul. But you are a white woman. He cannot own *you*." To Anna's great surprise, 'Bama reached out and squeezed her hand.

Anna responded with a smile, the first she had ever given Mrs. Alabama Fitch.

Caroline nodded emphatically. "'Bama's right, of course. But, Anna, you're behaving as if he does own you. The shock of that man's letters is so recent you haven't had time to think it through." She took up an apple muffin from a covered basket brought in by the multi-braided kitchen girl. "Answer me this, Anna: have you read Miss Bronte's *Jane Eyre*?"

"Yes." Realizing she hadn't eaten since last night's oyster stew, Anna took a steaming muffin from the basket and broke it in half.

Wiping buttery fingers on her napkin, Caroline continued, "Do you remember when Jane returns to Mr. Rochester—what she says to him?"

Anna shook her head, no, although she did remember it as having been a triumphant moment in the story. She bit into the muffin.

"She says," Caroline paused and took another small sip of her coffee. "She says, 'I am an independent woman now.'"

"Ha!" Anna sat up straight. *An independent woman*. The words strengthened her. Once again she had almost succumbed to Josiah's imperious influence! But now these friends had set her back on the right path. *An independent woman*. Henceforth she would live her life as such. In Caroline's breakfast room with its sunny furnishings, she was flooded with a renewed consciousness of her autonomous will.

"This is what I shall do," she said, slowly, as she finished the muffin. "I shall take ship for Calcutta as soon as it can be arranged. That's where Josiah will have gone. He knows the city and he has a community of fellow missionaries there. I'll confront him and recover—no, rescue, *redeem*—my daughter."

India Elizabeth was Ashok's daughter, as well, she thought, with a slight *frisson*. While in Calcutta, she would speak to her child's true father. What was in the letter Josiah had intercepted? He'd said something like, "the brute spoke of love." *Love*! Had Ashok written to her of *love*? If she did seek him out, after such a long silence, would she find a welcome?

As if from a long distance off, she heard Caroline speaking. "I would go with you, of course, as I did to Charleston, except for one thing."

"What is that?" She pulled her thoughts away from Ashok.

"Eben and I ... well ... we are expecting a child in the Fall."

The following morning Caroline went with Anna to the shipping offices on Hanover Square. At the third they visited, on the passenger list of the British ship *Blenheim*, which had just departed for Calcutta, the last ship of the season, they found the names of the Reverend Josiah Pierce Roundtree and his ward, Prudence Wheeler.

Anna booked passage on the first ship scheduled to leave in the spring.

She stood with Caroline and Eben on the broad East River quay in the midst of head-high stacks of boxes and bales, the spring morning air tainted by the stink of sewage, hot tar, and rotting fish, loud with sailor's rough shouts and the short, sharp clapping of the buoys, and she marveled at her own daring. It was not that she was brave; indeed she was all but immobilized with anxiety. A woman alone to take ship halfway around the earth! Was this an act of unfathomable folly? To travel unprotected in a company of strangers! But there was no help for it; her daughter awaited her, and she would go.

A five-piece German band blared out the first notes of "Auf Weidersein." Bridey came back from somewhere with a bouquet of paper roses for Anna. Eben jokingly offered her a sausage on a stick, but a thin black dog jumped up and snapped it out of his hand before she could refuse it. Rosie held out her arms to be hugged. At the last minute, Mr. Greeley, rotund and disheveled in his famous white coat, came huffing up with a copy of Mrs. Child's *Letters from New-York*. "In case you get homesick," he said.

Homesick? Yes, indeed. Once on deck, Anna took to the rail, waving the lace-edged linen handkerchief 'Bama had given her. This mismatched group of friends was the closest thing she had to family. She kept waving, although their faces were blurred through tears. When the ship began to steam out of the harbor, she remained at her place. They passed the crowded ferryboat from Brooklyn, passengers, with their eyes fixed on the Manhattan shore, oblivious of the departing ship. Further out, the Battery came into sight, ships of many nations riding at anchor. Despite the chill, the sun was bright and merchants had lowered their awnings. Myriad colors and stripes caught the brittle light. Flags waved everywhere. Lofty structures of five and six stories loomed in the distance, the modern steel framework transforming the skyline as modest frame buildings fell to the wrecker's hammers.

As Anna moved away from the rail, still clutching 'Bama's handkerchief, a sense of severance nearly overwhelmed her. This city, vast and impersonal, was now her home. She had made it such, and if the city had not exactly welcomed her, it had accommodated her. Homesick? Yes, oh, yes. She glanced back to the harbor, a grand half circle now, dark green and gray against the sea-blue waters. *Wait for me*, she breathed. *Wait*. Then she turned her face to the East. *India Elizabeth*, she thought, *where are you? Ashok*, she thought, *will I find you in Calcutta? Will you welcome me? Will you even remember me?*

FIFTY-TWO

Calcutta
1861

Calcutta

1 August 1861

My Dear Caroline,

I have been here in Calcutta for three days. You will call me foolish, I know, but since my arrival I have spent hours each day walking in the bazaars, searching the faces of the little children, even more futile an endeavor here than in New-York. Futile, futile! But, oh, the little brown faces are so beautiful! I have but to raise my glance from the packed earth of the streets and I see India Elizabeth everywhere. Running plump and dark and naked through the fish stalls. Clean and cosseted in a sari of white muslin, her ayah alongside with a silk parasol. Begging in rags on the steps of a Hindu temple.

I have decided now to call my daughter Elizabeth (without the India) in order to avoid confusion with the land of her conception. She would be—she is—three-and-a-half-years of age now. Walking, talking—thinking. What must she make of her life? Such abrupt changes—a home with loving parents, brown like herself; abduction by one cold, white stranger and, then, another; months and months of ocean voyage; then arrival in a loud and incomprehensible city. Is she frightened? Is she lonely? I fear so for her.

But, now as to my search. I have established myself in a hotel in Garden Reach, a most respectable address, and I have employed a banian, *a man of affairs. As an* angrezi *(English—here we are all "English") I require an intermediary to make inquiries and arrangements in the Indian community, and Mr. Satish Ghosh was recommended by the ship's captain as both honest and astute. He is Indo-Briton, a small, extremely proper man of few words and much efficiency, having fluent English. I speak some halting Hindustanee, so we get on together well enough.*

I've told him everything, and, even given my scandalous story, he has listened with a bland acceptance. I have been assured of his ability to keep confidence, and, certainly, I pay him rupees sufficient to buy his loyal silence. He has a large family to support, he tells me, and he bargained cannily until my initial salary offer was tripled. "Five daughters," he said, over and over. "Must provide dowry for five daughters." How could I—in search of my own daughter—deny him his just competence? He begins today to make inquiries among the servants of American missionaries to see if any have news of my child.

I shall write again as soon as I receive intelligence of either Josiah or my child.

Your Friend,

Anna

Post-scriptum: I post under separate cover a manuscript I penned on the journey, having had little else to occupy my mind. It is a long story called "The Girl in the Red Stockings," inspired by an audacious waif of about twelve I once saw in Paradise Square sporting a pair of crimson stockings and flirting with the men as if she were a hardened trollop. I hope this tale may call attention to the conditions that force children like her to such a life. I would appreciate it if you would try to find a publisher willing to bring out such a raw story. On my best days

I think of it as being something like Mrs. Stowe's Uncle Tom, *written in aid of the poor. On my worst days ... But that doesn't bear thinking of.*

Postmarked Calcutta
2 August 1861

New-York City
20 April 1861

Oh, Anna—we are now at war with the Southern states! I suppose by the time you receive this letter, you will know all about the bombardment by the Confederates of Fort Sumpter off the Charleston Battery—right there where you and I stood and looked out at the stars and stripes waving proudly from the battlements! But, Anna, the fort has been surrendered to those wicked secessionists, and at the moment we are all still in a state of absolute shock. President Lincoln has issued a proclamation announcing the blockade of Southern ports. Eben tells me that Mr. Greeley says this constitutes a de facto *declaration of war! Our nation is now riven in two—who could have imagined such a calamity? Even those wealthier, more powerful (and self-interested) New-Yorkers who have been advocating leniency for "our Southern cousins" have come to their senses. Today a mighty multitude gathered in Union Square in fervent support of our nation, everyone brandishing a flag or sporting a red-white-and blue-cockade. All around the Square there was such commotion—speechifying, hurrahing, and song. Flags flew from every building. What a show! Let us hope our fellow NewYorkers will volunteer to* fight *in similar numbers as they volunteer to* shout!

Which leaves me, Anna, to testify that I, selfishly, do not wish Eben to enlist. He is all aglow with patriotism and would volunteer at the drop of a hat. But I ... I ... what will I do if he goes to war?—one child already on hand, and another to arrive in four months? And 'Bama immersed in preparations for the opening of the Oyster Bay School.

Which brings me to yet another issue—pregnancy. I am as healthy as a brood mare, and no longer appear in public without my condition being noticed—and discussed! As if I have not already given Society enough to gossip about! But neither Eben nor I wish to marry. We have talked and talked about it, and have made a considered decision. He has no desire to be seen as a fortune-hunter—he feels strongly about that. And I take inspiration from Miss Margaret Fuller, who deemed marriage to be only one experience among many in a woman's life—not the be-all and end-all. And as I have no pressing need to ensure my future monetary security, Eben and I may live together in happiness without binding ourselves in law. And we are happy, Anna, very much so! I bless you every day for bringing Eben Garrett into my ken!

The Oyster Bay School of Superior Education for Friendless Colored Girls is, as you know, well in the works with 'Bama as Head of School. And, in a more controversial decision, we have this week hired our mutual acquaintance, Bridget O'Neill, to oversee the girls in their daily life—perhaps as Matron. Not a conventional choice, I know—but they will need someone who is frank and honest (and knowledgeable) about the trials and temptations of motherless young women in the bloom of their beauty—and about the consequences of their appeal to venal and selfish men. 'Bama and I have spoken with her at length, and we are comfortable that the girls' health and well-being will be safe in her hands. Bridey is intelligent, honest, plain-spoken, and bold. And she knows the fundamentals of the female body. I also search for a female physician—not so easy to come by. And, we will need a housekeeper—did you once mention a reliable house girl called Nancy?

Oh, Anna, how I miss you! Come home as soon as you can. Rosie is well and happy—and is turning into a terrible scamp!

She needs the calming influence of your dear India Elizabeth. May you find her soon! Lovingly, Caroline

Letter Arrived, GARDEN REACH HOTEL
20 August 1861
HOLD FOR RETURN OF MRS. ANNA WHEELER

Calcutta
7 August 1861,

Oh, Caroline, I should be ashamed to tell you this, but the handsome Bengali men in the bazaars entice me so! I see Ashok everywhere—and nowhere—immersed here—in this place—in India! It all comes back. Such joy! As if he had ripped a low ceiling from my sky! But, even more, the smile in his eyes when he gazed at me— The likeness of his beautiful face everywhere. I feel as if I am falling in love all over again, this time with a memory—or with a ghost.

*Twice I have visited the large mercantile establishment owned by Ashok's father on the pretense to myself of purchasing a length of taffeta, for which I have no need. And, even more shameful, the day of my arrival I hired a rickshaw to drive me past Ashok's home. It's more splendid even than I recall from my days there when Ashok brought me down from the tea plantation in the hills. I have been compelled by some mad instinct to return twice. Always the house has appeared empty, closed up, perhaps, for the season. But, today, as I passed in my conveyance, citing the roughness of the cobbled streets as an excuse for urging the rick-shaw-*wallah *to drive more slowly, the great door of the mansion opened, and a party of ladies and gentlemen emerged, surrounded by a host of servants. His father I knew at once, for he was white in a darker company. My heart rose painfully, and I strained my eyes to see—was Ashok among them? Too soon their carriages arrived and came between us, and the scene was lost to me.*

*Oh, Ashok, what if I had called to the rickshaw-*wallah *to stop? What if I had begged entrance at the gate? Would you have welcomed me? What if I told you of our child? Would you have joined me in my quest?*

But, no. If I approach you it will be only after your child is found.

Oh, Ashok, do you ever think of me? Intolerable thought, what if you have married one of those fluttering silk-clad ladies at your door?

Anna reread the letter, winced with embarrassment, and tore it into tiny pieces. In no way could she post such maudlin clap-trap to anyone, not even to such a close friend as Caroline Slade.

FIFTY-THREE

The brutal August sun was relieved only occasionally by a low cloud cover and accompanying thunderstorm, but Anna was used to this heat and had quickly reacclimatized. On the hotel verandah overlooking the Hooghly River she sat on a rattan chair by a low marble table, Josiah's crumpled letter clenched in a fist so tight that her fingernails cut into the heel of her hand. "This is what I must know," she said to Satish Ghosh. "Where is my daughter? Did Josiah Roundtree bring her to Calcutta? Did he meet with Mr. Montgomery? Which one of them now has the child?"

Anna's *banian*, a short man with shrewd brown eyes, perched on the edge of a bamboo stool on the wide hotel verandah. Satish Ghosh was some forty years of age and wore a suit of white nankeen. His waistcoat, embroidered with white thread on creamy linen, strained across a protuberant belly. It had been his intention to stand throughout the interview, but Anna's expressed impatience with the stiff Asian formality had at last convinced him into a semblance of ease.

Satish Ghosh, having been raised in the manners and languages of both Indian and British cultures, and with an extensive acquaintance everywhere, was proving invaluable to Anna as steward, go-between, interpreter, inquiry agent. Anna had known many Indo-Britons in the past, Hindu, Christian, even Muslim. Some were children of legitimate marriages, others of less permanent liaisons. People of mixed race participated in society in widely differing manners. A number of the men were clerks and teachers, some even missionaries, others were merchants on an extensive scale, as, of course, was Ashok.

Removing his steel-rimmed glasses, the man squinted at his employer. "I have a few answers for you, Madame, but not many. The reverend sahib is landing on the American ship in June, during Monsoon, is staying in Calcutta at the Methodist Mission several days, and then is vanishing. And from the Mission servants I am learning nothing of his whereabouts at this moment now." He polished the glasses on the lapel of his spotless coat. "They tell me only that during his stay here the reverend is going out wandering into the city and is staying out long times even in the wet weather. When he returns to the mission he is speaking without stop to all other reverend gentlemen about killing of the Europeans at Cawnpore. He gives bloody detail nobody wants to hear—the mothers shot, the little babies cut to pieces—just as it tells in the newspapers. He is talking so much, he never ceases. Missionary sahibs take to going out of room when he comes in."

"What about my child?" Reading again the letter she had received from Josiah in New York had raised her anxieties to a fever pitch. And now this—Josiah sounded half-crazed. What would her husband be capable of doing? Had he confronted Ashok? Had he ... offered violence? She opened her clenched fist so she could spread the crumpled pages out upon the low table and read them again. Was Ashok safe? Was Elizabeth?

It was late afternoon. Although Anna had sheltered herself deep in the latticed shade, the heat remained torrid, and she was bathed in perspiration. A boy in a loincloth squatted in the corner, pulling the rope of the overhead *punkah*. With each pass she felt the big fan's breeze prickle the exposed skin of her face and arms.

Satish waited to reply until she looked up from the letter. "They are telling me nothing other than that he traveled with a little one. They say that the child will not speak."

Anna's eyes suddenly were filled with tears which burned, but didn't fall. "What have you learned about Sahib Ashok Montgomery?" she ventured finally.

Satish dropped his gaze. He fussed with a gold watch chain clipped to one of his waistcoat buttons. "Sahib Mongomery is not at present in Calcutta. He departed this city months ago, before the Reverend Roundtree arrives here. A discreet agent of mine is informing me that the sahib travels often on business affairs, to England and Europe. His servants never know when he will return, but are not expecting him soon."

"Ah," she said, "then Josiah did not see him."

"No, Madame, that would be true."

Anna did not know whether to grieve that Ashok was still unaware of Elizabeth's existence, or to rejoice that he had not been told in Josiah's vicious manner. Unaccountably, she felt once again bereft. She had taken comfort in believing that she was on the same continent as the man who'd transformed her heart. She had hoped that he might help her find their daughter. She had hoped ... Struggling to keep the weight of loss from her voice, she said, "Is it usual for him to be gone from home so very long?"

"Always he is seeking new markets for the family's tea and spices. He started first for London, but my agent thinks even Sahib Montgomery's father is not at present knowing his whereabouts." The watch chain now arranged to his satisfaction, he once again allowed his gaze to meet hers.

She took up Josiah's letter and read the words again: *thrown out into the streets with the other beggar bastards*. When he had not found Ashok at home, would Josiah then have abandoned Elizabeth? Beyond the walls of the hotel compound, she heard the piteous cries of mendicants among the calls of vendors in the bazaar. She could scarcely control the fearsome visions that passed before her mind's eye. Yesterday she had seen one skeletal child, naked but for a carefully woven red thread around her neck. Anna had given the girl an overflowing handful of *pice*, but knew the money would do little to save her. Now she swept her arm in the direction of the bazaar. "I fear he may have discarded Elizabeth among the beggars." The *punkah*'s strong breeze threatened to scatter the letter's pages, and Anna took them up again in a shaking hand.

"Asking pardon, Madame," Satish replied, in his gentle manner. "Why would reverend sahib do such a thing, after bringing the child so far over the oceans to return her to her father?"

"To punish me," Anna whispered. Too well she recalled Josiah's disciplinary methods, which ranged from the monitory finger at the lips to those more intimate in nature which she shuddered to bring to memory. She twisted the letter into a tight spiral and dashed it down again.

"Would he be so cruel?" Satish pulled a large square of linen from his breast pocket and set it on the table. She allowed it to sit for a long moment before she took it. Neither she nor Satish acknowledged her tears. She did not answer his question.

In a corner of the verandah a sequestered musician played on a lute the lilting strains of an Eastern melody. A boy with a peacock-feather *chowrie* stepped closer and waved flies away, *swish*, *swish*. The raucous shouts of the bazaar, the screech of parrots, the monotonous cooing of the doves, the strained laughter of an English memsahib walking with a gentleman on the crushed stone pathway: the sounds of India absorbed her sorrow until once again she could speak.

She folded up the damp handkerchief, first into squares, then into a tight triangle, as if she were with this act momentarily containing her fears. She laid the fine linen item on the table in front of Satish, although she was aware that he would not take it back. To him as a Hindu she was unclean. He could not eat with her, touch her, or touch what she had touched, not without losing caste.

Now Anna had a delicate question she must needs ask: Had Ashok married since she had left him on the wharf to take ship home? Or was his heart still free? Whether she found her daughter or not, she would not leave India without informing Ashok of Elizabeth's existence. The answer to this question would determine how she would approach him when he returned to Calcutta, but she could not summon up sufficient breath to put the query into words. Should she speak to Ashok with even the most infinitesimal hope of taking up a life together as husband and wife, as companions and lovers, as mother and father to Elizabeth?

If she found Elizabeth.

Two servants in white sarongs and jackets arrived, noiseless on bare feet. One man carried a tea tray, the other a tiered dish of sandwiches and small cakes. She accepted the cup of tea poured by the waiter, but waved the sandwiches away. She had no appetite, and Satish, of course, could not eat with her.

"One thing more I am learning, Madame," Satish said, his intelligent gaze reading her aright. "At Sahib Montgomery's home, the servants tell me that Sahib Ashok does not yet take a wife to replace the mother of his son."

"Ah! Thank you, Satish. Thank you." Her body let loose a tension of which she had not previously been aware.

But now—once again—it seemed, her search had come to a standstill. Ashok was not in Calcutta, and neither was Josiah. Even Satish Ghosh could not learn their whereabouts. She gave a bitter little laugh, and her *banian* queried her with a puzzled look. She shook her head: *Pay no attention; I am lost in my thoughts.*

Her husband's masculine pride had been stung—even worse, his potency besmirched—and his first impulse was to strike out, not at her, but at the … *infidel seducer.* It was no longer a matter merely between Josiah and Anna, but something far more primitive: one male combating another over ownership of the female. And for that, Josiah, the civilized man of God, would sail eight-thousand arduous miles to claim vengeance.

But, once frustrated by learning that his rival had departed the country, where would her husband then have gone?

Home. An abrupt clatter of porcelain on marble as Anna set her cup and saucer down. One of the mute, motionless servants who stood ubiquitous in every corner glided up and rescued the fragile dishes. *Josiah would have gone home.* Not to America, but back to the mission where he and Anna had tried so unsuccessfully to bring a child into the world. He must be at Fatehgarh!

She jumped up from the rattan chair. "I will go to Fatehgarh! That is where he will have taken her. Satish, please prepare at once for the journey."

Satish Ghosh took his time replying. He smoothed his waistcoat over his substantial belly. Ran his fingers again over the gold watch chain. Looked at Anna owlishly. "Ah, Madame, such a trip would be arduous, as Madame must know—arduous and perhaps even dangerous. It is worth first trying other inquiries here in Calcutta before undergoing such risk. If Madame could manage to obtain an invitation to call upon the ladies at Government House, she would find herself among East India Company *memsahibs* of the most elevated rank, ladies who know all that occurs among the English-speaking society. If news of her daughter could be obtained thusly, Madame would not have to undertake such a riskful expedition as that to the North."

From where Anna sat she could see the great square polished-stone houses of the East India directors with their magnificent porticos, Grecian columns, and lawns running smooth and green down to the river. British society, she knew, was narrow and exclusive, an unending round of afternoon calls and formal dinners. Those events did not include missionaries. The Anglo-Indian elite despised the religious workers as lower-class, and had nothing but contempt for their proselytizing. She understood that Satish was right about pursuing inquiries first in Calcutta. But she also knew that for any information of Josiah and her child she would have to look in a very different direction than the glamour and glitter of the Raj.

"I would do better, I think, to go directly myself to the English-speaking mission community here in Calcutta before we travel north." She stood with her hands on the marble railing, looking out in the direction of the clamorous city. "Some will remember me as Josiah's wife and may speak to me freely." The Christian mission community of India was even more insular than that of New York, as religion in the provinces often tended to be. Approaching those upright men in their upright houses would be daunting, but she needs must do it.

FIFTY-FOUR

"You must understand," the Reverend Job Belding said, idly waving his silver-handled cow-tail *chowrie* at a buzzing fly, "we all thought Josiah Roundtree dead, massacred in Cawnpore with the others." His large, airy mission-house parlor opened in the Indian style through triple arches to a wide verandah. The furniture, however, was resolutely western: wooden straight chairs, massive cabinets, and a horsehair sofa in dark-blue plush. No Eastern exuberance of carpet, cushion, or silken panel here: even the flowers had been chosen for restraint, odorless lilies whose bulbs had been transplanted from some homely Massachusetts garden. Yet scattered around the room were curios from the good reverend's oriental travels: a mounted tiger head, a curved elephant knife in a silver-ornamented scabbard, a wooden tea chest surmounted by a large brass tray.

The Reverend Belding was white-haired, with gray eyes, a crooked nose and teeth that clicked when he talked—which was all the time. His mustard-yellow jacket covered a loose-woven linen shirt and, Anna was astonished to note, he wore sandals.

"But you, my dear Mrs. Roundtree," Reverend Belding said, "we'd heard that you'd departed for home just before the Mutiny in order to take a course of medical treatment. I must say, I was thankful for it."

With a jolt, Anna recalled the lie she had told an acquaintance met—ill-met, she'd thought at the time—as she attempted to depart without notice from the Agra train station.

"Fortunate timing, your illness, was it not, dear lady? The Lord certainly had you in his benevolent care. Are you quite well now?"

To Anna the flies were less annoying than the constant whisking of the *chowrie* so close to her face that it made her blink. *Whisk. Whisk.* "Yes, Mr. Belding, quite well."

She'd been relieved to find that it was Mr. Belding, an unusually mild and genial evangelist, who now directed the Methodist Foreign Missions Society of Calcutta. The long sojourn in the tropic sun had evaporated any Puritan bile from this missionary's New-England soul, leaving only essential Christianity. Mr. Belding was approachable, and well placed to hear any rumors of Josiah's presence here, thus her visit to him. But, as he chattered on, Anna found her attention wandering. Would this sociable clergyman never cease his talking so she could bring the conversation around to what really concerned her? *Whisk. Whisk.*

Her gaze skittered around the room, taking in a glass inkwell, a croctheted doily, a plain teak cross on the wall. Then, between one blink and the next, in the clutter of objects on the low table before her—oil lamp, brass candle snuffer, almonds heaped in a coconut-shell bowl—she saw, incongruously anchoring a half-written sermon against the *punkah*'s breeze, a small, round, polished monkey skull. Despite its innocuous purpose as a paperweight, the macabre object gave Anna a fascinated chill. All of a sudden she recalled the monkey skull Lallia, the village head woman, had given her to repel evil spirits and protect any yet-to-be-born children. At that time Anna, repulsed, had thrown the uncanny object into the jungle. Now she felt her gaze returning again and again to the little skull. She had ceased listening to her host.

"So," Mr. Belding went on, "when Josiah Roundtree walked in that door, plain as day, with that little half-blood girl, I said, 'My God!' If I were a man much given to superstitions, Mrs. Roundtree, I would truly have believed I was seeing a ghost."

Suddenly she paid attention. It was as if the air in the room were all at once charged with electric energy. "Did Mr. Roundtree tell you where he was headed with the child?"

"Ah." He gave her an enigmatic look. "So you already knew he had a little one with him. That was strange."

"But did he tell you—"

"He gave her over immediately into the care of our *ayah*, and didn't see her or speak to her the entire time they were here. There seemed to be no attachment between them, and we offered to take her off his hands. We place many such children, you know, at Mrs. Wilson's school for the education of native orphan girls—they train them to do the most exquisite needlework." The *chowrie* again. *Whisk. Whisk.*

"But—" Her gaze kept sliding back to the little monkey skull.

"But Mr. Roundtree said he already had a situation in mind for her. He went out into the city three afternoons in a row, dressed in the best broadcloth as if he was calling on people of consequence. Then he came home one evening in—if I may say it, dear lady—in a devil of a state. He packed up his trunk, had the *ayah* make the child ready, and they departed most abruptly."

Anna's attention was now fixed absolutely upon Reverend Belding. "But where did they go?" Finally she had gotten the entire question in. She leaned forward, every nerve intent, breathless for the answer.

"'Where did they go?' Oh, Mrs. Roundtree, what was I thinking," Mr. Belding said. "Of course—you wish to find him! To have believed him dead for so long ... Tsk. Tsk." The *chowrie* whisked within a hair's breadth of Anna's nose.

"Where did he take her?"

Reverend Belding regarded her gravely. It was as if he were reluctant to tender a direct response. "He told me it was only the Lord's saving hand upon him that allowed him to survive the massacre. He had been left to guard women and children. It was a tragic tale—his heroic struggle to protect those helpless innocents—but the vicious fiends struck them all down. He, too, was smote and lost consciousness. When he came to, he found himself miles away, on the far side of the Ganges from the field of slaughter. He did not know how he had escaped. He said it was a miracle."

Anna took up the cocoanut shell bowl from the table before her and cradled it in both hands. If only this too-affable clergyman would answer her one urgent question. "But, Mr. Belding, where has he gone with my—with the little girl?" She selected an almond and set the bowl back on the table.

Now the minister looked directly at her with his clear gray eyes. "Mrs. Roundtree, there is something I must tell you—Josiah Roundtree is not the same man I used to know. His horrific experiences during the mutiny have ... affected him most markedly. No matter how much you may long to be with him, my dear, do not seek Mr. Roundtree out by yourself. It might not be entirely safe. Wait a week or two, until I am free, and I will travel north with you."

"But. Where. Is. He?" Anna had no intention of waiting for Mr. Belding, of allowing even this well-meaning clergyman to know the true reason for her desperate need to find Josiah.

Job Belding sighed. "Ah, yes, naturally you wish to know his whereabouts. He said he was going—"

A loud voice brayed almost in their ears, ". . . the work of God in this Dark Continent." A stout, dimpled young woman in purple calico entered the room through the verandah arches.

Anna's breath was expelled in a great frustrated huff; she had been so close to getting an answer.

The plump woman had been sermonizing over her shoulder to a pale, melancholy-appearing cleric with short-cropped brown hair and beard.

"Ah," Miss Dilbert, Reverend Flint," Reverend Belding said, "come meet Mrs. Anna Roundtree, the helpmeet of one who formerly labored in the missions here." He turned to Anna. "Miss Matilda Dilbert and Mr. Gideon Flint are two of a contingent of men and women of God who have come out from America to take up the work of the martyred missionaries in the North-West provinces. I know you will have advice and wisdom to share with them."

From the garden, a half-dozen young Americans followed them into the room, two women in pale muslin and four clerics clad in unseasonable black. Their excited chatter, pink cheeks, and the gilt-edged Bibles the ladies carried made them seem to Anna less like the men and women of God Reverend Belding had declared them to be, than like overlarge Sunday-school boys and girls.

Anna sighed. Thus innocent and misguided must she and Josiah have appeared, as, buoyed by his enthusiasm, they had sailed up the Ganges in their leaky *budgerow* more than a decade since to convert the native Indian to Josiah's imported faith.

In the presence of these young missionaries, Anna could not inquire further about her daughter. As the slapping of bare feet on uncarpeted tile announced the arrival of servants with laden tea trays, she sat back with a great sigh, accepted tea in a Wedgwood cup, and drank it silently while the conversation eddied around her.

Even after all these months since she had received his letters in New York, she could not quite believe that her husband was still alive. How could the reports of Josiah's death have been so mistaken? Some few men were said to have escaped the slaughter. He must have been among them? What must he have had to do in order to survive? Reverend Belding's account of Josiah's tale was horrific, surely, but in his present, obviously disturbed, condition, was her husband capable of telling the truth, indeed of even knowing what the truth *was*?

Only half-aware of what she was doing, she set her cup on the cluttered table, reached out, touched the polished monkey skull—how cool and smooth it was! Abruptly she pulled her hand back. A current of energy seemed to have chilled her fingers. She stared at the skull, then reached out again, picked it up, fondled it. Her hand tingled.

Oh, Elizabeth—her poor child.

Anna caressed the cool, rounded dome of the monkey skull. She saw that the young people had no intention of leaving her alone with Mr. Belding. Replacing the artifact on the low table, she rose. Then, most abruptly, she resumed her seat, passed a hand over her hair, which as always in these humid climes was wantonly wayward, with damp curling tendrils falling over her forehead, shook the wrinkles out of her muslin skirts, took up her reticule, removed from it her thin cambric gloves, donned them carefully, making much of smoothing out each finger. Then, with a quick glance at the others (what had come over her?!), she plucked up the little monkey skull and slipped it into her brocaded bag. After a quiet minute or two, she rose again and began to make her farewells to the company.

Her host accompanied her to the door, where Satish waited in the courtyard with a hired carriage. "And where *did* my husband take the child?" she asked one last time, almost in despair of ever receiving a direct answer from this periphrastic clergyman.

"Oh, didn't I say?" Reverend Belding pressed her gloved hand. "Mr. Roundtree returned in a terrible state from the last of his afternoon visits, this time with his fine clothes all damp and wilted as if he'd been walking for hours in the monsoon rain. He announced that he was going north to Farrukhabad. When I pressed him as to his reasons, he said he wished to see if he could reclaim what was left of his ruined mission at Fatehgarh. He snatched up the child and left—without even the *ayah*. As I said, he was in a devil of a mood."

FIFTY-FIVE

At Calcutta Station Anna had been appalled to find her first-class train compartment reeking of lavender water and already occupied by Miss Matilda Dilbert, the fledgling missionary. The train was hissing and steaming, its whistle emitting a long mournful wail, too close to departure for her to change her tickets. She halted in the doorway. "Miss Dilbert, I believe I was to have this compartment to myself."

The young woman jumped to her feet and clasped her hands at her breast. "Yes, that's what they said at the ticket window, but, oh, Mrs. Roundtree, just think! When I spotted your name on the passenger list, I knew that God's Providence had led me to you. Now you will not be forced to travel alone. And ..." Her voice dropped an octave. "Perhaps I may be of some spiritual assistance to you."

Anna groaned aloud. With all the burdens she carried upon her heart must she be plagued with pious cant all the way to Agra? She sank onto the plush seat next to the window.

Miss Dilbert smiled beatifically. There was something of the jack o' lantern about her pudgy face. Oblivious to Anna's horror at her presence, she reached into her satchel and pulled out a book. "And look, I have this wonderful tale, *The Three Mrs. Judsons: The Celebrated Female Missionaries*. Here, you take it!" She thrust the small volume into Anna's hands, and her pumpkin face sagged into an expression of saintly concern. "The lives of these missionary wives will surely inspire you. The moment I saw you in the parlor at the Methodist Mission House, I recognized a spirit in turmoil. Oh, my dear Mrs. Roundtree, I do so fear for your soul. Are you truly saved? Are you safe in the arms of the Lord?"

Anna could not hold her tongue. For some reason Caroline Slade's acerbic tones seemed to animate her voice. "Our Lord Krishna, I assume you mean."

"Oh, no—" Belatedly Miss Dilbert understood Anna's intention and gasped. An entire stereopticon of expressions passed over her face until she reached the full realization of her sister traveler's apostasy. "Miss Wheeler! God will not be mocked!" In something approaching a most unchristian temper, the young proselytizer glared at Anna, rose stiffly from her seat, threw open the compartment door, grabbed her satchel, pivoted on her heel and began to flounce away down the narrow corridor.

When Anna realized she still held *The Three Mrs. Judsons* clutched tightly in her hand, rage ran through her. She rose from her seat, hurried out the compartment door, raised her arm and hurled the book at Miss Dilbert. It slammed into the missionary's nether parts, and, with a screech, Miss Dilbert picked up her pace, scurrying down the corridor toward her co-religionists' compartments. "And don't come back!" Anna whispered. She turned again to her compartment only to find her way blocked by Miss Dilbert's friend, the young Reverend Mr. Flint.

"Pardon me," she said, stepping to the right. But he sidestepped as well, and she was forced to come to a halt, facing him. "I saw that," he said. "You attacked Miss Dilbert without provocation. But, what else, Mrs. Roundtree, could I have expected. I have heard about you. You are the worst kind of sinner, for you have been trained in the ways of righteousness and have rejected them. You have spurned the very gospel into which you have been born. That in itself makes you more deserving of God's wrath than any benighted heathen."

Anna glowered at him. Gideon Flint reminded Anna so of Josiah that she felt suspended somewhere between hysteria and rage. "I must be reading a different Bible than yours," she said quietly, "because my Bible says, 'O give thanks unto the God of heaven, for his *mercy* endureth forever.'"

Rev. Flint tightened his lips, turned on his heel and followed in Miss Dilbert's wake.

Only Satish's arrival to see that she was comfortably settled prevented Anna from bursting into frustrated tears. He, too, was appalled at this disarrangement of his careful plans, but the train was already jolting its way out of the terminal, and nothing could be done. He advised Anna to lock the door on Miss Dilbert until she agreed to find lodging in another compartment.

In her ensuing days-long solitude, Anna was plagued with worries. Would she find Josiah still at Farrukhabad? If he had departed from there with no direction, how should she then proceed? Would he keep Elizabeth with him, when he could so easily abandon her? Elizabeth, an infant of three years lost in the vast country of village, jungle, mountain, and plain! Or did he intend to take the girl back to Calcutta when Ashok returned to India and confront him with her then?

Gazing out the sooty windows, she found distraction. Each thatched-roof village that passed brought her closer to her destination: each woman working in the rice fields, baby hung from a tree bough in a cloth sling; each villager gathering opium in the poppy fields; each troop of *nautch* girls traveling with sitars, tambourines, and drums. At station stops, peddlers passed sweet biscuits and tea in clay cups through the open windows, and that was one tea-time less until she held Elizabeth in her arms.

God willing.

On the fourth day the train halted at an isolated water tower. As was her custom, Anna stepped out on the station platform to take the air. It was a limpid blue evening, just before the abrupt descent of the dark, star-filled Indian night. At the far end of the platform, as the train began its whistle for all aboard, she turned back only to see Rev. Flint standing between her and the train. For a moment she felt paralyzed; she did not wish to walk anywhere near him for fear of what she might say to him. Then the whistle sounded once again, and the tea and sugar-cane vendors were scrambling from their low stools at the train windows, and she had to move. By the time she reached her carriage, the man had vanished.

Long years of domestic and spiritual subjection, she realized, had left scars upon her soul that seemed to become increasingly poisonous the nearer to Josiah's presence she found herself approaching. And yet his very presence was what she needs must seek. When she thought of his having abducted her daughter she frightened herself with her unspeakable—almost murderous—fury. If she felt so strong a desire to strike this importunate tin-pot missionary with whom she now traveled, what might she be capable of once finding herself in Josiah's presence?

FIFTY-SIX

Lafayette Place
New-York City
April 25, 1861
Anna—

Oh, dear friend, such an occurrence! Yesterday in the Arrivals section of the Tribune's Shipping News I spied Mr. Ashok Montgomery's name! I sought him out immediately at the Astor Hotel. Anna, what a splendid man! He has come to find you. I told him about the birth of India Elizabeth and your search for her. He was most affected, and has booked passage on the Silas E. Burrowes from Boston direct to Calcutta. Please God you two do not pass in the night once again. I have given him the name of your hotel. Stay where you are until he finds you.

I send this letter by today's packet ship to Liverpool, directing it thence to Calcutta, hoping it may precede his arrival.

So romantic! Just like a novel!

Love, love, love,
Caroline

Arrived GARDEN REACH HOTEL
11 August 1861
HOLD FOR RETURN OF MRS.WHEELER

Lafayette Place
New York City
19 June 1861

My Dear Anna,

Mr. Greeley has appointed Eben as the Tribune's wartime correspondent. He leaves soon for Virginia, some godforsaken place called Bull Run. He is gung ho *about the assignment, but I fear for him. He may not be an actual combatant, but he will be in the midst of everything, and bullets, as you well know, are blind.*

Baby grows well and has begun to move. It is big and active—I'm certain it is a boy! We are thinking of naming him Abraham, after our great national leader. And, oh, Anna, now I understand you even more acutely, how you are willing to move heaven and earth to retrieve your child. If our children are so much of our bodies, certainly they are of our souls!

And, under separate cover I send a copy of Josiah Roundtree's memoir. According to Reverend Pete it sells briskly to Sunday-School teachers and to the widows of impoverished clergymen, but not much otherwise. I am sorry to have to tell you that Rev. Roundtree sounds to me to be much unhinged in his intelligence. When he relates the horrors of the Cawnpore massacre, he says his survival is certain evidence of the existence of miracles. For him and him alone, he avers, God suspended the laws of nature, allowing him to escape the field of carnage by walking across the Ganges River. Anna, Josiah Roundtree believes that he has walked on water!

Arrived: GARDEN REACH HOTEL
3 October 1861
HOLD FOR RETURN OF MRS.WHEELER

FIFTY-SEVEN

"'The *memsahib* without a soul.' That is what the missionary *wallahs* are calling you," Satish Ghosh said, as he and Anna walked in the garden of her Farrukhabad hotel. All around them oleander bushes hung lush with clusters of pink and white blossoms and a delicate perfume suffused the air. "Or so the *kansamah* at the Baptist Mission House is telling me he has heard as he waits upon the dinner table."

"*Without a soul?*" She frowned, perplexed, then gave a short, bitter laugh. "Ah, a *lost* soul! The missionaries think I am a *lost soul*. That must be what the butler heard."

Satish looked at her sideways with his dark eyes. "Soulful, I am thinking. Not soul-lost. Madame is filled with soul."

She laughed again, this time without the bitterness. "Thank you, Satish." She smiled at him.

He looked astonished. "Thanking me? For what, Madame?"

"You have just said a lovely thing."

"Ah. I am meaning it."

"You!" bellowed the Reverend Gideon Flint, upon catching sight of Anna. "You dare to come here?"

In spite of Satish's cautions about the local missionaries, she had proceeded with hopeful mind to visit the Farrukhabad Methodist Mission House. Descending from a hired carriage, she had approached the city mission, a large, flat-roofed, *pukka*-walled building, only to find looming in the wide arched doorway the all-too-familiar figure of her nemesis from the train. Anna was plunged from hope into icy despair. She would receive no assistance here. Mr. Flint and Miss Dilbert had already poisoned local mission workers against her. Anna had become a *pariah*. In this place to which Josiah had been bound, the closest civilization to the settlement of Fatehgarh, Christian society would now scarcely acknowledge her existence, let alone provide information that might lead her to find him.

"Madame, what is this?" Satish Ghosh had been supervising the unpacking of Anna's trunks when a servant found tucked in a drawstring petticoat-pocket a small, round monkey's skull.

Anna blushed. She was embarrassed to see the primitive talisman in Satish's civilized hand with its gold rings and polished nails.

"Oh, nothing, really," she sputtered. "Throw it out. No, wait! Give it here. I'll pack it away. A curio for a friend."

"I see." Satish cast her a knowing look and slid the skull into his own pocket. "Leave it to me. I will prepare this ... curio ... for travel."

The following afternoon he handed her a teak cube carved intricately with a motif of jungle vines.

"What's this?" She revolved the peculiar object in her hands. It was exquisitely crafted, the corners turned seamlessly. There seemed neither top nor bottom. She could find no opening, no clasp. She gazed at him quizzically.

He took it from her. "See." With strong brown fingers he pressed the sides of the wooden cube, sliding them first one way, then another, until the little box popped open, revealing the monkey skull nestled on a brown velvet lining.

"Oh!"

"It is a puzzle box," Satish said. "For your friend."

"Thank you," Anna said. She knew it was absurd, but she would conceal the little talisman in her petticoat pocket once again as soon as she was alone.

Anna was composing a letter to Caroline when Satish Ghosh rushed into the hotel's library. "*Memsahib*! *Memsahib*! Strange news, but news nonetheless. Here is what they say in the villages—Sahib Roundtree haunts the ruined mission, day and night, night and day, moving between the fallen stones, pale and silent like a ghost. Because of his yellow hair they call him 'sun spirit.' They say he has returned from the dead."

Anna's pen ceased its motion. "He *is* at Fatehgarh! What of Elizabeth? Is she with him?" Her heart seemed as still as the pen.

"No mention of the child." Satish shook his head in commiseration. "Just that the Reverend Roundtree comes and goes, gliding through the ruins, always alone, speaking to no one but his gods." Anna's banian had somewhere acquired a stovepipe hat and now fingered its narrow brim.

"He will speak to me," Anna said, in an almost inaudible tone. Mechanically she sprinkled the page of her letter with blotting sand, blew off the fine white grains, folded it, slipped it into her reticule. She picked up the pen again, and for an interminable few seconds she sat at the desk with the ivory shaft immobile in her hand. Then, without warning, she slammed it down on the table, splattering ink over the polished wood, and jumped up from her chair, narrowly avoiding a collision with the room boy, who was on hand to carry her travel desk.

"We will go to Fatehgarh now, this very minute! We will compel Josiah to tell us what he has done with my daughter!" She almost grabbed Satish by the arms. At the last second, she stayed her hand; she did not wish to cause him to lose caste.

"No! Madame, no," her *banian* admonished.

She glanced at him in surprise. He seldom contradicted her directly. She began to speak, but he raised a beringed finger.

"Recall the Sahib Belding's warning—you must not approach Sahib Roundtree yourself. His is not the behavior of a sane person. Think of your safety. And, too, what would people say? Think of your reputation!"

"Bah! I am not afraid of Josiah." She removed her paper writing cuffs, dropped them on the table, and gave a short dry laugh. "And as for my reputation, it would seem I no longer have one to lose."

He shook his head.

She felt a spurt of irritation at his fussiness.

"It is not prudent for you to see him. It is not safe, truly. *Memsahib*, I am imploring you—allow me to proceed by myself. Tomorrow morning at first sun I will go out to the ruins. I will be taking a strong man in case he proves violent."

Anna was suffused by a passion of will that approached the irrational. "Now! Today!" She waved the room boy out of the library; it would not do for him to see her in conflict with her *banian*. "We will go now. I have never known Josiah Roundtree to be violent." Even as she spoke the words, she recalled that final beating.

And the rape that followed.

Satish pulled himself up to his highest stature, at which he was almost taller than Anna. His cream-colored vest swelled with self-determination. "Madame, I cannot go. I have business in Farrukhabad this afternoon." His mouth was firmly set.

Anna attempted to read his deep steady gaze aright. Did he indeed have good reason to remain in the city, or was this simply the unreasonable obstinacy of a recalcitrant subordinate? There was no knowing. She sighed deeply. She was not happy with Satish Ghosh. Her very feet in their soft kid shoes seemed intent on speeding her across the polished mosaics of the hotel floors and toward the rutted, dusty paths of the Fatehgarh mission. *Now! Now!*

Satish, still musing upon his plans for the day, continued, "It is too late for me to go this morning, and this afternoon I have ... crucial affairs to attend to. One more day will make no difference in approaching the Reverend Roundtree. I will go to the mission tomorrow. By then I will know—"

"Enough!" She stamped her foot.

Satish's expressive countenance at once became wooden.

Anna literally bit her tongue. She did not wish to alienate her *banian*, but she had lost patience with his overcautiousness. What if ...? What if ...? Anything could happen by tomorrow. Whole worlds could be lost ...

She did not need Satish Ghosh. She well knew how to get to the mission without him. She would wait until he left the hotel this afternoon on his "crucial affairs," whatever they were, and then she would act. He would be furious with her, she knew—as she was now furious with him. But she needed neither his assistance nor approval. If she was to be thrown back upon her own resources, so be it. It was only a few miles to the old mission, mostly over good roads. She had followed the route many times before by hired buggy and felt no hesitation now in doing so. She would brook no delay—not even a single day—in taking this crucial step to find her daughter.

FIFTY-EIGHT

The jungle seemed to have utterly reclaimed the mission compound, that one-time outpost of Christianity. The gates had fallen, and the long lane was choked with thickets of tall sturdy bamboo canes that clacked together in the light breeze. Anna told the driver to wait for her at the gates and made it well worth his while to do so. Avoiding the impassible lane, she wound her way through a neighboring mango grove in which she had often strolled during the coolness of the evening. In her plain travelling dress and stout boots, she was halfway through the grove when, among the dead brown leaves, she heard something slither close to her feet. She stepped back quickly. Cobra? Viper? She shivered—and searched the ground. A mongoose burst through the underbrush and scurried away. Harmless. She relaxed. Then a black-masked monkey dropped from an unseen height to a limb directly before Anna's face. She shrieked. The fierce little animal held its ground, chattering a reprimand at her impertinent intrusion. Snatching up a long length of fallen bamboo as a *lathi*, the sort of powerful weapon every villager carried, she chased him a few steps through the jungle undergrowth, frightening him off. In so doing, she lost her bearings and halted, disoriented in the midst of the thick mango grove. Just where was the mission compound?

Ah, finally—the far side of the grove. But she found there, too, bamboo lifting its tough, feathery branches in a tall close screen, obscuring her view. She could but guess at her destination and pushed through blindly, whacking with the *lathi* at the sun-drenched canes. Her sun helmet caught on an unseen branch and fell across her face. She resettled the *topi* and took a few faltering steps, still uncertain of the way. Of a sudden she found herself free of the obscuring thicket, not in the yard of her former home, but in the mission's little graveyard on the compound's outskirts.

The graveyard. Oh, the graveyard! She turned at once to the section where her stillborn sons were buried. All was destruction. Not a monument remained, simply the stumps of gravestones, like broken teeth. Grief swept over her—the last traces of her lost children vanished! She must reclaim Elizabeth, for her own sake, but also for the shades of her small abandoned brothers. She stood transfixed a moment, tears streaming down her cheeks. Then, vision still obscured, she followed the traces of a once-well-worn path and found herself facing—more ruin.

Where there had been a bustling compound—church, orphanage, hospital, a cluster of modest bungalows—nothing remained but fallen mud walls and heaps of stone—not a roof, not a door or window, not a table or chair. The church, with its gold-topped steeple, had been leveled, even the massive beams that supported its roof had been carted away. At the former hospital, in the angle formed by the broken infirmary walls, an elephant sheltered, asleep on its leathery, treelike legs. She could not but feel a jolt in her heart; it was just there—in that very spot—that she had first seen Ashok Montgomery, handsome in his gentleman's white coat, a benefactor touring the medical mission. She recalled his dark masculinity which had formed such a contrast to Josiah's radiant sinewy strength. *Ashok, where are you? I need you.*

She gave the hospital a wide berth and located the remains of what had once been her bungalow—hers and Josiah's. Three walls remained, half-broken and sun-baked, grown over by the small pink climbing roses she had so carefully nurtured. She stood still, in contemplation of the wreckage of a life. She had not been happy here, but had lived so much of existence —talking with the native women, nursing the sick, attending to her household duties, scribbling verses by the flickering light of an earthen lamp, fulfilling Josiah's marital demands and lying awake thereafter listening late into the night to the howls of the jackals, the doleful cries of the night birds, and the scrambling of green lizards across the walls. Giving birth. Giving away to death. And now nothing left of all her work. Even less of Josiah's, for at least her roses thrived.

Had Josiah been here this day? She glanced around for signs of her husband's presence. Broken branches? Footprints? But, no, the lush tropic verdure would all too quickly obscure any sign of alien passage. In the squawks, cries, and twitters of jungle life, she heard nothing but her own unwelcomed presence. But hadn't Satish said Josiah was to be found in the ruins night and day?

It was the hottest time of the afternoon; the tropic sun streamed relentless straight down upon the stony rubble. Thirsty and half-dizzy with the heat and memory, she determined to seek what shade she might find under the broad *neem* tree beside her vanished home. She would wait until dark if need be. Tomorrow she would return at dawn. Whenever Josiah came, he would find her there.

With the sturdy *lathi* she pushed her way through the tangled vines and bushes, rounding the corner where once had stood a door. In the wavering heat, something gleamed in the precise center of the roofless house. There under the merciless sun, in a posture of abject submission, his golden hair shining, knelt her once-beloved husband, his entire earthly form bowed deep in prayer.

"Josiah!" At her cry, a flock of parakeets burst screaming from their coverts.

His head jolted upwards, eyes following the emerald wings skyward, as if he thought the birds had spoken. He wore a garb of long white coat and leggings, native, but without the customary turban. Never before had Anna seen him attired in ought but the most severe of Western clothing. Today he also wore embroidered slippers, and a silver bracelet circled his wrist. The sun glistened on his brilliant hair and snowy raiment.

She stared at her husband in this new incarnation and did not know him. Indeed had she ever known him? What did it say about her that she had followed the Reverend Josiah Roundtree so slavishly? How could she have mistaken his rigidity for righteousness? She must have been mesmerized—or under a spell. During these past three years without him she had indeed become a new woman. Born again, yes, but not to any testament of his.

She called to him once more, running forward, half-tripping on the tangle of roses by the broken wall. "Josiah! Where is my daughter?" The trampled blossoms sent out an intense perfume, but she did not apprehend it.

He stared around, dazed, his attention drawn abruptly from infinity to earth. His gaze slowly fixed itself upon her. It was as if her image materialized beyond all rational possibility upon his vision.

"Anna?" he faltered.

At the sight of his face, she halted. It was the countenance of a man twice his age, drawn and lined, raddled with experience and care. His once-rosy cheeks, always so remarked-upon by his native congregants, were pale now, but his eyes remained bluer than the cloudless sky.

He stared at her, then shook his head. "You? You have come, then?"

"Yes, Josiah. I have come for my daughter."

It was as if she had not spoken. He passed a thin hand over his eyes. "I could find you nowhere." He hunkered on the ground, squatting like a native, and frowned up at her. "Our friends advised me that you must have been abducted by the mutineers. Then the revolt swept down upon us in the fullness of its fury." His tall frame was emaciated, whether by illness or by sorrow, she could not tell. He took up a handful of dust and let it fall slowly through his fingers. It blew faintly in the breeze. The lineaments of pain had transformed his face, their inscriptions harsh.

The awareness that Josiah, too, had suffered during the years of their separation came unwelcome to her; she wished to have no pity for this abductor of her child.

"I was shattered by your loss," he continued. "In despair, beyond what a faithful son of God should feel. And then," his voice was toneless, "I learned you had not died, but had betrayed me."

Her breathing halted. She stood motionless and silent at the ruined doorstep. What had once been a well-swept packed-earth floor was nothing now but disordered dust. The crooked trails of snakes and lizards dragged across paw prints of jackals and wild dogs. Doves in the bird-haunted *neem* tree began their steady wearying murmur. She noticed none of this; her attention all fixed on Josiah. She felt cut off from time in this place, suspended between the past and the present.

And the future? What of the future? It, too, was hovering in the cloistered tropic air.

"Josiah," she said carefully, "where is my daughter?"

Josiah rose to his feet and moved toward her. Anna shuddered, momentarily mesmerized in his presence, as if, once again, they had assumed their former roles. She took a step forward, then halted so abruptly that the toes of her boots were buried in the dust. She was no longer in thrall to this man. "Where is my child?" she asked again.

He halted an arm's length from her, his expression bemused. In the branches above him, the doves continued their mournful calls.

"Elizabeth! Elizabeth, my daughter." Impulsively she clutched him by the arms. "What have you done with her?" Indeed it was all she could do not to shriek at him. Oh, she must tamp this fury searing her veins, or she would estrange him—and lose all hope. "Josiah, you took my daughter from New York. You wrote to me about her. Your landlady told me you named her … ." She searched her memory for the name the landlady had mentioned. "Prudence! That's it! What have you done with Prudence?"

She did not wish to think too closely upon just what he might have done—or might yet do—with the child. If he was feeling merciful—perhaps an orphanage or church school. If he had no mercy, abandoning her in the bazaar would rid himself of his unwelcome charge. If he were to wax vindictive, there were the child brothels— But, no! No. He must have her hidden away somewhere safe, against Ashok's return.

"Yes," he reached over to cover her hand with his, "the small brown girl—her existence the bodily emblem of your blasphemous sin. Did you love her father?" He searched her face. She recoiled, letting her hands fall from his arms. "Or did the black brute savage you?"

She felt as if he had struck her. "If anyone has savaged me, it is you, Josiah." She spat out the words.

His eyes widened. "Me? But, Anna, I have loved you so … dutifully."

Dutifully? "Where is she?" Her voice shook.

Josiah sat on the low stone wall. "I brought Prudence home to India. What else was I to do with the little pagan? Not a pleasant child at all, but what could one expect from an infant of such sadly promiscuous background. She belongs here." He gestured around at the broken walls, the dusty ground, the over-lush verdure swarming with life. Then he gave Anna a sudden penetrating glance. "With her … goddamned … heathen father." He shook his head, and the fine blond hair haloed out with the movement. "Sahib. Ashok. Montgomery. That I should be so deceived in a man." His voice remained toneless. His sharp gaze had not left her face. "And in a woman."

She stared at him. "Josiah, do not do this!"

The hot air was stirred by a light wind, but she smelled neither the ripe sweet decay of the mangos' fallen fruit, nor saw the cat-like slink of a pink-nosed mongoose. The groves surrounding them were thick with the cacophony of life: cracking of branches under the hyena's foot; the scolding of peacocks and squawking of parrots. And hushed in the dry fallen leaves, a slithering, as of a snake. She heard the latter with only half an ear, yet she gripped her tall *lathi* more tightly.

She saw a stillness come over Josiah.

"Do what, my dear?" He rose from his seat on the wall and stepped toward her. No expression crossed his face save that of the most saintly concern. He reached out, as if he would caress her, then let his hand fall. The silver bracelet winked in the harsh light. "You always were a disobedient spirit," he said. "I knew it from the start, and it was only my carnal weakness that persuaded me otherwise."

"I will have my daughter." A fly landed on her forehead, and she did not brush it away, her concentration all on keeping the fury from her voice.

"Even so, I will have my wife. 'What God hath joined together' …," he stared at her with eyes so intent they glittered. Some force of will was being exerted against her soul; she could feel its heat upon her skin. He held out his hands in supplication, thin and pale. "Let us pray, Anna, for your repentance as a sinner. If God so wishes it, I will struggle to find forgiveness in my heart that we may resume our lives together."

She returned his stare and swallowed hard, striving for a tone of dispassionate reason. "Josiah, I have not come to 'resume our lives.' If ever you loved me—or if ever you knew the meaning of Christian mercy—you will tell me where my child is."

Josiah was not an evil man, Anna knew. He was something infinitely more dangerous—a weak man, a man incapable of living in a world that offered no absolutes. He was feverish with the desire for salvation. He was sick with it, mad perhaps. But, at that moment, even compassion could not keep her from hating him.

His gaze was still fierce upon her. "Wife, you have sinned grievously, and nothing but eternal fire and suffering awaits you. Unless, that is, you repent and plead for God's forgiveness."

"I do not require forgiveness," she said quietly. "No one's eternal salvation is at stake, but something far greater."

"And what could that possibly be?" He looked genuinely bemused, as if he truly did not know.

"Life! My child's life. *Each* small life." An over-ripe mango fell from a tree and splattered on the ground between them. Once again, a slither in the dust.

He frowned again. Something departed from his eyes. "One small life? How could *that* be enough?" His normally mellifluous voice was of a sudden as dry and barren as the destroyed walls surrounding them. Then he reassumed his preacher's edifying accents, but his words now seemed spoken by rote. "Wife, I have done my best for you. Since you do not return to me, to whom God hath wedded you, you must ever mourn your ... misbegotten brat." On the latter word, he could not maintain the admonitory tones and spite embittered his words. "As to the little heathen's whereabouts, it is not the Lord's will that I tell you."

With a swift movement he bent, reached down to the ground, scooped up something from the dirt, and stood, all in one smooth motion; a bluish-black snake embellished faintly with thin white lines was clutched in his hand, its flat head just beginning to rise from the torpor of sleep. He smiled beatifically. "Do not fear for me, my dear, it will not harm me. The Lord has given me power. 'In my name,' he has said of the saints, 'they will pick up snakes with their hands.'"

"Josiah ..." She stepped back. Her eyes were fixed on the writhing serpent, its polished scales reflecting the harsh sunlight. She whispered, "Josiah, throw it off. It is a krait. You know its bite will paralyze." She had seen any number of villagers die from krait venom, their faces stiffening, their limbs gradually losing power, their breathing slowing almost imperceptibly, drowsiness encroaching. It was a long, sluggish, unhurried death.

He spoke as if to himself alone as he watched the long serpent twist in his hand. "I thought you dead, you know. One of us should be dead. God hath joined us together. Only death can part us." Suddenly he thrust the snake toward Anna, as if offering an impulsive gift. A flick of his wrist, and the krait came to full life, its head turning this way and that, seeking whom it might strike. Josiah looked up at her—and smiled.

She raised her sturdy bamboo *lathi* and struck the madman with all her furious strength, just as the deadly krait twisted back and buried its fangs deep into his upper arm. But that small happening Anna did not see. Nor did Josiah, in his greater torment, feel it. At the impact of her blow, the lithe snake flew in a wide arc out of his hand and vanished deep into the thick vegetation.

Josiah reeled, then righted himself against the stone rubble of the walls, stunned and uncertain. "Anna?" His expression was stiff and still, but was that anything new? In his white Indian raiment, with his bright blue eyes, he appeared translated, as if death had passed him by and he was truly already changed into his eternal state. A ghost, as the natives had said. A visitant from among the damned.

She tossed away the bamboo rod. "Tell your God I do not need him. I should never have needed *you*; that was only my weakness. As for you, you are no Christian—you have neither love nor mercy in your heart." As she turned from him and from their destroyed abode, she did not note the sudden bleak devastation of his countenance.

"I will find the child myself," she said. Her words rang of defiance and certitude, but in her heart she feared that Elizabeth was now forever lost.

"If you walk away from me," his words came in a monotone, "you never will see her. Not in this world. Or the next."

She stopped, stone still, confused and dizzy in the heat, tempted to turn back. Then she grew aware of a sudden commotion in the brush, the sound of someone shouting her name, of men slashing through the thick bamboo of the mission lane.

"*Memsahib? Memsahib?*" She recognized Satish Ghosh's voice, frantic. He pushed into the clearing, a large brush knife at his side. "Ah! There you are."

She pivoted to see Josiah's reaction to this intrusion, but he was gone.

It was just a fisherman's boat poling out into the Ganges. Anna would have paid it no attention save for the sunlight glinting off the golden hair of the fisherman's passenger.

"Stop," she yelled, and the carriage driver yanked on the reins. She and Satish were returning from the ruined mission to Farrukhabad on a road that closely hugged the river side.

"*Memsahib*, no!" Satish Ghosh cried as Anna jumped from the abruptly halted carriage. Stumbling across the river stones toward the water, she called, "Josiah! Come back!"

But the little boat continued steadily on.

"Josiah," she screamed, wading into the water, her voice shrill with frenzy. "Please. Please." Her wet skirts were heavy now, beginning to drag her into the river's current.

The boat paused, not as if at her plea, but rather as if predestined to exactly that watery midstream point. Slowly, the Reverend Josiah Roundtree stood up, shakily, from his seat and gazed toward the shore. If he had heard her and could now see her, Anna would never know. But he held his arms out, as if seeking—or bestowing—a blessing. He didn't so much jump out of the pinnace, as he quavered out of it, struggling to take a step toward her.

At Anna's side, pulling her back toward safety, Satish gasped. "Does he think he can walk upon Mother Ganga's waters?"

There was no struggle; as Josiah sank, the waves scarcely registered his passing.

"Oh! No!" Anna cried. Her hands flew to her heart, as if she had received there a mortal blow. She began to wail like a mourner at a funeral pyre, throwing herself down, pounding her fists upon the rocky shore.

"*Memsahib*, do not grieve so." Satish squatted beside her. "Look, Mother Ganga receives the Reverend Roundtree as if he were a jewel, tucking him peacefully into her bosom."

But Anna did not grieve for Josiah. No, not that. Never. It was simply that now, irretrievably, the last tie was severed to the knowledge of her daughter's dwelling place.

FIFTY-NINE

She recalled little about her return to the hotel, nor of the days she lay prostrate and confused in her darkened room, treated with cold baths and the *punkah's* cooling breezes. Satish Ghosh came and went during that time, busy with much else it appeared besides the care of her. But at one moment she seemed to awake from slumber to see him burst into the room clutching a telegram, and the maid, Shanti, bustling him off with much scolding.

On the fourth day she felt sufficiently recovered to rise and dress herself. While she sat writing at the desk in the curtained window alcove, Satish announced the arrival of the Reverend Job Belding, come up from Calcutta in haste when he learned that Anna had ignored his cautions and gone to Farrukhabad without his protection.

Today, perhaps due to the solemnity of his errand, Job Belding wore clerical garb. "I have learned of your husband's suicide, Mrs. Roundtree. Most regrettable news. I wish I could somehow have shielded you from the sight of that drastic act." Anna shrank from the compassion in his weary gray eyes. "And I fear I have further bad tidings for you."

Elizabeth, she thought. *They have found her. She is dead.* "My daughter ..."

"Daughter? No. It is about the Mutiny. I have been tempted to keep this disquieting news about your husband's duplicity to myself, dear lady, but, upon reflection, feel that you should know the entire truth."

"What *is* it?"

"I have learned that Mr. Roundtree never reached Cawnpore."

"What?"

The clergyman leaned forward, his hands upon his dark-clad thighs. "I don't know how much you know about the plight of the Fatehgarh refugees, or, indeed, how much you wish to know. But, upon arriving near Cawnpore, the Europeans, a hundred or more of them—missionaries, merchants, civil servants, and their families—took refuge on an island across from the city. Starved, thirsty, and exhausted, they attempted to negotiate safe passage with that traitor, Nana Sahib. According to a faithful *ayah* who remained to the end, Josiah Roundtree was left to guard a group of women and children while other men talked with Nana Sahib's representatives. When the *sepoys* swarmed the island with their guns, the male missionaries put up a struggle, but Reverend Roundtree leaped into the river and swam away, abandoning his charges. All else were taken prisoner to Cawnpore, then executed."

"Oh."

"When he told me in Calcutta about the massacre," Mr. Belding continued, "he spoke as if he had been there, heroic, on the bloody field. But—no. He must simply have read about it, like the rest of us.

"Mrs. Roundtree, I am so sorry. Do not weep."

But weep she did, although she did not take again to her bed. Reverend Belding's news sat heavy on her heart. *Duplicity*, he'd said. Madness, she had seen. And malevolence. What had transformed her radiant young husband into the vindictive wraith he had become? Was it she, herself? Had she shattered him in leaving him? Or was it India? Had he from the start not been sufficiently strong to endure the bright sunshine, and the seductive spices, and the indelicate hues of the flowers, and the insistent *tum*, *tum*, *tum* of the drums? Had these dark people and their sensuous ways breeched some chill redoubt within him in which he had long kept his soul secured?

The *tum*, *tum* of the drums. Recalling the incessant village drumbeat, brought Lallia, the village headwoman, to mind. Lallia? Would she be still alive? And the other villagers with whom she had worked for so long? How had she forgotten them? She loved them. She would go at once and visit the native village.

Contrary to all common sense Anna had determined to remain in India, a pilgrim wandering in search of her child. It was not that she had a particular bond with this country; she detested the imperious and vapid manners of the British rulers, but to a highborn Indian, whether Hindu or Muslim, she would be something close to a barbarian. To the lowborn native she was a *memsahib* only. She did not wish to be a *memsahib*; she had no desire for the petty domestic tyrannies of the white expatriate.

New York City had become her home. It grieved her to lose her abundant life in that great metropolis: her writing, her friends, the air of vibrant possibility. She would miss the brisk breeze off the harbor and the whiff of roasting chestnuts, the brawling manners of the freeborn citizens. She would miss Caroline, her friend. And ... never to see Bridey, again, or 'Bama, or to know what little Rosie made of her life. Or to meet Caroline's child. And, how would she support herself here? Her money was going fast. Perhaps Mr. Greeley would take two or three pieces about India, but what then?

Nonetheless, as hopeless as the quest had become, she could not abandon her daughter. Satish Ghosh, she knew, thought that Anna now found herself in the grip of a hopeless monomania. But he humored her, as Indians tended to do with the mad *angrizi*, and had prepared everything for a return to Calcutta. He told her that they had exhausted all possibilities of finding Elizabeth on their own, that now they needed Ashok's help and must call upon him when he arrived back in India. And she, with both longing and trepidation, concurred.

SIXTY

In a murky evening haze, the smoke of cooking fires hung heavy and low over the village. In times past Anna had paid many visits to this community near the mission compound. Here she had delivered babies, treated fevers, nursed the injured, and eased the passage of the elderly and ill into the company of whatever gods awaited them. Now she and Satish Ghosh approached the place on foot by a muddy path from the main road, past the crumbling stone of an old tomb and villagers bathing in a sluggish stream.

"Our *memsahib* returns," a tall boy shouted as they entered the village. Anna stared at him; could that be little Chathan—the boy who had so loved candy? A thin white cow meandered across their path. The village *tum tum* drums kept up a low and steady beat. Somewhere in the surrounding wilderness a jackal began to howl, then another. Village dogs joined the cacophony, attempting to overcome the threat of the jackals by outhowling them.

"*Salaam*," Anna said, as she approached a group of men hunkered around a bubbling *hukka*. "I greet you in remembrance of our days together." Her use of the local dialect was halting, as it had ever been.

Before anyone could reply, the woven palm-frond curtain covering the door of the largest hut parted, and a woman in a blue patterned skirt and green jacket appeared, her white headcloth hanging to the waist. "Anna, *Memsahib*," the woman said, and bowed in ritual greeting, "to whom I owe my life. Welcome."

Anna smiled. "Lallia, do I find you still in health?"

Lallia twisted the copper bangle at her wrist. "I knew you would come ... for the girl."

"Pardon?" Surely Anna had not heard aright. "The girl?" She couldn't understand what had happened to her ears; they seemed all of a sudden to be packed with cotton batting.

"Roundtree, *sahib*," Lallia explained. "He said she would be ours, but I saw you in her eyes. I take good care ... for you."

"The *girl*?" Anna repeated, her heart lurching.

"You did not know?" the head-woman asked, frowning at the disorderly mob of curious children pressing around the strangers as if drawn by a magnetic impulse. They were everywhere, the younger ones mostly naked, the bigger boys and girls only half-clad. Lallia made shooing motions and the children fell back to let the visitors pass. A brown waif in a short vest attached herself to Lallia's skirt, gaping at Anna, her big eyes wary.

"Then, *Memsahib*," Lallia continued, "I will tell you. But, come, surely you will partake of food with us." She uttered a sharp command. Women rushed to spread a cotton cloth on the ground and offer *chapatees* on plantain leaves with gourds of buffalo milk.

Anna stared at the plump and grubby infant who clung to the elderly village woman as if her life depended upon never relinquishing the printed cotton fabric of the colorful skirt. She was transfixed. At first glance the child had looked like any one of the other Indian children, but upon closer scrutiny Anna could see her complexion was a lighter hue, there was a rounder cast to her eyes. The child was a girl, as the scanty clothing made apparent, about three years of age. Dark hair oiled and pulled into a tight knot on top of her head. Ears pierced with small silver rings. Sweep of dark lashes against a soft tan curve of cheek. Bright eyes. Large, bright gray-green eyes.

Anna's eyes.

Anna both heard and did not hear Lallia's tale. It had been months earlier when the Reverend Josiah Roundtree had suddenly reappeared in the village bringing this half-blood child. Lallia spoke of how little

Sarmani—no one could pronounce her ugly English name—had shied away from all but Lallia, who had taken her on as a charge of her old age.

"And here is the child," Lallia said, detaching Sarmani's hand from her skirt. "I deliver her at last to you." She urged the little girl forward, appearing to be at once relieved and desolate to be free of the burden.

Instinctively, Anna lurched toward the child, consumed by an emotion both miraculous and terrifying. Satish grasped her arm. She whipped around to glare at him. He held up a finger: *Wait*. "She will be frightened. She does not know the white memsahib." That her *banian* had actually touched her in itself alerted Anna to the seriousness of his admonition. Nonetheless Anna thrust his restraining hand away and reached out to the little girl.

And Sarmani drew back, her regard suspicious.

With all the love so long and painfully repressed, Anna attempted to clasp her daughter in her arms. Little Sarmani recoiled. She hid her face in Lallia's skirts. She outhowled the dogs, outhowled even the jackals.

SIXTY-ONE

In the first-class compartment of the train to Calcutta, the child was now unrecognizable as the waif Anna had found in Lallia's village. They rode together, Anna, Elizabeth, and Lakshmi, the *ayah*. Lakshmi had washed the girl's dark hair and arranged it in the English fashion, long curls tied back with a bow. The child wore a white muslin dress with a satin sash. Her complexion was a milky tan, her gray-green eyes stubborn under straight silky brows like Ashok's, her nose a button, like Anna's, her mouth small and piquant. When she forgot to scowl, she was a beauty. Anna's arms ached to hold her, but the child would not allow it, clinging to her *ayah*, refusing all overtures from the white *ferenghi* who seemed so passionately intent upon her. By the time they'd boarded the return train to Calcutta, Anna was at her wits' end with this small fierce stranger who screamed each time she tried to touch her, who would not speak a word, who fought sleep, who ate only rice, and that in the most meager of portions.

At each town of any size, Anna left the train, searching the bazaars for fruit and cakes and toys to alleviate the child's sullen spirits. But nothing comforted India Elizabeth Sarmani Prudence Grace: not a paper elephant with a movable trunk; not a red and yellow whirlygig; not a doll in the sari of a Hindu girl. Did she not know how to play? Was she not capable of childish joy? At one of the larger towns, where they made an hour's halt, Anna purchased a set of nesting blocks. Bright animals were painted upon the surfaces of each block: tigresses and tiger cubs, homely she-camels and their babies, mother elephants and elephant calves, mother monkeys and their ugly little babies. The little girl took the blocks apart again and again, stacked them up, knocked them down and then nested them back together. She seemed to find comfort in their ability to be realigned in their never varying order, of the mothers and babies to be reassembled in their unchanging pairs.

The train slowed as they approached yet another station. As they jolted to a halt at the platform, the car jerked and Elizabeth's blocks went flying. The air in the compartment was thick with the humidity of the day and the never-acknowledged human pong of long monotonous travel. Vendors scratched at the closed windows of Anna's compartment, offering coconuts, fresh fruit, steaming tea in clay cups, and small sweet cakes. Despite the danger of cinders, she pushed up the window and purchased tea for herself and Lakshmi and coconut confections wrapped in paper for Elizabeth, who had painstakingly begun restacking her blocks.

Satish emerged from the station house deeply engaged in reading a telegram. Really, the man never stopped, Anna thought. She imagined him with business affairs from Bombay to Delhi to Lahore. If it were possible to lay telegraph lines across the ocean, he'd be receiving messages from New York and London as well. Folding the paper with an automatic motion, the *banian* glanced up and saw Anna watching him from the train. He stopped still, the dust swirling around his booted feet, and granted her a wide, spontaneous smile. She could not have been more surprised if this exceeding sober and proper man had broken out into the whirling dance of a dervish.

A long wail from the engine, and the train started up with another jerk. Elizabeth had built a tower with the blocks, and it fell.

Anna sighed and turned to the window. Green parakeets skimmed along banks of wild blossoms. Beyond thickets of flowering bushes, the countryside stretched away featureless to the hazy hills rimming the horizon. It was still oppressively hot. Now the tracks crossed a high bridge and swerved to run alongside a well-traveled sandy road. Riders on horseback smartly outpaced those on elephants, who lumbered past crude bullock carts crowded with women and children. "Elizabeth," Anna said, "see the elephant?"

Elizabeth ignored her.

The moment Anna had learned of her existence, she had given her heart to this child. Nothing, not even the most persistent or cruel rebuffs, could cause her to renounce that love. But, oh, what was ahead for them? Life-long anger, resentment and conflict? There must be something she could do to ease her little daughter's sad history of loss. She sighed again and settled herself into the window corner of the green plush seat. "See the elephant?" she asked one more time, as they passed a line of the beasts laden with a carpet merchant's wares. She had no hope of a response.

"*Memsahib*," Lakshmi whispered. "Look."

Elizabeth was holding up the block with the picture of the mother elephant. She did not look at Anna or indicate in any other way that she had heard. She simply held the elephant block up where Anna could see it ... if she happened to be looking.

Anna's heart leapt. "Yes," she said. "Yes, that's the mama elephant." Then she, Anna, reached down and secured another of Elizabeth's blocks. "And, see, Elizabeth, I have the baby elephant. Would you like to hear a story about this baby elephant?"

No response from the little girl. "Once upon a time," Anna said, gazing out the window so as not to alarm the child with the intensity of her feeling, "there was a baby elephant who lost her mama. ..."

After a minute or two of baby Ellie's adventures in the jungle looking for her mother among jeweled cobras and golden eagles, Anna felt the cushion sink ever so slightly as Elizabeth climbed up onto the seat beside her. She smelled of the sweet talc with which Lakshmi had powdered her. Anna did not look at her, did not breathe. She felt as if she were taming a wild bird.

They were traveling through a forested valley, and Anna held the baby elephant block up to the window. "See, Ellie, somewhere out there is the mama. Do you think she is behind that big *neem* tree? No? What about under the banyan tree? Do you think an elephant could hide in those big roots? No?" She felt a small warm hand on her arm, and her breathing halted completely. Elizabeth climbed up on her lap so she too could see out the window. Anna placed an arm lightly around the child's shoulders and, still addressing the little elephant, continued her tale. "Maybe the mama elephant is right here on the train with us." With the gentlest of movements, she turned to the child on her lap. "Do you think so, Elizabeth?"

The girl turned from the window with an expression of horror—she was on the *ferenghi's* lap! "No!" she cried. She jumped down and buried her face in Lakshmi's cotton skirt.

Anna stared out the window as the train flashed through yet another small village, another miniature world. *No*, she repeated to herself. Elizabeth's first word. And in English! *No*. She stared at the passing jungle and smiled. *No*: It might not articulate a smooth start to their life together, but she felt a thrilled confidence that this was the first word in a long conversation.

"Stay seated, *Memsahib*," Satish Ghosh commanded, as passengers streamed off the train in Calcutta, pushing, jostling each other, bickering. "The little one will awake frightened if we go out into that unruly mob. We must wait until the way is clear."

Beneath the cavernous glass and steel arches of the Calcutta Railway Terminal, the air was thick with cinders and sooty steam, jittery with trapped, filthy sparrows. Engines chugged, whistles screamed, bells rang, and porters shouted in a hundred dialects. It was night, and the vaporous gaslights added to the general locomotive stench.

Anna, clad in a fresh sand-colored linen travelling dress and a green straw hat with a veil, remained seated in her dingy, ill-lit compartment. Elizabeth, bundled in Ashok's worn Kashmiri shawl, slept beside her. Lakshmi had already left the car in search of fresh milk for the child, and Satish fussed with bags and bundles. Usually the soul of imperturbable competence, the *banian*, this night, dashed in and out of the train in an agitated manner, searching up and down the platform, shouting for porters, for baggage carts, for rickshaw-*wallahs*.

Boys with bundles of straw and firewood clambered down from the tops of the cars. Bearers passed on the platform with bags and bundles on their heads, then farmers leading bleating goats. A train steamed in on the opposite track, grinding to a halt with a drawn-out screech and the smell of water dousing ashes.

After days of stifling in this cramped compartment Anna was anxious to remove herself and Elizabeth to their hotel. "Now," she said, pulling the veil over her eyes to protect from cinders, "now we will go. The way is clearing."

Now that she had found Elizabeth, Anna intended to remain in Calcutta until Ashok's return. It might be months, for all she knew; nonetheless she would scan the shipping news in the Calcutta papers, watching for his name on the passenger manifests. When she found notice of his return, she would dress herself and Elizabeth in their very best and call upon him. ... If Ashok still wanted her, she would remain with him—she and Elizabeth. She would become his whole-hearted and willing mistress. But would he want her? Beyond the moment when she would see him coming through a doorway, hear the sound of his step moving toward her, she dared not think.

Satish blocked the door with his slight frame. "No, wait, *Memsahib*. I beg you, remain as you are. You must go into the city refreshed. I will send for tea. 'Tea-*wallah*!'" he called, and three responded with their braziers and steaming pots. "Here, drink this."

The crowd had begun to thin, and Elizabeth was snoring lightly beside her. Anna reached the end of her patience and rose from her seat. She pushed aside the proffered cup. "Satish, I wish to get to the hotel," she grumbled. "Enough of this nonsense. We will descend right this moment from the train."

Satish, staring down the platform gave a sudden exclamation, but Anna refused to be deterred. She turned to the overhead net to secure her handbag, lifted her shawl-wrapped daughter in her arms, resting the quiescent weight against her shoulder, and pivoted back to the compartment door. "Now, Satish," she ordered, "let us delay no longer—"

But the man in the doorway was not Satish Ghosh. He was, at first sight, a stranger. Sturdy, tea-brown, broad-shouldered, in a white linen suit, holding his tall hat in his hand, he appeared for one blank moment, through her thick green veil, to be just another Anglo-Indian *pukka sahib*. The train compartment's dim flickering lamplight fell obliquely across his face. She could see black shiny hair curling down upon a forehead. Dark, almond-shaped eyes. Tinge of smoky shadow in the long plane of a cheek. In the hollow beneath one ear, a white birthmark blossoming against brown skin. She threw her veil back. Involuntarily she reached halfway out to him. "Ashok!"

"Anna," Ashok said. He, too, stretched out a hand, hesitated, and then withdrew it, as if fearing rejection. There passed between them a long sober look, heavy with years and distance, freighted with a multitude of unasked questions. The rest of the world seemed to fall away. There was no other reality—simply Anna, Ashok, and, of course, their child.

She shifted Elizabeth against her shoulder: other than that, she could not move; she could not breathe; she could not tear her gaze from her lover's face. He reached out again and caressed the child's curly hair, studied her sleeping face. Then he took up the soft fringe of the shawl, letting it fall through his fingers like water. His eyes found Anna's. Their gaze held, thick and sweet as honey. "Come home with me?" he asked. He pled. "Will you? Will you come? I have yearned for you so. Oh, Anna, will you marry me?"

"Yes," she said. "Yes. Oh, yes, I will."

EPILOGUE

Many months later, Anna pulled her shawl closer as their ship, the North-American, steamed into New York Harbor, smaller craft scattering out of its way. Anna was once again pregnant—this time gloriously, happily so. The atmosphere was autumnal, fresh and brisk—New World air, she thought. In the morning sunlight, windowpanes glinted in the tall brick buildings that were fairly outnumbering the decrepit wooden houses with which she was familiar. From the wharf, families and friends waved handkerchiefs and bouquets. Idle gawkers, too, watched the big ship approach the city, whistles blowing, signal pennants flapping. To one side, cabs, coaches, and drays awaited their freight. Many, many more flags—Union flags they would now be called—whipped in the breeze than when she'd departed a year and a half earlier. They were entering a nation at war. She knew the risks of bringing into this bloody maelstrom of civil strife a dark husband and a child of ambiguous race. For Elizabeth's sake, they had considered remaining in London, but the British were clamorous partisans of the American Confederacy. Anna could not tolerate any support for the slaveholding states.

The cargo hold was crammed with aromatic crates of tea and spices and with bundles of shawls and silken sari lengths. With an appraising mercantile eye, Ashok now surveyed the warehouses and the small, ridged mountains of barrels, sacks, and boxes stacked along the docks and streets. It was his purpose to extend his family's export business to New York.

Elizabeth, in her *ayah's* arms, dangled a favorite cloth monkey in one hand; with the other she waved a "Namerican" flag on a stick. Like little Rosie Slade and like Caroline and Eben's baby son, Abraham Lincoln Garrett, Elizabeth Grace Sarmani Montgomery would grow up American. In England, Anna had met Arvind, Ashok's son from his first marriage, who was studying at Eton. Arvind, too, planned to come to New York when his education was finished, and work with his father. Yet another young American.

According to Caroline's letters, the Oyster Bay School was thriving. Now, after a year and a half in operation, they housed and educated twenty-five girls from fourteen years to eighteen years of age, under the tutelage of three young female graduates of Oberlin College, two of whom were among the college's first colored alumni.

Anna planned to keep on writing. So many untold stories had she stumbled upon in her search for Elizabeth, and she would tell them all. Stories in lust and money, in hope and hopelessness, in blood and passion. Her novel, *The Girl in the Red Stockings*, which Caroline had seen through publication, had appeared here and in London to great controversy, a mixture of acclaim and outrage, and Anna's visit to her British publisher had yielded a draft upon a London bank in an amount that had astonished her.

The ship docked with a series of thumps, followed by the chattering ring of pawl and ratchet when the mooring lines were secured. As the gangplank was lowered, Anna took Ashok's arm. Her husband was particularly handsome today, his skin darkened to a deep shadowed sepia by the sunshine of the weeks at sea. As first-class passengers, they would be among the first to disembark, a spectacle indeed for gawkers. White and black is what the onlookers would see. White and black married, in a nation at war. In Calcutta, even in London, such a pairing would not be unknown, might even, in Society, be somewhat sought after. But here? ... She held Ashok's arm tightly and smiled up at him; she might as well begin with audacity, begin as she meant to go on.

ACKNOWLEDGMENTS

During the many years it took for *The Kashmiri Shawl* to gestate, I've had generous advice and support from a number of friends, family members and fellow writers, especially Beverle Graves Myers, Kate Stone Lombardi, Sandra Robinson, and Sandra Zagarell. Others who read various versions of the draft are, Marie Laure Degener, Bill Cosgrove, Myriam Dobson, Diana Healy, Lisa Kohomban, and Patricia O'Gorman.

And a heartfelt thank you to the American Antiquarian Society, for the Robert and Charlotte Baron Fellowship for Creative Writers, 2004. The depth and breadth of their book collection and the knowledge and generosity of their staff is reflected in every scene of this novel. Especially, thanks to Su Wolfe for the hands-on lesson in 19th-century writing implements.

And to my loving family: especially Dave Dobson, who is the most patient and supportive person I have ever known. Thank you!

AFTERWORD

For *The Kashmiri Shawl* I have done so much research over the past ten years in so many sources, both nineteenth-century and modern, that it would be problematic for me to attempt the compilation of an accurate bibliography. Readers familiar with the period will recognize in some places spellings and usages from contemporary sources (for instance, the hyphenated *New-York* that appears in written documents included in the text, but not in the text itself). Perhaps those readers might also hear echoes of catchy nineteenth-century voices that colonized my imagination without leaving mental citations.

My apologies for anything problematic in the Indian sections of the novel, as my sources were mostly nineteenth-century missionaries and travelers with their particular take on things. I trust I have avoided their biases, if not always their misspellings. For narrative reasons, I have taken liberties with the location of early Indian railway lines. Although I have run the manuscript past a specialist in Indian Studies, any errors are, of course, my own.

ABOUT THE AUTHOR

Joanne Dobson is a mystery novelist and a scholar of American women's literature. Her six-book Professor Karen Pelletier mystery series won her an Agatha nomination and a Noted Author of the Year award from the New York State Library Association. **THE KASHMIRI SHAWL** is her first venture into the genre of historical fiction.

Formerly a tenured professor of American Literature at Fordham University, Joanne is a specialist in Emily Dickinson and in the work of nineteenth-century American women writers. Currently she teaches in National Endowment for the Humanities and Fulbright Fellowship International summer programs at Amherst College. She also teaches Creative Writing at the Hudson Valley Writers Center.

Made in the USA
Middletown, DE
01 September 2015